THE DOOMSDAY TESTAMENT

D0987996

THE DOOMSDAY TESTAMENT

James Douglas

CORGI BOOKS

TRANSWORLD PUBLISHERS
61–63 Uxbridge Road, London W5 5SA
A Random House Group Company
www.transworldbooks.co.uk

THE DOOMSDAY TESTAMENT
A CORGI BOOK: 9780552164801

First publication in Great Britain
Corgi edition published 2011

Addresses for Random House Group Ltd companies outside the UK
can be found at: www.randomhouse.co.uk
The Random House Group Ltd Reg. No. 954009

The Random House Group Limited supports The Forest Stewardship
Council (FSC®), the leading international forest certification organisation.
Our books carrying the FSC label are printed on FSC® certified paper. FSC is
the only forest certification scheme endorsed by the leading environmental
organisations, including Greenpeace. Our paper procurement policy can be
found at www.randomhouse.co.uk/environment

Typeset in 11/14½pt Sabon by
Kestrel Data, Exeter, Devon.
Printed and bound by
CPI Group (UK) Ltd, Croydon, CR0 4YY.

2 4 6 8 10 9 7 5 3 1

For Kara

I

1937, Changthang Plateau, Tibet

Ernst Gruber squinted into the ice-flecked wind, gritted his teeth and kept his eyes firmly on the retreating figure ahead. The muscles in the backs of the German's legs felt as if they were on fire and his chest like he was breathing hydrochloric acid, but the pain gave him a certain sense of masochistic satisfaction. If *he* was suffering, how much more so were the lesser men following the near vertical scar in the sterile, corpse-grey rocks that provided them with a path up the mountain?

Not the Drupka guide, Jigme. Like all his people, the nomads who scratched a living in one of the most inhospitable environments on earth, he was a wiry urchin of a man capable of incredible feats of endurance. His metronomic step didn't falter – no matter how steep the incline or difficult the footing. It had been five days since the expedition set out from their base camp by the freshwater lake. Today they had already marched for four ankle-crushing hours across country devoid of either water or vegetation, but still he showed no sign of tiring. Gruber, a vastly experienced explorer who had climbed some of the highest mountains in the Himalayas and ten years earlier had led the first German expedition across the Gobi Desert, delighted in testing himself against such men, but he knew his companions would be destroyed if they maintained this pace.

'*Bkag pa! Gcig chu tshod.*' He shouted the order to halt for an hour, but it must have been lost in the wind for the guide maintained his pace, or perhaps he just didn't want to stop. These people were like that. Stubborn. Like a donkey he would plod on until his stomach told him it was time to eat one of the barley dumplings that were the only sustenance he appeared to need. Gruber increased his pace until he was close enough to grasp the Drupka tribesman by the arm. '*Bkag pa!*' he repeated.

The guide grinned and nodded, although he was puzzled why the loud European with the frightening eyes and unhealthy red face persisted in addressing him in his unintelligible Tibetan. 'We stop soon. Very close,' he assured Gruber in bastard English.

'No. Stop now,' the German ordered.

The grin didn't falter, but Jigme wondered again what had made him agree to take these demanding, ill-mannered foreigners to the special hole in the ground. His cousin, now a Buddhist monk in far-off Lhasa, had told him of it when Jigme had made his solitary visit to the Tibetan capital on a pilgrimage to the Jokhang

Temple. The Germans had sought him out at his village because of the English he had learned from a Yakshir holy man who had been trapped for a season on the plateau and died of hut fever wishing he was back in a country called Leds. Normally the parties he led were only interested in finding special rocks to hit with their little hammers, or to shoot the gentle Kiang, the wild ass which didn't have the sense to run away from a man with a rifle. The Germans were different. They had asked him about the old people, which amused him because, in the village, they had been surrounded by old people. It took time before he realized they meant the enlightened ones, who had passed beyond life, which was even more amusing because the enlightened were spirit creatures now, their earthly bodies exposed and consumed by the vultures, the buzzards and the foxes. How could one find a ghost, especially if the ghost didn't want to be found? But the large foreigner insisted that these old people had lived in holes far below the ground. Did he know of any such holes? Now they were a few hours from their goal and he wanted to stop. Truly they were beyond comprehension.

'Stop now,' he agreed at last, pointing to a piece of stony but relatively flat ground just ahead on the left. 'You rest, eat, look at rocks.'

Jigme carried on a few paces before settling comfortably on the steep path with his pack beside him. He sat, cheerfully considering the twenty goats he had been promised, and the handsome wife they would bring him. The wind had dropped now and a watery sun blinked myopically through the thin cloud, showing the surrounding hills in all their arid magnificence. Far to the south-east was just visible the vast, snow-crusted bulk of Quomolonga, which the Europeans spoke of as Everest. One by one, the five members of Gruber's research team staggered to the rest area, leaving the porters, carrying their sixty-pound loads of supplies and equipment, to crouch where they halted.

Gruber assessed his companions as they passed, searching for signs of weakness or injury that would slow them down later in the day. The group had been put together to provide a broad range of expertise. As well as being the expedition leader, Ernst Gruber doubled as the team's zoology and mapping specialist. Berger, the ethnologist; Rasch, the anthropologist, and Von Hassell, the cinematic cameraman, were all reliable mountaineers and experienced explorers, wiry, tanned and bearded. After them came Junger, the security man who always had something to smile about, even if the smile never quite reached his pale eyes. A few yards behind, and looking like a city accountant who'd taken a wrong turn, struggled Gruber's deputy, Walter Brohm.

The men were of a similar age and had one other aspect in common. They were all officers of the SS Ahnenerbe – the Nazi Ancestral Research and Teaching Society – personally appointed by Reichsführer Heinrich Himmler. During the five day trek through the mountains they had conscientiously recorded and photographed the wildlife and fauna, studied the ethnic make-up of the local tribes and taken geological samples like the naturalists they appeared to be. The true reason for their mission was Himmler's obsession with the occult and his personal quest to discover the origins of the lost city of Atlantis and the ancient civilization of superhumans who had given birth to the Aryan race. According to ancient legend, these earliest Aryans, the Vril, practised a sophisticated form of mind control and had been led from the city before Atlantis drowned in the flood. After travelling through Asia they had created the legendary underground kingdom of Thule. If the expedition could find the entrance to Thule, Himmler believed he would gain access to all the secrets of the Vril.

As he distributed the rations, Gruber revealed for the first time that they were close to their destination. Walter Brohm noticed the eyes of his companions light up with anticipation and allowed himself a smile. They were the true believers, he was a realist – only here out of necessity, in the pursuit of advancement. A physicist with a fascination for geology, Brohm had no interest in lost cities, which was just as well because he very much doubted they were going to find one. He would loyally accompany the others into some dark cave where they would discover a few animal bones, or perhaps a Yeti, which Gruber would hail as the first Atlantean, and then he could go home to the comfort of his office and his laboratory. He knew Gruber didn't like him, but that was of no consequence. The cloth-headed adventurer was one of those National Socialist enthusiasts who would run through a brick wall for his

Führer – and was probably capable of doing just that. Walter Brohm was only interested in Walter Brohm. He had joined the Nazi party when it became clear nothing could stop Adolf Hitler from taking and holding power, and the Schutzstaffel, the SS, because he looked better in black than brown and it was the quickest way for an ambitious man to get on. He would never admit it, but he looked upon the secret rituals of the SS as a joke, although no worse than the Masons. With Germany expanding economically and militarily, the future had never looked brighter for a pastor's son from stuffy old Dresden.

Two hours after they resumed their march, the expedition reached the edge of a gigantic depression several hundred feet deep and perhaps two miles wide. Brohm couldn't suppress a flutter of excitement when he recognized what it was, but he guessed even now that Gruber was destined to be disappointed.

'Where is the cave?' the expedition leader demanded.

Jigme's deep-set eyes, the product of a hundred generations of staring into Himalayan blizzards, twinkled and his grin grew wider. His cousin's instructions had been very clear. 'Secret place. You follow. I show.' He skipped off down a barely visible track, with the rest of the group treading warily in his footsteps on the perilous slope.

The cave – more of a tunnel – lay hidden at the bottom of the eastern wall of the crater, partially screened by a rock fall and only visible to those standing directly opposite it. In any other part of the world it would long since have filled with rotting vegetation or silt washed down by the rains, but little vegetation grew on the Changthang and the plateau's annual rainfall measured around ten centimetres and was absorbed instantly, as if the land were a giant sheet of blotting paper.

In front of the entrance, Brohm was amused to see Gruber and the others lose some of their former spark. They were big sky men, mountains and deserts were their natural habitat, not this wormhole. Yet he could hardly blame them. There was something menacing about that brooding black portal that would make even an expert caver hesitate. The curious thing for Brohm was that the entrance appeared to be almost exactly circular, so perfect that it might have been man-made. Beyond it, as far as his torch would reach, the tunnel floor descended at a fairly steep angle of about thirty degrees. From a geological viewpoint he found it fascinating.

Gruber studied the entrance somberly. 'We'll make camp for the night and go in tomorrow. I want everyone up at first light.'

After a meagre breakfast of barley dumplings and yak butter tea, Gruber made his dispositions.

'Rasch, Brohm, Junger and I will make the initial descent, along with the guide, who will lead.' Von Hassell, the cameraman, protested that he should be involved but Gruber waved him away. 'You will have your opportunity. We'll rope together as if we were on a climb and take it slowly, a foot at a time – we don't know what the ground will be like. I don't want to lose anyone. Berger will command on the surface.' He raised a hand holding a whistle. 'If there's an emergency I'll blow on this, but your first duty will be to ensure the porters don't desert us.'

Berger nodded, his face a frowning mask of concentration, the expression he thought conveyed ideological commitment, but which only made him look as if he suffered from chronic constipation. Brohm was surprised at his own feelings. He should be anxious at being volunteered for such a hazardous enterprise. Instead, it was as if this cave had been waiting for him all his life. It held no terrors, quite the opposite. He felt as if he were being welcomed.

Gruber checked their bindings and roped himself into line behind Jigme. Twelve-foot lengths of hand-tested climbing rope linked the five men and each had been issued with a torch and spare batteries. Like the others, Brohm's pack contained food and water for three days. The Germans carried side arms, although for the life of him he couldn't think what they were going to shoot. With a nod to Berger, Gruber jerked the rope linking him to the Tibetan. 'Go,' he ordered.

They walked in reverential silence, like pilgrims entering a cathedral. Jigme's steps were tentative, as if every footfall had the capacity to plunge him down a shaft to the centre of the earth. He swept the ground in front of him with the torch and then swept it again. The beam lit up the tunnel for ten or twelve paces ahead, but beyond it lay the darkness of the tomb, unforgiving and eternal. Superstition was as central to Jigme's life as it is to every Tibetan, but nothing had prepared him for the inner terror he felt as he inched his way forward. Familiarity brought no lessening of the fear, because each step took him further from safety and closer to the demons that inhabited this place. He knew nothing of Atlantis, but his finely tuned senses told him they were not alone in the darkness. If he could, he would have broken free and fled back to the surface, but Gruber had tied his knots with a climber's efficiency. There was no escape.

Roped behind Gruber, Walter Brohm could feel his leader's impatience at their slow progress, but it was clear no amount of threats would make the Tibetan guide move any faster. A barely discernible draught tickled the back of Brohm's neck and made him think there must be another opening somewhere ahead. Given the angle of their descent it seemed unlikely, but at least the draught meant the air down here was relatively fresh. Most of Brohm's senses, though, were concentrated on his immediate surroundings. He allowed Gruber to pull him along and used the torch to study the tunnel walls. What could have created a shaft as uniform as this? He would have expected some signs of erosion, most probably from an ancient water source, but there were none. Instead the walls, which surprisingly dripped with moisture, appeared as smooth as glass. And the perfect circle was an illusion. Beneath his feet the floor of the tunnel was horizontal, though uneven. In the torchlight it looked like the petrified surface of a lake.

As he marched, his mind discarded the possibilities one by one until he was able to see the tunnel in an entirely different way. The walls didn't just look like glass, they *were* glass, or at least vitrified stone. Whatever had made this passage had created a heat so intense that it had actually *melted* the rock. He had recognized the great saucer in the plateau above as the impact crater of a meteorite, a celestial object, in this case a very large one, which had struck the earth several thousand years earlier. It appeared that some element within the meteor had survived the impact, retaining enough mass, heat and power to allow it to cut through the solid rock in much the same way as the new armour-piercing shells from the experimental weapons facility at Stuttgart cut through layers of metal. The possibilities were fascinating.

He couldn't be certain how far they had travelled when he heard the sound, but his disbelieving brain told him it must be more than a mile. At first it was just a whisper in the still air that brought Jigme to a faltering stop. Gruber snarled at him to go on, but it took a sharp push in the back with a pistol barrel to encourage the Tibetan's feet to move. Brohm felt the tension grow with every step and the sound increased in volume until it became hauntingly familiar. It was impossible. What they could hear was the solemn rhythmic chant of the Buddhist monk. A few steps later they saw the flickering yellow shadow light of an oil lamp ahead, accompanied by the faint, rancid scent of yak butter oil.

Gruber pulled Jigme to a halt and untied him so that

they could move forward side by side, signalling with the pistol for the others to follow. By now the musical chanting echoed from the walls and it was clear it came from more than one voice. Astonished, they approached the small chamber that marked the end of the tunnel. It was wider than the shaft and Brohm noticed evidence of tool marks that told him this, at least, was man-made. Gruber muttered what might have been a curse or a prayer and Brohm heard gasps from behind as the others reached the chamber. What he found there made him wonder if he had gone mad.

Against the far wall, at the end of a passage more than a mile below ground, three ancient, milk-eyed Buddhist monks sat cross-legged in saffron robes. Their lips moved in an unceasing incantation that made no allowance for the entry of the strangers.

'They're blind,' Gruber said incredulously. Then after a second's thought, 'Why do they need lamps?'

'For the air.' Brohm found himself whispering. 'The flames burn off oxygen and draw air from the surface. Without the lamps the air down here would soon become unbreathable.' He saw now that the side of the chamber was stacked high with stocks of food, water and dampened sacks of yak butter, which meant these ghostly cave dwellers were resupplied from the outside world at least every few months. But his eyes, like all the others, were drawn to the centre where an ornate golden casket sat upon what could only be a ceremonial altar.

'Why don't they acknowledge us?' Junger hissed. Like a man in a dream, Brohm moved towards the altar.

Second by second a realization had been growing in the geologist that made him want to shout out loud. Sweat ran down his back and his hands were clammy as he reached for the casket.

'For them you do not exist,' Jigme answered Junger's question, his voice shaking like an old man's, 'except as demons. They are chanting a spell to make you vanish.'

'What is it?' Brohm found Gruber at his shoulder, his eyes fever bright. Atlantis was forgotten. All that mattered was the casket.

Obviously of great antiquity, it was about two feet long by eighteen inches wide and eighteen deep. At first Brohm thought it was made of solid gold, but the moment he laid hands on it he realized it was actually wood covered in gold leaf. Representations of the Buddha and various Indian deities had been carved along its length. What puzzled and then excited him was the fact that when he picked it up it *weighed* as much as gold. He didn't dare answer Gruber's question truthfully. For one thing he still wasn't certain yet, for another Gruber was too stupid to understand.

'We can't afford to open it to find out, but I believe what this box contains could be of vital importance to the Reich. It must be returned to the homeland immediately. And in absolute secrecy.'

Gruber stared at him, then nodded. 'What about the monks?'

Brohm had already decided. 'Kill them.' Junger drew his pistol.

Together, they turned to Jigme. 'And him?'

The tears running down the Tibetan's cheeks turned the habitual grin into a tragic mask. He was still wearing his smile when Walter Brohm shot him between the eyes.

II

2008, Welwyn Garden City, England

Jamie Saintclair knew instantly that something was wrong because of the smell, or rather the lack of it. When he arrived at the house on a Sunday afternoon he could expect to be met by the comforting, salty-sweet aroma of roasted beef. Today all he could smell when he opened the back door was sour milk from the open carton beside the stainless-steel sink.

'Granddad?'

He walked through to the front room his mother had grandly called the lounge, with its fussy ornaments, drab, functional wallpaper, and decades-old furniture. It was cool in here, but that was normal; the old man never turned on the heating before October. What concerned Jamie more was the stillness. The house was always quiet since his mother had died. But never this still.

'Granddad?'

He opened the door that led to the stairs.

'Oh, Christ.'

Something sucked the contents of his stomach into his chest and he struggled for breath. He felt as if his feet had been kicked from under him and the roof had fallen in at the same instant. His eyes automatically looked away, as if his mind was convinced that what he'd seen wouldn't be there when he looked back again.

But it was there, in a tangled heap lying inside the front door at the bottom of the stairs. The long arms and legs that had always reminded him of a demented stick insect splayed at impossible angles and the neck, in its plastic, clerical collar, twisted so that the old man's dull blue eyes seemed to focus on his left armpit.

'Granddad?' Instinct made Jamie reach for the throat to check for a pulse, but he stopped halfway when he realized how pointless the gesture was. If the broken neck wasn't evidence enough of death, the yellowy-grey pallor of his flesh and the way it seemed to hang off the bones confirmed that Matthew Sinclair had been lying here for days. It looked as if he'd lost his footing on the stairs. Just lately he'd been having trouble moving around, even with the walking stick that Jamie's subconscious mind noted should have been lying somewhere, but wasn't.

Jamie slumped down on the bottom stair and closed his eyes. No tears. Not yet. Because the prevailing emotion wasn't grief, but loneliness. His grandfather was – had been – his last living relative. No uncles or aunts. No cousins, at least that he knew of. He tried to imagine the old man as he had been, and came up with a narrow, bony face dominated by a Belisha beacon of a nose whose rosy light was fuelled by the cheap Scotch he claimed was the only thing that helped him sleep. Grey, thinning hair and benign, kindly amusement in eyes shadowed by the tropical diseases that were the legacy of his years in Africa. A prayer formed in his head, but he knew the old man was already with the God who had sustained him for so long. Matthew had been a 'good' man in the truest sense of the word. Every waking hour and spare penny dedicated to helping others. Every new day an opportunity to be a better person.

Jamie put his hand to his mouth and choked back a sob. The guilt that had been lying dormant was growing now – why hadn't he insisted on staying with him? – but the shock was wearing off. A switch clicked in his head telling him to move: to *do* something.

He knelt beside the still figure and bent to kiss the cold brow.

'Goodbye, Granddad.'

It was ten days before he felt strong enough to return to the house, his mind still numbed by that peculiar detachment that follows a period of intense grief. Only now had he been able to overcome the dread that had been keeping him away from the unwanted, but necessary task of sorting out his grandfather's papers and putting aside anything of monetary or sentimental value before the house clearers came in.

This had been his home for eighteen years, shared

with his mother and grandfather, before he'd left for university. Like his mother, the house was a product of the fifties; a functional five-room cube of brown pebble-dash with a tile roof, neat windows and a small, carefully tended garden. Semi-detached, of course; she could never have afforded what she called a 'proper' house in Welwyn, and Matthew's meagre church pension didn't stretch far. He remembered the day she'd died and the unexpected sense of release he'd experienced. At last he'd been free of the smothering influence that had kept him wound tight since the day he was old enough to understand it.

Matthew had changed nothing in the year since she'd gone. The house had become a shrine to her. Every corner had memories for Jamie. Strawberry teas at the kitchen table where she'd wiped jam from his face with a damp facecloth. The scent of her perfume as she'd leaned over him in twin-set and pearls to complete a jigsaw in the front room. His grandfather helping with an elusive Latin verb when he was about twelve, at what must have been one of the hardest times. He shook his head. Where to begin? The papers, he supposed, which were stored in the polished bureau in the corner.

He kept it up for half an hour, sorting through insurance documents and gas bills, before boredom inexorably drew him to a collection of his mother's leather-bound photo albums. He flicked through the pages of regimented pictures, each perfectly positioned and in its proper place. The early ones were mostly photographs of him as a baby, alone or with his mother or grandparents. But here was five-year-old Jamie, deadly serious, ready for his first day at school in cap, purple blazer and tie, with his proud mother at his shoulder. In the picture, her hair was a dark, lustrous brown. How could he have forgotten that? Margaret Saintclair had been a snob, an unbridled and unapologetic snob who had somehow kept her status as an unmarried mother from her toffee-nosed acquaintances as she'd clawed her way to become chairwoman – not chairperson, God forbid – of the local bridge club. For all her faults she had loved him, and loved him as only the single mother of an only child can show love: single-mindedly to the point of obsession. It had taken him a long time to understand what she and his grandfather had gone through to ensure that he was equipped to take on the world. In a way, she had donated thirty years of her life to him. She'd even given up her name – plain old Sinclair – as part of the plot to give him the best possible chance when he went to Cambridge: driven, almost bullied, by her to win a scholarship from the local grammar school.

As he leafed through the pictures he realized that he'd always thought of his mother as old, but she hadn't been old at all. She wasn't quite sixty-three when she died.

Another picture. Her proudest moment, his graduation with a First in fine arts and modern languages. Jamie barely recognized himself in the stern-faced young man in the one-size-fits-all, hired robe, even though the photograph had been taken less than ten years earlier. While the other students had spent most of their time drinking and carousing, he'd never been able to escape his mother's telepathic control. If he remembered correctly, the popular term for the image he'd created for himself had been 'Young Fogey' and he'd cheerfully embraced it, right down to the tweed jacket and briar pipe, for Christ's sake. Oh, he'd had his moments, and the girls who seduced him, usually for a dare, had gone away pleasantly surprised and reasonably well-satisfied, but he'd never indulged in that relentless pursuit of the female flesh his fellow undergraduates felt was their duty.

He shook his head at the memory and, still carrying the album, climbed the narrow stairs past the row of plaster flying ducks that guarded the hall like a flight of Spitfires. He knew he should be doing something more productive, but he was unable to break the lethargic grip of the past.

Matthew's bedroom door stood ajar and he walked through with the feeling of a child entering a forbidden garden. It was years since he'd been inside this room. Perhaps fifteen feet by twenty, the only furnishings were a white melamine dressing table, a shallow cupboard where the old man kept his shoes, and an enormous, clumsy oak wardrobe that must have come from a second-hand shop. The room still carried a faint, sweetish scent of ill-health and when he lay back on the quilt he was surrounded by Matthew's presence. He felt a sharp prickle behind his eyes. *Pull yourself together, Saintclair.*

He sat up and reopened the album. A newspaper cutting with a photograph of an adult Jamie holding a small painting in a gilt frame. Had he really made them proud? He supposed the cutting was proof that he had, but it was a pride built on false pretences. When his mother heard he had set up his own business after eight years jobbing for Sotheby's and moved into an office in Old Bond Street, she'd insisted on opening a bottle of her carefully hoarded Asti Spumante. He'd never invited them to the office and hadn't had the heart to reveal it was little more than an extended cupboard with a posh address. A decanter of whisky stood on a bedside table. He smiled as he heard Matthew's soft voice – *'purely medicinal, my dear boy'* – and poured himself a small glass. He studied the photograph more closely. The painting had brought him short-lived fame, and even shorter-lived fortune.

It was one of Rembrandt's earlier works, a portrait of some rosy-cheeked Dutch merchant and not a particularly impressive one, but a Rembrandt nonetheless. Until 1940, it had hung in solitary splendour in the Paris mansion of the Mandelbaum family, cloth exporters for five generations and proud of it. Over the centuries the Mandelbaums, French Jews of German extraction, had weathered many storms, but the hurricane that blew in from the Third Reich that summer had well and truly sunk them. Monsieur Mandelbaum, who had waved away offers of sanctuary from his customers in England, took one last look at his Rembrandt on Friday 14 June as the Germans marched into Paris, then blew his brains out, leaving Madame and five little Mandelbaums to be evicted, registered, classified and eventually deported, via the transit centre at Drancy, to the extermination camp at Auschwitz. By the time the fighting ended, only a single little Mandelbaum, Emil, had been left to emerge miraculously from amongst the corpses and the living dead, like a ten-year-old version of one of Lowry's matchstick men.

After the war Emil was claimed by relatives in the United States and he spent the next sixty years trying to forget the screams, the sight of hanged men and women and the never-ending stink from the crematorium chimneys. But a year earlier he had been tracked down by the son of an old business acquaintance of his father's who suggested he reclaim the Paris property and asked what had become of the celebrated Rembrandt. Emil had only a vague memory of the painting, but by then being a retired stockbroker, he certainly knew its potential worth.

For a successful art dealer, tracking down stolen property, especially property stolen half a century earlier, is the professional equivalent of walking blindfold through a minefield. So it was unsurprising that Emil had trouble finding someone reputable to help him seek out the Rembrandt. At the time, Jamie was conspicuously lacking in obvious signs of success and the jury was out on his reputation after a series of auction ambushes that had left both him and his clients out of pocket. The two men had been introduced by Simon Marks, a merchant banker and former Cambridge classmate of Jamie's, who had watched and despaired at his friend's pitiful efforts at building a business.

'Either do it to make money or don't do it at all, old son,' Simon had advised him. 'Emil is rolling in cash, he'll pay you a daily stipend and your expenses while you look for the bloody thing, and a whacking great finders' fee in the unlikely event that you ever lay hands on it.'

Luck, his languages and what he liked to think was a modicum of good judgement had all played their part in what followed. As he told Simon: 'The Nazis were just as efficient at cataloguing what they pinched as they were about everything else. Emil's Rembrandt was one of thousands of artworks hoovered up by Hermann Goering's Reichsleiter Rosenberg Institute for the Occupied Territories. Once I discovered that, there were three possibilities. First, it could have been destroyed during the war: possible, but most stolen artworks survived. Second, some resourceful, high-ranking Nazi could have smuggled it out as working capital using one of the Odessa escape pipelines: again possible and if that's what happened the most likely route was by Spain or Switzerland to South America. The third option – less likely – was that it ended up stored in a big cave in the Bavarian Alps and some enterprising GI lifted it to take home to his ma in Pittsburg.'

Good fortune came when investigating Option Two. He had followed a trail from a Madrid art house that led him by a circuitous route to Option Three and the jackpot. An auctioneer in Santiago knew a dealer in Buenos Aires who thought he had seen the self-same painting on the wall of the Argentine Embassy in

Panama. A trip to the Canal Zone and a friendly cultural attaché who was terribly proud of the embassy's prized artwork confirmed the identification. The look on his young host's face when he suggested the Rembrandt might be stolen property almost broke Jamie's heart. It was the first of many moments of unease created by his new career path. Tracing the painting's course backwards led him to an American veteran who had indeed taken the Rembrandt home to show Ma, only in Omaha, not Pittsburg, then sold it on. The chain included a respected New York art dealer who had been creative with the Rembrandt's provenance and whose reputation was now damaged beyond repair. Jamie had savoured his moment of triumph – but it was short-lived. Only too quickly he realized that it made him about as popular in the tight-knit art community as a dose of bubonic plague. Suddenly the small galleries, which had once greeted him with a sympathetic smile and had always been happy to throw him a few crumbs, didn't want to know him. The big dealerships didn't even return his phone calls. Still, he had the money to tide him over. At least he did until the New York dealer's lawyers got involved. The suit never came to court, but keeping a lid on it had cost him most of what he'd been paid to find the painting. His only consolation was that the publicity the find generated and Emil Mandelbaum's endorsement resulted in a slow stream of commissions from Jewish families who likewise wished to be reunited with their treasures. The work kept him afloat and occupied, but he had never been able to repeat that initial success and he was beginning to wonder if the luck that had brought him the Rembrandt was the beginner's variety.

He pulled himself off the bed and tentatively opened the top drawer of the dressing table. No hidden surprises. Carefully folded handkerchiefs, socks laid out just so, uniformly white vests and pants that probably dated back decades. He'd wondered if the old man still kept his mother's correspondence, perhaps a perfumed love letter from Jamie's father whose name she had never revealed, but there was nothing.

He turned his attention to the wardrobe, breathing in a mouthful of mothballs and well-worn tweed as he opened it. At the same time he caught a glimpse of himself in the full-length mirror on the back of the door. The man staring out at him was tall, angular and still carried the vaguely foppish air cultivated at Cambridge. His grandfather's death had marked him in some way, but he couldn't really say how. Perhaps it was the slight bruising below the eyes that made him look older than his thirty years, or a set to the thin lips that hadn't been there previously. Wholesome, verging on handsome, with a steady green-eyed gaze that was more shrewd than intelligent; dark, unruly hair that flopped over his eyes and a hard edge that, strangely, only women seemed to notice. Who are you? he asked the man in the mirror. Where did you come from?

He rummaged through the dark suits, threadbare white shirts and ancient clerical gear, checking pockets, then began on the wardrobe floor, where Matthew had stored his supply of gardening magazines. Nothing there for him to worry about. He turned away, his mind already on the next room. As he did, he caught the faint gleam of metal in a tiny crack at the junction of the floor and the walls. With growing puzzlement he crouched to identify it, but it was only when he removed the magazines and tested it that he realized the floor consisted of a removable plywood panel. His heart beat a little faster. As he raised the wood his eye found a sharp-edged metal box in the darkest corner of the recess.

The box was about the size of an old-fashioned biscuit tin and covered in chipped dark green paint, which gave it a distinctly military look. A patch of bare metal had revealed its hiding place below the wardrobe. When he lifted the box the contents rattled intriguingly. He placed it on the bed with the same feeling of anticipation as when he'd first laid eyes on the Rembrandt, like a clock wound too tight with the springs threatening to explode free. A rusting metal clasp held the box closed and with a deep breath he carefully unclipped it, levered the lid free and lifted it open.

His first impression was of a hotchpotch of army memorabilia; a few tarnished medals, dusty strips of ribbon, worn badges and scraps of time-stained paper. But as his eyes took in the individual elements he realized it was much more than that. The maroon booklet half hidden among the medal ribbons could only be a soldier's pay book. What he had before him was a man's whole identity. He felt a surge of exhilaration and had to suppress a shout of triumph. This was his *father's* identity. With shaking hands he lifted the booklet and opened it, eyes greedily searching for the name. 'Shit!' The word echoed from the walls and he could feel his mother's posthumous disapproval.

Matthew Sinclair.

Not the father he'd never known, but the grandfather he had. Dotty old Granddad Matthew who had sat Jamie upon his knee quoting endlessly from the scriptures and expecting him to enjoy strange stories told in his fluent German. Who had taken him to his first art gallery and taught him the importance of composition, form and line as they stood in front of an enormous Civil War portrait of some curly-wigged knight. His gentle, kindly grandfather, who quite literally would not have squashed a fly, had been a soldier. It didn't seem possible, but the evidence was here on the bed.

He laid the pay book aside, picked up the medals one by one and placed them on the quilt; two silver circles about twice the size of a ten-pence piece, three bronze stars differentiated only by the colour of their ribbons, and – he hesitated, half-recognizing what he had in the palm of his hand – a fine silver cross with a crown embossed at the end of each arm. He turned the cross over and read the inscription on the reverse side: *Cptn M. Sinclair (Royal Berkshire Regiment) 8 May 1945.* The cross, though Jamie could only hazard a guess at which award it was, meant Matthew Sinclair had not only served in the army, he had fought, and fought well. And there was more. Now that he'd almost emptied the box he found two small scraps of cloth nestling at the bottom. One was a set of parachute wings and the other the instantly recognizable winged dagger of the Special Air Service.

Jamie stared at the badge in disbelief. He felt excited and robbed at one and the same time. 'Why didn't you tell me?' he demanded of the empty room. His mother had not just cheated him of his father, she'd cheated him of his grandfather as well. The sweet, eccentric old man he'd lived beside all those years had been a war hero. Yet neither of them had ever mentioned it.

He was so angry he almost missed the battered journal that had been hidden beneath the box.

III

2008, Menshikov Palace, St Petersburg, Russia

The six men in black overalls sat bathed in dim red light in the rear compartment of a large van parked on Vasilevskiy Island diagonally across the Neva from the Hermitage museum. Their leader was very pleased that the vast, imposing building on the far riverbank wasn't tonight's target. When it had become clear that what his client sought was in St Petersburg he had reconnoitered the six buildings of the main complex and discovered exactly what he'd known he would: the Hermitage was as tough a nut to crack as the Bank of England or Fort Knox. Fortunately, he didn't have to crack it. Like every major museum in the world, the Hermitage is home to far more treasures than it can ever display at one time and those treasures are dispersed among its sister museums. It also holds several thousand items whose origins and ownership have been subject to dispute since the end of the Second

World War. As greedy for retribution as he was for power, Stalin insisted that Germany's art and historic artefacts should make up part of the blood price to be paid for Mother Russia's suffering. When his generals closed in on Berlin, special NKVD trophy brigades spread across the country plundering carefully chosen paintings, books and sculptures, taking home with them between three and twelve *million* artworks, depending on who you believed, including paintings by Botticelli and Van Dyck. Some of those artefacts were almost certainly not far from where he sat with his assault team, but tonight only one of them interested him. He looked at his watch. 01:55.

'Get ready.' He pulled a black ski mask over his head. The others followed suit, automatically checking their weapons and equipment.

Dimitriy Yermolov stifled a yawn and struggled to keep his eyes open. Time to take another look around. If one of the supervisors came in – admittedly unlikely – and discovered him even half asleep he'd be out of a job by morning, and then who'd pay to put his wastrel son through university? He was getting too old for this night work, but what else could he do? The New Russia had been just as tough on Dimitriy as the Old Soviet Union had. That was the problem with being an honest man in a country where corruption was an essential element of any successful career. It didn't matter whether it was turning a blind eye to some Mafia drug dealer from Kazakhstan or keeping your mouth shut about a party functionary selling off state alcohol, it was the same old stink. Trouble was, being a lowly security guard, even in one of Russia's most prestigious museums, didn't pay well and never had. And let's face it, this was just a sideshow compared to the Hermitage across the water. Don't get him wrong, the Menshikov Palace was impressive enough, a glorious Baroque mansion house overlooking the river in one of the world's prime locations. It was probably the oldest surviving building in the best city in Russia. Forget Moscow, 'Piotr' had always been the capital and always would be, and he loved it, even if that bastard Vladimir Vladimirovich Putin had also been born here. But compared to the State Museum or the Winter Palace, the Menshikov was just a collection of pretty rooms really, with the odd Old Master here and there to give it a wafer-thin veneer of distinction. Nobody would rob *this* place.

The leader looked at his watch again. 'Two minutes.' He'd put together a team of five Russian-speaking professionals carefully selected for their skills and ruthlessness and with ancestral DNA linking them to the mountain passes where the Kremlin's conscript army fought their perpetual savage war against the mujahideen fighters and the Black Widows of Chechnya. Add a few shouted words of classroom Chechen and you'd created a terrorist smokescreen that would keep the investigators busy for months if things went wrong. They were all mercenaries, but each was a special forces veteran. Between them, the six men had served in

Grenada, Panama, Iraq, Afghanistan and a few other places the world wasn't supposed to know about.

The security systems protecting the Menshikov Palace differed from those of the Hermitage only in scale. Each floor had its cameras, alarms and motion sensors, infrared and laser. The instant an alarm was triggered the whole building would go into lockdown and in less than ten minutes the place would be crawling with St Petersburg cops. The only weakness was during those vital minutes between alarm and response, when the museum's security guards were expected to deal with any developing crisis. At the Hermitage, several dozen guards were on duty during the hours of darkness. At the Menshikov Palace, the men on the night shift numbered just six, and the red dots on the laptop in front of him showed him precisely where they were.

Dimitriy used his radio to inform Yuri in the control room that he would be patrolling the lower floor and basement for the next fifteen minutes. He heard the other man's knowing chuckle. 'Sure, Dimi, see if you can shoot some of those fucking rats when you're at it.' Dimitriy smiled. This close to the river the black rats that swarmed from the sewers and culverts in summer were forever tripping the alarms or chewing through the electric cables. Not that he was going to shoot anything. He'd never used the heavy six-round RSA Kobalt revolver that hung so uncomfortably in the holster at his waist. They'd put poison down, but the slippery bastards seemed to thrive on it. He wandered cheerfully through the pillared main hall and under the big staircase, allowing the torch beam to wash over the portrait-covered walls under the eyes of the classical statues and busts of stern-eyed tsars. His rubber-soled shoes made no noise on the stone floor. Sometimes being alone in the palace could be a little spooky, but tonight he felt he was among friends.

'One minute. Night vision. Lights off.' Inside the van the leader felt the tension grow as if it were a gathering thunderstorm. Each man locked his goggles in place and stared ahead, wound tight but lost in his thoughts, mentally going through his movements over the next ten minutes. Three months they'd been training for this. Three months of sweat and endless repetition – all for ten minutes that would change all their lives. Yet success or failure depended on a man they had never seen who sat in an office seven thousand miles away.

The security system that protected the Menshikov was as good as any in the world, but, like every security set-up, the alarms and the cameras and the detectors and the automatic door locks were all controlled by a central computer heavily dependent on technology and software originally developed in the United States. In the wake of the 9/11 attacks, senior US government officials held secret talks with the heads of the country's top-ten computer manufacturers. The White House was, and is, concerned about the use of computer technology for recruitment and secure encrypted communication by al-Qaida and its associated terrorist networks. Post-9/11, the big corporations also recognized that the world had changed, particularly when it was made clear that the lucrative government contracts that helped boost their stockholder profits were dependent on a new level of cooperation. In return for increased research and development funding they agreed to provide privileged access to, and information on, all new and forthcoming technological developments. The most significant effect of this pact was to provide a small offshoot of the National Security Agency with the ability and technology to infiltrate, and if necessary control, any computer on the planet. Of course, the client couldn't buy the US government, but he did have the resources to identify and purchase the services of a software developer and computer engineer at the heart of the new system: a man whose pension arrangements had been boosted by multi-million-dollar payments to a private bank on the Cayman Islands. By now the engineer would have remotely entered the Menshikov computer system and made the necessary undetectable change to its emergency reaction procedures.

'Thirty seconds.'

In a major incident, the computer controlling the Menshikov's security system would automatically restrict access to all areas of the museum, securing every door and window. A similar reaction would take place in the event of a power cut. In this case, the leader knew it would take ten minutes for the museum's emergency generator to provide enough power for the system to be reset. Loss of power wouldn't be enough to trigger a mass call-out of police, unless it was accompanied by an emergency signal from the control room. Which was why the lights were about to go out in this particular sector of St Petersburg.

'Ten.'

A red dot crept slowly across the screen of the laptop. One of the guards was on the move, but the others were exactly where he wanted them.

'Nine.'

He looked around the van at the intense eyes staring at him from behind the night-vision goggles.

'Eight.'

His hands ran over the equipment on the belts and harnesses strapped to his body. Stun grenades, taser electric dart gun, Russian-made GSh-18 pistol and ammunition.

'Seven. Remember, from now on we speak only Russian.'

He closed his eyes and, for the final time, visualized the interior of the museum and the route he needed to take from the van to the side door.

'Six.'

'Street clear,' the mercenary seated beyond the partition beside the van driver announced.

'Five.'

He reached for the door handle.

'Four . . . Three . . . Two . . . One . . . Go!'

They leapt from the van into the darkness, and as he sprinted towards the Palace he could see – half a mile away – the spot-lit frontage of the Hermitage dappling the calm waters of the Neva. He didn't need to hear the soft thud of boots on the tarmac to know the five men were following close on his heels. Seventy-five paces to the side entrance. Ignore the CCTV cameras, which would still be powered by their batteries, but would be sending their pictures to blank computer screens. The double oak doors. This was the moment of truth; what the client had paid all those millions for. The minute the power had been cut the computer would normally have locked down the entire museum, but the state-of-the-art software uploaded by the engineer had *reversed* the procedure. The Menshikov Palace was wide open and there for the taking. Still, he couldn't resist a soldier's prayer as he turned the handle. Now!

The six men burst inside where the familiar interior was bathed by an eerie underwater green in the prism of the night-vision lenses. No orders were needed. Three men to take care of the guards, two, including the armourer, to follow him to their target. The security staff would still be under the impression that they were in lockdown and would stay in position until the back-up generator restored power. Thanks to the client this was the third power cut they'd experienced this week and they'd have no reason to be concerned.

A harsh voice sounded in his earphone. 'Item Six still outside rear of building.' The two men left behind in the van were continuing to monitor the guards' movements. The sixth guard was a nuisance, no more. Not even that, if he stayed out of the way.

Moving purposefully, but not running, he reached

the end of the corridor and turned right, with the two men keeping pace and the others peeling off. Behind the mask he couldn't help smiling. He recognized a Rubens, a Caravaggio and a Raphael. A hundred million dollars and then some and he couldn't lay a finger on them.

'Item One down.' This was the operative tasked with dealing with the guard at the front entrance. If everything had gone to plan he would have first stunned the man using his taser then disabled him with a spray that would keep him unconscious for at least two hours.

'Item Three down.'

He reached the stairway leading towards the cellars.

Even in the most well-protected buildings a man who knows his way around will find a route in and out that bypasses all that tiresome security. Especially a man who needs a smoke.

Dimitriy Yermolov cursed when the lights went out. Bloody power company again. Things were better under the fucking Communists. He had arranged for Yuri to unlock the steel door leading from the basement to the gardens and had been enjoying a quick Sobranie. Standing in the dark under the old linden tree beside the door, he lit another cigarette and felt a complete idiot. The power cut would have over-ridden the instruction and locked him out until the back-up kicked in. He thought of calling Yuri, but that would just make him look stupid. Even though he knew it wouldn't do any good, his hand automatically reached for the handle. It turned easily. Strange . . .

*　　　*　　　*

'Item Five down.' Which only left the fool outside to the rear of the building. Maybe he'd been checking some earlier alert. Well, he could stay outside.

They reached the cellar level and he turned right. Below the Baroque splendour of the palace lay a rabbit warren of former kitchens and wine cellars from the days when the fabulously rich Prince Alexander Menshikov had entertained his friend the Tsar. Now they were disused boiler rooms and storage areas that held a share of the 95 per cent of the treasures the Hermitage didn't have the space, or the will, to display. There were literally dozens of rooms, but he had studied floor plans of the museum and he knew precisely where he was going. They reached the door he was looking for. Still seven minutes before the power returned.

As he walked though the corridor between the cellars, Dimitriy was more puzzled than alarmed by the ease with which he'd been able to get back into the building. 'Dimitriy to control. Dimitriy to control.' He tried to call Yuri to let him know he was back inside, but the basement was a notorious radio blackspot. No reply, no real surprise.

The commander studied the long corridor of packing cases and badly wrapped parcels. 'Row four, section B,' he said to himself. He'd memorized the shape, size and number of the package he sought and it took him no more than a minute to track it down. Despite the tight schedule, he allowed himself a few seconds to enjoy the moment. Finally this was the reward for years of searching, planning and training and the client's enormous investment. He knew he could probably carry it alone, but he gestured to the man beside him to help. Then, a moment of unfamiliar doubt.

'Hold it,' he said. The other operative stepped back, his surprise hidden by his night-vision gear. 'Let's make sure we got what we came for and not some old guy's favourite piss pot.' He produced a knife from his belt and levered free the lid of the packing case with a splintering of nailed wood. The object inside had been packed in straw and he pulled it aside to reveal a glint of gold. Exactly what he expected to see. He grinned at the other man, then replaced the lid, hammering in the nails with the butt of the knife.

Behind them, the armourer had been working to place a series of what appeared to be large upturned soup plates among the boxes and crates, linked by wire to a central mechanism that sat on the cellar floor and included two tubes of liquid, a large battery and an old-fashioned mobile phone. 'I'm done,' he announced.

'Good work,' the leader said. 'Cover the rear.' He inspected the bomb. The explosion would conceal what they had stolen. If the security guards were lucky, they'd survive along with most of the main palace, but the six Russian anti-tank mines would sure blow the hell out of the east wing and the cellars.

'Go.' He picked up one end of the packing case as his subordinate manhandled the other. The case felt heavier than he'd imagined, but it was nothing for two fit men. They sidled through the door of the cellar and made their way to the stairway, followed by the armourer. Before they reached it a sharp order rang out in Russian and they were blinded by a searing light.

Dimitriy had been approaching the cellar when he heard the voices. His first thought had been to go for help, but logic told him these men wouldn't be here if Yuri and the rest of his shift were still free. Still he could have turned and walked away, but this was what he was paid for. He pulled the gun from its holster, checked the ammunition and flicked off the safety catch.

'Halt! Stay where you are or I shoot.'

The shout and the beam from the powerful torch froze the men in place. 'Shit,' the leader muttered beneath his breath. He squinted into the glare past his black-suited subordinates and saw a fat man in an ill-fitting blue security guard's uniform standing by the cellar entrance pointing a gun in his direction. Black patches of sweat stained the armpits of the tunic and the guard was breathing hard, but he held the pistol steady and from here the mouth of the barrel looked like a cannon.

'Take it easy, friend. Nobody needs to get hurt here,' the leader called. The pistol swung towards him. In a whisper, he ordered, 'Get ready.'

Dimitriy was angry. The night-vision goggles puzzled him, but the dark boiler suits and ski masks told him only one thing. He had watched and wept when the Moscow theatre siege ended in explosions, clouds of poisoned gas and gunfire. He had no doubt the rescuers

45

had been incompetent, but the reason 129 innocents had died was because men like these brought terror into his country. 'Move and I shoot,' he warned and he meant it. The torch moved between the three men, the light magnified and eyeball-scorching in the lens of the goggles, but the leader saw his opportunity. The armourer partly shielded the mercenary carrying the other end of the crate. 'Hit him when you get a clear shot,' he said calmly in English.

'What did you say?' Dimitriy demanded. 'You—' He didn't have the opportunity to finish the sentence. The man in the centre of the trio moved faster than he'd ever seen a man move and he flinched at the muzzle flash before the bullet from the GSh-18 hit him low in the belly. Despite being half-blinded by the torch the soldier had had a clear aim and he believed to his last heartbeat that he'd fired a killing shot. But Dimitriy wasn't just a fat man in a bad suit. He had once been a thin man wearing the uniform of the Guards Airborne Assault Brigade among the super-heated rocks of the Panshir Valley and as his body absorbed the energy of the bullet he got off a round that took the other man in the right eye and dropped him in a spray of blood and brains. Dimitriy knew the damage the bullet had done to his insides but, even with his strength failing, he tried to raise the gun for a second shot just as the armourer fired his first. The 9mm parabellum round left the barrel at a muzzle velocity of 1,100 feet per second and hit the cylinder of Dimitriy's Kobalt revolver. It struck at an angle which made the grotesquely misshapen bullet ricochet upward with a force that blew off most of Dimitriy's lower jaw and part of his left cheekbone before hurling his body off the door jamb into the cellar.

'Fuck,' the leader cursed, now struggling to hold the crate on his own. He willed himself to be calm. Everything had turned to shit, but that was nothing new in his world. The key was to keep a lid on it and to get the fuck out before things got worse. He shouted an order to the armourer. 'Make sure of that bastard and get back to help me with this.' But before the man was halfway to the cellar door he took another glance at his watch. They had just over one minute before the lights came back on. The clock was ticking, their timings out. 'Belay that. He's dead or close enough. We need to move *now*.'

Abandoning their comrade's body they struggled up the stairs and through the museum. The others were waiting in the van as the leader and the armourer pushed the packing case into the rear. They didn't ask where the third man was, they didn't have to.

'Drive,' the leader shouted into his throat mike.

Inside the cellar Dimitriy was only vaguely aware of his terrible wounds. His world came and went in alternating waves of trauma-induced shock and agonizing pain. He still had eyes though, and his conscious mind identified a sight that had been common enough in the Russian-occupied rear area of Afghanistan. The object in front of him was certainly a TM-57 anti-tank mine. Normally it would take the weight of a large vehicle to detonate it, but he noted the wire leading from it to the contraption in the centre of the floor. He knew the damage it would do. Dimitriy began to claw his way towards the trigger mechanism.

When the assault team reached the outskirts of the city, the leader ordered the driver to stop the van. He nodded to the armourer, and the bomb maker retrieved a mobile phone from the breast pocket of his overall. By now the men had removed their masks and they leaned forward in anticipation as the armourer punched in the number. When the signal reached the phone it would complete a circuit which would mix the two explosive liquids and send an electric charge to the anti-tank mines.

Dimitriy studied the mechanism with the bemused concentration of a drunk man peering at a keyhole. He was lying in a pool of his own blood and his vision had begun to fade. He knew he hadn't got long. He looked at the mobile phone. It was of a type more familiar to his son, but some instinct told him to remove the battery. He reached out towards it. Maybe now they would give him a raise.

The leader opened the van door and listened for the familiar muted thunder of the explosion. After two or three anxious minutes he turned accusingly to the armourer.

'I can go back . . .' the man offered.

The leader shook his head. The helicopter would be at the rendezvous and they could be in Finland and home free within the hour. He banged on the partition between the rear and the driver's seat and the van took off.

'We've got what we came for.'

IV

In his Old Bond Street office, four storeys above the well-heeled shoppers who could afford to buy from the expensive shops he walked past every day, Jamie cleared a space for the maroon pay book and the journal among the auction catalogues and art history books piled haphazardly on the desk.

He hesitated, torn between the fascination of the journal's ruled pages and the pay book, which he knew would give him an immediate insight into the grandfather he had never truly known. The journal must once have been an expensive purchase and was of a type he guessed had been used to record the meetings of exclusive gentlemen's dining clubs. It was three-quarters of an inch thick, A5-sized and bound in what had once been fine quality blue leather, now scuffed and faded with age. There had been a clasp to hold it shut, but that had long since disappeared and the book was now held closed by a piece of tightly knotted silver cord. The pages appeared well-thumbed, but something told him it hadn't been opened for many years.

Reluctantly, he laid it aside and opened the little maroon pay book.

The first page came as a surprise. Jamie knew that most soldiers who served in the Second World War had been volunteers or conscripts, civilians in uniform who reluctantly stepped forward to serve their country against the Nazis. He had expected his grandfather to be one of them, but Matthew George Sinclair had signed up with the Royal Berkshire Regiment on August 17 1937 at the age of nineteen. The pay book recorded his height as 6 feet, his chest expansion as 40 inches and his weight as a 180 pounds. His appearance was described as – eyes: green; hair: dark; no distinguishing marks. Jamie felt a slight shiver as he recognized himself in his second year at university as a member of the Officer's Training Corps. On graduation, he'd had an offer from the Royal Military Academy at Sandhurst and he had almost completed the selection process before his mind had rebelled against the lifetime of discipline he was letting himself in for.

Other dog-eared pages contained information on Matthew's pay and allowances, deductions, training received and courses taken (rifle shooting/rated sniper) and his commission with the rank of lieutenant in September 1939. But the most interesting was 'Record of Specialist Employment Whilst Serving'. Here was revealed the mystery of the awards he'd found in the metal box. The African Star and clasp, the France and

Germany Star, the 1939–45 Star, the Defence Medal and the War Medal, all dated and initialled by his commanding officers. And finally, the Military Cross for 'acts of gallantry in the area of Augsburg, south Germany'.

But who was the man behind the medals?

Only now did he feel able to pick up the journal and work with his fingers at the knot holding it closed. He opened the book at the first page. Each entry was preceded by a date and laid out in the neat copper-plate writing he remembered from the few letters and cards he had received from his grandfather while at university. Some of the wording and phraseology seemed quaint to him, as if it had been written in Victorian times. The first few entries were dated in the days just after Matthew's promotion, when war was declared in the late summer of 1939, and reflected the gung-ho enthusiasm of a young man on the brink of his greatest challenge; along with a frankly stated unease about letting 'the men' down. How would he be affected by fear? Matthew was reticent about his horror of being maimed, but death appeared to hold no terrors for him. There was also a tacit acknowledgement that keeping such a journal was frowned upon and that the writer would have to suspend it when he went overseas, which seemed imminent. But it quickly became clear that Matthew Sinclair had become so involved in recording his thoughts that he had ignored the restriction, risking reprimand or even court martial, an act of rebellion that revealed something else Jamie hadn't known about his grandfather.

The phone rang at the other end of the desk and Gail,

his secretary, answered. 'Saintclair Fine Arts, may I help you?' She listened for a few seconds, before placing her hand over the mouthpiece. 'A call from a hospital in the Midlands. Can you take it?'

Reluctantly, he laid the journal aside and accepted the phone. 'Jamie Saintclair.'

'Is this the grandson of the late Reverend Matthew Sinclair?' a serious female voice demanded.

'That's correct.'

'Only the names confused me.'

'They often do.' Jamie smiled wryly. 'How can I help you?'

'My name is Carol O'Connor. I'm a nurse at the St Cross Hospital in Rugby. I'm sorry to bother you, but one of our long-term patients says he knew your grandfather and is very keen to talk to you.'

Jamie raised his eyebrows and Gail smiled. 'I'm pretty busy at the moment. But put him on the line. It's always nice to speak to one of my grandfather's former parishioners.'

Carol O'Connor's tone turned apologetic. 'I'm afraid that, like many of our elderly clients, Stan is very strong-willed. He will only talk to you face to face.'

Jamie sighed. 'I don't think—'

'And he isn't one of your grandfather's parishioners. He says he served with a Matthew Sinclair during the war.'

Jamie's heart gave a little flutter. 'What did you say his name was?'

'Stan. Stanislaus Kozlowski.'

*　　*　　*

'I read 'bout Matthew Sinclair's det in *The Times* newspaper and I tink, maybe this is same Matt Sinclair from vor. Carol she a good girl, do anytink for us inmates. She check wit' undertaker and now you are here.' Sixty-eight years in Britain had failed to take the edge off Stan Kozlowski's Polish accent; indeed it had added a nasal West Midlands twang that made his words barely comprehensible at first hearing. Jamie suspected it was an old man's indulgence and about as authentic as Stan's hair, which swept back from a wide brow, an unlikely crow-black helmet that gleamed like a guardsman's toecap. Shrunken and plainly exhausted, the old man lay back in the tentacled embrace of a kidney dialysis machine, surrounded by coils of tubing which pulsed to the rhythm of a beeping monitor. The Pole saw Jamie's look. 'Four hour a day. Real pain in de ass, eh? But worth it. You comes back later, maybe Stan take you dancing?' A shaking hand reached into the top pocket of his pyjamas and pulled out a faded black-and-white photograph. 'See, me and Matt. Late 'forty-four. Maybe 'forty-five?' Jamie accepted the picture. Two soldiers in camouflage jump smocks standing beside a jeep. Stan was instantly recognizable as the bare-headed young man on the right: short, dark and with a fierce scowl on his pinched, unshaven face. The tall, rangy lieutenant in the paratrooper's pot helmet could have been Jamie's twin brother. 'Me and Matt, ve lose touch after ve comes back from vor, but Matt, he tells me had enough of fighting. He go into Church.' The old man laughed. 'Me, I can't go back Poland cos Reds vill shoot me, so I go into car factory in Solihull. One minute officer and gentleman and genuine heroic Polish ally, next minute job-stealing Polish bastard, eh?'

'I'm sorry,' Jamie apologized. 'I've heard that Polish soldiers weren't treated particularly well after the war.'

Stan laughed again, a raking cough that sounded painful to the ear. 'Dat *lizus* Churchill, he sell us down river. But you don't feel sorry for Stan. Had good life. Lots of whisky. Lots of girls.' The old man's voice faded and he lay back, breathing noisily through his nose, but after a few moments he opened his eyes again. 'How Matt die?'

Jamie told him about the accident. 'Look, Mr Kozlowski – Stan – I'm tiring you. Maybe I should come back later, or tomorrow?'

Stan shook his head. 'Is OK. Not a bad way to go, eh? Just one snap and you're in heaven. Better than this. I know. Broke lots of necks during war, me and Matt.' Jamie opened his mouth to protest, but the Pole spat words like three-second bursts of automatic fire. 'Quick and clean.' He raised his hands as if he held a head between them, and twisted with a single sharp movement, at the same time making a distinct tick through his teeth. 'Old Stan he still got it, eh? I remember the first time . . .' Without warning, his eyes dropped and he began to speak softly in a confused mix of Polish and English. Jamie could make out enough to understand that he was hearing the story of Poland's fall. After a few minutes the voice faded again and he realized Stan had fallen into a doze. Half an hour later, the old man was still asleep, and Jamie watched his body twitch and jerk as he refought the war.

A nurse inspected the monitors before rearranging the old soldier's blanket, tucking it around his neck and shoulders.

'Stan's a bit restless today, I'm afraid. I'm Carol, Mr Saintclair, we spoke on the phone.' She offered him her hand and he shook it. She was tiny, but heavy breasted, with strawberry-blonde curls and that confident, un-flappable air the best nurses cultivate. 'I should have warned you about this, but he was very keen to see you. Morning is a much better time for him.'

'I'm glad I came.' Jamie hid his frustration behind a smile. 'But I think I've tired him enough for one day. Maybe I can come back again another time?'

'Of course, we always encourage visitors and Stan doesn't have anyone nearby. His children both emigrated to Australia, I think. He's a remarkable man. You're seeing him at his worst. The machine takes a lot out of him, but he still insists on a walk along the stream every morning and he plans to march in the parade on Armistice Day.'

Jamie thanked her and picked up his coat. A drowsy voice interrupted his departure.

'You come back tomorrow, then ve talk about Matt, eh? I tell you what I told other guy. About last mission with the *szkopi*. Goddam disaster. Brass called it Operation Equity, but Matt he had other name for it. Operation Doomsday.'

V

On his way back to the train, Jamie debated whether to bother coming back the next day. He had plenty of other things he should be doing and the Polish veteran's ramblings, though interesting, were sometimes ludicrous. What was that stuff about Matthew breaking necks, for God's sake? Still, he wouldn't decide immediately. Once he was settled in his seat he opened the journal at the page where he'd left off.

As the rampaging *Wehrmacht* finished off the scattered remnants of Poland's destroyed army and the Soviet Union joined in, feasting on the defeated nation's carcass, the Royal Berkshires had embarked for France along with 150,000 soldiers of the British Expeditionary Force. The initial overseas entries, as the battalion deployed inland, leapfrogged erratically between the wide-eyed wonder of a youthful tourist and the excitement of a professional soldier desperate to get to grips with his enemy. Lieutenant Matthew Sinclair also had a touching regard for his soldiers' welfare. His relationship with his sergeant, Anderson, a man old enough to be his father, seemed to have been particularly close. The cosy, confessional tone of the diaries ceased on 10 May 1940 when the *Wehrmacht* attacked France and Belgium. Matthew Sinclair was about to get his baptism of fire. His Berkshires were part of the 2nd Infantry Division and on the far right of the British line, south-east of Lille, defending the flatlands around the River Dyle and in the direct line of General Erich Hoepner's rampaging XVI Panzer Corps.

The first entry of the shooting war was almost comically indignant.

My initial experience of battle was entirely farcical as we weren't allowed to move to our positions in Belgium until the Germans attacked first. As a consequence we were quite ill-prepared for them. Nevertheless, I feel very excited because this is what IT has all been for. First bombs fell during afternoon stand down.

But the horrors that followed chilled Jamie's blood. The bombs fell so frequently in the following days that Matthew stopped recording them. Meanwhile, the tone of the diary became ever more disjointed and frenetic. Jamie imagined the brief sentences being scribbled in the dark as the writer lay cowering in some water-filled ditch with his ears tuned for the slightest sound of an approaching enemy. Snatches of personal shorthand recorded what may have been momentous happenings, but were forever unintelligible. These pages were torn and mud-spattered and some were missing altogether. On one, Jamie noticed a fine spray of what could only have been blood. Within six days, the BEF was surrounded and fighting for its very survival. The Berkshires were ordered to fall back towards the Channel ports, and Lieutenant Sinclair tersely recorded the disintegration of his battalion as it was chewed to pieces by the panzers, entire platoons and companies wiped out in savage minor engagements that would never appear in the history books.

18 May 1940 (near Mons). Cut off from battalion. Sergeant Anderson killed today. Shot through head while counter-attacking German tanks armed with hand grenades. Not sure I can get through this without him. I wept. Hope nobody saw me. We are now just twelve men.

Jamie read on. Hunger, thirst, strain and exhaustion took its toll on the retreating British soldiers, and his grandfather's morale collapsed as he played a deadly game of cat-and-mouse amidst the chaos of defeat. At one point it was clear he had to be persuaded not to surrender. That entry was followed by a gap of several days. Then:

2 June 1940 Reached Dunkirk perimeter with one sergeant and three men, none from 1st RBR. Waited seven hours on Mole for evacuation. Eventually picked up from beach by chap with motor boat 0100 hours and transferred to destroyer HMS Whitshed. Bombed continuously. Must sleep. God, how good that word sounds. Sleep.

The words began to blur and Jamie noticed with surprise that the train was drawing in to Euston station. He felt utterly drained, as if he'd been fighting side by side with the men whose dramatic lives and deaths the diary chronicled in the final days of Operation Dynamo, the evacuation of the Dunkirk perimeter, when Matthew had been among the very last of the three hundred thousand French and British soldiers to leave the beaches.

One thing was certain. He had to know more about Matthew Sinclair's war.

He phoned ahead next morning to confirm his arrival and found Carol waiting for him at the hospital entrance before she started her shift.

'You're a little early. He's out walking. He likes to take the path through the fields to Dunchurch Road then back again. He should be on his way back now.'

Jamie remembered the pale figure hooked up to the dialysis machine. 'Does he go alone?'

'Please don't underestimate Stan.' She smiled. 'The treatment is hard on him, but he's as tough as a pair of old army boots.'

'Maybe I could go and meet him?' he suggested.

'I think he'd like that. It's just around the corner and

across the main road. You can't miss it. The path that runs beside the stream.'

He followed her instructions and found a track between two fields. Ahead he could see where a line of trees flanked the stream – actually more a sluggish canal – and beyond them an estate of substantial houses. He would have expected to meet the old man by now, but it was a warm morning and Stan must be close to ninety; maybe he had stopped for a rest? The further he went from the hospital the more his concern grew, but he wasn't truly worried until he reached the road at the far side of the field. There was no reason the Pole couldn't have taken a different route back, or been given a lift, but . . . As he retraced his steps Jamie found himself searching among the tall grass on the verges of the path, and in the glittering shadows beneath the trees.

Stan had worn a black overcoat despite the heat of the day and that was why Jamie had missed him on his first pass. He had to look twice before he climbed down to the river's edge on legs that seemed to belong to some-one else. Gradually, his eyes adjusted to the gloom and realized what he was seeing. Christ. This couldn't be happening. Not again.

The old man lay face down in the shallows beneath an ancient willow, his body weighed down by the waterlogged cloth of the coat. The black overcoat looked like just another shadow on waters the colour of stewed tea, its folds billowing gently in the almost non-existent current. Jamie struggled through the water until he could take a handful of cloth and heave the body over. As he turned, Stanislaus Kozlowski's bespoke artificial hairpiece detached itself and floated sedately downstream. Reproachful eyes stared back from features set in the same fierce scowl they had worn in the wartime photograph.

'You'd be amazed how often it happens, sir.' The middle-aged constable's voice was almost resentful, as if the dead man had deliberately spoiled his day. 'Elderly person goes out for a walk and doesn't come back. No rhyme nor reason to it, they just decide it's their time. We find them days, sometimes weeks, later, and there's always water involved. The young ones, they'll step out in front of a train, but the old, they head for the sea or the river. Primeval instinct, I reckon.'

'So you're certain Stan – Mr Kozlowski – killed himself.'

The officer's look hardened and Jamie realized he'd overstepped some invisible mark. 'Based on our initial investigations and unless you have reason to believe otherwise, sir?'

'No, of course not.'

'No immediate signs of violence visible on the victim. You'd have noticed if there had been undue disturbance of the grass, wouldn't you, sir, when you marched through our potential crime scene in your size-ten boots?'

Jamie bridled at the implied criticism. 'I thought my first priority was to help Mr Kozlowski.'

'Of course you did, but then he was already dead.'

He raised a hand to forestall any argument. 'It'll be up to the Coroner to decide cause of death. We have your address, sir, in the event we have to contact you again? You'll probably be called as a witness.'

Back at the hospital, Jamie tracked down Carol to the ward where he'd first met the Pole. It was obvious she'd been crying.

'Not very professional, is it?' she said with a wet smile. 'But I'd grown very fond of old Stan. He could be sharp, but he was also brave and generous and kind.' She shook her head and he wondered if she had been half in love with the old man.

He told her what the police had said and she nodded distractedly. 'That's true. You can never tell with the elderly. Sometimes it's as if a switch has been flicked. But Stan, he seemed so keen to continue his talk with you. I just can't . . .'

She sniffed and Jamie laid a comforting hand on her arm. 'I got the idea he had a lot to tell me. It crossed my mind that he might have written some of it down?'

'I can have a look,' she said warily. 'But I'm not sure I'd be allowed to hand it over to you even if he had. It would be the property of his next of kin.'

'Don't worry; it was just a thought. I'm sure you have enough on your plate already.'

She pursed her lips. 'There'll be some kind of inquiry. Should we have allowed him out on his own? I'm not certain now, but he was so insistent.'

'Maybe this isn't the time for it, but I had one other thing I wanted to ask,' Jamie said. 'Stan mentioned that he was going to tell me what he had told the other guy. Does that ring any bells with you?'

Carol's face set in a frown. 'Actually, it does. About ten days ago he had a visit from a Polish gentleman doing some sort of research on the lives of exiles still in this country. I wasn't on duty, so I didn't see him, but afterwards Stan became quite animated. It was obvious that he'd stirred up memories Stan had buried a long time ago. I think it was one of the reasons he was so determined to get in touch when he heard your grandfather had died. He said he and Matthew had been part of something important and it was time to tell the story. I have a friend in the local newspaper and he'd agreed to come here to interview Stan about it.'

Jamie thanked her again and set off along the corridor, his head filled with that first glimpse of the old man's body and weighed down by the questions that would now never be answered.

'Mr Saintclair?' He turned to find Carol bearing down on him. 'I think he would have wanted you to have this.' She placed the faded photograph in his hand, closed hers over it and walked away before he could say anything.

He looked down at the square of creased paper and wondered what secrets the blank-eyed young faces were hiding.

VI

A night searching the internet drew a disappointing blank on anything called Operation Equity that wasn't about spending billions to rescue banks. By the time he woke the next day Jamie's hands itched to get back to the diary, but he still had a business to run. He spent the morning working on the itinerary for an upcoming trip to Switzerland to check out the sale of what might be a Watteau once owned by an Alsatian industrialist and his family. Economically he had to find other reasons to justify the expense. That meant checking out auctions and galleries in Geneva for acquisitions that might yield a small profit. The Watteau itself was such an ugly painting he wondered why anyone would want it back.

At lunchtime he changed from his suit into casual jacket and jeans and took the train from Victoria station to Welwyn. He still had too much to do before the clearers arrived, and the discovery of his grandfather's journal had set him back at least twenty-four hours. As he changed trains at Finsbury Park he couldn't get the diary out of his mind. Nothing had prepared him for the sheer awfulness of his grandfather's war. He tried to remember Matthew's eyes. Was there any evidence there that the man behind them had killed and killed again? It was never stated directly in the journal, but there were plenty of hints that couldn't mean anything else. Hints that put Stan's boast about breaking necks into perspective. Lieutenant Matthew Sinclair had been forced to kill to survive, and it had changed him. Jamie's walk from the station to his house took less than ten minutes and on the way he enjoyed the sun on his face and the sound of the birds singing. This was home, familiar and comforting. Welwyn Garden City was well named. It had been planned with wide, tree-lined boulevards radiating from a central square. Of course, it had developed and grown since Ebenezer Howard had designed it in the 1920s, but the original principles still held sway and no one who lived there wanted to live anywhere else.

Before he got started, he switched on the heating and filled the kettle. While it boiled, he leafed through the newspaper he'd bought, which, as it had been for months, was full of the credit crisis. Jamie tended to bypass bad news stories, but he took a certain doom-laden satisfaction that house prices were in free-fall just when he had one to sell. On the upside, if there was an upside to the death of a family member, the place should still provide him with enough money to survive for a few years, even in his present state of semi-permanent business doldrum.

A story on the Foreign pages caught his eye. A security guard at the Menshikov Palace in St Petersburg had died a hero fighting off an attack by suspected Chechen terrorists. Something flared inside him. What did these people think they would gain by destroying some of the most beautiful things in the world?

The puzzling element of the attack was that the terrorists, one of whom had been shot dead, had taken only *one* item before they set their explosive charges and escaped; a Tibetan artefact that appeared to have little value and even less real interest. Why that, when there were so many more valuable things they could have fenced on the international black market to help fund their cause? The piece was said to have no national or cultural importance, so the authorities were working on the theory that it had some sort of religious significance. In the meantime, a minor international row had broken out over the casket's ownership. China, which now controlled Tibet, had demanded its return on the grounds that it had been looted from the territory before the war, while Germany claimed that the then Dalai Llama had given its 1937 expedition permission to remove it from the country. A German spokesman said that if found it should be sent back with all the rest of the artworks the Red Army had pillaged on their way to Berlin. The Russian president condemned the outrage while threatening the usual bloody consequences and said the return of the Tibet casket was not subject to discussion. It might have been comical but for the death of the poor guard.

Jamie was upstairs when he heard the sound of a door opening and closing. The only person with a key for the house, apart from himself, was Mrs Jenkins next door who had been Matthew's housekeeper. He grimaced at the thought of wasting an hour chatting to the old busybody while he should be working. The way things were going he'd be lucky to finish before he flew to Geneva.

Reluctantly, he dragged himself downstairs, hesitating as a thought occurred to him at the spot where he'd found Matthew, before rounding the corner with a welcoming smile that instantly froze on his face.

In the centre of the living room, with a pile of papers in his hand, stood a hard-eyed older man wearing a black leather bomber jacket and dark trousers. In other circumstances, the almost uniform and the close-cropped hair might have marked him as a plain-clothes cop. But, if he was, how did he get into the house? The man stared. Everything about him now: the look on his face; his stance, balanced on the balls of his feet; the way he held his hands, said one thing – ready.

'Can I help you?' Jamie said warily.

'You can fuck off,' the intruder suggested in a flat accent that originated somewhere east of London's docklands.

The dismissal was meant to intimidate him, but Jamie felt only a curious thrill of anticipation. He had missed out on a light heavyweight boxing Blue at Cambridge after coming up against a combative South African with a titanium chin and a punch like a steam hammer. That, and the close combat training he'd been given in the OTC, had nurtured an unlikely, but surprisingly fierce taste for moderated violence. The only drawback to a fight was the size of the room and the furniture, which precluded any of the Ali-style dancing he favoured. Still, he was certain he could take this guy, even if he was a few pounds heavier and looked as if he could handle himself.

'I believe you'd better leave before I call the police,' he said politely.

'Why don't you make me . . . ?' He launched himself across the room, swinging a telegraphed right hook designed to break the younger man's jaw. Jamie saw it come and timed his response to perfection. With a twist of his body, he swayed clear and stepped aside, allowing his attacker's momentum to take him past. When he was placed just so, Jamie rammed a lightning one-two into his kidneys that brought a grunt of agony.

The intruder turned and stretched, rubbing at his lower back. He was hurt, but he'd been hurt before. Warier this time, he tested Jamie with a couple of jabs, one of which stung the younger man's shoulder. So, he fancied himself as a boxer? That suited Jamie just fine. He hunched his shoulders and raised his guard. In the next minute and a half he connected with two good shots to the head that left the other man bleeding from the nose and lip, following them with a right to the solar plexus that doubled him in two. Jamie stepped forward to finish him off, but the intruder had other ideas. The twinkle of a knife point betrayed the blade in his right hand and Jamie felt a surge of adrenalin as he understood the battle was now in deadly earnest. He was close to the kitchen door, but there was no question of retreating. Dropping into the classic self-defence crouch, the voice of his close combat instructor whispered in his ear: *It's all about the timing, laddie. Let him make his move, then use his own momentum to hurt him.* But his opponent was better with the knife than he had been with his fists. As he feinted a darting jab to the body, the point came slicing up towards Jamie's eyes. Forced to retreat, he stumbled on a chair and fell to the carpet. As he tried to squirm away, he found the other man looming over him and probing for the opening he needed. 'Now we'll hear you squeal, you bastard.' Helpless, Jamie waited for the knife to plunge. Instead, the man glanced away, distracted for a vital second. Jamie saw his chance and brought his heel up hard into his opponent's unprotected groin. With a groan, the intruder doubled over and dropped the knife. Jamie hauled himself to his feet. Very deliberately he brought his knee up into the man's face, sending him backwards over a chair.

'Right you bastard,' he said. 'What—'
The whole world went dark.

He found himself hovering just below wakefulness. He couldn't be entirely certain where he was, but a combination of scents, sounds and the feel of threadbare linen sheets told him it must be hospital. The pain was out there waiting for him. He decided to let it wait a little longer.

The next time he came to, he realized how sensible his earlier decision had been. From a delicate point just below his waist to the top of his throbbing head, his body was one big ball of suffering, an all-over toothache only time would cure. He had a vague memory of being in a fight, but felt as if he'd been run over by a bus. He risked opening his eyes, or, rather, an eye singular; only one appeared to be working. A female figure rose at the end of the bed and he recognized his secretary. 'Hello, Gail,' he croaked. 'Are we still in business?' She looked up in alarm and he saw something in her eyes. He wondered why he'd never realized how much she cared for him. As he tried to think of something clever to say, she waved to someone beyond his line of vision and a large, uncomfortable-looking man hove into view, accompanied by a young nurse.

The nurse placed a cool hand on Jamie's brow, shone a light in his good eye and asked with a professional smile if he felt up to answering a few questions from Sergeant – a cough from the background – sorry, Detective Sergeant Milligan.

'Tell him if he's here to arrest me, I surrender.'

She laughed in a way that he found reassuring. 'It may not feel like it, Mr Saintclair, but your injuries are mostly superficial bruising. No broken ribs or internal injuries, thankfully. The blow to your head was the one we were worried about, but any concussion you have is mild.'

'They gave you a right going-over,' DS Milligan confirmed. 'You were lucky.' Jamie had a flash of his attacker's face as he stood with the knife at the ready and silently agreed. He was lucky to be alive. Whoever had hit him from behind must have hauled the knife-man off before he could do any real damage, then allowed him to have a little fun just to even things up.

'Why . . . ?'

'That's what we're trying to find out, sir. I'm afraid the house is a bit of a shambles, although you won't be worrying too much about that just now. This sort of thing often happens after the death of someone who lives alone. The crooks see the notice in the paper and reckon the house will be empty. We'll have to ask you to check if anything is missing, but for the moment all we know is that they didn't take any of the valuables that would normally be targeted by people like this. Very professional. No stone unturned, if you see what I mean, but it appears they were after something *specific*. You wouldn't know what that might be? No Picassos stored at your granddad's, given your profession and all? No little stashes of diamonds the taxman doesn't know about? Not that it would be any business of mine.'

Jamie tried a smile, but it was too painful, and he had a feeling that shaking his head would be worse.

Milligan got the message and nodded sympathetically. 'Well, if anything does come to mind . . .' He asked for a description of the attacker, which Jamie gave him, and left.

Jamie asked the nurse to prop him up in a sitting position and he and Gail talked about his trip to Switzerland – postponed – and the other appointments she'd have to cancel. 'I thought you might need this.' Gail handed over his antiquated leather briefcase. When she had gone, he opened it and pulled out the journal.

It was only when he had it in his hands that he realized just how *specific* it was.

VII

The British Expeditionary Force which landed in France
lost thirty thousand men defending Dunkirk. Lieutenant
Matthew Sinclair had come close to losing his sanity.
Matthew recorded his landing on British soil in a flat,
laconic single sentence that was followed by one of the
now familiar gaps. The next entry revealed that, while
Winston Churchill was exhorting his countrymen
to fight on the beaches and the landing grounds, the
journal's author had been lying in a hospital bed not
dissimilar to the one presently occupied by his grandson.

After a short leave spent with his parents in
Kidderminster, in the summer of 1940 Matthew was
posted back to his battalion at a bleak training camp
somewhere in the Midlands. The 1st Royal Berkshires
had ceased to exist as a fighting unit and all Lieutenant
Sinclair's energy was devoted to reforging it. It was
exhausting work, with few opportunities for relaxation,
but during that time something wonderful happened.
Matthew Sinclair fell in love.

Now the journal transformed from a record of military life to the diary of a love affair. The girl's name was never mentioned, but Matthew's heart soared and his prose soared with it as he attempted to articulate the strength of first his attraction, then his affection and finally – and when he read some of the entries Jamie found himself blushing – their mutual passion.

The intensity of Matthew's love grew so powerful that it was painful for Jamie to relive, and he had to skip over the next few entries. Then, at some point in the late spring of 1941, it vanished. What was more, it vanished in a flurry of violence, the ferocity of which was still evident in the ragged edges of pages torn from the spine of the journal. Jamie found himself mirroring the pain Matthew must have felt in that moment when his fingers had brutally removed the evidence of the final months of the affair. The next entry might have provided some kind of explanation, but it had been written by a man either drunk to the brink of insensibility or distressed beyond despair. Words had not been written, they had been smashed into the page, only to be scored out with enough force to tear through the three following pages, or smudged by some liquid whose origin Jamie could only guess at. But if the words were unreadable, the emotion Matthew Sinclair was expressing in his savage frenzy was clear. Hatred. A murderous unquenchable, all-consuming hunger for revenge.

Two days later he had requested a transfer to the Commandos.

The Commando special service brigades were born out of Churchill's impatience at being unable to retaliate at the Nazis poised on France's Channel coast. Thousands of men from the remnant saved at Dunkirk volunteered for the chance to get their own back and by 1941 the unfit and the unsuitable had been weeded out at secret camps in the Highlands by the toughest training regime in the British army. Now they were an élite service, ready to fulfil the prime minister's vow to 'set Europe ablaze' and the perfect haven for a man bent on bloody murder or getting himself killed. Yet Matthew's time with the Commandos was short-lived and characterized by frustration, self-pity and heavy drinking that was evident in the number of pages stained by the bottom of a glass. Whilst Matthew fretted to get at the enemy, Churchill limited Commando incursions to pinprick operations for which he was never chosen. By August his patience had run out and he volunteered for a new and untried outfit called the Special Air Service, then operating in North Africa. Jamie had the impression Matthew's superiors were glad to see him go. You had to be even crazier to volunteer for the SAS than the Commandos.

Disappointingly, it rapidly became clear that his secretive new employers were a great deal more stringent about diary keeping than the regulars. Between August 1941 and October 1944 the journal contained a single entry – a cryptic reminder, at the end of 1943, for an appointment:

M suggests meeting at Baker Street re: Jedburgh
after I've knocked the sand from my boots. 10 a.m.
Sounds interesting.

The war ground towards its inevitable end, with the
Nazis squeezed between the twin jaws of the Allied
forces and the Red Army. Now the regular entries
resumed. Lieutenant Sinclair had been promoted to
captain and placed on light duties as a liaison officer
in northern Holland, and then in Germany where his
fluency in the language would have been invaluable. No
mention of Stan, but Jamie had an image of him looming
in the background, a permanent reminder that war was
no laughing matter. He flicked over the following pages
until he reached the entry for 1 May 1945.

News of Hitler's death came through this morning
when we were close to Leipzig, where we are work-
ing with Patton's Third Army. There is a feeling
that it is all over and that we will soon be going
home. I suffer it as much as anyone, but I must
ensure the men don't drop their guard. It would
be stupid to get yourself killed now, after all we've
been through.

Jamie lay back and closed his eyes. Reading the journal
had affected him like no other book had. When he'd
started, it had been in the hope that it would bring him
closer to the grandfather he'd never truly known. Yet he

found he still had more questions than answers. There was anger, too, real anger, at the true scale of their deceit. He knew it was selfish, but he felt that Matthew and his mother had not only robbed him of a hero, but of a father figure who might have shaped his identity in a different way, perhaps even changed the course of his life. Each individual is unique, but they are as much the products of their upbringing and childhood influences as they are of their DNA. What type of man would he have become if he'd known his grandfather had won the Military Cross? It would have given him something to look up to, perhaps made him strive harder. He would have approached challenges in a different way. He knew now he could have beaten the South African who had given him a battering in the boxing ring if only he'd known how much aggression he was truly capable of. His rejection of Sandhurst had been partly, maybe mostly, because he didn't think it was *his kind of thing*. But it *was* his kind of thing. Soldiering was in his blood. If they had only shown him the journal when he was eighteen he wouldn't have become the frustrated failure he feared, deep down, he really was.

Just as maddening were the questions that remained unanswered. The gaps that persisted in his knowledge were as wide as those in the entries in the book. Was it only fatigue that caused the breakdown at Dunkirk? What had happened during the three years of silence in the SAS? What had ended the love affair that promised so much? And what was the significance of the Baker Street entry? He knew those questions would continue to haunt him. In some ways, he wished he'd never found the journal. Life had been simpler before he'd opened the blue leather covers. Lost in thought, he flicked over the next page.

2 May 1945 As the German army began to collapse in front of us I was summoned to Major Fitzpatrick and briefed for one final mission . . .

VIII

'You call yourself professionals? I could have picked a child from the street to do a better job.' The figure behind the desk stared at the two men in a way that made them feel as if he was sizing up their organs for a transplant. They called themselves Campbell and McKenzie, but their closest contact with Scotland had been through the mouth of a whisky bottle. McKenzie raised a hand to gingerly touch his bruised nose, but dropped it when he noticed the pale lips tighten in the unlined, expressionless face. It was a face that might have belonged to an albino, but for the eyes, which were points of lifeless pewter. When you looked again you realized that the odd colouring of the skin was less a matter of pigment than of a life lived in permanent shadow. Despite the setback at the target house the two men regarded themselves capable of handling any situation that could be resolved by force, but from the first they had sensed something in this man that made them wary. A dangerous stillness that took them back to days in South Armagh. Days when shadowy men whose abilities they'd learned to respect appeared from nowhere for operations that resulted only in clean kills. The leaden eyes pinned them remorselessly as the pale man continued in a deliberate, faintly accented English. 'This was to be a discreet, low-profile operation with minimal disturbance to the house and no – I repeat, no – violence. Yet what do I read on the police computer? A man we may require to cultivate is assaulted and taken to hospital with concussion. The property ransacked and overrun with investigators – now wondering why someone would go to so much trouble without stealing a single item. Any fool would have understood the need to take a few pieces of jewellery or the television set.'

'He hit Mac and—' Campbell, the man who had brained Jamie with his grandfather's ceramic tea caddy, was silenced by a raised hand.

'That is of no consequence now. What matters is that you will stay within reach of the grandson, but not so close that he might be alerted. If the journal exists, the chances are that this Jamie Saintclair now has it. For the moment, we will maintain electronic surveillance. When the opportunity arises you will enter his apartment and his office and carry out a search. Do you believe you can achieve that, gentlemen . . . discreetly and without violence?'

The question was delivered softly, but the unspoken threat was clear. The two men nodded.

'Then we'll say no more for the moment.'

When they left, he stared at the door for a long time.

Not quite sure. It might be better to be safe than to take the chance. He picked up a secure satellite phone from the desk and punched a speed-dial button. It was answered after two rings.

'Well?'

'I think it may have been a mistake not to bring in our own team.'

The man at the other end gave a faint snort of irritation. 'We talked about that. The risks outweighed the advantages.'

'Perhaps we are pushing forward too quickly and too hard,' the pale man persisted. 'We have waited a long time for this opportunity. What is another few months, even years, when balanced against the possible rewards?'

They had also talked about that, and he knew bringing up the subject would annoy the other man. Old men were always in a hurry, trying to make up for the time they had wasted in their youth and fearful that their next breath might be their last. Ever ready to snatch at opportunities. He was different. He had been taught patience from the day he was born, groomed to take advantage of the chance that might be about to present itself.

His listener chose to ignore the question. 'What are your specific concerns about these men, Frederick?'

The younger man smiled, amused by the use of his work name. Their dealings were conducted by single-use satellite phones using software that scrambled their voices, but the employment of the name was still a threat and they both knew it. 'They were recommended to me by a security company on the basis of their local knowledge and past record. I fear their talents may have been exaggerated.'

'They dealt with the old Pole discreetly enough.'

'That is true, but I questioned them again about Saintclair's grandfather. Campbell claimed it was an accident, but I think there may be more to it than that. They knew how vital he was to the operation. They knew he was an old man. They should have treated him with more caution. Either they were careless or they overstepped the mark. Campbell says he squirmed free as they were taking him upstairs. Perhaps that is true and perhaps it is not, but the fact is it should never have happened.'

'Do you believe lasting damage has been done?'

'No,' Frederick admitted. 'The police are treating it as a household accident and are not linking it to the burglary. There is no reason Saintclair should be alerted.'

'But?'

'But perhaps Mr Campbell and Mr McKenzie should be given a demonstration of the consequences of any further mistakes.'

The shortest of pauses. 'Arrange it.' Despite the scrambler, he could hear the grim smile in the other man's voice. 'What is your feeling about the journal?'

Frederick frowned, annoyed by the question. He didn't deal in feelings. He dealt in facts. That was what made him different from the other man. For the moment, he was the junior, but there was no telling when that might change. 'If,' he placed heavy emphasis on the word, 'the journal exists, then Saintclair is the way to get to it.'

'Very well.' Were the words followed by a period of hesitation, or merely contemplation? 'As long as Saintclair is useful to us I want him protected. Once we have what we want, get rid of him.'

IX

Jamie's heart quickened. He was closing in on Operation Equity.

I have a great deal of respect for Fitzpatrick. He has led three Jedburgh operations in France and Holland, and I know only too well the kind of strength, physical and mental, that is required to survive that kind of test. Still, it is difficult to describe the loathing I felt for him at that moment.

For weeks we have been swanning around Germany in the wake of the Allied spearhead, strong-arming German mayors and interrogating hundreds of suspect men and women. Strange that not one of them had ever been a Nazi, in a country where the majority of people who weren't Nazis ended up in the awful concentration camps we've liberated. After Belsen my German tastes like vomit in my mouth. We still lose a few men to ambushes and accidents, but we regard this holiday from

the war as just recompense for our earlier efforts,
which were considerable. Compared to Malestroit
and Arnhem this was a picnic.

Frowning, Jamie tapped the word 'Jedburgh' into the
laptop Gail had brought to the hospital. Pages and
pages on a quaint historic market town in the Scottish
Borders. Puzzled, he added the word 'operations' . . .
and was invited into a deadly new world.

Jedburgh was the code name for small teams of highly
skilled clandestine soldiers, operated by the Special
Operations Executive and the American OSS, who were
dropped by parachute into Occupied France prior to
the D-Day invasion. This also explained the reference
to the meeting in Baker Street – the location of SOE
headquarters. Unlike SOE's undercover agents, the first
priority of the Jedburghs, normally a three-man unit
composed of experienced special forces soldiers from
the United States, Britain and the host country, was not
to gather information or carry out sabotage. Instead,
their primary purpose was to liaise with local resistance
movements and provide guidance, training and access
to weapons. Sometimes this would involve a few dozen
men, but in one well-recorded case, in Brittany, more
than a thousand resisters supported by Jedburgh teams
and a squadron of French SAS, had fought an entire
German regiment to a standstill.

Now Jamie knew how Matthew had been employed
after he returned from North Africa. He could only
imagine the strain of hiding for weeks on end behind

enemy lines, under the constant threat of betrayal or discovery. The Jeds dropped in uniform, but that meant little after Hitler's 'Commando Order' in October 1942, which sentenced captured Allied raiders to death without trial. The war had almost run its course, but now they had a new and unwanted mission to complete.

Fitz at least had the grace to look embarrassed when he handed over our orders. Two three-man teams, codenames Dietrich and Edgar, commanded by Captain Matthew Sinclair, will proceed southwest to a given map reference, where they will be issued with further orders. This mission, Operation Equity, is to be treated with the utmost secrecy – which I took as the greatest insult of all, since I have been operating in the utmost secrecy for the last four years. I should tell him I am the wrong man for this job. That I am burned out and numb, and that I welcome the numbness because it protects me from the man I have become. The war has drained me of all humanity. I feel like a boxer at the end of a fifteen-round contest. I have nothing more to give.

What is war? War is chaos and stupidity as the norm; hunger as a constant companion; death – non-judgemental, arbitrary, messy death – everpresent and around every corner; a callous disregard for life or the living, ingrained so deep a more religious man would call it evil. And of course hatred. Hatred for the people who made you like this, hatred for the enemy who wants to kill you, hatred for the bovine civilians too stupid to run away, hatred for the mines and the bombs and the bullets and the shells and the flame-throwers, that will castrate, mutilate, eviscerate or incinerate, just state your preference. Oh, yes, you can hate an inanimate object, just as you can hate the dead for making you kill them. You hate the tanks and the planes and the guns, as long as they are the other side's tanks and planes and guns. You very quickly learn to love your own tanks and planes and guns in the same way you love the soft, red Saxon earth that crumbles beneath your entrenching tool to give you sanctuary, right up to the moment it buries you alive. You hate the trees, for giving shelter to the enemy and for those great, jagged, TNT-propelled splinters that can tear out a man's eyes or his throat. You hate the birds for giving away your position. You hate the weather, in all its many forms, because heat and thirst can kill you just the same as damp and cold. You hate your friends, because you know they are going to die all too soon. But most of all you hate yourself.

I could tell him all that, but I won't because I know it won't do any good. Whatever the mission, I am the best man to complete it. I know it as well as he does.

Jamie paused and re-read the last passage. He had believed he had no illusions about war, but the war Matthew fought was one he struggled to comprehend. This was victory, the Allies had cut deep into the Third Reich and the outcome was no longer in doubt. Yet his grandfather recorded it with all the pain and despondency of a defeat. Travelling in two armed reconnaissance jeeps, a subdued Matthew and his five companions – two British SAS men, an American, a Frenchman and a German-speaking Pole, who had to be Stanislaus Kozlowski – had set out at dawn.

Progress is slow because the Yank columns we drive past are nervous. Like us they feel it would be silly to be killed when the war is almost over. The remnants of the Fourth Panzer Army are heading our way with the Russians on their tail and we are meeting local opposition. Some of the Gerries still don't know when they are beaten. Our American allies have an interesting way with snipers. We were stopped for an hour near Jena while they dealt with some chap who'd taken a potshot at a convoy from an isolated farmhouse. A British unit would have sent in a patrol to flush him out. The Yanks called in an air strike by three rocket-firing Typhoons and then sent in Firefly tanks to finish the job with their flame-throwers. By the time the shooting stopped, the farmhouse was just a blackened pile of bricks. A GI major emerged grinning from the smoke with the sniper tied to the front of his jeep like a hunting trophy. The Gerry must have been thirteen years old.

Their destination was close to a pretty Bavarian town that had been left eerily untouched by the war.

We drove west out of Coburg into a heavily wooded area where the Americans have set up a reception centre. It isn't a prison camp, at least not so you'd recognize it. No machine gun towers or searchlights, just a group of wooden huts hidden behind a barbed-wire fence among the trees. I handed over my orders at the gate and was told to report alone to a building at the far side of the complex. The officer behind the desk had the coldest face I'd ever seen; a long nose and thin lips, eyes like ice-chips. The kind of face that would send a man to his death and not even blink. He wore the uniform of an American colonel, but I doubt he'd ever been on a parade ground. I loathed him on sight. Behind him stood two others, dressed in civilian suits but with military haircuts. I recognized the breed immediately. I was back in cloak and dagger land, but these cloak and dagger types weren't the usual enthusiastic SOE amateurs, they were genuine hard-eyed, government-sponsored killers. The officer didn't introduce himself. 'You're familiar with the area around Lake Constance, Captain.' I admitted

I'd done some walking there before the war and he nodded. He handed over a sealed envelope and without another word one of the civilians escorted me to a door at the rear. Beyond the door, three seated figures in khaki overalls were waiting on a bench by the far wall. One had a leather briefcase perched primly on his knees and looked up with a wide smile. Two of them were the most evil men I would ever meet. The third was Walter Brohm.

X

Jamie paused. Walter Brohm? The context and the way the name was mentioned suggested it should be signifi-cant – someone well placed in the Nazi hierarchy – but it meant nothing to him. His research into looted artworks had given him a working knowledge of the coterie of top Nazis around Hitler and he could name every senior officer in Herman Goering's semi-official looting organization, but that was the limit of his expertise.

He needed more information.

He checked out of the hospital after a brief physical inspection, but didn't feel ready to go back to work. Instead, he retreated to his flat in Kensington High Street. When he opened the door he had a sense of things not being as they should be, a kind of alien presence hovering over the multitude of books and pictures stacked carelessly in every room apart from the kitchen. A quick check showed no evidence of anything missing or noticeably out of place and he shrugged off the feeling as a symptom of attack-induced paranoia.

He reached for the laptop, then had a better idea. He picked up the phone and dialled the university friend who had first put him in touch with Emil Mandelbaum.

'Simon?'

'Jamie! I heard you were in hospital. Bloody awful thing to happen, and in your old granddad's house, too. I meant to visit, but you're out, so you must be feeling OK. I hope you are?'

Jamie looked at himself in the living-room mirror. His face was comically one-sided because of the swelling to his right eye and the pain in his ribs made him move with a slight crouch. 'I look a bit like Quasimodo's uglier aunt, but apart from that I'm fine. Nothing that a good belt of Macallan won't cure.'

His friend laughed. 'If you feel up to it we could go somewhere tonight, somewhere quiet?'

Jamie winced. 'I don't think I'm ready for that yet. Look, I'm sorry to bother you at work, but I'm after a favour.'

'Nothing new there, old son. I'm your man.'

'Er, I'm trying to find someone in London with a specialist knowledge of high-ranking Germans during the war, maybe even some kind of Nazi hunter.'

'And you think that because I'm one of Abraham's chosen I might know someone like that?' Jamie sensed an unfamiliar wariness in Simon's voice.

'It was a long shot,' he admitted. 'If I was wrong, I apologize. It really doesn't matter. I can look it up on the internet, or something. I'll give you a bell about that drink another time . . .'

'No, wait. Look, there is somebody, but he's often out of the country. Old Nazis and their whereabouts are a kind of hobby of his. It depends if he's around?'

'Yes, of course.'

'So I'd have to check with him to see if he's willing to talk to you.'

'Any time would be perfectly fine with me.'

'Great. Let me have a word with him and I'll get back to you.'

Jamie thanked him and when he'd hung up he returned to the journal. With the war drawing to a close, the danger less ever-present and more time on his hands, Matthew seemed to have a desperate need to record the final days in the kind of detail that had been denied to him for five years. He'd been reading for half an hour when the phone rang.

When he picked it up it was Simon. 'That was bloody quick.'

'He was very keen to see you after I explained about Uncle Emil and the Rembrandt, and he'll be happy to help in any way he can, although, naturally, he can't promise anything.'

'That's brilliant, Simon, I owe you one.'

'Do you know the Builders Arms on the corner of Thackeray Street and Kensington Court Place?'

'Sure, it's just along the road.'

'Of course it is . . . Can you meet him there in half an hour? He's off on a business trip first thing tomorrow, but he can spare an hour this evening.'

Jamie hesitated. He'd been thinking in terms of days,

possibly weeks. 'It's a little sooner than I expected, but sure. I'll grab a quick shower. How will I know him?'

Simon thought for a few moments before Jamie heard him laugh. 'He'll be the one all the girls are eyeing up. He answers to David.'

Despite the name, the Builders Arms had long since cast off its working-class origins. Now it was comfortable and trendy, tight-packed leather sofas nudging glass-topped aluminium tables, with an emphasis on food and the designer beers that Jamie loathed but always found himself drinking. The place was almost empty when he arrived, with the few staff gratefully taking advantage of the lull between the lunch crowd and the after-office crowd.

A casually dressed, tanned young man sat at a table against the far wall with a perfect view of the door. When Jamie walked in he looked up and smiled in recognition even though they'd never met. Jamie saw immediately what Simon had meant. 'David' was of medium build but had the kind of strong features that would appeal to the ladies, thick dark hair and a chin that needed shaving twice a day. He rose from his seat and shook hands with a weightlifter's iron grip.

'Thanks for agreeing to see me at such short notice,' Jamie greeted him. 'What can I get you?'

They settled for two Stellas and wandered back to the table, where David took the seat with the same view of the door he'd had earlier. As they sipped their beers the younger man studiously avoided mentioning Jamie's battered face and chatted in accent-free English and with a diplomat's ease about the weather and London and the world in general. It became clear he was Jewish, but that came as no surprise given his friendship with Simon.

Jamie was perfectly happy to allow David to make the running and it was a few minutes before he quietly steered the conversation to business.

'Simon said you were interested in Nazis. May I ask why?'

Jamie surprised himself with his reply. 'I specialize in hunting down artwork stolen during the war. Perhaps Simon mentioned the Mandelbaum Rembrandt?' David nodded. 'This is in connection with another missing painting, but I'm afraid my agreement with the client means I can't say for whom.'

David smiled, a man who could appreciate confidentiality. 'Nazis in general, or a particular Nazi?'

'Not Nazis in general, no, I could get that information from a book. A particular Nazi, but not one of the better known names.'

'And the name is?'

'Walter Brohm.'

The two words hung in the air between them like a dangling noose.

'Walter Brohm?'

Jamie nodded. 'The name is familiar?'

The other man studied him before making up his mind to continue. 'Not one of the better known Nazi personalities, but an interesting character, nonetheless. Yes, I am familiar with Brigadeführer Walter Brohm.'

'Brigadeführer?'

'The SS equivalent of a brigadier in your British army. Son of a pastor, born in Dresden, nineteen thirteen. University educated. Joined the Nazi party in nineteen thirty-one at the age of eighteen and was accepted into the SS in September nineteen thirty-four; his SS number, by the way, is 39520. You are impressed so far?'

'Very.' It struck Jamie that whatever other talents he possessed, David was one of those extraordinary people blessed with a photographic memory.

'Such information is available if you know where to look,' he said modestly. 'It is a little hobby of mine.'

Jamie accepted the unlikely statement without comment. 'Please carry on.'

'Brohm studied applied physics under Erich Schumann at the University of Berlin – Schumann was one of the top Nazi physicists – graduated in nineteen thirty-four, and was awarded his doctorate two years later. In nineteen thirty-nine, along with other Nazi scientists, he began work on the *Uranverein* project at the Kaiser Wilhelm Institute. Simon said you speak German, you understand *Uranverein*?'

'Uranium Club?'

'Correct, and you make the proper connections from this, yes?'

'The Nazi nuclear project.'

David took a sip of his beer. 'Ten out of ten, Mr Saintclair. Brohm continued to work on the project until nineteen forty-one, at which point it was downgraded when it became clear the *Uranverein* would not bear fruit in time to help the Nazis win the war.' He noticed Jamie frowning. 'You are surprised?'

'Yes, I thought the nuclear race continued right up to the last days of the war.'

'A popular notion, but not correct. The Nazis critically damaged their nuclear effort in nineteen forty-one. That was the year they sent many of their best scientists to Auschwitz.' His smile lost its warmth. 'You see, their fondness for killing Jews may actually have lost them the war.'

'Do you know what happened to Brohm after nineteen forty-one?'

David hesitated and his dark eyes narrowed. 'I still don't quite understand your great interest in this man. There is no record of him being involved in any of the art theft or looting that so many high-ranking German officers carried out. No link to any particular painting.'

Jamie smiled disarmingly. 'Come on, David, we both know that just because there aren't any records doesn't mean it couldn't have happened. There are still thousands of pieces of art that haven't been traced. Probably nothing will come of it, but if my clients say it's possible, it's my job to follow it up.'

He could see David was unconvinced, but after a moment's hesitation the younger man nodded. 'Very well. We have very little information about his work. There are fragmentary records, including a suggestion he may have been in Poland in nineteen forty-four, but they are too limited for our purposes.'

'Then why do you know so much about him?'

'A good question. You ask why, not how. I congratulate you. Why? Because Walter Brohm was a fanatic, one of their worst. Because one of those fragments, though unsatisfactory, is extremely important. In late nineteen forty-two, just before the camp was cleansed of Jews, Brigadeführer Walter Brohm supplied radioactive material and carried out certain experiments on female inmates at the Ravensbrück concentration camp. The women involved in these trials wore a yellow triangle, denoting their Jewish origins. The experiments resulted in the sterilization of all the subjects and the death of many. We know so much about Walter Brohm because he is a war criminal, Mr Saintclair, and he is still wanted by Israel, Russia and the United States.' He reached into his pocket and produced a business card with his name and phone number. 'Should you discover anything more about Walter Brohm or require any further assistance, please contact me.'

'You say he is still wanted. Does that mean you believe he's still alive?'

David frowned. 'No one knows whether Walter Brohm is alive or dead. He escaped from a prison camp in April nineteen forty-five and has never been heard of since.'

XI

We left the camp at dusk, nine of us in two jeeps, with the three Germans now dressed in British battledress, but without rank or unit insignia. The instructions pointed us south, towards Nürnberg, but only I knew our final destination. I had orders to avoid contact with military officials of any nation or service. We were on our own. Cut adrift in a Germany tearing itself apart in its final death throes.

Jamie took a deep breath and laid the journal down. He had returned from the interview with David more disconcerted than illuminated and with the feeling of having thrown a stone into a dark and dangerous pool. Walter Brohm's past both fascinated and horrified him. He'd heard about the experiments carried out on inmates in the concentration camps, but the thought of Matthew riding in the same jeep as a man such as Walter Brohm brought the war – and its atrocities – closer than he felt

100

comfortable with. It was as if a door had blown open to allow in the smoke from a crematorium chimney. There was also the puzzle of the amount of information David had provided. The sheer detail was astonishing, yet, like the missing years of Matthew's diary, it left a large gap in the story that needed to be filled. What had Brohm done in the three years after he left the Kaiser Wilhelm Institute? And if his fate was such a mystery, what had been the purpose of Matthew Sinclair's mission? He stared at the book. Were the answers in those final few dozen entries?

He picked it up again and scanned the pages, not reading now, searching, but his brain must have continued to soak up the words because, gradually, he became consumed by a sense of impending disaster that crept up his spine like a python slithering towards its prey. The realization grew with each page he turned. It couldn't be? Not Matthew, the man whose newly discovered heroism had given Jamie a whole new belief in his own worth. But there couldn't be any doubt. It was all there in those neat, tightly spaced sentences, as good as a handwritten plea of guilt.

Captain Matthew Sinclair and his men were helping three notorious Nazi war criminals to escape justice.

He flicked through the pages again, desperately hoping to find something, anything, that would prove him wrong, but there was nothing; no plea in mitigation apart from the five mealy-mouthed words of the Nuremberg defence – 'I was only obeying orders'.

As he read on, a single word leapt into his head and he

was astonished that he could have missed it on the first reading. It was never mentioned specifically by name, but the clues were all there. He felt like a man who had walked into a pyramid and triggered the mechanism that opened the pharaoh's undisturbed tomb. The pain of Matthew's betrayal was replaced by a feeling of breathless wonder and his memory took him back to an Italian hilltop town; cool, narrow streets beneath a sun-baked henna roofscape, and a house with a brass plaque engraved with the same word that now made him react like a love-struck teenager.

Raphael!

Raffaello Sanzio di Urbino. Artist and architect. The only man who could stand side by side with Leonardo and Michelangelo and not be dwarfed by their greatness. Raphael's name might not be as well known, but those with vision recognized his genius and his paintings were characterized by a serenity that was unmatched, even in Leonardo's *Mona Lisa*. Those paintings were now valued in their tens of millions of pounds, and from what he was reading it appeared that one of them might have been the price of the three Germans' lives.

More importantly, this wasn't just any Raphael.

Jamie carried the journal through to the spare room that doubled as a home office and rummaged beside his desk until he found what he was looking for. It was a scrapbook he'd started when he had been commissioned by Emil Mandelbaum to find the Rembrandt. He quickly turned the pages to three cuttings from a Sunday colour supplement on the world's top ten missing works of art. *There*, among the Cézannes, the Degas and the Picassos, was a single work by Raphael.

Portrait of a Young Man. Painted in oil on wood panel and regarded as one of the sixteenth-century Italian artist's finest works. It had been the prize exhibit at the Czartoryski Museum in Cracow, hanging alongside Leonardo's *Lady in Ermine*, and another Rembrandt, *Landscape with Good Samaritan*, until the first week of September 1939, when, along with the rest of Poland, the museum had found itself under new management.

Even before the invasion of Poland, Hitler had decreed that the great artworks of Europe should be confiscated to hang in a grandiose Führermuseum at Linz, his birthplace in Austria. Teams of collectors followed the *Wehrmacht*'s armoured spearhead like hunting dogs, sniffing out paint and marble. One of them, Kajetan Mülhmann, an SS officer and the Nazi Special Delegate for the Securing of Art in the Occupied Territories, had tracked the three paintings to their hiding place on the Czartoryski estate. Later, they had become the subject of a three-way tug-of-war between Hans Posse, Hitler's art curator, Hermann Goering, who naturally wanted them for himself, and Hans Frank, the governor of Poland. Perhaps surprisingly, Frank won the contest and had hung the paintings in the Wawel Castle where he could enjoy them as he organized the massacre of the Polish intelligentsia and the enforced segregation of the millions of Jews under his control.

When Hans Frank left Poland in 1945, a few steps ahead of the avenging Red Army, his paintings went with him. But after his capture by the Americans in Bavaria only the Leonardo and the Rembrandt were among his hoard of looted treasures. Frank claimed he had given the Raphael to Reinhard Heydrich early in 1942, but despite confessing to war crimes and converting to Catholicism before he was hanged in 1946, his interrogators refused to believe him. There was no record of Heydrich ever possessing the picture.

Portrait of a Young Man was the most important masterpiece still missing from the Second World War. According to the article it had a potential value of one hundred million dollars but that had been three years ago. Jamie reckoned that, given the way people were now pulling their money out of plummeting shares and investing in art, it was certain to be a great deal more.

Somewhere in Matthew Sinclair's journal were the only known clues to its whereabouts. It was all there. A portrait by one of the big three, the one Leonardo feared. Oil on wood. One of his later works.

Jamie felt as if his heart might burst; an almost sexual feeling of anticipation. With shaking hands he picked up the book and flicked through the remaining pages . . . only to find what he least expected.

Twenty leaves at the end of the journal had been carefully removed.

XII

His head felt as if it was about to explode. For a few frustrating moments he had been within inches of one of the world's greatest missing artworks and a coup that could have made him a fortune and restored his battered reputation. Just as quickly, it had been stolen from him.

After the shock, came the questions, so many of them; like an avalanche. Who had – so carefully, with scalpel or razor blade – removed the key pages? Not Matthew, who had somehow safeguarded the journal through six years of war and kept it secret all this time. His mother? Had she found it and read it; discovered some awful family secret? If she had wanted to hide something why not destroy the whole book? And if it had been someone else, why leave the journal behind with all its tantalizing clues? The more he considered it, the greater became his certainty that those final pages contained some momentous revelation.

In an explosion of sublime clarity he felt the old man's

presence beside him and he understood. *The journal had always been meant for him.*

Now he found himself able to look at the blue leather volume in a different way. If Matthew had always wanted him to have it, did he not also want him to have the treasure at its very heart: the Raphael? Perhaps there were other clues he'd missed. He would read it again with fresh perspective, go through it line by line. Matthew Sinclair's life had been changed irrevocably by his meeting with Walter Brohm and that was where the key to the mystery lay. Poor Stanislaus Kozlowski could have given him the answers he needed. Now there was only one road to follow. To understand Matthew, he must understand Walter Brohm.

Almost reverentially, he picked up the journal and opened it where the pages had been so clinically removed. He'd been so infuriated by the discovery that he hadn't inspected the damage as closely as he might. Now that he did, he was struck by something curious. It was as if his subconscious was sending him a message in an indecipherable code. He'd had a similar sensation when looking at paintings that were later revealed as fakes; he just hadn't had the wit or the insight to comprehend them. This was subtly different. An alarm bell was ringing . . .

He reached for the magnifying glass on the desk and focused it on the roots of the missing pages. It confirmed his original suspicion that the removal had been carried out with great care and in a way that did minimal damage to the journal. The responsible party had valued what he was removing and what he was removing it from. That realization brought him back to Matthew. But why? If he had wanted Jamie to have the book why not give it to him in its entirety?

As he weighed the open journal in his hands he felt a prickle of anticipation as he realized something that had originally eluded him. The book balanced almost perfectly between his palms, but it shouldn't. The missing pages should make it slightly lighter at the back than the front: only a little, but enough to be noticeable. Now he closed it and looked at it side-on. The missing pages weren't the only difference between the front and the back, the endpiece was imperceptibly thicker than the frontispiece. Was that usual in a book? He couldn't be sure. He chose a title at random from the shelf nearest to him, wondering at the coincidence that placed a leather-bound copy of Pope-Hennessy's *Raphael* in his hand. He studied it from the same angle he'd looked at the journal. No, the front and back covers were identical in thickness. He stood up and walked to the window. This was when he needed to be at his calmest, but the adrenalin rushing through him made the whole room spin. He took a deep breath and returned to the journal. He prodded the blue leather of the back cover. Almost undetectable, but it was definitely more cushioned than the front. But when he looked at the interior board under the magnifying glass he could see no evidence that it had been tampered with.

He took the book back through to the front room with its packed bookshelves and little-known, haphazardly hung works of art, placed it on the coffee table beside the window and poured the large glass of Macallan he'd promised himself earlier. Sitting back, he studied the journal from a distance for a long time, sipping the mellow malt whisky and feeling the burn rise to wrap itself around his heart. When he made his decision it was surprisingly easy. He hunted through the nearby drawer for the scalpel he knew was there somewhere, and worked the blade carefully around the half inch of stretched leather that overlapped the heavy card on the inside of the back cover. He found himself sweating. One part of him worried he was committing sacrilege, but another insisted he had his grandfather's permission, his encouragement even. When he'd peeled back the torn leather, he very gently worked the point of the knife beneath the card so he could prise it clear.

Jamie hardly dared breathe as he levered back the covering. His first reaction was disappointment. Not the missing pages. Of course, they would never have fitted into the space he had uncovered. Then came dry-mouthed anticipation. Whatever this was, it was important to Matthew Sinclair. *It* was a neatly folded piece of what appeared to be fine cloth. Carefully, he drew it clear and unfolded it on the coffee table.

A perfect square of silk tinted in dull shades of green and brown. At first it meant nothing. A cheap scarf or a watchmaker's cloth? After a moment of careful concentration he found himself staring at a faded map of Germany's land mass. Bending low he searched it for any markings or symbols. It couldn't be that simple – X only marked the spot in pirate fiction – and it wasn't. Apart from a few tiny broken stitches the silk was unblemished. So what was its purpose? Very slowly suspicion became certainty. It was an escape map. He'd seen enough war films to know that every airman who risked being shot down over Occupied Europe had been issued with one like this, along with a compass and enough local currency to give him a chance of reaching the nearest safe haven. It was only natural that the Jedburgh teams, parachuted into the very heart of enemy territory, should be similarly equipped. He ran his hand over the silk. This had been Matthew's. He might even have worn it around his neck. It made him feel closer to his grandfather than ever. But why, when it apparently contained no information, had it been hidden inside the book cover? He had his answer when he turned it over.

On the reverse was a crudely sketched symbol of a type he'd never seen before.

XIII

Central Germany, 7 February 1945

It was over. SS Brigadeführer Walter Brohm couldn't pinpoint the exact moment when intuition had become truth, but he knew the war was lost. He could taste defeat in the air he breathed and smell it on the people who surrounded him. As a physicist he understood the concept of critical mass better than most. He wondered why he hadn't recognized earlier the moment it had all turned to dust. Perhaps he could blame the fact that he had been trapped in this enormous concrete prison for most of the past two years, but he knew that wasn't true. The evidence had been there for all to see despite the Führer's grandiose promises. Goebbels could trumpet Wehrmacht success as loud as he liked, but anyone who could read a map knew that each 'victory' brought the enemy ever closer to the heart of the Reich. Brohm had watched the Ami bombers making their stately, invulnerable way across sacred Germany's skies like shoals of tiny silver fish through a pale blue sea. Only a few weeks earlier he had seen the results as he flew into Berlin across whole districts reduced to barren fields of crater and rubble. Everyone knew a family who had lost a loved one at the front. The truth was, like everyone else in Hitler's Germany, he had deluded himself that it could never happen. The promised wunderwaffen existed; the unstoppable rockets and jets that could fly faster than any Allied plane, the pulse cannon and the new tanks and improved U-boats. But there had never been enough and now there never would be. The Reich's industrial base had already been crippled beyond repair. Not even Speer could make artillery shells with dead engineers in a factory that was just a pile of bricks.

He looked around the office that had been his home for the last twelve months. Wood-panelled walls, works of art and Persian carpets couldn't disguise the chill reality of a subterranean existence and the all-pervading damp earth scent of quick-drying cement. He lit one of his little black cigarettes to mask the smell, the smoke swirling through the glare of artificial light to be consumed by the extractor fan in the ceiling. Beyond the internal window SS troopers from the security battalion hurried back and forth helping his research staff carry boxes of files and records to be burned in the furnaces two floors below. The occasional metallic crash told him that the work of dismantling or destroying the plant and removing the experimental machinery was being carried out as he had ordered.

Such a waste, after all the years of struggle and effort.

This bunker's existence was known only to the highest ranking members of the SS hierarchy and had been built to last for a thousand years, but he had never truly believed the Reich would survive that long, and had never much cared. What mattered was his work.

At first, no one would even consider his theory about the material in the casket from Tibet. It was beyond the intellectual capacity of even the finest minds. Schumann and von Braun had looked at him as if he were mad. In the two years leading up to 1939, the theoretical and the experimental were only of interest if they applied to technology that would help Germany win the war everyone knew was coming. Even in 1940 the High Command had issued an edict banning research and development that would not produce military results in four months.

Chastened by the professional setback, Brohm had been recruited to work with Otto Hahn, Fritz Strassmann and Lise Meitner on a project that involved bombarding uranium with neutrons, continuing the work begun by the New Zealander

Ernest Rutherford who had split the first atom. Meitner, a chain-smoking dynamo of a woman, was undoubtedly the brightest of the team and the acknowledged leader, but as an Austrian Jew her genius could not offset the massive disadvantage of her tainted blood. In 1938 she had fled Germany for Sweden. A year later Brohm had watched as Hahn discovered barium in a uranium sample. They had achieved what would become known as nuclear fission.

But that had not been enough for Walter Brohm. During the years with Hahn and Meitner, he had continued with his own experiments to discover the exact nature of what he had found in the casket. He worked at night, pushing himself to the point of exhaustion and mental breakdown, driven by the absolute conviction that this substance had been placed on earth for him and him only. He understood that his quest went beyond obsession, that it took him to the very brink of madness, but he revelled in the pain and disappointment as he rode ever closer to his goal on a tidal surge of anticipation. Eventually, he had come close enough to be sure of what he had. Now it was a matter of examination, analysis and theory as he tried to understand where the material took its place in the periodic table of earthly elements, if it had a place there at all. Row upon row of calculations on a blackboard concluded, studied, then dismissed. At first it had been as if he was wandering through a jagged, fissured landscape in a dense fog, each step uncertain and fearful, but gradually his mind had cleared. Eventually, he realized that he'd wasted hundreds of hours trying to peer forward into the unknown when he should have been looking back at the celestial origins of what the casket contained.

A timid knock at the door interrupted his thoughts and he looked up as a lovely dark-haired girl of about nineteen carried a tray into the office.

'Your coffee, Herr Direktor.'

'Thank you, Hannah, that is kind of you.' He smiled. She truly was beautiful. Even wearing the dowdy, striped grey shift, Hannah Schulmann radiated a kind of inner tranquillity that always made him feel at ease with himself. And she was as talented as she was pretty; he had never heard the piano played more movingly than when her supple fingers moved over the keys. Her presence in his bed had made the last few months almost bearable.

The girl flinched as a guard dropped a box of files and he stood up and put a reassuring hand on her shoulder. 'Don't be frightened, my dear. You must go and join the others now.'

He watched her leave and experienced a painful twinge of what, in another man, might have been conscience.

It had been the late summer of 1941 before he had felt confident enough to approach Himmler with his findings. He found it difficult to think of Heini as the bogey man who had terrorized Europe. The intense, myopic stare and the unnatural stillness could be unnerving at first, but the Heinrich Himmler he had come to know was an affable dinner companion who called him by the familiar du and had always shown a genuine interest in his work. Himmler, who delighted in anything mysterious or enigmatic, had been fascinated by the Changthang casket, and when Brohm presented the paper outlining his discovery's possible potential the owl's face shone with excitement. As the panzers probed the suburbs of Leningrad, threatened Moscow and completed the encirclement of Kiev, Brohm received a call telling him to report to Templehof aiport. Two hours later he was on a Junkers 252 transport to Rastenburg for a personal interview with Adolf Hitler at his Wolf's Lair headquarters. It was the only time he had met the Führer and he had emerged both hugely impressed and hugely disappointed. With the war all but won, Hitler had been at his most affable. In person, he had none of the enormous presence he projected at the great rallies Brohm had attended, but the scientist found himself mesmerized by the aura of power surrounding the man. To meet him was to truly believe. Hitler had clearly been well briefed on the subject and had immediately grasped its potential, but, just when Brohm believed he had received agreement to proceed, the Führer had called a third man into the room. The moment he recognized the visitor, Brohm realized he had been outmanoeuvred. Six years earlier Werner Heisenberg had been involved in a scientific scandal that had brought him into conflict with Himmler. Brohm had supported his chief and Heisenberg had been fortunate to survive. Now he was back in favour and Brohm knew he was in trouble.

Heisenberg went over the arguments for and against Brohm's project and then pointed out the potentially catastrophic consequences of an error. Brohm had been forced to acknowledge the hazards and argued that no scientific experiment was without risk, but he knew he had already lost the battle. The Führer had brusquely shaken his head, too timid to truly appreciate the capabilities of what Brohm was offering. He left the meeting in a rage. Hitler had cost him his place in history.

But he had underestimated Heinrich Himmler.

When he met Himmler two weeks later, the Reichsführer-SS had been at his most charming. Since the launch of Operation Barbarossa, the Führer had a great deal to occupy his mind and could not be expected to oversee every tiny detail of national policy. Brohm's project would go ahead, but under the auspices of the SS-WVHA, the economic and main administration office of Himmler's vast organization. It was only now that

Brohm was given an insight into just how vast. The SS had developed from Hitler's bodyguard into a state within a state and with the financial power to match. After years of fighting for funding and laboratory time, Brohm now had everything he wanted, and more. More staff and more funding meant he could make greater progress, which in turn increased the project's importance. When the bombs began to fall on Berlin the scientists and engineers had been evacuated to the bunker, the most advanced research facility in the world, and Brohm had been able to experiment on a scale that would previously have been unimaginable. And with each experiment he moved a step closer. Closer to harnessing the power of the stars.

And just as he had it within his grasp, it was over.

He felt a surge of anger that restored his resolve. His work was too important to stop now. Much more important than petty considerations like nationhood.

'The Sun Stone is ready to be transferred, Herr Brigadeführer.'

Brohm looked up at his aide, Ziegler, in the doorway. He nodded. 'Good, and you have my personal documents and records?'

'Yes, Herr Brigadeführer. They have been placed in fireproof security boxes as you ordered.'

'Very well.'

He could trust Ziegler. The Sun Stone and

the records, the bargaining chips that would assure his future, would travel by convoy to the armoured train which would take them to their final secret destination. The Ivans and the Amis were closing in. Free Germany was like a piece of ham between two slices of pumpernickel and the ham was getting thinner with every hour. Still, he'd left enough time for the move. He would make his own personal arrangements for escape. It was time to go.

The grey-clad commander of the security detachment appeared at the door, his face red from the exertions of the morning and one of the new Sturmgewehr automatic rifles on his shoulder.

'Shall we take the Jews outside?'

Brohm considered for a moment. The Jews. Such an all-encompassing, unsatisfactory and entirely fatal classification. In reality many of the three hundred scientists, engineers and technicians in the barracks below were men and women he had worked with long before the war, people he had come to like and respect. People like Hannah.

'No, do it where they sit. It will cause them less anxiety.' The SS man frowned; what did he care about anxiety? They were only Jews. Nobody had bothered about anxiety on the Ostfront. Brohm saw the look. 'It will save time,' he suggested. 'And this place will make a very appropriate tomb.' The frown was replaced by puzzlement. 'They will be like three hundred of the pharaoh's servants,

118

buried in memory of his achievements,' Brohm explained wearily.

He risked one last look at the painting on the wall. A pity, he would have liked to take the Raphael. It had been a birthday gift from poor old Heydrich, who had somehow, in his sinister way, prised it from Frank's grubby little fingers. But he wasn't going to escape Germany's Gotterdamerung carrying a large piece of wooden board. He would be travelling light; just his new identity and the secret that would change the world.

XIV

Jamie's heart beat faster as he studied the drawing. Something about it felt familiar. It was in the shape of a wheel, with nine articulated spokes that met in a geometric pattern in the centre. Below were three words – *In Faust's spuren* – which, if Jamie had the translation correct meant, 'In Faust's footsteps', and a date: 1357. They obviously had some sort of significance, but it was the larger significance of the symbol that drew Jamie's attention. The composition looked vaguely South American; some sort of abstract solar symbol? But he wasn't dealing with Aztecs or Mayans, he was dealing with Nazis. He ran a finger slowly down one of the articulated spokes and felt the room go cold. The almost savage way it changed course drew another shape in his mind; a sinister emblem that had brought terror and darkness to two continents.

He tapped a few words on the keyboard of his laptop and hit enter. Plenty of options. He placed the arrow of his mouse over the word 'Images' at the top of the screen, clicked and hit enter again. This time his screen filled with monochrome thumbnail pictures of soldiers. They stood in their long, orderly ranks, hard-eyed, unsmiling faces showing what? Determination? Discipline? Severity? The determination of the fanatic. The discipline of the automaton. The unbending severity of the executioner. He saw the picture he was looking for, but curiosity made him ignore it for the moment. He double-clicked to enlarge a photograph in the top row. Some kind of parade. They had been chosen for their square-jawed features and Nordic perfection; proud, confident, blood untainted by any undesirable element. Even a missing tooth would have denied a man a place in this picture, taken around 1939. Their defenders claimed that, man for man, they were the finest soldiers the world had ever known. Their detractors decried them as butchers who killed without a shred of conscience. Their superiors had demanded 'unparalleled hardness' and they had willingly provided it. They had died in their thousands and their tens of thousands in the snowy wastes of the Russian steppe, in the hedgerows of Normandy, the forests of the Ardennes and the burning ruins of Berlin.

The mouse hovered over two more photographs, but he didn't have to enlarge them. He knew the precise wording that hung below the stark iron gateway in what had been some Polish backwater before it had become a factory of death. And who would ever forget the boy in flat cap and short trousers as he raised his hands in surrender to the laughing jackbooted warrior liquidating the Warsaw Ghetto?

One final picture. A close-up, head-and-shoulders shot of a uniformed man with wide-set eyes and narrow, fine-boned aesthetic features. It was a medieval face, the face of a scholar, or of a monk, but where a monk's eyes might show compassion this man's lacked any semblance of pity.

The men in the pictures all had one thing in common. They wore the twin silver lightning flashes of the SS – the *Schutzstaffel* – Heinrich Himmler's private army.

Jamie looked again at the symbol on the back of the map. Yes, it was there. The same coarse, almost brutal, simplicity of design, as if they had been created by the same hand with the help of a blunt bayonet.

A sharp knock at the door interrupted his train of thought and he felt a momentary flutter of panic that he instantly dismissed. Idiot. They wouldn't knock. If you're not safe here where are you safe? Still. He picked up the heavy crystal whisky glass and wrapped it in his fist. With a last glance around the room he reached for the handle . . . hesitated, retraced his steps and retrieved the journal and the escape map and put them in the nearest drawer. Only then did he open the door.

'Hey, how are you?' A grinning face peered through the narrow gap and Jamie relaxed his death grip on the glass. Simon's eyes were drawn to the movement and he waved a tawny bottle with a white label. 'I see you're prepared. Couldn't manage the Macallan, but I thought you might fancy something a little more robust. Islay's finest. Enough peat to bury you in.'

Jamie waved his friend inside, accepting a bottle of

whisky almost as old as he was. Simon had always been generous, but even for him this was a little excessive. 'I don't suppose you're here for a cup of tea?'

Simon surveyed the semi-organized chaos with a practised eye. 'I doubt if you could find the pot even if I did, old boy. No, I'll have whatever medicinal tincture you're having. I just came round to make sure you were OK.'

Jamie searched for a second cleanish tumbler. Simon wandered the room casually, picking up a book here, surveying a painting there. His eye settled on a tank of tropical fish that Jamie had bought a few weeks earlier in a moment of misguided enthusiasm.

'Haven't these bloody things died yet? My goldfish never lasted more than a week.'

Jamie looked up. 'They're not goldfish, they're freshwater exotics.'

'Christ, what's that?' Simon's attention had switched to a vividly coloured rural scene in a plain frame. 'Planning to sell it?'

'No. I like it.'

'I would if I were you. The market for contemporary regional tosh is moving in the wrong direction.'

Even at university Simon's interest in art had been purely economic. He treated it the way he now treated the stocks and bonds he dealt with each day at his bank, as a commodity to be bought and sold at a profit.

'Are you still going to the gym?' Jamie asked innocently.

'What?' Simon blinked like a startled owl behind his designer spectacles. 'Oh, this?' he said guiltily, running a hand over the bulge above his belt. 'Couple of weeks of circuits will soon get rid of it. I'm considering hiring a personal trainer, what do you think?'

Jamie grinned. 'Can't do any harm, especially if she's a looker. Who needs circuits when you could be chasing a plump Lycra-encased backside round the park for an hour? Cheers!' He handed the other man a glass filled to halfway with glowing amber.

Simon sighed as he took his first sip of the malt. 'Christ, I needed that. How's your research going?' The tone was casual enough, but the words gave Jamie the odd sensation he was in the room with someone else. It only lasted a split second before he mentally discarded the thought, but it had definitely existed. 'Only I couldn't help noticing the picture on your computer,' Simon continued, waving his glass at the spare room. 'The uniform seems familiar.'

Jamie led him through just as the screen-saver turned the monitor blank. He tapped the mouse and restored the aristocratic face with the cold, certain eyes and an expression a calculated millimetre from a sneer.

'Fuck!' Simon stepped away from the computer as if it was contaminated.

'You recognize him, then?'

All the bonhomie had been stripped from Simon's voice by the image on the screen. 'The Devil Incarnate. I'm a true Brit, albeit of the mongrel variety, Jamie, but first and foremost I'm a fucking Jew. You'd never forget the man who sent your grandparents and eighteen of your other relatives to the gas chamber. Reinhard

Heydrich. If Hitler was the chairman of Holocaust PLC, Heydrich was the chief executive. You know he was the first person to use the words *Final Solution*?'

'No, I didn't.'

Simon drained the rest of his whisky in a single swallow. 'A complete bastard of the first water and a remarkably thorough man. Even Himmler feared him. Once he had his murder squads up and running in Poland and Russia, he banned Jews from the occupied western countries from emigrating and effectively made Europe their prison. When he had them trapped, he created an enormous Nazi killing machine that first processed, then murdered them. At the Wannsee Conference he estimated that they would have to "deal with" eleven million Jews. Fortunately, I suppose, he could only get his hands on half of them. When he was killed in Prague the Nazis murdered or deported thousands of innocent people in retaliation, but ask any Jew and he'll tell you it was worth the sacrifice. Look,' he placed his empty glass beside the computer, 'this has put me off my liquor. I have to go now, but let me know if you need anything. Enjoy the whisky.'

Jamie held the door for him. 'There was one point. Do you know anything about the relationship between Heydrich and a man called Hans Frank? Frank was an SS bigwig who ruled over most of Poland for four years of the war. He was hanged for war crimes at Nuremberg.'

Simon frowned. 'No. But David would. You should stay in touch with him. He's a handy man to know. Look after yourself, laddie.'

When he was gone, Jamie sat down at the computer and stared at the man on the screen. The words beneath the picture confirmed most of Simon's chilling biography. Heydrich's subordinates went in terror of him and had nicknamed him The Hangman. How he came by it was never properly explained, but Jamie could hazard a guess. Heydrich had been cleverer than Himmler, Goering and Goebbels combined, more cunning than Bormann and saner than Hitler, if your definition of sanity encompassed an anti-Semitic mass murderer with ice-water in his veins. If he hadn't been killed he would undoubtedly have become one of the visionaries of the Nazi regime, taking his place among the coterie of thugs and bullies who clung to Hitler like lice, even a possible successor to the Führer himself. Where Hitler saw the destruction of the Jews as a means to an end, Heydrich had been taught to hate them from the cradle and approached their extermination like a Holy War. Kicked out of the German navy in 1931, for seduction of all things, he'd thrown in his lot with the Nazis, making himself indispensable to Himmler while the future Reichsführer-SS was still a Bavarian chicken farmer. Heydrich had created a political power base in the *Sicherheitsdienst*, Himmler's feared security service, used the Night of the Long Knives and the corpse of Hitler's former ally Ernst Rohm as stepping stones to help him up another few rungs of the ladder, before, with the Führer's blessing, making it his business to rid the world of the Jewish race. When he had been rewarded with the Protectorship of Bohemia-Moravia, it must have seemed just another step in the right direction. But two British-trained Czech agents brought his career to an abrupt close with a couple of hand grenades on a warm spring morning in Prague. The date was 27 May 1942. No wonder Hans Frank's interrogators hadn't believed him. If he'd made a present of the Raphael to Heydrich early in 1942, surely it must have been in his possession when he died?

It was all very interesting, but it wasn't getting him any closer to the painting or his grandfather's mission. He retrieved the journal and the silk map from the drawer and placed them side by side on the desk in front of him. When he looked at it now he wondered why he hadn't seen the similarity between the design of the wheel and the SS lightning-flash runes immediately. Runes? The word stirred something in his memory, something he'd read about Heinrich Himmler.

He brought up Google on the computer and typed in the words *Schutzstaffel* and *symbolism*.

There were thousands of hits, but a name and a place drew his attention as if they'd been written in lights. He clicked on the link and there it was: a large room with a marble floor surrounded by pillars. In the centre of the floor was a circular symbol identical to the one on the reverse of Matthew Sinclair's silk map. The place was Wewelsburg Castle, the very heart of Himmler's SS empire. The symbol was known as the Black Sun.

A few miles away the search results were replicated on another computer screen.

XV

'We have what we need. The package is no longer required.' The disembodied voice crackled in their earphones.

'About time.' The younger of the two Chinese men parked in a blue Ford across the street from Jamie's flat reached below his seat and fitted a silencer to the pistol hidden there. The driver put a hand on his arm.

'Wait.' He punched a number into the hands-free phone on the dashboard in front of him. 'Please confirm.'

'Are you questioning my order?'

The driver, Li Yuan, who used the work name Charles Lee, was a senior operative of the Second Bureau of the Chinese Ministry of State Security. He bit back the comment that threatened to get him into further trouble. Who was this pup they'd parachuted in from Beijing to treat him like one of the waiters in the upmarket Cantonese restaurant he ran? Lee had been trained in assassination and covert operations, but his primary function was intelligence gathering, and ten years of work was in danger of being compromised by this cowboy from the Fourth Bureau. It was a measure of the importance of this mission that they were even prepared to consider what they were about to do, but if he was going to terminate this Saintclair he wanted to be certain.

'Seeking clarification. If the subject is making progress, perhaps—'

'Perhaps he will help others make progress?' The voice had grown sharper. 'He is attracting too much attention. We have a location and we have far greater resources to find what we seek than a second-rate salesman of paintings of dubious provenance. There are other lines of inquiry with which you need not concern yourself. We no longer need Saintclair. Confirm, please.'

The driver shrugged. Idiot. 'Confirmed.'

His passenger grinned and clicked off the safety catch on the silenced automatic.

The older man shook his head. 'No, not that way. Better if it's an accident.'

Jamie didn't notice the blue Ford with the tinted window as he left the building to go to his office later that afternoon. Neither did he notice the young Chinese in the leather jacket who dogged his footsteps on the way to the Tube.

At this time of the day more people were coming out of Kensington High Street station than going in and Jamie quickly made his way through the ticket barrier and down to the platform. As he stood among the crowd on the platform edge, his mind was on the breakthrough he had made and what his next step should be. He now knew where the original of the symbol was located, but what should he do about it? Yes, it was a potential link to the Raphael, but how much time could he afford following a trail that was sixty years old and likely to lead nowhere? He had his grandfather's story. Maybe he should just be happy with that? But then there was the not knowing. Not knowing whether Matthew Sinclair had been a war hero or some callous gun for hire. The latter didn't seem possible, but the moment he'd opened the journal Jamie had entered a world where the certainties of the past no longer existed. *Anything* was possible. And what if the Raphael was just beyond his fingertips? In his mid-teens Jamie had become obsessed with discovering the identity of his father and he felt the same compulsion now. He needed time to think. He needed to take a good look at what resources he had. Did he have enough money to give a month of his life to this mad quest? He did if the house sold, but the market was dead and didn't look as if it was going to get any livelier for a while.

'Sorry.' Someone nudged him in the back, but he couldn't identify who because he was surrounded by commuters. He looked to his left, where the train would be arriving and six feet along the platform his eyes caught those of a slim young woman – a girl? – with distinctive red streaks in her dark, shoulder-length hair. She returned his gaze and he could have sworn he saw a twinkle of amusement, even recognition. He smiled and turned away. It was strange how you grew accustomed to the suffocating proximity of other people. Up there, in the natural light, you fought for your personal space. Down here, in the dusty, ill-lit depths, breathing in lungfuls of chewy, overused air, you spent an hour with some big Romanian housewife camped in one pocket and an African busker in the other and were happy to pay for the privilege. The big digital counter at the far end said the next Circle Line train was due in forty seconds. He moved nearer the edge of the platform.

Nobody talked, but it was always noisy; the echoing halls of one of Tolkien's cavernous subterranean cities. A muted dragon's roar and the familiar change of pressure told him the train was approaching. He took a deep breath and closed his eyes. The movement at his back increased as people nudged forward in anticipation and he soaked it up, his toes inching a little closer to the edge. Something, he wasn't quite sure what, made him smile. The lunatic optimism of a man standing in a grubby London Tube station who thought he was about to discover one of the world's great missing masterpieces? The feeling that old Matthew was up there somewhere daring him to follow the trail he had left? Maybe this was all a delayed reaction to his death. A sort of pre-mid-life crisis. The roar changed to a demonic, rhythmic clattering of steel on steel as the train approached along the tunnel.

He never felt the push. One moment he was on the platform, the next he was in the air, falling and twisting, his eyes wide open and the postered walls spinning. A freeze-frame moment when a female face gaped at him from the opposite side of the track, the mouth torn by a silent scream. At her side a dapper man in a dark suit and a red tie wore an annoyed frown, as if a demented circus performer had leapt out from nowhere to spoil his lunch break. Jamie knew he should move his arms to cushion his fall; do *something*. But they might have belonged to someone else. His shoulder struck first with a sickening crunch that sent a fireball of pain through his left side, but at least it absorbed most of the impact. When his cheek bounced off concrete with a rattle that loosened his teeth, he knew it could have been worse. A steel rail shone two inches from his eyes. Only now did it register where he was and what was about to happen. His feet. His legs. Where were they? Terror engulfed him like quicksand, forcing its way into his eyes and his mouth and his ears. He lost any sense of self, any control of body. He didn't hug the concrete, it absorbed him. After a millisecond the lights went out with an explosive whoosh of whirling air that threatened to pick him up, buffeted him as if he was head down in a wind tunnel, tugging at his clothes and tearing at the bond that held him to the oily concrete. He screamed, louder than he'd ever screamed before, fighting with the sound of a million nails being scraped across a million blackboards, magnified a million times. Then it stopped. Dead.

XVI

Was he dead? The question took time to answer. There was a long, breathless pause; an in-between time where he wasn't quite sure. No, because he could feel his heart beating like a roadman's jackhammer, his shoulder hurt like hell and a metallic taste told him his mouth was bleeding. For some reason it seemed important that he hadn't lost any teeth and he ran his tongue over them, checking the molars one by one.

Someone was screaming quite close by and he could hear a voice shouting for help. He moved his arms and legs. Surprisingly, they were all present and correct. The inky blackness seemed terribly extreme until he realized his eyes were screwed tight shut. Very carefully, he opened them and a low, gloomy tunnel appeared ahead of him split by three rails that ran parallel with his face. He lifted his head an inch to get a better view and clattered his skull against something unyielding and metallic. So that's what the underside of a Tube train looked like? It came to him in a rush. In that second he realized how close he had come and he had a vision of an alternative end that featured ragged lumps of flesh, splinters of bone and a single eyeball discovered some way down the track.

That was when the shaking started.

'So you didn't jump?'

Jamie looked up at the florid features of the British Transport Police sergeant and answered the question for the fourth time. 'No.'

'And you don't think you were pushed?'

'I don't know. One minute I was standing on the platform, the next minute I was doing a double somersault with back flip in front of forty tons of Tube train.'

'Only the CCTV is pretty poor quality. In the frames that matter there are maybe eight people in close contact with you, but most of the faces are indistinct. It doesn't show anything except you taking a flyer and none of the passengers we've been able to interview noticed anything helpful. Most of them cleared off when they found out you were still alive and kicking. That's Londoners for you. Always got something better to do.'

They'd reversed the train from above the spot where he lay and three Tube workers had helped him up from the pit below the track and carefully past the electrified centre rail. After he'd been checked over by a paramedic they'd brought him to the station supervisor's office that served as the BTP team's temporary interview room. The walls had recently been painted a dazzling daffodil yellow and the over-heated atmosphere combined with the paint fumes made him feel sick.

The sergeant studied the report in front of him and shook his head. 'What I'm saying, Mr . . . Saintclair,' he pronounced the name with a tight smile that said he didn't quite believe what he was reading, 'is that unless you can give us a little more detail, or a reason to think otherwise, at the moment we're looking at an unfortunate accident that will look bad on our statistics, but won't require any further investigation. Are you with me?'

Jamie nodded, not trusting himself to speak. The sergeant was staring at his black eye. Should he have mentioned the attack in his grandfather's house? If the men who'd beaten him up had wanted to kill him they would have done it there and then, not waited until they had a hundred potential witnesses. Maybe it *had* been an accident. Even as the thought formed he knew it wasn't true. There'd been too many accidents lately. The bottom line was that if he told them about the attack he'd have to tell them about Matthew's journal and the Raphael. For reasons of his own, he didn't want to do that.

He declined the offer of a cup of tea and the chance to have a friend collect him. At the sergeant's request, he signed a health and safety form confirming he was fit and well enough to be released under his own steam. The policeman ushered him to the door. 'I'd say you used up a couple of your nine lives there, Mr Saintclair,' he said cheerfully. 'If you'd landed on the rails instead of in the suicide pit, you'd probably have been electrocuted and you'd certainly have been killed by the train. If you hadn't stayed still like you did it would have had your head off. Have a good day, sir.'

Jamie managed a shaky smile of thanks, but by the time he reached the station's main hallway his head felt as if it belonged to somebody else. Maybe he should have accepted the tea after all? There was a sandwich bar in the foyer, but he wasn't far from the flat. What he really needed was a seat and some fresh air. He headed for the exit.

'Wait up!' She was at his shoulder before he registered that the words were aimed at him.

He stopped and turned towards the voice. The first thing he noticed were the red streaks in her hair that told him she was the girl from the platform. Mid-twenties, dressed in denim and leather, with an attractive face that might fairly be described as elfin, tilted slightly as it looked up at him. On closer inspection she had the kind of skin that shone with a sort of subdued golden light, like the setting sun through thin summer cloud. Eyes a little too wide apart, pencil-thin arched brows and a snub nose that didn't quite fit with the rest, but somehow added to the charm of the whole. She was frowning and pearly, slightly protruding front teeth nibbled her lower lip. Despite his condition, he found it incredibly sexy. He realized he was staring, but her eyes held his and he was reluctant to break the moment.

'Can I help you?' His voice sounded weary in his own ears. He tried to offset it with a smile of encouragement that, he decided on reflection, probably made him look like Mr Bean.

'I thought you were a goner.' The words contained the slightest American drawl. New York? No. A bit too refined. Something inside his head said Boston, but he didn't know why. 'You didn't look as if you had a chance. I almost fainted.'

'So did I.'

She smiled and he noticed for the first time the sparkle of a tiny diamond stud at the edge of her left nostril.

'Sarah Grant.' She held out a slim hand. 'At least you've kept your sense of humour.'

He took it, surprised at the strength of her grip. 'Jamie Saintclair.' When he tried to focus on her eyes the world started to come and go in waves. She said something and the words floated away before he could absorb them.

He shook his head to clear it. 'Sorry?'

'I said I wondered why someone would want to kill you.'

'Excuse me.' He staggered past her and vomited copiously in the general direction of a nearby waste bin.

'Feeling better now?' She had found a park bench in a small, rather unkempt public garden not far from the station, where they sat drinking coffee from over-sized cardboard cups and watching the late-afternoon traffic stream by.

'Mmmh. Sorry about that. Not the most pleasant way to introduce oneself.'

She shrugged. 'You never know when the shock will hit you. You didn't get much sympathy, though.' She had the kind of voice he associated with dental nurses, soft and reassuring, with just a hint of welcome authority.

'No,' he said, remembering the large and very outraged cleaning lady who had looked as if she was about to brain him with her mop. 'Why didn't you tell the police?'

She chewed her lip the way he'd discovered she did when she was thinking. 'The usual reasons. I didn't want to get involved. You give a statement and your name goes on a list. You never know when it's going to come back and bite you on the ass. Then again, what could I tell them? I had an impression of someone in the crowd pushing in your general direction. I couldn't tell them who did it; in fact, it wasn't until after they'd taken you away that I realized what I'd seen. Once you disappeared under the train it was as if my brain was encased in concrete. I couldn't even scream.'

'I could,' he said with conviction.

'A big crowd gathered, but once they found out you were alive they drifted away.' She stared at him. 'I think some of them were disappointed.'

Now it was his turn to shrug. 'It's human nature. If there's a disaster, people want to say they were there. Bad news is like a magnet if you're a certain kind of person. You see a crowd and you join the back of it. You work your way to the front. You don't know if you're going to see somebody pull a rabbit from a hat or a man lying bleeding on the pavement. You're disappointed if it's the magician.'

She nodded. 'Anyway, I made myself scarce, but I kinda felt an obligation to make sure you were all right.'

'Why?'

'You smiled at me.'

He laughed. 'What makes you think I don't smile at everyone?'

Her expression stiffened and she moved to get up. 'If you're going to make fun of me . . .'

He put a hand on her arm. 'Please, I didn't mean anything. You're the only one who's given me a thought since it happened and I appreciate that. And you're . . .'

'I'm what?' she demanded.

'Er . . .' Christ, thirty years old and he was still acting like a tongue-tied teenager around an attractive woman.

She raised an eyebrow. 'Yeah?'

'I appreciate your . . . concern.'

She studied him and he noticed that her hazel eyes had flecks of gold around the pupils and the skin around them crinkled when she grinned. 'Well, a girl does like to be appreciated.'

He took a deep breath. 'Look, you don't even know who I am, apart from the fact that I smile at pretty girls and I have a predilection for jumping in front of trains, neither of which is much of a recommendation.'

'Pre-dil-ection.' Her slow drawl stretched the word out on a rack. 'I like that. All right, Mr Jamie Saintclair, who are you and why would someone want to kill you?'

XVII

4 April 1945

Walter Brohm huddled miserably in his commandeered greatcoat among five hundred other men in a makeshift prisoner of war cage north of Leipzig. He had traded the black and silver of the SS for the uniform of a Wehrmacht private, hoping that such a lowly rank would allow him to slip through the Allied net, or, at worst, secure his early release if he was captured. The fighting had pushed him south into the path of the American Third Army, but that had suited his purposes perfectly. He'd met Americans before the war and knew them for a kindly, quite innocent people who'd believe anything as long as it was accompanied by a convincing smile. How wrong he had been.

His problems had started when his staff car had been strafed by a rocket-firing American fighter.

He'd only just escaped with his life by diving into a nearby ditch and had watched as the Mercedes was turned into a fireball along with his driver and his carefully hoarded supplies. All he had been left with was his pistol and his briefcase and he'd almost lost that to some cowardly scum of a deserter who thought it must contain food and got a bullet in his guts for his trouble.

After that scare he'd kept off the road, but he soon realized that the stamina that had taken him across the Himalayas in the thirties was long gone. After three days he was a stumbling wreck on the brink of starvation, forced to drink from stagnant pools in the forest. The water had saved him from dying of thirst, but within hours of consuming it he had come down with dysentery. He was finished.

He'd hidden his briefcase and pistol and, nearly shitting himself with sickness and terror, given himself up to an American combat patrol. They had first lived up to his earlier hopes by providing him with food and water and telling him to hand himself in to one of the supply units following them, but it wasn't long before a staff officer appeared and demanded to know why they 'hadn't shot the Nazi bastard'. For a few minutes his fate had been in the balance, but he had cut such a forlorn figure that the officer had eventually relented and put him in a jeep to be taken to the nearest collection centre.

Now here he was with his arse in a puddle and the rain dripping from his nose. His comrades, who could sense he was no more a landser than a chimpanzee, watched him suspiciously. It was only a matter of time before someone gave him up to the guards.

And it was about to get worse.

He hadn't realized the screening would be so thorough. This hunger for revenge and determination to ensure the Nazi hierarchy had no possibility of escape seemed very un-American. Every prisoner was being strip-searched and interrogated, regardless of rank. It wouldn't take the Amis five minutes to find out that he didn't know a machine gun from a panzerfaust, even if they didn't find the SS tattoo that verified his blood group. They might very well shoot him on the spot.

Well, if he couldn't trick his way out he'd buy his way out. The key was to convince them to let him recover the briefcase and, even in his current pitiful state, Walter Brohm was capable of that. It contained only a general summary of his research and findings, but it would be enough to save his neck if he could get it into the right hands. Of course, they would be able to do nothing without the stone and his detailed notes. He would only hand over their whereabouts when he was somewhere much safer than this. He had heard Rhode Island was pleasant at this time of the year.

He pushed himself to his feet and approached the nearest guard, who eyed him suspiciously and kept the muzzle of his carbine pointed exactly at Brohm's midriff.

'I would like to speak to your commanding officer. I have information that will be of considerable interest to his superiors.'

XVIII

'So you hunt down pictures and stuff stolen by the Nazis?' He knew she was trying to sound enthusiastic, but he heard the doubt and he could hardly blame her. It didn't seem like a very grown-up occupation.

'It's not even as exciting as it sounds,' he apologized. 'I read catalogues, check out art sales and spend most of my time on the phone. I'm more likely to be looking for a pair of candlesticks than a painting.'

He was usually shy at first with women, but she was deceptively easy to chat to. Maybe it was because she was American; open, talkative, interesting and interested. They discovered they had shared likes: climbing and walking. And pet hates: anyone who wandered around listening to rock music on earphones when they could be listening to the birds singing. Their musical taste differed, but there were areas for negotiation. Sarah liked the new album by Robert Plant and Alison Kraus, although she thought Plant was talented but ancient. Jamie confessed to a secret hankering for old Johnny

Cash standards and a love of Mahler inherited from his mother. He found himself relaxing and revealing things he hadn't even told his best friends.

'Do you think your work could have anything to do with why whoever it was tried to whack you?'

Her words produced a photoflash memory of the train thundering by an inch above his head. All it would have taken was a single hanging wire . . . She noticed his look, and placed a hand on his arm; the warmth injected new life into him and for the first time since leaving the Tube station he felt like facing the world.

'What are you smiling about?' He shook his head and she turned a quizzical eye on him. 'OK.' She shrugged. 'I don't mind a man having secrets. Makes him more interesting. But you didn't answer my question.'

'About my work?' She nodded. 'I doubt it. I'm sort of between jobs at the moment.'

She grinned. 'Me too.'

'Hold it,' he said. 'I notice all we've done is talk about me. Your turn.'

'OK, but I'm hungry; how about lunch?'

'I'm sorry, I was certain he was dead.'

Charles Lee tossed the remains of his cigarette from the car window and studied the couple talking together on the bench. He should have done the job himself. His partner had been too impatient – a young man's flaw; one learned patience as one grew older. He would have shadowed Saintclair and bided his time until he was certain of the outcome. True, the attempt should have succeeded, but that wouldn't be in his report to the agent from Beijing. Better that the younger man was at fault. There would be a little residual fall-out, but he would survive, and that was what mattered.

'It couldn't be helped,' he lied. 'We know where he lives. We'll go back tonight and do the job properly.'

'Ninety per cent of accidents happen at home. Perhaps he'll drown in the bath?'

Charles Lee didn't smile. 'As long as we take care of it this time, no one needs to know.'

The younger man nodded, visibly relieved.

'What about the girl? Who is she?'

'She wasn't with him when he went into the station. Maybe someone he knows who witnessed the . . . accident?'

Lee reached behind him and picked up a black SLR camera from the back seat. The lens appeared normal, the kind any tourist would use for photographing London's sights, but it had been specifically designed to provide the same results as a much larger telephoto. He homed in on the couple and took a series of shots.

'Well, we'll know by tomorrow morning.' If the girl had a passport or any form of picture identification anywhere in the world, the Bureau's sophisticated photo identification software would find her.

'What if she's there tonight?'

Lee put the car into gear and moved carefully out into the traffic.

'That would be too bad.'

Ten minutes later the Ford pulled up at a set of lights

by a row of derelict shops. Beyond the shops stretched a broad empty space where a factory had stood, but which now contained a few burned-out wrecks that had once been automobiles. They had made the journey in silence, Lee allowing his colleague to contemplate his failure and formulating in his mind how to ensure the man from Beijing saw his own part in the best possible light.

'I thank you for your forbearance and support, comrade,' his partner said.

'I've told you before, don't call me comrade. You are in London now.'

The younger man nodded. He looked up as a motorcycle and pillion passenger drew up beside them, noting faded jeans and a fringed leather jacket. 'If the commander heard how we'd failed . . .'

The helmeted rider turned his head towards the car and an alarm rang in the younger man's head. He reached for the pistol below his seat. 'Drive!' he screamed.

Lee reacted as quickly as any driver could have done. Even the man from Beijing would have been impressed. He was still too slow. His hand had barely touched the gearstick when the pillion passenger calmly raised a silenced Mach 10 machine pistol and kept his finger on the trigger until the bolt clicked on empty. The Mach 10 is an old design, developed by Gordon B. Ingram as far back as 1963, but it is remarkably efficient and remarkably quiet. If someone had been close enough to hear, the only sound they would have registered was that of the thirty-two 9mm hollow-point rounds thumping against the interior of the Ford after passing through their victims, and even that was drowned as the motorcyclist revved his engine. For these particular assassins, the hollow point had two advantages over normal jacketed ammunition. When the bullet hit soft tissue it was designed to mushroom, thereby creating extensive damage along a wider path through the body and a significantly larger exit wound. Trapped by their seatbelts the two Chinese agents jerked and shuddered as almost half a pound of metal travelling at a thousand feet per second punched into them and the interior exploded into a charnel house of blood, bone and ragged flesh. The same mushroom phenomenon slowed the velocity of the bullets so that, although they tore up the plastic trim, none pierced the metalwork to leave outward evidence of the hit or inconvenience passers-by. When the bodies stopped twitching the pillion passenger leaned over to place a package inside the Ford. He gave the driver the OK to move off. From the moment they had pulled up beside the car it had taken less than ten seconds.

'So what's wrong with being a freelance journalist? Somebody has to do it, right?' Sarah went quiet for a few seconds as she chewed her burger. Jamie was fairly certain he'd never eaten a Big Mac before, but there was a first time for everything. It was worth enduring the soggy cardboard-textured bun to be in the company of this mercurial girl-woman with a point of view so different from his own. He sat back as she drew breath and continued the broadside that had been provoked by nothing more than a look of mild disquiet. 'If you're thinking scavenger, think again. I did a Masters in English Literature at Harvard. I'm a writer, and what I really want to do is write novels. But even writers have to eat, and a hundred thousand words is just so much computer crap until somebody wants to publish it, right, so I do features; homes and gardens, fashion, that kind of stuff.' She reeled off an impressive list of publications. 'OK?' The final word was a challenge and he could almost feel the heat from the fire in her eyes. He wondered what would happen if that level of passion was channelled in a different direction.

'So what brings an aspiring novelist from Boston to London? I'd have thought there was as much, if not more, inspiration in the States. Isn't Greenwich Village the place to be?'

'Jeez, Jamie, you must be older than you look. You'll be telling me next you were at Woodstock.'

He ran a hand though his hair and slouched in his plastic chair in a vain attempt to appear what people called cool and she laughed, a deep-seated, unashamed proper laugh. 'Hey, you almost made it to the eighties there. A new haircut and full wardrobe change and I might let you take me out.'

Ouch.

She noticed his look. 'Hey, I'm only kidding, right?' She threw a handful of fries into her mouth and managed to make it look elegant. Swallowing, she took a drink from what looked like a gallon cup of diet

Coke and produced a gentle belch. 'To get back to your original question, I'm not here for inspiration, I'm here for the atmosphere. My book is a time-shift thriller.' His mystification must have shown. 'Happens now and way back in history? Simultaneously. Barbara Erskine?' He nodded, the name was familiar. 'Same theory, different execution. Mine will be tougher, grittier. Elizabethan London. You'll be able to smell the sweat and the cat pee.'

'Sounds great.'

Her eyes narrowed. 'You're kidding, right?'

'Not at all,' he said, and meant it. 'I'm fairly sure that anything you write will be worth reading.'

'Anyway, I've just finished the first draft and now I'm looking for another feature assignment to help keep my foul-breathed landlord out of my face for a while.'

Jamie hesitated for a full five seconds. The decision he was about to make was like stepping off a cliff just to experience what it was like to fly, and he suspected he was going to regret it when he hit the bottom, which was bound to happen sooner or later. He took a deep breath.

'Er, there's this rather wonderful stolen painting and . . .'

He told her about the Raphael. But not about the journal or Matthew. Not yet. When he'd finished, her eyes shone and the words bubbled from her like water from a mountain stream. 'Now that's a story. You think you might be able to track it down? Maybe I can help you. I'm good with research and I'll pay my way. Anyway, you need somebody to watch your back.'

Which was true. He'd also convinced himself he was attracted to her in a way that went beyond the purely physical. That would take time to confirm and he had a feeling he'd need to approach things slowly. On the other hand, working together, even if it was on a wild-goose chase, would at least give him a chance to find out. He grinned. 'OK, you're hired as my acting, unpaid researcher, but if there's a story in it, I get copy approval.'

Now it was her turn to grimace, but she nodded.

'What do you know about Heinrich Himmler?'

XIX

4 May 1945, somewhere south of Nürnberg. Walter Brohm was probably the most self-centred human being I ever met. Anyone else would have been cowed by the situation in which he found himself – a prisoner travelling under guard and with an uncertain future – but all Brohm could see was opportunity. We travelled together in the second jeep and he talked and talked, about his work, about his genius and about the conflicting ideologies that had brought about the war. For Brohm, our war was the inevitable continuation of that 'War to end all Wars' both our fathers had endured; a necessary reconfiguration of national boundaries, power and influence to redress what had been taken – he said stolen – from Germany two and a half decades earlier. 'You may take a nation's resources, but its pride is inviolable, Leutnant Matt. You would have done the same.' Calling me Leutnant, though he knew I was a captain, was his idea of poking fun. That was Brohm's way. 'But we could never have produced Hitler,' I countered. 'Pfaw! You created Hitler with your merciless peace, you and the French and the Americans. Hitler was just a politician taking advantage of his people's prejudices and fears. Every country has its own Hitlers. Wait until your middle classes are without jobs and forced to watch their children go hungry,' he said. 'Then you will see your Hitlers.' He told me that Hitler's only mistake had been to declare war on America. Not Russia? 'Of course not. Communism was the ideological counterweight to Nazi-ism, for one to prevail the other must fall. It was a question of natural selection. With France neutered and powerless, Hitler had to attack Stalin before Stalin attacked Hitler.'

He trusted me because he had cast me in the role of his saviour. 'The Nazis,' he said, 'had just been a means to an end – Ein mittel zu einem ende, Leutnant Matt.' All that mattered was his work. He could have gone to the Russians, but for all their power and resources they were a stupid people who wouldn't have treated him correctly. He would work with the west and the world would be a better place for it. We talked about art. 'I have a great painting,' he said, 'very famous.' From his loving description I worked out that it must be Italian, perhaps by one of the big three. 'Where?' I asked, joking. 'In a safe place.' He winked and his hand strayed to his breast pocket.

*When he was bored, he would pass the time
with riddles. 'My journey begins at Heini's centre
of the earth. You must look upon the faded map
for the sign of the Ox.' He laughed, because that
was the name he had already conferred upon his
fellow prisoner, Strasser. I was never sure whether
he was making fun of me, and he was insulted that
I did not play his little games. Of course, every
man has his own centre. Walter Brohm claimed the
centre of his world would always be his mother's
spiritual home. Sometimes, I thought the war had
driven him mad.*

'Where did you get this?'

Back in Jamie's flat Sarah studied the symbol on the
reverse of the silk escape map. Jamie noted approvingly
that she was now all business. He pondered just how
much to tell her about the map's provenance.

'I suppose I inherited it. My grandfather was in
the war.' He turned the cloth over to the escape map.
'Every Allied airman carried one of these. He must
have drawn the symbol on the reverse of it. I think
it's a copy of something he was shown by a German
prisoner.'

'And you think it might lead you to the painting?'

A catch in her voice said she didn't quite believe it.
'According to family legend, the prisoner he was guarding mentioned the Raphael.' He felt a sharp pain like
a knitting needle in the chest as he lied. 'Now we have
this.'

154

She frowned. 'So it's a clue. Kind of X marks the spot?'

'Right. Only by my count, X has nine arms and the spot looks like a spider's web. And what about the words and the date?'

'*In Faust's footsteps.* D'you know anything about Faust?'

'Only what I remember from school. Didn't he sell his soul to the devil?'

'That's right. Old, old story, but a guy called Christopher Marlowe made it famous round about the time of Good Queen Bess, called him Faustus, though. The date thirteen fifty-seven doesn't mean a lot.'

'Edward the Third was on the throne of England, but most of what is now Germany was ruled by the Holy Roman Empire. What relevance can it have to the Second World War?'

'Or Raphael?'

'He lived between fourteen eighty and fifteen twenty; about a hundred and fifty years too late.'

'So not much of a clue, huh?'

'Maybe. But the original of this symbol is out there somewhere.'

She looked up. 'You mentioned Heinrich Himmler.'

'That's right.' He showed her the pictures of marching SS men on the computer, the lightning-flash runes and a picture of a Swastika flag. 'Notice any resemblance?'

'Uhuh.'

'So I dug a little deeper into Himmler and the SS. It turns out that Himmler was obsessed with the occult.'

He smoothed the silk so the full effect of the symbol was visible and she gave a little grunt of recognition. 'Like a pentagram maybe, but different?' A pentagram was a five-pointed star associated with freemasonry and paganism that had sometimes been hijacked by Satanists. 'Sir Gawain and the Green Knight, and all that. It might tie in with the Faust angle, too?'

Jamie nodded, impressed. 'Could be. I hadn't thought of that. But one of the things I discovered was that Himmler was so taken with the Arthur story that he had his own round table built. And that took me here.'

She squinted at the blurred picture on the screen, trying to make something of it.

'Some kind of great hall?'

'That's right, but look at the floor, just off-centre.'

Her hand reached out and squeezed his and he knew she had seen what he had. Slightly indistinct, but still recognizable as the twin of the one on Matthew's map, the marble sun symbol with its spray of articulated arms and its sinister presence dominated the room. That was when he made his decision. The sun symbol led them to Wewelsburg. Wewelsburg could lead them to the Raphael. He would accept Matthew Sinclair's challenge.

'How would you like to do some European sight-seeing?'

XX

'The victims are two men of Chinese origin who we believe earlier attempted to eliminate our target. The police are investigating a Triad link, apparently they found a large quantity of heroin in the car.'

Frederick waited for the inevitable explosion and was rewarded by a single word. 'Clowns.' He wasn't sure whether his superior was referring to the dead men or to the police.

A long silence followed while the other man considered the question Frederick had already asked himself. 'Do we think Saintclair was involved?'

'It does not seem likely. They were each struck by approximately twenty rounds of soft-point ammunition. Whoever made the hit knew what they were doing. Our people tell us Saintclair has weapons experience, but only at cadet level,' he said dismissively. 'He was a toy soldier at Cambridge. I doubt he would know one end of an automatic weapon from the other.'

'So, the opposition, but which part of the opposition?'

'Is it significant that they were Chinese?' The man at the other end of the phone frowned. It was very significant, but Frederick would never know that. Frederick was commander of the society's military wing, like his father before him. But the ideals that drove him were old-fashioned and, in his leader's view, no longer relevant in the twenty-first century. *He* had a very different agenda. Frederick, and the men like him, were a means to an end. Nothing more. The Tibetan casket wasn't Frederick's problem. It appeared that the men in Beijing who believed they were the rightful owners of the casket were much better placed than he had realized. Someone had done him a favour, but that same someone might very well have the opposite effect in the future.

'I'll instigate some investigations at this end. In the meantime, are we still on Saintclair?'

'He should be boarding the Air Berlin flight to Paderborn with his girlfriend in exactly five minutes.'

'Girlfriend? The file said no significant others.'

'It appears she is new on the scene. We are checking her out.'

'Do that, and get back to me. I don't like loose ends.'

'Hey, could that be it?'

Jamie leaned across so that he had a view from Sarah's window as they made their final approach to Paderborn-Lippstadt airport. Through the shimmering translucent disc of the propeller he made out the regular street patterns of a small German town scattered around a wooded height. On the summit of the hill stood an enormous, oddly shaped castle constructed of grey stone. It had been built in the shape of an elongated triangle, with a large twin-towered building across the apex and two wings that converged on what looked like a huge drum. At first glance it reminded Jamie of the *Starship Enterprise*. He stayed a little longer than he needed to, enjoying the proximity of the slim body and the fragrance of the perfume she wore.

'That's it. Wewelsburg Castle. The centre of Himmler's empire.'

He gave her a reassuring smile and leaned back in his seat ready for landing. The knuckles on her left hand showed white where she gripped the rest between them. Most Americans he'd met treated flying the same way Londoners did the Tube, as a necessary inconvenience that brought them closer than they liked to people they'd never met and probably didn't want to. Sarah Grant was different. She'd taken one look at the twin turbo-prop plane and almost refused to board.

'I came across on a 747 and I didn't like that much. You're not getting me on a boxkite the Wright brothers flew in. I'll wait until something bigger comes along, huh?'

Eventually, Jamie persuaded her it was all part of the big adventure and once they were in the air she'd opened her eyes and almost relaxed. Now they were approaching the runway she closed them again. 'Wake me when we've landed,' she ordered.

Wewelsburg lay less than two miles from the airport,

but Jamie resisted her suggestion that they take an immediate look at the castle and, instead, drove the hire car to Paderborn, where they were staying at a cheap hotel on the outskirts.

'I've booked us in for three nights, so we'll have plenty of time. No need to rush things,' he said airily, ignoring the look of suspicion she directed at him. The look told him everything he needed to know about the coming seventy-two hours. This was going to be a strictly professional trip. He forced his libido back into cold storage and concentrated on getting them the nine miles to the town.

But she had another surprise as they checked in that had him questioning everything he thought he knew about women. He had booked them adjoining rooms, but she made a point of asking if they were connecting and the look she gave him made his stomach lurch. In the corridor there was a moment when he thought she was waiting to be invited inside, but it passed before he could take advantage.

'We'll split the bill, OK?' she insisted. 'I told you I'd pay my way. I'd like to freshen up; maybe we can meet downstairs in an hour and go into town for something to eat?'

'Of course, but I thought you wanted to see the castle later?'

'No point, it's Monday and the castle's not open on Mondays.'

He looked at her in surprise. 'How do you know that?'

She grinned and waved a tourist brochure she'd picked

up at reception. 'You gotta be prepared, Jamie, isn't that what you Boy Scouts say. Or maybe you weren't in the Boy Scouts?'

When the door closed behind her he hesitated for a few seconds, struggling to break the invisible elastic cord that drew him towards it. He'd been in the Scouts for four years, but it seemed he hadn't learned one damned thing that was worthwhile.

The food, at a back street restaurant off Friedrichstrasse, was surprisingly good, as was the light German beer that washed it down. Sarah seemed sombre, which was unusual for her, but she came to life when he remarked on the number of English voices at the tables around them. 'Didn't you know? This is an army town, kinda like Colchester in England. Your Twentieth Armoured brigade does its exercises on the plain just to the north. Ten thousand Brits live round here, five thousand of them just up the road in Sennelager. People from England come to visit all the time.'

'You've done your research.'

'That's what I'm here for.' She smiled. 'We'd better get back, breakfast is at eight.'

They said goodnight in the corridor and she reached up and kissed him on the cheek. He could still feel the heat of her lips as he lay awake three hours later.

Next day, they parked in the village and walked up through the narrow streets to the castle. It was still only nine-thirty and the museum didn't open until ten, so they used the time to inspect the building and its surroundings.

'This was the centre of Himmler's power.' Up close, the castle was enormous and Jamie felt dwarfed by the sheer scale of it. 'It was to be a shrine to the Aryan race. Under the cover of an *SS-Führerschule*, an officer's school, the SS leadership would have gathered here to study mysticism and the occult and to enact ancient long-forgotten ceremonies.'

'I hate the place already,' Sarah said, and he was surprised by the passion in her voice.

'The castle was built by some German aristocrat in the seventeenth century, but it was more or less a ruin until Himmler took an interest in the early nineteen thirties. What you see is just a fraction of the complex he wanted to build here,' Jamie continued earnestly. 'It would have extended for miles, with eighteen separate towers and a huge SS barracks, all connected by roads laid out in a precise geometric pattern. You can read conspiracy theories that suggest it was going to be a landing ground for UFOs or the doorway to Nilfheim, one of the nine worlds of Norse mythology. No claim is too wild where Wewelsburg Castle is concerned. The SS attempted to blow the whole place up at the end of the war, but even with every explosive they had they barely made a dent in it. Eventually, they tried to burn it down, but the Yanks – sorry Americans – arrived before the fire damaged the main buildings and—'

'And no one knows exactly what they found when they got here,' she interrupted, determined not to be outdone. 'Himmler had ordered that the Death's Head rings of every fallen SS man should be kept here. He had some crazy idea that they absorbed the strength and courage of the soldiers who'd worn them. Eleven and a half thousand rings were believed to be stored in the castle's crypt and vanished without trace at the end of the war. Hey, I can read, too. Look, the gates are open.'

They paid for tickets to the memorial museum and were directed to what had once been the castle guard-house. A statuesque blonde girl in a white blouse and knee-length black skirt met them at the door.

'English?'

'How could you tell?' Jamie asked. The two women looked at each other a certain way, like strangers who'd come across an injured rabbit and were debating whether to take it to the vet or put it out of its misery.

'Maybe we should get on,' Sarah said, smiling at the German girl.

'Would you like a guided tour? Normally we only take parties of ten and more, but as you can see it is quiet this morning. I'd be happy to show you round.'

'How much would that be?'

'We usually charge forty-five euros, but since there are only two of you I could do it for twenty?' She saw Jamie's grimace. 'Including your entry fee?'

He opened his mouth to say no, but Sarah spoke first.

'That would be lovely,' she said, unhitching her ruck-sack and pulling out a wallet to hand over two ten-euro notes.

While their guide went to inform the ticket desk,

she hissed at him, 'If I'd known you were this cheap I'd have paid for my own schnitzel last night. I thought we were here to find out about the castle and the symbol and their relationship to Himmler? We won't do that stumbling around on our own looking at the walls. This way we'll discover more than is in any guidebook.'

Jamie soaked up the rebuke. 'I thought, if we were on our own,' he explained with exaggerated patience, 'we might be able to spend a little time alone with the symbol and get a really close look at it. There was method in my meanness.'

Her lips made a perfect circle. 'Oh!'

'This is the former gymnasium and the room the officers used for fencing practice.' The girl, whose name tag said Magda, spoke a clipped, very formal English. 'In nineteen eighty-two work began to transform it into a permanent museum to highlight the ideology and terror of the SS. As you see, it is an exhibition which encompasses the experiences of both the perpetrators and the victims.'

The exhibits and photographs were displayed on clean whiteboards beneath strip lights that gave the museum the atmosphere of a hospital operating theatre. Magda led them through a labyrinth of cubes and corridors, talking continuously and stopping occasionally to ask if they had any questions. The Death's Head and lightning-flash runes attacked them from every angle and Jamie noticed that Sarah seemed almost cowed by the constant bombardment of evil. In one picture

Heinrich Himmler, looking like an office clerk in a soldier's borrowed uniform, chuckled with the architect of his Wewelsburg vision, Hermann Bartels. In another, Jamie noticed Heydrich's elegant figure among a group who had come to the castle to discuss the creation of the *Einsatzgruppen*, the killing squads who had murdered one and a half million Jews, partisans and Communists in Russia and Poland.

'Here you see the plan formulated by Bartels for the expansion of Wewelsburg.' Magda pointed to a framed architect's drawing, which showed the castle as a small element in a much larger complex. Broad avenues radiated from a semicircular compound surrounding the northern and western sides of the hill and what appeared to be blockhouses and bunkers dominated every crossroads and approach road. From the east, a single roadway approached arrow-straight to meet the base of a huge triangular building complex of which the castle, enormous in its own right, was only the tip. The scale of the project was astonishing and all the more so when you realized it was to be funded not by Germany's Nazi government, but by the SS alone. 'You will notice the shape of a spearhead and the shaft, which was to be a tree-lined avenue two kilometres in length.' The guide pointed to the roadway. 'This is said to be a portrayal of the Spear of Destiny, the legendary weapon that was used to pierce the side of Jesus Christ and which Himmler went to extraordinary lengths to find. The spear would be precisely aligned from south to north. He intended Wewelsburg to be the final repository of the spear. Work began on the redevelopment in nineteen forty, but it was never completed. This was fortunate for the villagers, whose homes were to be destroyed and whose land was to be flooded to form an artificial lake. Of course, such a project would require many workers. To this end Wewelsburg had its own KZ or concentration camp, Niederhagen, which provided slave labour.'

Dispassionately, she reeled off a string of statistics, from which Jamie picked up a single fact: of the close to four thousand prisoners held at the camp, one third had died of sickness or starvation or were worked to death in the quest to create Himmler's dream.

'Niederhagen was also used as an execution site by the local Gestapo,' Magda continued. 'It is recorded that fifty-six people were shot to death here, but we suspect the true figure may be much higher. You have heard the expression *nacht und nebel*?'

'Night and fog. Code for people who disappeared without trace.' Sarah's voice sounded strained. 'How did the local people feel about this?'

Magda looked puzzled. 'Of course, they knew. How could they not? But there was nothing they could do. This was Hitler's Germany. To voice dissent was to join the victims.'

'No, I meant about this.' The American waved her hand at the pictures of hollow-eyed men in striped suits labouring under the castle walls. 'This was *their* shame. They couldn't have enjoyed having it shoved in their faces fifty years after the war ended.'

Magda's smile was shut off as if by a switch. 'There was opposition, yes?' Her English lost its assurance, the words thickening on her tongue. 'Many people protest against the plans for an exhibition. They wish to forget. To – how is it you say? – sweep under carpet.'

'And you, Magda?' Jamie put a hand on Sarah's arm as a signal to back off, but she shook it away. 'What do you feel?'

The German woman stared at Sarah. 'I have my own reasons for believing it is important to remember. One of my great grandfathers carried a knife just like that,' she pointed to an SS dagger in a glass case, 'and wore the Death's Head on his collar. He served with the *Das Reich* panzer division in the Soviet Union and in France. For the first fifteen years of my life I was brought up to think of him as a hero. But then I began to read and to understand what happened in my country, and the things that were done in my country's name.'

'I'm sorry, I shouldn't have . . . I understand.'

'No, you do not understand. I had another great grandfather, a pastor in the town, and one of the few who did protest at the treatment of the prisoners in the camp. He was not a brave man, but felt he had an obligation to help these people. He is one of the fifty-six shot by the Gestapo. They burned his body and ground his bones into the dust. Now do you understand?'

Sarah nodded wordlessly.

'One a hero and the other to be forgotten. But I will not let them forget. To us, the people of my generation, this is not just history. It is a lesson that we must never allow anything like it to happen again. We will go to the castle now.'

She led the way over the drawbridge and into the triangular courtyard. Jamie could see the German girl was struggling to control her emotions.

'What the hell was that all about?' he whispered.

'I just wanted to know.'

'Know what? None of this is new. You must have heard stories like that a hundred times.'

'Yes, but this isn't stories. This is where it *happened*. People died to create this monstrosity for a megalomaniac. This place is evil. Can't you feel it? It's as if the spirits of the SS are still here in the walls all around us. They should have blown the whole damned thing to kingdom come.'

Jamie stared at her.

'Look, I'm sorry. Maybe it's something in the air. I'm over it now. Forgive me?'

'OK,' he said, and took her hand as they walked through the door of the north tower and into the heart of Himmler's Camelot.

XXI

'This was to be the centre of the world.'

The phrase stirred something on the outer limits of Jamie's memory, but he struggled to place it as Magda's hypnotic voice echoed eerily around the walls. Inside the crypt the only light came from a series of small windows set in the domed ceiling. Out there in the sunlight, Himmler's obsession with the occult might appear foolish, even comical, but here in the darkness it took on a frightening reality. The room was empty but a shallow basin five paces across and surrounded by a low concrete wall dominated the centre of the floor.

'Above you, the *hackenkreuz*, the swastika symbol of the Nazi party.' She pointed to an ornate carving in the centre of the ceiling. 'It is physically linked to the famous Black Sun which is the centrepiece of the room above us.' Jamie tensed at the mention of the sun symbol and his eyes met Sarah's. The American girl's face appeared unnaturally pale in the gloom. He was reminded of an image he had once seen of an avenging angel with a fiery sword; firm of purpose, grim and unyielding. Something had changed since they had left London. This had been his quest and she had tagged along more or less on a whim. Yet with every hour that passed it was clear her emotional commitment to the search increased. It was as if the only way she could combat the aura of evil around them was by creating a super-hardened shield of her own. He had felt her strength right from the first, but he began to understand that this new Sarah Grant had a core of steel.

'Here were to be stored the Death's Head honour rings of every SS officer who fell in battle. You see.' Magda knelt by the basin and indicated a short piece of copper pipe just visible in the very centre. 'An eternal flame would have burned to prove that the spirit of the SS warrior was unquenchable. The rings were the personal gift of Himmler and as well as the *Totenkopf* they were also engraved with rune symbols and the name of the bearer. It is said that the crypt was to be Himmler's last resting place, but as you know, that was not to be.'

Jamie struggled to contain his simmering impatience. Sarah hovered by the doorway and he could see that she, too, was desperate to reach the sun symbol. Now that he was within feet of the symbol itself, he felt the chilly fingers of doubt close around his heart. Every inch of this vainglorious Nazi monument had some sordid story to tell of murder or madness, slavery or repression, but what was the secret behind Matthew Sinclair's silk map? What if there was no message? What if the Black Sun was simply a decoration? No, his grandfather wouldn't have left him the map unless it contained some kind of clue and the clue had to be visible in the original.

'Now we will proceed to the *Obergruppenführersaal*, the Hall of the Generals.'

Magda led the way to the ground floor and through a doorway – where they were met by a barred metal grille. Behind it Jamie could see a large empty room encircled by stone pillars and windowed alcoves. He held his breath as he prepared to look upon the true Black Sun for the first time. The guide's next words made him feel as if he'd been kicked in the stomach.

'Unfortunately, the hall is closed for special cleaning, but if you move to the front you will be able to see everything and I will explain it for you.'

Jamie felt Sarah stiffen beside him. He turned on Magda and gave her his hundred-watt smile.

'But we've come all the way from England to see this.' He sighed. 'The Hall of the Generals was always going to be the highlight of our trip. Surely you could let us in for a few minutes?'

'Please?' Sarah added. For a moment he thought that membership of the sisterhood would achieve what charm was patently incapable of doing. Magda retrieved her keys from her jacket and fiddled nervously with one that was large and silver. He saw the conflicting arguments race across her face. She was a nice girl who enjoyed helping people. Truly, she wanted to help them. But she was also a good German girl, and despite all her unease about the war and what had happened here, a good German girl still obeyed orders. If her manager said this gate stayed closed until Thursday, then that's what would happen. She shook her head and returned her keys to her pocket.

'I'm sorry, I cannot.' Her face mirrored the genuine regret in her voice. 'But please, ask me anything you wish.'

They looked through the bars at the Black Sun twenty feet away in the centre of the marble floor and as available for close inspection as if it had been on the moon. Jamie was surprised when Sarah smiled and enquired what the room had been used for.

Magda smiled back, relieved the moment of confrontation was past.

'The *Obergruppenführersaal* and the crypt below are the only two rooms in the north tower known to have been completed to Himmler's satisfaction. This was to be the meeting hall of the twelve generals, the *Obergruppenführer,* who commanded the Allgemeine-SS.' She saw Jamie's puzzlement. 'What one might call the civil SS, as opposed to the Waffen-SS, who were the military arm. You will count twelve alcoves and twelve pillars, perhaps the alcoves would have contained statues of these men, yes? Twelve generals, as there were twelve Knights of the Round Table. If you half close your eyes you will be able to imagine a round table in the centre of the room and beneath it the Black Sun, the centre of Himmler's universe.'

'Are you saying that Himmler really thought he was King Arthur?' Jamie laughed.

172

Magda smiled again. 'Perhaps that is more difficult to imagine, he was such a . . . a *kümmerling.*' The word meant runt of the litter, but more besides. 'But his interest in the occult was very real. It extended even to the search for a forgotten race of superhumans who were the forerunners of the Aryan people.'

Something puzzled Sarah. 'What was it that made the Black Sun so important? If it was the centrepiece of Himmler's world it must have been of enormous significance?'

Magda frowned. 'It is one of the enigmas of Wewelsburg,' she admitted. 'No one knows for certain. This was to be the room of the great mysteries. The inner sanctum, like the *cella* of a Roman temple. To understand the significance of the Black Sun, you had to be one of the twelve men versed in the mysteries. It is certainly a form of sun wheel, perhaps of pagan origin. As the planets of the solar system revolve around the central figure of the sun, so Germany, and perhaps the rest of the world, must revolve around Himmler and his SS. At one time a gold disc formed the centre of the Black Sun. The sun is the giver of life, so the Black Sun could give life or take it away. But that is only my own theory.'

'Perhaps if we could get a closer look we could come up with an alternative?' Sarah suggested.

Magda gave her a tight smile. 'One of the reasons this door is here is that, for certain people . . . certain organizations . . . the Black Sun is still important.'

'Nazis?'

173

'I believe they are now called neo-Nazis. Certainly groups who still follow the Nazi ideology, perhaps worship the memory of Adolf Hitler, and believe in the same mysticism in which Heinrich Himmler believed. There have been several instances in the past of these groups holding ceremonies here.

'But not now.' She shook the bars of the gate. 'It would take someone very strong and very determined to break through here. And first they would have to get into the castle.'

Jamie smiled, but his heart was somewhere near his boots. If a bunch of neo-Nazi fanatics couldn't get inside the north tower to see the Black Sun, how the hell was he going to manage it? Magda escorted them back to the gate. They thanked her and declined her suggestion of lunch at the museum's café. Jamie stood back as Sarah apologized for her earlier behaviour. She whispered something in Magda's ear and the German girl wrapped her arms round her in a tight hug. When they parted, her cheeks were damp with tears.

They walked back down towards the car. 'What did you say to her?' he asked.

'You wouldn't understand.'

He stared up towards the north tower. 'I'm going back tonight.'

'I know. I'm coming with you.'

He shook his head. 'It's certainly illegal and it could very well be dangerous. You're my researcher, remember, not my accomplice. And . . .'

'And I'm only a girl?'

'What?'

'That's what you were thinking. I could tell.' He shook his head, but she continued before he could deny it. 'How are you going to get inside? After all, it is a fortress and then there's that *big metal gate* to get past.'

When she said *big metal gate* she mimicked a child's voice. Christ, she could be infuriating. Not for the first time he decided he would never understand women.

'I'll make up my mind once I get here. There has to be a way. Maybe through one of the windows.'

'Wow! What a master plan. The Pink Panther strikes again. Raffles has a rival.'

He turned to ask whether she had a better idea, and blinked.

'Perhaps these would help.' She held up a bunch of keys that were suspiciously similar to the ones the guide had carried.

'How . . . ?'

'I grew up in a rough neighborhood.' Sarah smiled. 'You had to be kinda tricky to get by. I didn't think Magda would miss them for one night.'

'But . . . ?'

'Do you have a better idea?'

XXII

5 May 1945 We camped for the night on the outskirts of Ingolstadt. We were in the middle of the American sector now, but we kept our distance from any other units we met on the way. While we ate, the two other Nazis sat apart like ghosts at the feast. They despised Brohm and didn't care that he knew it. The tall thin one is Gunther Klosse, some kind of medical genius. Klosse has the gloomy demeanour of an undertaker and is filled to bursting with suppressed fury. Strasser, the third of my precious charges, seldom speaks, even to Klosse, but cries out in his sleep in a language, Stan, our Polish paratrooper, says is Russian. Brohm pulled a bottle of brandy from somewhere – he is that kind of man, always finding a way to provide life's little comforts – and insisted I share it. He teased me about the painting. 'Perhaps, when it's over, I will take you to see it, Leutnant

Matt.' 'See what?' I asked. 'My masterpiece,' he says. 'It is beautiful, but to reach it you will face the traditional fearsome challenges. Where Goethe met his demon, avoid the witches' trail. Below the water you will find it, but you must look beyond the veil.'

He grinned, a drunken Germanic bard, pleased with his atrocious poetry. I said I didn't understand, but he only smiled and shook his head. I was a clever man; perhaps I would solve the riddle in time. It was not like any of the painter's earlier works, but had the beautiful simplicity that characterized his best portraits. He tried to persuade me to guess the artist. I wouldn't play his games, but by now I was close to knowing. Not Leonardo, but one of his contemporaries, the one he feared. It made me smile to think that he believed he could tempt me with his non-existent masterpiece. Art had once been my passion, but I had watched whole galleries burn and not felt a scratch on the flint surface of what was now my soul. When a man has seen people burn, what are a few scraps of oily canvas?

Later, Brohm got very drunk, perhaps we both did, but what he revealed that night was a stronger brew than the brandy, and I'd never felt more sober in my life. He began to speak about his work, about a force so powerful that even Hitler feared it, a force that could change the world or destroy it.

Back in his hotel room, hunched over the journal, Jamie frowned as he contemplated the two puzzles the short passage had spawned. Phrase by phrase, his unconscious mind worked its way through the words until it felt as if the blood was fizzing inside his head.

Where Goethe met his demon, avoid the witches' trail. Below the water you will find it, but you must look beyond the veil.

Could this be *it*? The first real clue to to the Raphael's location, rather than just its continued existence? But what kind of clue was it? What did it mean? Unless he could decipher it, he was no closer to the painting than he had been before he turned the first page of Matthew Sinclair's journal. From across six decades it was as if he could hear Walter Brohm taunting him.

Reluctantly, he turned to the second mystery. *A force so powerful that even Hitler feared it?* This was something new. Or was it? David had said Walter Brohm had been involved in the *Uranverein*, the Uranium Club, and the project's goal had been to create a force capable of changing the world or destroying it. But surely Hitler had been aware of the bomb's potential? He had embraced it, not feared it, at least until it had become clear it wouldn't win the war for him and he'd diverted the resources to other, more readily available, *wunderwaffen*. Perhaps Brohm had been closer to Hitler than anyone knew and had recognized something no one else had seen. After all, what was it Robert

Oppenheimer had said about the Manhattan Project? *Now I am become Death, the destroyer of worlds.* In 1945, nobody, certainly in Germany, was aware of the bomb's true power. Hitler would have been well within his rights to fear it.

He was about to put the book away, but the next passage caught his eye because the tone was so different from those he had read so far.

> *6 May 1945 I dreamed of Peggy last night. She had the most beautiful hair, soft and flaxen, and the colour of spun gold. It was silhouetted against the sun, so that it made her appear like some haloed Madonna. I went to take her in my arms, but it was as if I had run into some sort of invisible barrier. I called out her name and she smiled at me.*

He read the words twice, flicking back to Matthew's doomed love affair and confirming that the description of Peggy matched the unnamed lover of the earlier pages. This was wrong. Peggy had been his grandfather's pet name for Jamie's mother, but . . . He shook his head in frustration. He didn't have time for another mystery. He already had too many things to think about.

He dug out the paperback copy of Marlowe's *The Tragicall History of the Life and Death of Dr Faustus* he'd bought in the hope that it would help him decipher the meaning behind 'In Faust's footsteps'. So far it was hard going and he'd discovered nothing that seemed to be relevant. Faustus had sold his soul to the devil in exchange for increased power and knowledge. Walter Brohm had sold his soul to the twin devils of Nazism and science. Was that the message? And if it was, where did it take them? Or could it be some sort of *mea culpa* from beyond the grave by Matthew Sinclair for his part in Operation Equity? Somewhere in these pages were the clues that might lead him to the Raphael and bring him closer to Walter Brohm's great secret. The problem was that there were too many of them. Brohm had created a blizzard of riddles to camouflage the truth, whatever the truth was. Jamie desperately needed time to sit down and unpick them. He picked up the diary again and turned the page.

We are south of Augsburg now, heading west, and our little unit is increasingly nervous. For months this area has been cast as the great stage for a suicidal last stand by Nazi fanatics still loyal to Hitler's shade, who operate under the codename Werewolf. The Final Redoubt. By now we knew the Redoubt was probably just wishful thinking, but the mountain roads are just a little too narrow and the twisting valleys too ambush-friendly for us to relax. Nobody wants to die now, when it is clear the war has only a few days at most to run. The tension affects us all and the division between Brohm and the two other Nazis grows ever deeper. He sought me out last night and nodded towards fat little Strasser. 'To look at him,' he says, 'you would not believe that he holds a world record; like

Jesse Owens, but a little different, eh?' He saw that he had aroused my curiosity. 'It's true, Leutnant Matt. In September nineteen forty-one, just outside Kiev, our friend Strasser personally shot eleven hundred and sixty-five individuals in a single day. Extraordinary, no? But I have seen the papers. They gave him a medal, I think. And more extraordinary still that he is now accompanying a man like me to a new life thanks to our American friends. Why? you ask. I will tell you, Leutnant Matt, because you and I should have no secrets. Our Strasser discovered that killing made him nervous, so they transferred him to the Ausland-SD, where he became most adept in counter-intelligence against the Soviet Union. My good friend Strasser, the Ox, knows more about the NKVD than any other man alive, so he will not hang, as he deserves, but will sunbathe overlooking Long Island Sound as he sips his whisky sour. And Klosse? Look at him,' he spat, 'a monster who carried out experiments in the camps, even on children. The very sight of him makes me ashamed of the uniform I once wore. And why does he deserve your charity, Leutnant Matt? Because he knows things that would make your flesh creep. What civilized person would make war with germs that are capable of wiping out entire nations? Bubonic plague, anthrax and awful things that don't even yet have names. Gases that strip a man's flesh from his bones in seconds. You have read Frankenstein, of course, Leutnant Matt.

Compared to Gunther Klosse, Dr Frankenstein is a kindergarten teacher.' What bothered Brohm most, was that, as he saw it, Klosse's work had no benefit for mankind, whereas Brohm's, of course, did. I asked him how he knew these things. He shook his head regretfully, all part of the performance: 'Once I was an important man, Leutnant Matt, and I made it my business to know things.' What he was telling me was almost certainly the truth, but the reason he was telling me was to set him apart from these other men. The guilty. If Walter Brohm was guilty of anything it could only be of genius, which he then went on to reinforce. When I think of all we have suffered and all the men who have died, I can't get Brohm's words out of my head. He talked of things I didn't fully understand; a 'Nuclear Age' that was over before it had begun, superseded by this thing he was on the very brink of creating. Something that was beyond the comprehension of most ordinary men – though not Walter Brohm. He painted an image of himself as a great Germanic hero. Another Humboldt. Before the war, he had walked in a land of giants, seeking the heart of Aryan purity and there, in the most unlikely place on earth, he had found it. His only regret was that he did not dare stay longer, because he was certain there was more to find. When the Americans gave him the resources he would replicate its qualities. It would be the wonder of the age ...

More clues and more riddles. And a tantalizing possibility. He read the last paragraph again. Another Humboldt? The only Humboldt he could think of was the German voyager and naturalist. So Brohm had been an explorer. And from there, the rest was simple. Jamie's researches had uncovered the pre-war SS expeditions sent to seek out the origins of Aryan civilization. Those expeditions had travelled to Finland, the Middle East and Siberia. But to only one land of giants.

He reached into his wallet and pulled out a card, then dialled the number into his mobile phone. It was late, but he had a feeling the man he was calling wouldn't mind.

XXIII

Jamie had just replaced the phone when he was interrupted by a knock. When he opened the door, Sarah was waiting, dark hair tied back, dressed all in black and carrying her own rucksack.

'Ready?' she asked.

'Ready as I'll ever be.' He switched off the light and closed the door behind him.

Wewelsburg Castle by day intimidated, by night it had all the charm of a Transylvanian keep under a full moon. They parked beside the road circling the base of the hill and stood for a few moments in a tense, nerve-tingling silence. Sarah bowed her head and he wondered if she was praying. He remembered what she had said – *This is where it happened* – and he knew she was thinking about the men and women who had died here. This was the very ground where the pictures had shown the Russian prisoners, the homosexuals and the emaciated shells of Hitler's political enemies toiling to make Heinrich Himmler's crazed dream of an SS Disneyworld a reality.

Jamie had identified a track that wound across the tree-blanketed slope. It was less a path than an unofficial shortcut created by wandering deer and children on mountain bikes, and he cursed silently as unseen brambles clawed at him and nettles whipped his face. A few feet behind, he noted tetchily, Sarah moved easily, as if darkness was her natural element, a silent shadow that treated the fierce incline as if it didn't exist. When they reached the top of the hill, he began moving to his left. She placed a hand on his arm.

'Not by the museum, there'll be some sort of security.' She led him through an arch and into the shadows. 'I told you I was good at research.'

'If you're so good at research what *is* the penalty in Germany for breaking into a national monument?'

'You should have thought of that earlier, but I'm fairly certain you wouldn't get away with anything less than being put up against a wall and shot.'

'You're right, I should have thought of it earlier. Where now?'

'This way avoids the museum.' The grounds of the castle were on two levels. She led them to where a narrow stair led up to the roadway and the main gate. 'Just pray there aren't security lights with motion sensors.'

For once, he found the intellectual high ground. 'Rabbit burrows.' He pointed to the dark shadows in the grass. 'They'd never be off, think of the electricity bill. Bugger.'

Sarah stopped. 'What is it?'

'I've left my rucksack in the car.'

He heard a soft mutter that might have been 'idiot'. 'We can't go back now. We'll just have to get by with what's in mine. Come on.'

They trotted to the gateway with Jamie in the lead. At one point the clouds parted and he felt as if he was the focus of a hundred eyes as moonlight reflected from the castle windows, but soon they were across the bridge and inside the internal courtyard.

At the far end of the triangle lay the wooden door to the north tower. It had been open earlier, but now it was locked and Sarah pulled the stolen keys from the voluminous pocket of her hooded jacket. Jamie used his own anorak as a shield and switched on his torch. She studied the lock and speculatively dangled the keys. They'd discussed the likeliest ones for each door, but now, faced with the choice, she was uncertain which to try.

'OK, baby, which one are you?' She chose one of four similar black keys designed for mortise locks, and tried the first. It slid easily into the lock but didn't turn. She repeated the process with the second with a similar result.

Jamie fretted. She was taking too long. 'Let me try?'

The darkness hid her face, but he guessed that the look she gave him would leave a permanent scar. Fortunately, she thrust the keys into his hand without argument.

He worked the next key into the lock, but it barely

fitted. One last try. As he juggled the keys in his hand they rattled like a prisoner's chains.

'Jeez, next time I'm going to commit a burglary I'll make sure my partner's a rhinoceros. He'll make a darn sight less noise. Try the first one again. I had the feeling it might just be stiff.'

'Maybe we should have brought some oil?'

'Just try it,' she snarled.

This time it turned easily and the door opened with a slight creak. 'You just have to have the knack.' He was glad she hadn't brought a knife.

The barred door to the inner chamber was much simpler. Only a single key in the bunch, the big silver one Magda had brought out earlier, looked capable of fitting the ornate lock and the gate swung open without complaint when Sarah turned it. They slipped inside and stood in the darkness. Jamie knew the exact location of the Black Sun, but for some reason he found it difficult to move. It wasn't fear, he told himself, just a sensible precaution. This was a chamber where only the initiated were meant to feel at home. He'd expected there to be at least a little light from the windows in the alcoved niches, but it seemed someone had closed the shutters. Still he could visualize the *Obergruppenführersaal* from their previous visit. Twelve large pillars circled the room, and twelve empty niches that had never been filled. He knew that the number twelve played a major role in Nazi mythology; just as the twelve apostles served Christ and twelve knights followed King Arthur, so an inner circle of twelve *Obergruppenführer* served Himmler. The only sound was Sarah's steady breathing. He knew they were alone, but in the darkness of the chamber it was as if the ghosts of the past stalked them.

Forcing his feet to move, he walked slowly to the centre of the chamber and with a soft click his torch illuminated the marble symbol on the floor. The first surprise was that it wasn't black, it was green, a mottled greyish green the colour of the *Wehrmacht* uniforms he'd seen in colour newsreels of the Russian Front. The second, that it was much bigger than it had looked.

'The Black Sun,' Sarah whispered.

'But not our Black Sun. This is different.' He felt a moment of confusion, uncertain whether to be disappointed or not. The symbol from his grandfather's diary had nine arms, this had twelve, and there was no message or number.

By now Sarah had pulled a large piece of tracing paper from her bag and was hurriedly copying the design. As an afterthought she shaded in the centre of the sun with the pencil as if it were a brass rubbing. She had just finished and was in the act of replacing the paper when the beam of a powerful torch trapped them in its spotlight.

XXIV

Silicon Valley, California

'The artefact is of very ancient construction.' Six men in white protective suits stood over the golden casket inside the 'clean' area of the laboratory complex, but only one spoke into the microphone. Speakers relayed his emotionless voice to the glass booth where the man who had initiated the raid on the Menshikov Palace now stood. He cut an incongruous figure in his T-shirt and jeans, with the thick-lensed rimless spectacles that reminded people of a short-sighted cartoon character and his long grey hair tied in a ponytail. He knew he was a throwback to another era, but he had never cared what anyone else thought about him. Money allowed you to make your own decisions and he'd long ago made more than enough money to tell the world to go screw itself. He listened intently as the scientist continued.

'Tests conducted on the base of the object confirm it is manufactured of mahogany wood, probably imported from India, overlaid with a thin sheet of beaten gold which chemical analysis suggests is of similar origin. The gold is embossed with extensive symbols and patterns. Several letters are visible, but these are in a very obscure and venerable form of Sanskrit, possibly even pre-Sanskrit, and are indecipherable to me.'

He paused and looked up at the watchers. 'I understand more expert eyes are already studying this aspect of the investigation.'

He turned his attention back to the casket. 'The lock has a fairly complex twin-barrel mechanism, but we have been able to manufacture a key that should allow me to open it. Radiation levels are normal for an object that has spent many years in the mountains of Tibet, however our X-rays indicate the box may be lined with lead or some other similar material, so before I begin, please seal off the room.'

Metal screens rose up in front of the booth window and the man inside concentrated on the voice. 'Check suit integrity. Yes? I will commence to open the box.'

The words were an inane catchphrase from some long-forgotten TV game show. Did the scientist have a sense of humour? It seemed unlikely. The pony-tailed man had known him for fifteen years and he could barely remember seeing him smile. Nerves, perhaps. That was more likely. Whatever was inside the casket, even if it only held a tiny trace of what they hoped, could change their lives. The scientist would hold the key to the last great secret of nuclear physics and the man in the booth would take a decisive step towards his goal of becoming the most powerful person on the planet. He held his breath and it seemed that the silence that preceded the metallic click of the lock's engagement was the eternal silence of the grave.

'I will now lift the lid of the casket . . . which contains a . . . a . . .'

The scientist's words tailed away and the man ground his teeth in frustration.

'A what, goddamit, Jensen? Lift these goddam screens.' He did not normally use profanity in public, but many years earlier when he had been a packer in the loading bay of a television factory in Mesa, Arizona, he had been an inveterate cusser, and his choice of words reflected the tension of the moment.

The metal screen withdrew to expose the brightly lit scene below. He saw that the six white-suited men had all taken a step back from the casket and were staring in astonishment at whatever was inside. He craned his neck to get a better view, but he could still see nothing because of the ring of hooded figures.

'For Christ's sake.' He hammered the reinforced glass and six pairs of eyes turned to him.

The men moved apart, like a white flower opening in the sun, and at last he saw it.

For a moment he couldn't speak. He felt a hammer blow in his chest that might have been the prelude to a heart attack. The hammer blow of failure. All that time and effort and investment and the sacrifice of other men's lives had achieved nothing but to uncover some sort of macabre joke. It had never been likely that the casket would contain the material itself, but he had hoped for some sort of residue, some hint of its nature or potential. The Sanskrit symbols might still provide a clue, but surely he deserved more than this?

'The casket contains . . .' Jensen resumed his commentary, but now his voice crackled with nervous energy, '. . . what appears to be a representation of a human skull . . .' He held up the object in gloved hands and the over-bright artificial light of the laboratory caught it, so that the man in the booth was almost dazzled by the reflected brilliance. 'It appears to be made of . . .'

'Silver,' the man in the booth said decisively. 'After sixty years old Heini is still playing with us. Who would have thought the chicken farmer had a sense of humour? Don't you recognize it, Jensen? Christ, your old man probably had one just like it.' He studied the empty eye sockets and the mocking seven-toothed smile. 'It's a replica of the skull on an SS Death's Head honour ring. Get me the file on the nineteen thirty-seven expedition to Tibet.'

Five minutes later he was leafing through the thin folder. Most of the documents were original and in German, but German had been his first language in the clapboard house in East Brunswick where he had been brought up. The original family name hadn't been Vanderbilt, of course, but there had come a point after December 1941 when the old man decided it was more sensible to be Dutch than Deutsche. His German had come in useful when he was drafted, because it allowed him to spend the dangerous Vietnam years at a NATO headquarters near Hanover instead of crawling around some swamp in the DMZ getting shot at by Stone Age sub-humans. That was where he had learned to love electronics and had spotted the potential of the new-fangled tape cassette players. When he returned to the States he'd bought a licence and mortgaged himself ten times over to create a manufacturing facility. Within a year he'd made the first of his many millions. Another opportunity had come with the rise of video tape technology in the early seventies, but he'd remembered how the eight-track player had once looked as though it would cost him everything, and foresaw that this new race would develop into a battle of formats. Instead, he decided to focus on the components that would be needed in *every* machine, whoever made it. By the time the boom in home computers took off he'd been perfectly placed to take advantage. And that was just the start. He'd made and lost fortunes along the way, married and lost wives, but there had always been one constant in his life. Membership of the Vril Society had come via his father and grandfather, influence in it had come with his growing fortune. Influence had inevitably led to the leadership, the first time the position had been held by a member outwith the Fatherland. Half of his life had been devoted to the search for the Vril, the race of ancient supermen who had survived the Great Inundation and sought refuge deep in the earth, where their powers still lay untapped. He had sponsored years of research, expeditions to the Arctic and the Gobi

Desert under the guise of scientific fieldwork, and he had pinpointed sunken Atlantis to the Bay of Naples, in Italy, on the edge of the Phlegraean Plain. His fortune funded Frederick's private army, which ensured that the potential advances made under Adolf Hitler would remain within the control of those pure enough to merit the rewards they promised. He had believed. But the Brohm papers had changed everything. Now he understood that the Vril would never be found within his lifetime. The strange thing was that it didn't matter because he had discovered that the power of the Vril already lay within him. All he needed to tap into it was the Sun Stone. He snapped his fingers and an aide placed a mobile phone in his hand, the preset number already ringing.

XXV

'Please place the paper back on the floor.'

The flat voice had a distinct Berlin accent and came from the direction of the torch. Jamie became aware of shadowy figures moving inside the ring of pillars. Twelve of them. Why wasn't he surprised. Somewhere within him a dangerous stillness developed. He recognized it from his OTC days and an escape and evasion course that had gone wrong. He had fallen into the hands of three ugly Paras who thought it would be fun to haze a posh boy for a change. They told him what they were going to do to him and showed him the broomstick they were going to do it with. They'd expected him to piss himself with fear, but all he felt was the stillness. And from within the stillness the beast had emerged. He remembered an arm snapping and yellow teeth flying. They'd got him in the end, of course, and they might have killed him if the marshal hadn't appeared. Instead, he'd been given the option of joining them. That was then. This was now. He began backing towards the doorway, but two of the shadows moved to block the only exit. His first priority was to protect Sarah, and for the moment the only way to protect Sarah was to submit. Or at least appear to submit. He willed the beast back into his lair and nodded to her to do as the voice ordered. She glared at him, but retrieved the tracing from her bag and reluctantly placed it back over the sun symbol before stepping away.

A tall man in a dark suit entered from the direction of the torch, stooped to pick up the tracing and returned the way he came. He was silhouetted against the light and Jamie couldn't see his face, but he had an impression of absolute control and athletic strength. A grunt of acknowledgement seemed to indicate satisfaction.

'This is a sacred place. Why are you here?'

'I see nothing sacred about a Nazi chicken farmer's obsession with King Arthur.' The beast might be docile, but he still had a tongue. 'And judging by the fact that you haven't put the lights on, I'd say we have as much right to be here as you have. Who are you people, anyway?'

For a moment the hatred in the room was so palpable he could feel the fingers reaching for his throat, but the insult seemed to have no effect on the man who had spoken. 'You may call me Frederick. As for my friends, they would prefer to remain anonymous for now.'

Something told Jamie that Frederick's willingness to be candid wasn't good news and the German's next question confirmed the suspicion. 'What is your interest in the Black Sun?'

'As you can see,' Jamie pointed towards the paper in Frederick's hands, 'our interest is purely artistic.' Frederick didn't laugh, but then it hadn't been much of a joke. The silence that followed was more eloquent than any words and Jamie sensed Sarah moving closer and slightly behind him. She froze as the double click of an automatic pistol being cocked split the graveyard atmosphere and Jamie's body did its best to disappear into itself as it awaited the strike of the first bullet. Frederick continued as if nothing had happened. Either he enjoyed the sound of his own voice or somebody somewhere was checking that the interlopers didn't have back-up who might arrive to spoil the party.

'You went to great lengths to keep your visit here secret; for us that is not so necessary. Did you think that those for whom this castle holds the same reverence as your St Paul's Cathedral would be kept from it by a few provincial bureaucrats? We belong here. We are the inheritors. The keepers of the truth. The mysteries enacted in this room are beyond your capacity for understanding. If our predecessors had succeeded in what they attempted here the world would be a different place. A better place that would not have had to endure sixty years of the corrupt, putrescent influence of Communism.'

'A world ruled by Nazis?' The inner stillness returned and the monster took a distinctly human form. He focused on Frederick. When the time came, he would take him first. 'I don't think I would have liked to live in that world.'

'Do not be confused by labels, Mr Saintclair.' Jamie winced at the sound of his name. Clearly this wasn't the chance encounter Frederick had let him believe. But what else did he know? And how did he come to know it? The German's voice took on a new authority as he continued. 'Let us say a world ruled by those with the qualities to rule: authority, resolve, organization and ambition. Men of pure heart and pure vision. Men with the courage to remake the world. Men like those who stood where we stand now more than half a century ago. When the time came they did not hesitate. They stepped forward to take their place in history, because it was their duty.'

While Frederick talked Jamie allowed his senses to absorb the changing dynamics of the situation. He could sense the dark shadows moving closer: the slightest hint of movement against the faint blur of a pillar; the soft shuffle of a rubber-soled shoe on the marble floor. He tried to focus his mind. There had to be a way out of this trap. Negotiation clearly wasn't an option, but at least he could try to buy more time. He remembered his grandfather's journal entry about the camps. *My German tastes like vomit in my mouth.* If he could provoke them, or at least surprise them, maybe he could give Sarah the chance to get clear.

'Was it their duty to kill millions of innocent people and destroy the lives of tens of millions more?' He allowed contempt to saturate his words. 'The only place they have in history is in the chapter reserved for cowards and murderers. And they failed in the end. This room is an illusion, an architectural conjuring trick. It is no more sacred than a multi-storey car park. The power of the men who created Wewelsburg was smashed, the way evil will always be smashed. This so-called Valhalla was never anything but a building site. The SS no longer exists except in the minds of a few misguided idiots, and Heinrich Himmler and those he led are long dead.'

The expected reaction didn't materialize. Frederick wasn't finished with his lesson.

'You misunderstand the situation, just as you misunderstand the true meaning of the Black Sun. You talk of Nazis and the SS as if they were somehow central to our aims, but they were only a vehicle for their times. Adolf Hitler allowed his vision to be distorted by fear and hatred and in doing so he betrayed his legacy. His fear led him to go to war five years before he was ready. His hatred made him focus on the extermination of the Jews and the Slavs to the exclusion of all else. He should have enslaved them or conscripted them into expendable penal battalions, the result would have been the same in the end. Instead, he wasted irreplaceable resources on their destruction, when those resources were needed here to achieve something truly important. That opportunity was missed, but we are patient men, Mr Saintclair, and it will come again. Now, where is the journal?'

Jamie had no time for surprise at Frederick's mention of the journal. Suddenly there was movement all around him. 'Go!' He shouted the warning to Sarah and threw himself towards Frederick. It had always

199

been a long shot and it lengthened further when a leg stuck out and knocked his feet from under him. He hit the marble floor with enough force to jar his teeth and kicked out frantically at the nearest solid form. Someone cried out in pain, but any satisfaction was buried by the realization that they were now making a determined effort to kill him. He tried to roll clear of a glancing blow from a heavy boot that made his ears ring. Another knocked the wind from him as it crunched into his ribs. He called desperately to Sarah to get out and he could hear the fear in his own voice. A muffled scream answered his plea and he knew they had failed. Now the boots were arriving in earnest, a relentless businesslike rhythm that sought out his most vulnerable parts. He squirmed and twisted, but his racing mind told him he was dead unless someone intervened. A heel that had been meant to crush his skull emerged from the darkness and missed his nose by an inch. He had a vision of other helpless men who had died in this very place, beaten to death by the predecessors of the men who were killing him.

'Enough!'

Strong arms hauled him roughly to his feet. His head still spun from the blows and his body was a mass of pain, but at least he was alive. He winced as something hard and metallic was rammed into his bruised ribs with enough force to make him grunt.

'Search them, and the bag.'

He heard Sarah hiss like a trapped wildcat as coarse hands made a rudimentary check of his body.

'Nothing but more paper, a length of rope and a lap-top.'

'It does not matter. It will be in the car or one of the rooms.'

'It isn't.' Jamie's words seemed to freeze the darkness. 'Let the girl go and I'll tell you where the journal is.'

Frederick, he assumed it was Frederick, brought his face close enough so Jamie could smell the mix of beer and garlic on his breath. Half a head taller, with cropped, sandy hair, the German's calculating grey eyes studied him from a face that was as flat and as expression-less as a marble statue and with the complexion of a day old corpse.

'No,' the other man said eventually. 'I believe you are bluffing. In any case, we will soon find out. Gustav?' Another figure detached itself from the outer shadows. 'Gustav has recently returned from duty in Afghanistan where he was able to refine his interrogation techniques with a remarkable degree of success.' A hand like a shovel pulled Jamie's arm backwards and before he knew what was happening his wrists had been cuffed and he was spun to face his captor. Gustav was short, but with a chest that strained the buttons of his shirt, a face that seemed too small for his head and wide-set eyes like quarry chips. He gave Jamie's cheek a playful slap with his left hand and drove his right fist deep into the Englishman's stomach. A man who enjoyed his work. Jamie struggled for breath as his captor drew him upright again.

'That's on account, yeah? We don't want no trouble.'

The German picked up Sarah's rucksack and put it over his left shoulder.

'Take them to the cellar below the bridge. I will join you there in a few minutes.' As Gustav and another man led them away, Frederick turned to Jamie. 'There is no escape for you, Mr Saintclair. You will soon tell us where the journal is, I assure you. Gustav not only enjoys what he does, he is also extremely adept at it. He understands the psychology of torture as well as the physical mechanics. He will use the woman to cause you pain.' His voice rose a fraction. 'He will hurt her and make you watch as he humiliates her, sexually.'

Gustav chuckled his appreciation and ran coarse, butcher's hands over Sarah's body; an appetizer for what was to come.

'You bastard.' She tried to snap at his face with her teeth, but the German only laughed all the louder. Jamie struggled against his cuffs until the big man turned and slapped his head hard.

'Please, don't hurt her. I'll tell you everything you want to know.'

Frederick motioned to Gustav who produced a roll of parcel tape and slapped a short length across Jamie's mouth before repeating the exercise with Sarah.

'That would be very sensible, of course, but I'm afraid it is not possible. This is the holy of holies. We of the Vril Society have protected its secrets and maintained its purity since the beginning. You and your woman have desecrated it and you must be punished. Once you have everything you need from him, you may do what you wish with the girl,' he said to Gustav. 'When it is over bury them in the north woods. They will be among friends and I doubt a few more bones will be noticed.'

XXVI

Sarah cursed behind the tape and kicked out as Gustav and a taller, dark-haired man armed with a pistol hustled them out into the V-shaped courtyard of the main castle. Jamie bowed his head as if he couldn't take any more punishment, but his eyes studied his surroundings. Gustav was the greatest physical threat, but if it came to it he'd have to take the man with the gun first. He was resigned to the fact that he probably wouldn't succeed, but the alternative didn't bear thinking about. If he was going to die, he would go down fighting, it was just a question of choosing the right moment. Frederick had mentioned a cellar, which meant some kind of slope or stairs. It would be awkward. A little cramped, maybe. That might give them their best chance. Their only chance. If they could somehow disable their guards and reach the trees. But there were too many ifs. He realized now why they had found it so easy to get into the castle. Frederick must have come to some sort of arrangement with the night security guards who would surely have been alerted by the noise Sarah was making even with her mouth taped. Gustav must have been thinking the same because he grunted something and his comrade took over Jamie's arm while the stocky Nazi grabbed a handful of Sarah's hair and almost lifted her off the ground.

'I told you. No trouble, or it will be all the worse for you.'

It struck Jamie that it was unlikely things could get any worse, but the German's words seemed to have an effect. Sarah went limp and allowed herself to be pulled along. They had barely exchanged glances since the moment the torch beam had trapped them, but now her eyes met his. Two dark streaks marked where tears had smudged her make-up, but the eyes held no fear. The message he read in them was that whatever he tried, she was with him.

The main door was unlocked and wide enough to allow them through as a group. Gustav walked to the left with his hand still in Sarah's hair. Jamie's captor was to his right with one hand on his arm and the other on the butt of the pistol. As they emerged into the night Jamie sensed a blur of movement to his left and the air rang with the resounding 'clang' of metal hitting something solid and unyielding. He felt the tall man tense and begin to turn, the arm coming up and the pistol drawing clear. But Jamie was quicker. With a flying butt that almost dislocated his neck he smashed his skull sideways into the tall man's face and felt bone cracking as the head snapped backwards. At the same time he used all his energy, like a rugby forward hitting a tackle bag, to propel his captor towards the bridge parapet. He had a vague notion of a second clang behind him, but by now the tall man's legs had caught on the low stone wall and he was going. Jamie scrabbled with his feet for balance and if his hands had been free he might have saved himself. Instead, his weight took him over, still tight to the other man's chest. He felt himself falling and tried to remember distractedly how high? What was at the bottom, grass or more of those bloody hard looking cobbles? As if it mattered. He held onto that thought until the lights went out, all the breath was knocked from his body and his head seemed to be detached from his neck. He heard a sharp crack that might have been a rib breaking, but he wasn't sure whose. It seemed odd that he should bounce, but for a second he was in the air again and this time he had a harder landing. Definitely cobbles. For a few seconds he lay back and watched the stars spin. A little rest didn't seem too much to ask after all the excitement.

A hand ripped the tape from his mouth.

'Get up,' Sarah hissed. 'We don't have much time.' She turned him over and worked at the cuffs that were biting into his wrist. Christ, Houdini had nothing on her. With a click they came free. Then he remembered Gustav. Of course, Gustav would have had the key.

'Gustav?'

'He's out, but not for long. Not like this guy.'

Jamie sat up and she helped him to his feet. Only now did he notice that the tall man was beside him, lying very still and with his head at an awkward angle. He had blood on his face and more was leaking from the back of his head to form a dark pool on the cobbles. He heard a gasp from above, and turned to find the German museum guide Magda looking down from the bridge, the expression on her face a mix of fear and horror. She was out of uniform in jeans and a tan jacket over a white T-shirt, and still held the shovel she must have used to brain Gustav. His mind told him she shouldn't be there, and neither should the shovel, but Sarah didn't give him time to think about it. She hauled him up the slope and across the road towards their escape route.

'Hurry.'

Magda dropped her ironmongery and took Jamie's other arm. 'I came back for my keys,' the German girl explained breathlessly. 'I thought I had dropped them somewhere. Then I heard noises from the *Obergruppenführersaal*. I was frightened, but I decided to check. It was my duty, yes?' Yes, Jamie thought, and thank Christ for that. 'These men, they were saying terrible things. I think they would kill you both. So I had to do something. I am not brave, but I could not let it happen here again. You understand?'

Before he could answer Sarah muttered a curse and turned back.

'Keep going,' she whispered. 'I'll catch up.'

While Magda kept him upright on legs that still felt like rubber bands, Jamie glanced back to see Sarah rummaging beside the dark lump that must have been

Gustav. As she did, a lamp clicked on in the courtyard and she was instantly bathed in bright yellow light. She straightened and ran towards them carrying her rucksack by its straps in her right hand. They had almost reached the trees and the slope that would take them back to the car, when they heard the first shout. Jamie would have stopped to help Sarah, but Magda pushed him forwards over the lip of the slope and into the first bushes. As he raised a hand to help her down, the blonde girl turned to check Sarah's position. Apparently satisfied that the other girl would make it safely, she reached out to take Jamie's hand. Her eyes met his and he could have sworn there was a twinkle in them; the eyes of someone caught in a great adventure and not quite sure what to make of it. Lips pursed as if she was trying not to smile at the ludicrousness of their situation.

It was just the faintest noise. A soft thud and the sort of 'pffff' you hear when compressed air escapes as a mechanic tests tyre pressure. Jamie felt fine liquid spray his face and Magda let out a short, outraged gasp. He would swear that he never heard a shot. A small spot of red appeared over the left breast of the museum guide's T-shirt and he watched disbelievingly as it grew wider. Without another sound Magda toppled forward into his arms.

'Move. They're coming.' Sarah came down the slope at the run, but slowed when she saw Magda's limp body.

Jamie shook his head. 'I—'

'We have to keep moving, Jamie.' Urgency made her breathless. 'And you need to keep it together. It won't do

Magda any good if Frederick gets his hands on us again. Take her to the car and I'll try to slow them.'

'How?'

She shook her head. 'Don't argue. Just go.'

Reluctantly, he stumbled down the hill with the injured girl in his arms. His storm-battered mind fought to understand everything that had happened. A few minutes earlier they were about to be tortured to death. He had killed a man, or he might have killed him. Magda had been shot. He tried to check her pulse, but there was no response and he could feel the dampness on his chest where her blood had soaked through his shirt. With a feeling of hopelessness, he laid the body at the base of the slope, avoiding the dull, accusing eyes. My fault, he thought. I killed her. Not Frederick. Not Sarah. Jamie Saintclair killed her with his idiotic quest. And now . . . ?

The firecracker snap of a small-calibre weapon, followed instantly by a scream of agony, broke through his grief. It was a man's scream. He bundled himself into the car and a moment later Sarah tumbled out of the darkness and jumped in beside him, throwing her rucksack on the floor at her feet. He put the engine into gear, accelerating away before the door was properly closed and praying that Frederick hadn't left anyone to watch the road. Sarah glanced into the back seat and choked back a sob. 'Where is Magda?'

He kept his eyes on the road. Couldn't have met hers even if he hadn't been driving. 'I thought it was for the best. We wouldn't . . . She was dead. Frederick will have ways of tidying things like this up. He can't afford to have his holy of holies splashed all over the front page of *Bild Zeitung*. Magda . . .' He shook his head. What else was there to say?

The adrenalin surge from whatever had happened on the hillside was fading and Sarah slumped forward with her head on the dashboard. Her voice was muffled so he could barely make out the individual words.

'I shot a man.'

'What?' His voice sounded shrill in his own ears, but he remembered the scream and realized that he'd already known. He modified the question. 'Why?'

'To delay them. They were coming. They would have got to the car before we could escape. So I shot him in the leg.'

'That seems fair enough.' Not in the real world, maybe, but certainly in this madhouse they had stumbled into.

She raised her head and he knew she was looking at him. 'I took the gun from the one you . . . the one who fell. I grew up with guns. I learned to shoot when I was just a kid. I hid behind a tree and when he came past I pointed it at his leg and shot him.'

'Frederick?' he said hopefully.

She shook her head and began to cry. 'Poor Magda.'

'Yes, poor Magda.'

He drove for an hour, but the road signs might as well have been invisible. His eyes were more on the mirror than the road ahead and he switched between the autobahn, major roads and minor ones, taking exits and turns at random. He was confident they weren't being followed. Hopefully.

'Where are we going?'

'I don't know.'

'Not back to the hotel?'

'No. They'd be waiting for us.'

'Unless they thought we'd gone to the police?'

He shook his head. 'The one I . . . the tall one. I think I recognized his face from earlier today. Near the hotel. He was in one of those blue and white police cars they have here.'

'What do we do now?'

'I don't know.' It was the second time he'd admitted as much. The truth was that he hadn't known what he was doing right from the start.

'So when are you going to tell me about this journal?'

XXVII

They must have travelled south, because by the time they reached the outskirts of the small German town the sun was coming up over the hills to their left. A sign informed him he was entering Fulda, but left him little the wiser. He avoided directions to the town centre and instead looked for an industrial area where he knew he'd find one of those cheap hotels that lorry drivers use when they don't want to sleep in their cabs; the type that caters for arrivals at any time of the day or night and the receptionist is too bored or too tired to ask questions. When he found it, he parked the little Japanese compact in the corner furthest away from the hotel building and part-shielded from the road by a pair of green recycling bins. Sarah's face was deathly pale and from the set of her lips he knew she was thinking about Magda.

He switched off the engine and they sat in a silent purgatory of exhaustion and disbelief, allowing the minutes to pass.

'Do you feel up to booking in?' he said eventually.

212

'They may not be too fussy here, but I doubt I'll be welcome looking like this.'

She turned to look at him, and he saw her flinch as she took in the blood that stained the front of his shirt and jacket. Her dark hair hung lank across her cheeks and weariness and grief had sharpened the planes of her face making her look like an urchin from a Dickens novel. She reached into a pocket to retrieve a tiny white handkerchief, spat on it and wiped at his face and cheeks. The gesture was almost motherly and he would have smiled except the linen came away pink and he remembered the wet spray as Magda had been shot. He felt as if he was going to be sick. Sarah's frown deepened as she noticed something else. She reached up to the side of his head and gently searched amongst his hair. He felt a sharp pain as she tugged at some object embedded in his scalp and her hand came away holding a sliver of white.

'Bloody hell.'

'Upper left incisor, I'd say.' They stared at it and suddenly they were both laughing, at first almost hysterically, but gradually the tension drained away as if someone had opened a valve.

'Book a room for a week. If they're suspicious they'll want to get a couple of nights' rent before they turn us in to anybody.'

'You mean the cops?'

'No, I mean anybody.'

*　　*　　*

The room was modern and clean. It had one double bed with a single bunk above, and just about enough room to sidle between the bed, a small chest of drawers and a sink that comprised the rest of the furniture. A sign informed them that the communal bathroom was along the hall. Jamie would have preferred a room on the upper floors, but this had been the only one available. It had a small square window, set high enough for privacy, which faced on to trees beyond the car park. Once Sarah had booked in and smuggled him past reception they had been too tired to feel anything but relief. Jamie closed the curtain while Sarah kicked off her shoes and lay back on the bed and closed her eyes. For a few moments he stood over her, wondering at the sheer resilience packed into that small, almost childlike body. He looked from the bed up to the bunk bed. To hell with it. He peeled off his bloodstained shirt, replaced it with the slightly less stained jacket and lay down beside her. Before he lost consciousness a little voice kept demanding: What the hell are we going to do now?

He was woken by someone blowing gently into his ear, which was a pleasant contrast to the dream where he had just been placed into an implement of torture straight out of the *Pit and the Pendulum*. Blearily, he opened his eyes and found himself under the scrutiny of two liquid orbs of gold-flecked walnut.

'I hope you didn't take any liberties while I was asleep, Jamie Saintclair.' Sarah lay on her side with her head supported by her right hand, but he knew she hadn't woken in that position because it was clear she had washed her hair and done those things that women do to their face that turns attractive into beautiful. She spoke lightly, but he felt a sizzle of electricity in the air that had nothing to do with the fact they were on the run. It struck him that now was the moment to act on the impulse he'd felt since virtually the first moment he'd cast eyes on her. Then he was struck by something even more fundamental.

'What's for breakfast?'

She swung herself off the bed and he raised himself as she produced two enormous pastries from a paper bag and complemented them with two cardboard cups that contained, if his nose didn't deceive him, about a gallon each of tarry German coffee. 'I've been busy. We're in a town called Fulda.'

He nodded, remembering the sign from yesterday, or was it last night, or possibly this morning?

She nibbled delicately on her pastry. 'Nice place, lots of great architecture according to the girl at the coffee house.' Jamie stared at her. He'd assumed the food had come from somewhere in the hotel. He stood up and pulled back the curtain a fraction of an inch so that he could see across the gravel car park. She glared at him. 'I'm not stupid, Jamie. I didn't take any chances and nobody followed me back.'

He ignored her and continued his check. There didn't seem to be anything unusual. No one sitting in cars reading yesterday's newspaper. 'It was still a risk.'

'You'd rather not eat?'

He laughed and bit into the *kuchen*. It was sweet and flaky and when he added a tentative sip of scalding liquid he felt instantly revived. 'I don't plan to be here long enough to see the sights.'

'I guessed that. So I washed your shirt – just don't expect service like this every day, OK. But maybe you should . . . umm, clean up first and see what you can do with the jacket before you put it back on.'

The hint made him suddenly aware he was wearing yesterday's underwear. He sniffed and caught a whiff of stale sweat and something else that was instantly recognizable, a mixture of rotting fish meal and wet metal; fear and blood. His fear. Magda's blood. 'We need new clothes.'

She nodded. 'And a lot of other things. When we've eaten and you've freshened up, maybe we could talk about it?'

An hour later they were sitting on opposite sides of the bed with the two rucksacks between them. Sarah pulled out her laptop and linked to the hotel's wi-fi connection.

'I did a little research on this Vril thing our friend Frederick mentioned. It's another of Himmler's pet cults and all tied up with his obsession with the creation of the Aryan race. The cult was founded by a bunch of guys who'd read a nineteenth-century book called *The Coming Race* by some crazy English baron called Edward Bulwer-Lytton. It was a work of fiction that speculated on a long lost master race emerging to rule the world. You can see where we're going here, huh?

The Vril Society ticked all the boxes for Himmler, but the important thing for us is that the energy that gave the Vril their mythical powers was said to be from the Black Sun and the aim of the Vril Society was to find the key to that power.'

Jamie felt the room go cold. 'So what exactly was the Black Sun? Obviously it wasn't just a symbol.'

'Nobody knows, but it sure spawned a lot of conspiracy theories. Look.' She brought up another internet page. 'Remember Magda talked about Wewelsburg being a landing site for UFOs? Crazy, huh? Well, here's a story that claims the Nazis actually made contact with the Vril and they cooperated to build a fleet of flying saucers at a secret base in the Antarctic. It sounds nuts, but the United States government were convinced enough in nineteen forty-seven to put together Operation Highjump under a respected admiral and former polar explorer called Richard E. Byrd. Admiral Byrd commanded a task force that included an aircraft carrier and four thousand men. They combed the ice shelf from one side to the other and it's claimed that Byrd actually found the base. After he returned to the States he was hospitalized and when he died in nineteen fifty-seven there's speculation that he was murdered.

'What I need to know is where we go from here.' She spoke slowly, choosing her words with care. They were at a crossroads, she was saying, and not just in their quest. Jamie held her gaze as she studied him. 'My take is that this has got way out of our control. What happened back there has taken it beyond a fun jaunt looking for a painting that may not exist and with a little sexual tension thrown in to make it spicy.' She saw his look. 'Come on, Jamie, don't tell me you didn't feel it too. Anyway, people have died and we're on some Nazi's hit list and on the run. This isn't a game, it's the real thing. These people are cold-blooded killers. The sensible option would be for both of us to get the hell out of here, find a way back to London and disappear for a while.'

Jamie nodded, acknowledging she was correct in every particular.

'You're right. You should go. There's bound to be a train from Fulda to the north coast. You can jump on a ferry and be home by Friday. But I have to stay here. I have my own reasons for keeping going.'

'And those reasons are?'

He took a deep breath. 'Magda for one. I'm to blame for what happened to her, no one else. She was a nice kid, trying to make a better world. She didn't deserve to die, but she was as good as dead the minute we walked into that museum. It's not about anything as melodramatic as revenge, though I'd surely like to see Frederick behind bars, or better still, in a coffin, but at the very least I need to know *why* she died. And that's the second reason. I can't let Frederick get away with whatever he's doing. Not now.'

She nodded. 'I kinda guessed that would be the argument, and it answers one of the questions I was asking myself: what makes it worth going on? You're right, Magda does. We can argue about who's to blame when this is all over, but she sure as hell deserves some answers. My second question is, if this is out of control, how do we get back in control?' She allowed the question to hang in the air and develop an energy of its own. He sensed that the answers she sought went far beyond the meaning of the words she'd used. He had a decision to make.

He reached for the rucksack.

'Maybe the answer to that is in the journal.'

XXVIII

She closed the book and laid it back on the bedcover.

'So this isn't about the Raphael at all?'

'Not just about the Raphael, no,' he admitted. 'I suppose it's always been about my grandfather.'

'But Frederick and his Nazis aren't interested in the painting or your grandfather. They're interested in this other thing that Walter Brohm discovered.' She seemed very calm, which struck him as unlikely and possibly ominous. He picked up the journal and flicked through the pages to avoid meeting her eyes.

'We don't know that for certain. All Frederick did was confirm he knew about the journal.'

'I thought this was supposed to be a team effort, but you've been holding out on me.'

'I . . .'

Her face was turning pink below the light tan. 'All this time we've been working together and you've got this cute little guidebook while dumb old Sarah has been groping around in the dark. Christ, I've only got your word for it that there is a painting. This could just be some kind of elaborate dodge to get me into the sack. But then it couldn't be, could it? Because you haven't been trying very hard. How many times does a girl have to wave a Goddam flag before a stiff-necked English-man finally notices?'

'But you didn't—'

'Shut up.' She was crying now and the tears turned her mascara into dark blobs around her eyes. 'Where I come from a girl likes to be asked. But you didn't have the balls. Just stood there like some Goddam ruptured goldfish with your mouth opening and closing. Well, you've had your chance, Mr Saintclair. Sarah Grant isn't going to play second fiddle to no colouring book.'

He stared at her, not sure how to react. In another time and another place those words would have torn him apart, but the way she said them, a certain inflection buried deep in the rage, made them more consoling than angry. She was letting him know he had let her down, but she wasn't going to walk away from this. Not yet.

'I needed to be certain. The same way I needed to be certain about the book. I didn't know you. I didn't know where this was going to end up. Let's face it, I'm not some kind of super-sleuth. I've been completely use-less; a danger to you and everybody else we've come into contact with. And I'm not sure where to go next. The book is all we have now, but without getting a closer look at the Black Sun maybe it's not enough.'

She sniffed and shook her head. 'That's where you're wrong, buddy. You're not the only one who can pull a rabbit out of a hat.' There was a rustle as she retrieved something from the rucksack. 'I made a mistake. Two sheets instead of one. If I leaned heavily enough we should be able to retrace the lines . . .'

Between one breath and the next she was straight back to business. They laid the tracing paper flat on the wooden floor, pushing the chest of drawers aside to make room. Sarah's pencil had left a barely visible impression when she'd drawn on the top sheet Frederick had confiscated. She began highlighting the faint lines. It wasn't easy, sometimes a mark that looked significant was only a crease where she had folded the sheet into her rucksack. It took twenty minutes before they had a semblance of the original.

'It's a pity the paper wasn't big enough to cover it all.' She brushed the hair out of her eyes. 'But I think I got the centre pretty much mapped, apart from the section that's missing.'

As they worked over the paper, they moved closer together until their heads touched above the centre of the drawing.

She pulled back, smiling nervously. 'I think that's us about done.'

Reluctantly, Jamie drew away. They studied the diagram she had created, and he felt the excitement growing in him like a bottle of champagne about to pop.

'You said mapped. Can you see it?' It hadn't been visible on the marble of the castle floor, but the tracing had brought out faint lines on the symbol's twelve spokes, spaced by unidentifiable blobs. 'The guide said the castle was to be the centre of the world. Well, this is a map of the SS world. Twelve spokes of the Black Sun. Twelve *Obergruppenführers* to do Himmler's dirty work. Twelve departments. I bet if you had enough information you could identify each one and its headquarters.'

'That means . . .'

'If the Wewelsburg Sun is a map, so is ours.'

Sarah frowned and bent low over the paper.

'I think . . .'

'What?'

'Look closer. Those blobs are symbols of some sort.'

He got down beside her. His hip nudged hers, but she didn't seem to notice.

'You're right. These are runes, like the SS lightning flashes, but much more complex. See, there's a kind of upturned Z in a square, and a pair of what look like arrowheads in a circle. There could be twenty different variations here and we're only looking at one small part of the Black Sun.'

'And they seem to be linked by the lines.'

'Maybe, it's difficult to tell. But if they are . . .'

'And this *is* a map . . .'

'The placing of each rune would correspond to a location and the rune itself would tell whoever knew the code what is being stored or kept there. This was the place of secrets. No one but the twelve SS generals were meant to see this, and only they knew the meaning.'

'And now Frederick must know. He said they were the inheritors.'

Jamie shook his head. 'Not necessarily.'

Her eyes lit up. 'Because something's missing.'

'The golden disc at the centre. What if the disc was the key? It disappeared at the end of the war, but did the SS take it when they abandoned Wewelsburg? Or did the Americans loot it with everything else?'

'It could have been melted down, or it could still be out there somewhere.'

Jamie studied the detail of the Black Sun again. It was like a star map and if it continued over the entire marble circle it was huge and incredibly complex. Looked at in different ways it could have many different meanings.

'This is why Frederick couldn't allow us to have the tracing. He couldn't afford to let us go with the Black Sun's secret. And what if there was more? What if the gold disc wasn't fixed, but rotated? It's possible that the orientation of the disc opened up another set of secrets to those who could read the runes. Perhaps the Black Sun isn't a single map, but layers of maps.'

He sat back and found he was breathing hard. 'This could unlock the whole underworld of the SS. Who knows what mysteries are hidden there? If we could track down the gold centrepiece . . .'

'If we could decipher the runes,' Sarah agreed. 'But we can't. And this is just a part. We would need it all.'

'You're right. We don't have the time to do this. It will have to wait. We already have enough mysteries to solve, but maybe, some day?'

'Some day.'

The excitement was still on them as Jamie fetched the silk map with the original Black Sun and spread it beside the tracing. Compared with the drama of the last few minutes, the drab, poorly drawn image seemed to smother their enthusiasm.

'It's impossible,' Sarah said. 'This is just a drawing. Perhaps if we could find the original?'

'Well, we don't have it. There has to be another way.' He struggled with the possibilities for a few moments. 'Can you get the road map we brought, please?'

They studied the two suns and the map, seeking out any similarities.

'Hey! You're a genius, Saintclair.' Sarah broke the silence. 'Pick a town. Any old town. See the way the roads radiate from the centre the way rays shine from the sun.'

'So we're looking for a town with nine roads?'

She looked at the silk Sun again. 1357. 1357?

Jamie watched her elation grow as the permutations went through her mind. 'Not necessarily. Remember we're dealing with the same people who drew that map on the Wewelsburg sun. Nothing is what it seems.'

She pointed at the spokes on the drawing. 'One. Three. Five. Seven. Not nine roads, four, and in this very distinctive configuration.'

He saw it, but he was still sceptical. 'So we study every city, town and village in Germany, until we find the right one?'

Sarah's eyes met his, and he recognized the challenge there. 'I did my bit. Your turn now. Let me see that book again.'

'OK.' But after half an hour of staring his vision began to blur.

'Your granddaddy had quite a war.'

He nodded. 'I grew up without a father, so it came as a shock to find that the only father figure in my life wasn't the man I thought he was. I need to *know*, but I'm still not certain exactly what it is I need to know, even now. Until I read about Walter Brohm's great discovery I'd only been kidding myself I was trying to find the Raphael. If that sounds like I was leading you on, well, as I said, I'm sorry.'

She leaned forward and he thought she was going to kiss him. Instead she stared into his eyes as if she was looking for something there. Eventually, she must have found it. 'At least now we know why someone would go to the trouble of pushing you under a train. The big question is do we believe it?'

'That Brohm discovered something during the war that has stayed hidden for sixty years? On the face of it, that seems unlikely,' he admitted. 'From what's recorded in Matthew's diary, we know Walter Brohm was an egotistical dissembler who exaggerated his capabilities, sucked up to his superiors and would have shopped his own granny.'

'Shopped?'

'Betrayed. But stranger things have happened. If Brohm did make it to the States it's possible he passed on his formula, but that the Yanks – sorry, Americans – for their own reasons either suppressed it or discovered that it didn't work in the first place.'

'Why would they suppress it?'

'For any number of motives, most of them economic.

They'd spent hundreds of millions developing nuclear technology and along comes this new wonder-power that makes it redundant about sixty years before they've recouped their investment. Maybe it's sitting in a wooden crate in some big warehouse, like in that Indiana Jones film.'

'This isn't Indiana Jones, Jamie, this is real life, but I take your point. What do you think *it* is?'

And there it was. The sixty-four million dollar question. The problem being that he didn't have an answer. Not yet. 'I don't know and I don't think we can even make an educated guess. If you believe Brohm, it was a one-off discovery that paved the way for a great scientific breakthrough; something of enormous power that even Hitler feared. Since Hitler was willing to do anything to win the war, we can assume that whatever it was it must have had a fearsome potential to make him walk away. Greater even than the nuclear capability he'd just given up on.

'That's why it's so important to find out where this map takes us and what happened at the end of my grandfather's journal. If Brohm didn't reach America, then the great secret is still hidden in Germany.'

The question was where.

Sarah read the diary with a frightening intensity, as if she was trying to force the answer from its pages with the power of her mind. 'Was this why we came to Wewelsburg?' She pointed to a paragraph and he looked over her shoulder.

'No, it was a wild shot. I looked up Himmler and the

227

occult on the computer, I found the photograph with the Black Sun and it seemed the most likely place to start. Why?'

'Because Walter Brohm pointed you towards it. And I think he gave you the first clue to the Raphael.'

'Where?' He made a grab for the book.

She drew it away from his hands. 'You had your turn, Saintclair. What is Wewelsburg?'

'The centre of the SS world?'

'Exactly.' She read from the page. *My journey begins at Heinrich's centre of the earth.*'

'Christ, how could I miss that?'

'There's more: *You must look upon the faded map for the sign of the Ox.*'

Simultaneously, they looked towards the tracing paper still lying in the middle of the floor. Jamie reached it first and Sarah quickly knelt beside him.

'The faded map is the Black Sun.'

'Yup, has to be.' She nibbled the inside of her lip. 'But what is the sign of the Ox?'

'Get your laptop.'

She stared at the screen. 'The runes on the Black Sun all seem to be from some kind of runic alphabet called the Elder Futhark. There are other Futharks, but this one is what's called proto-Germanic. The Elder Futhark has twenty-four runes broken up into three groups of eight.' She looked up at him, her brow creased in concentration. 'Jeez, this is complicated. Each rune has dozens of entirely different meanings, depending on how it's used.

228

It would take years to decipher the stuff on the Black Sun even if you knew what you were looking for.'

'But we're not interested in the Black Sun, are we?' he pointed out. 'We're only interested in one symbol. Which one is the Ox?'

She shot him a poisonous look and bent over the screen again. It took only moments before she cried out triumphantly. 'Here! It's kinda like an n or a sort of inverted U. Uruz, sign of the aurochs, which this says is a kind of giant cow or oxen.'

'Let me see.'

She showed him the screen and they both turned to the traced drawing.

'You've done it.' Jamie hugged her to him and the feel of her body sidetracked him for a second. 'There it is.' The Ox rune lay a short way from the centre of the drawing on one of the legs of the sun symbol. 'Now all we have to do is translate it to the silk map.'

'How do we do that?' She frowned.

'Magda said the spear of destiny was aligned north to south. That means the point of the castle is north.' Suddenly he saw what she meant. 'The spear must align with one of the legs of the wheel, but which one?'

'There's no way to tell.' She shook her head. 'It's a circle. It doesn't have a top or a bottom, a left or a right. If we could find one point of reference . . .'

'Bugger,' he said quietly. 'We're so bloody close, I can touch it.'

Sarah shrugged. 'Nobody said this was going to be easy.' With a last glance at the tracing she returned to the journal. She'd been reading for fifteen minutes while Jamie continued to stare in frustration at the drawing when she suddenly stiffened.

'Idiot.'

Jamie turned to her. 'Don't be too hard on yourself. It's not your fault.'

'I mean you. Why didn't you show me this damned book earlier? Walter Brohm may have been a great scientist, but he was a lousy poet. Listen to this: *Where Goethe met his demon, avoid the witches' trail. Below the water you will find it, but you must look beyond the veil.*'

'You're right,' he said cheerfully. 'It's rotten.'

'You are an idiot. *Where Goethe met his demon.* Don't you know who Goethe is?'

'Some kind of German writer, wasn't he?'

'Yes, he was.' Her voice was dangerously patient as she handed him the journal. 'He also wrote a version of the Faust legend. Remember Faust? In Faust's foot-steps?'

Jamie winced. 'You're right, I'm an idiot. But what does the rest of it mean? Witches and water and beyond a veil. It's just gibberish.'

'One step at a time, lover boy. First we need to find where Goethe met his demon.' She began a search on the laptop, while Jamie retrieved the *Tragicall History* from his rucksack.

'According to Marlowe, Faustus met the devil's representative in a place called Wittenberg, which . . .' he exchanged the book for the road atlas they'd used to

230

cross-check the escape map '. . . is here, about a hundred miles to the north-west. We could be there in about three hours.'

'Uhuh, but we'd probably be going in the wrong direction. Remember, this isn't about Faustus, it's about Goethe. Goethe based his Faust on Marlowe's play. His demon is the same Mephistopholes who visited Faustus in the original and gave him twenty-four years of access to absolute power in exchange for his soul. But if I remember rightly the two stories are very different. Marlowe's Faustus began by wanting to do good, but Mephistopholes ensured he wasted his opportunity. Goethe's is a much deeper and more complex tale. They only have one thing in common. Nothing good can come of doing deals with the devil.'

'I'll remember that. OK, it's interesting, but where does it take us?'

'Precisely nowhere,' she admitted. 'I can't find anything about Goethe meeting up with Mephistopholes. What we need is a really good biography. I doubt if the hotel will have one.'

'No, but there'll be a library in town . . . I think one of us should stay here and keep checking online, while the other finds the book.'

'I'm the one who graduated *summa cum laude*. I'll take the library,' she said grandly. 'You can stay here with the laptop, but no peeping at my Facebook page.'

He opened his mouth to say something, but she put a finger to his lips. 'I know. I'll take care.'

* * *

231

It was three hours before she reappeared. 'Remind me never, ever to volunteer again. When I got there, this greasy librarian looked down his nose at a pesky foreigner speaking lousy German, but after I asked him for books about Goethe he couldn't get enough of me. I'd get started on one, then he'd come along with another. Have you seen the size of German biographies? I could have built a cabin. He started talking and boy that guy could talk. Goethe and politics, Goethe and philosophy, Goethe and religion. When he got to Goethe and sex, I was outa there.'

Jamie waited patiently, familiar enough with her now to know she was toying with him. 'But?'

She grinned. 'But I got it. Walter Brohm was a little cavalier with the facts. Goethe never actually met Mephistopholes, but he decided to write Faust after a scary encounter in the mist on a big ol' hill somewhere in the Harz Mountains.'

'The Brocken?'

'Now how did you know that?'

'Because I found a version of the Faust play on the internet. The Harz Mountains were where Mephistopholes took Faust to see the devil. Listen to this: *The witches hie to the Brocken top, yellow the stubble and green the crop.*'

'Avoid the witches' trail, huh.'

'I think we should pack.'

She looked at him a certain way and he felt something melt inside.

'I have another idea.'

XXIX

Sex, when you're new to each other, can sometimes be awkward. It all gets hot and heavy a little too quickly and unless you're a proper Casanova, no one's quite sure what to do precisely when. The result is that you spend so much time wondering if the other party is having a good time that you don't have a good time yourself. It wasn't like that at all.

Jamie was astonished at the emotions Sarah stirred in him; a raw carnality he'd never experienced before, allied to a profound tenderness that couldn't be far short of what he presumed was love. Her lips tasted somewhere between sweet cinnamon and heather honey and her skin was as soft and downy to the touch as his imagination had told him it would be. They had been sharing kisses for a few minutes when she drew in a deep breath, her eyes opened wide and her body gave a long shudder.

'No,' she said, loosening her grip on him.

Inwardly Jamie groaned. Christ, what had he done wrong?

'Not like this. Like this.' Her fingers flew to the buttons on her black cotton shirt and with remarkable speed they were undone and the shirt thrown aside. As he watched with his heart pounding somewhere in his throat, her hands reached behind her and with a single movement her bra was gone. She stood before him for a second, allowing his eyes to feast on her body and his mouth felt as if it was filled with sand. The clothes she wore had camouflaged the full wonder of her breasts, which were heavy and rounded for such a slim figure, with small dark nipples engorged to the size of ripe blackcurrants. Her eyes were wild and amused and inviting all at the same time. He moved towards her.

'Wait!'

Now her hands were at her belt, and the button of her black jeans. She bent and slipped them over her hips, sliding one leg down at a time and kicking them off. Her underwear was black and silky and he wondered if she'd been prepared for this to happen and cursed himself for not making it happen sooner. Now she teased him, half turning while she slid them down her long legs so that it wasn't until she turned back that he had a view of her sex, which was blush and swollen and partially hidden by a thin line of sparse dark down. She stood before him, hands hanging loose, hips thrust forward as if she was offering herself. He found he could barely breathe. Again he moved, tugging at his shirt, but she shook her head and glided across the silk map and the tracing paper, which crinkled beneath her feet with each step. She wrapped herself around him, like a beautiful python coiling itself around its prey, and drew him to the floor on top of her.

'All in good time,' she whispered hoarsely.

He was never quite certain what came off when, but it happened after a prolonged period when the eroticism of his fully clothed body against her nakedness drove him almost to the brink of violence. His hands were able to rove at will over her nakedness, while hers teased at his shirt and his jeans, now plucking at a button, now moving a zip half an inch downwards. At one point she moved away from him and he noticed the raw red mark where his belt buckle had forced itself into the taut flesh of her stomach. It was an age before she allowed him to reach down and stroke her, but when he did it was like touching molten fire.

He had his revenge when they finally came together. Now it was he who controlled the rhythm, taking her to the brink, then back again; first slow, then fast, then faster still, inspiring an earthy profanity he wouldn't have believed could come from that sweet mouth. When they arrived together at that moment of mindless oblivion it seemed entirely natural. Her eyes rolled into her head and her lips clamped on his and she began to buck and heave beneath him until he was driven to an equal, stallioned frenzy and their frantic cries mingled.

Afterwards, they lay entangled for a few minutes, still touching and stroking, whispering the endearments and compliments that are the expected aftermath of love in the afternoon, before the ludicrousness of lying naked on a hardwood floor when there was an alternative available struck them and they moved to the bed.

The second time was even better.

When Jamie opened his eyes, he could tell by the fading light that it was still only early evening. He turned to find her on one elbow looking down at him, pert breast peeping out from under the bedcover like an interested spectator. She smiled demurely.

'Now we should pack.'

7 May 1945 It just came across on the radio. The war is OVER. The Germans have agreed to surrender unconditionally. It will not come into effect until tomorrow night but everyone agrees the fighting is finished. Strangely, the mood among the men is sombre. After a moment of celebration everyone went silent, almost crushed by the unreality of it. This has been our life, this constant fear, days and weeks without proper rest, and the tension that eats you from the inside like a cancer. To have fought for so long and seen so many friends die and to have survived? It scarcely seems believable. Despite the fact we've known it was coming, our minds are having difficulty accepting that there isn't another battle to fight or another man to kill. We've been living on benzedrine pills and hot tea for two weeks, averaging about two hours' sleep a night. For the past few days I've been able to feel the fractures developing in my brain. Little fault lines cracking through the thin membranes, as if someone has stepped on a sheet of ice. But I can't give in now. The war may be over, but I still have a mission to complete. Tonight I watched the distant mountains turn smoke blue in the twilight, then fade to pale silver before transforming into insubstantial wraiths which finally vanished entirely, like soldiers marching into cannon smoke. I experienced a strange, dizzying, unnatural sense of lightness and it was only later that I realized what it was. For the first time in five years I can close my eyes without wondering whether I will be alive to open them in the morning. The sun will rise, the mountains will return, the guns will be silent.

XXX

Starting early next morning, they retraced their route fifty miles due north to Kassel, a sprawling district capital on the Fulda River that owed its startling modernity to the fact that it had been wiped off the map by Allied bombers in 1943. When they arrived in the city centre, the shops were just opening and the streets lay empty apart from a few early-bird office workers and the street cleaners without whom no German dawn is complete. Sarah bought a few basics to replace the clothes and toiletries they'd been forced to leave behind in Paderborn, while Jamie watched her from a distance until he was satisfied she wasn't being followed. Still, he had an uneasy feeling. Someone like Frederick would undoubtedly have contacts in the Bundespolizei. Their little hired Toyota was as anonymous as any car on the road, but it could only be a matter of time before someone noticed it. Sarah had suggested abandoning the Japanese compact in Fulda, and he'd considered it. But the car would have had to be replaced by something else and if the opposition were looking for it, they'd also be checking the hire firms. On balance, it was better to stay below the radar for as long as they could.

From Kassel the road took them on a long sweeping curve through Gottingen and Gleboldehausen, until about another hour into the journey they could see the Harz Mountains on the horizon.

'They look kinda pretty,' Sarah said, when they were about twenty miles from their destination, the spa town of Braunlage. Jamie saw she was right, from a distance and in the golden light of the afternoon sun, the mountains appeared benign and unthreatening, their sharp edges dulled by the spruce, oak and beech that cloaked their flanks. But by now he knew differently.

'If you imagine a sliding scale of mountain ranges and the Himalayas is ten, then the Harz is probably less than one. The Brocken is the highest peak, but it's only eleven hundred metres, and the land mass is about equivalent to England's Lake District. But what these hills lack in scale, they more than make up for in atmosphere. Goethe didn't set Faust here by accident. This is a land of forest and bog, witches and devils, mist and mystery; a place where anything can happen. Heinrich Heine described the mountains as "so Germanically stoical, so understanding, so tolerant", but it's doubtful whether the concentration camp prisoners who were held there until nineteen forty-five or the East Germans who were shot attempting to cross the Iron Curtain death zone that cut through those hills would have agreed.'

'My, we are poetic today.' She said it with a smile. 'Any particular reason for that?'

He grinned at her. Last night, they had proved to their mutual satisfaction that the previous afternoon had been no fluke. He looked back with a mixture of weary delight and awed wonder at what they had created. A coupling of the soul as well as the body, a ferocious contest of will as they attempted to outdo each other in imagination and intensity . . . He forced himself to concentrate on the road.

'All I was saying was that they may look pretty, but they are actually pretty bloody dangerous. The terrain is what you might call fractured. Craggy gorges and deep, steep-sided lakes. The place is honey-combed with caves and pits. It's also probably the wettest place in Germany.'

'You make it sound so welcoming.'

He didn't reply. After the encounter with Frederick and his fascist friends in Wewelsburg the best he could hope for was no welcome at all. They covered the last twenty miles on winding, narrow roads through a tree-blanketed wilderness. If Walter Brohm had wanted to hide something, then this was the perfect place. Jamie had chosen Braunlage because it was the closest town to the mountain, but he had no idea what would greet them there.

'It looks like an Alpine ski resort, only without the Alps. I kinda like it. Reminds me of Colorado in the summer.' Sarah studied her surroundings as they entered the town, a sprawling community that flowed like a red-roofed glacier down the valley. It had a manufactured tourist prettiness that Jamie guessed would be more inviting in the winter. The websites said it was predominantly a ski resort, but also a popular summer destination for hikers.

He spotted a shop where they could purchase walking gear. An ominous mass of dark cloud piling up on the eastern horizon meant two good quality anoraks and decent hiking boots were going to be essential. They'd also be able to buy a large-scale map of the area that he'd compare with the silk drawing. Still, he had a feeling tomorrow was going to be a long, tough day. The only consolation was that he couldn't spend it in better company.

They booked into a gabled hotel on the main square and kitted themselves out from the outdoors shop at an eye-watering price which reminded Jamie just how badly the pound was doing against the euro. Europe, and Germany in particular, seemed to have weathered the banking crisis much better than Britain. The thought prompted an image of his dwindling bank balance and he reminded himself to check for progress in the sale of his grandfather's house. Braunlage seemed benign and unthreatening and it would be easy to forget Frederick and his sinister friends had ever existed. But as he sat at a restaurant overlooking the artificial lake in the town centre, Jamie's eyes never stopped searching for potential threats among the multi-coloured weather-proof jackets.

It wasn't easy. A tall man on the far side of the square

seemed to be staring at them until his face lit up and he walked forward to meet a woman with two young children. Did the danger come from the four hikers who walked with the straight backs and measured stride of the military? Or was it more likely to be from the couple at the next table who seemed to take a little too much interest in what Sarah was ordering? Eventually, he forced himself to relax and concentrated on his food.

When they'd finished their meal they spread the walking map out on the table. Jamie pointed to the approximate centre. 'Here's the Brocken. Remind me what the journal said.'

'*Where Goethe met his demon, avoid the witches' trail, below the water you will find it, but you must look beyond the veil.*' As Sarah recited Walter Brohm's riddle her finger traced a red line that meandered horizontally across the map with the Brocken at its centre. 'I thought finding the Witches' Trail would be the most difficult part, but it's the biggest thing on this map. A whole network of hiking trails through the Harz. Look, there must be sixty miles of it. That's a lot of ground to cover. Too much.'

'Maybe we don't have to cover it. Excuse me.' He called to a passing waiter, a young man in a white shirt and dark trousers. 'We were thinking of doing some walking around the Brocken. If we wanted to bypass the Witches' Trail what would be the best route to take?'

'That would depend on how far you wanted to go and what you wanted to see, sir.'

Jamie was stumped for an answer, but Sarah cut in. 'Somewhere scenic with lots of water. A lake or a river.'

The young man laughed. 'Then that is simple. Here.' He put his finger on the map at a point west of the mountain and conveniently just north of the town. A thin ribbon of bright blue amongst the green and the grey of the mountains. 'It's a popular walk for people who want to branch off the main trail and take in Braunlage. The Oderteich and the Oder gorge. Lake and river.'

Sarah turned to Jamie with a wry grin. 'Did you pack your swimsuit?'

When they returned to the hotel more than one pair of eyes watched them cross the square.

At ten the next morning they were gazing across the glittering expanse of the Oderteich lake. The guidebook said the dam where they stood had been built three hundred years earlier to create a reservoir for the area's mining industry. Now it powered a hydro-eletric scheme. The reservoir was close to one mile long and perhaps two hundred paces wide. For once, it was Jamie who chewed his lip. Sarah leaned against the wall, dejection written plain on her face.

'OK, I'll rephrase my question of yesterday. Did you pack your diving gear? Because it looks like you're going to need it. We always knew this was a potential wild-goose chase, but at least there was a chance we'd find something. Now,' she waved a despairing hand at the acres of grey water surrounded by pine trees, 'now this. If they've sunk the painting in here we haven't got a hope in hell of finding it. Not without a boat and a diving team.'

But Jamie only continued to gaze out across the rippling surface. 'I don't think so,' he said distractedly.

'You don't think we should give up?'

'No, I don't think I'll need my diving suit. Not even my swimming trunks.'

'But you read Brohm's words: *Below the water you will find it*. Well, there's your water and if you want to find the Goddam thing you'll have to find it yourself.' She turned away and would have walked back towards the car, but Jamie put his hand gently on her arm.

'You're forgetting who we're dealing with here. With Walter Brohm nothing is ever quite what it seems. This is a riddle within a riddle. No one in their right minds would hide a painting worth millions of pounds underwater. Gold, yes. Jewels, yes. But not something delicate, like an Old Master.

'So we have to start with the premise that it's not there, and ask ourselves what Walter actually *was* telling us. Think. He's a scientist, a man very precise with his words. He would say *Below the surface* or *Under the water*, maybe even *Below the water line*, but never *Below the water*.' He led her by the arm across to the opposite side of the road, where the Oder gorge cut through the trees as if it had been hacked out by a giant with a knife. 'Unless he meant below the dam.'

'Down there?'

'Down there.'

*   *   *

'What are we looking for?'

It was a question Jamie had been asking himself as he studied the map and tried to make it work with the shape formed by the four legs of the Black Sun symbol on the silk. They were sitting in the hired Toyota in a walkers' car park, three miles downstream of the Oderteich, and it was only now that they'd begun to realize the true scale of the task facing them. He had never expected it to be easy, but, on paper, it had looked relatively straightforward, if strenuous and time-consuming. Find a track that would take them in to the general area pinpointed by the maps and then cover the ground until they discovered . . . what?

'I don't know. A sign, another symbol, a message painted on a rock. I don't think we're going to find the Raphael nailed to a tree. Walter Brohm says: *'you must look beyond the veil'*, which I suppose means whatever we're looking for isn't what it seems. But the diary says it exists and the map says it's around here somewhere.'

'That's helpful,' she said in a voice that reminded him of nails dragged across a school blackboard.

Somewhere. That was the problem. The forest around them would have been all but impenetrable except for the woodsmen's tracks and walking trails carved into it. Low cloud the colour and consistency of gun-cotton added to the gloom, providing a thick mantle that brushed the treetops and wept a steady drizzle of misty rain that made it difficult to see more than fifty paces. Not that the visibility mattered. Even on a good day the view would have consisted of mile upon mile of grey-green spruce and the odd patch of bare granite. Somewhere behind them in the fog he could feel the great stubborn mass of the Brocken looming like a fox waiting to pounce. It wasn't a nice feeling.

'Well, whatever it is, we aren't going to find it in here,' Sarah said decisively. She zipped her black and green Gore-tex jacket to the neck and dragged the hood over her red-streaked hair. He followed suit and they got out of the car into the rain. The rucksacks were stowed in the boot and they checked the contents before setting out. They decided to start their search in the centre of the gorge, on the grounds that whoever had hidden the painting would have done so at one of the less accessible spots. 'You're sure you've got the compass? I have the feeling that once we get into this shit we're going to need it.'

He showed her the perspex-encased dial and a pack of sandwiches wrapped in plastic. 'We've enough food so we won't starve to death until next Tuesday.' He wiped the rain from his face. 'I don't think we'll have to worry about dying of thirst.'

'You don't say.'

Their route took them along a forest track that led in the direction of the river. Five minutes after they set out, a white minibus drove into the car park and eight men in wet-weather gear jumped from the rear led by a man almost as broad as he was tall. Ensuring the minibus screened him from the road, Gustav took a Heckler and Koch MP5 machine pistol from the floor of the bus, rotated the selector lever to 'safe' and pulled the cocking handle back to empty the chamber. Guns were the tools of his trade, but he thought the compact, matt-black Heckler had a rare dangerous beauty. This model, the SD1, had been developed for use by border guards during the Cold War and was fitted with a suppressor. It weighed less than three kilos and was small enough to be easily concealed. The stubby silencer added three inches to the length of the gun, but was remarkably effective, as he'd found when he'd topped four ragheads in a row outside Fayzabad. Stupid bastards stood around like dummies while he took them out one at a time. Frederick wouldn't have been happy to see so much firepower, but Frederick wasn't here. Gustav didn't intend to take any chances with Saintclair and the girl. The purple bruise over his left eye was a throbbing mass of pain. These people were owed. He slung the weapon around his neck by its leather strap and zipped his jacket over it. The others were armed with pistols, the Sig Sauer 266, standard German police weapon. Gustav ordered them to gather round as he spread a large-scale map of the Braunlage area on a nearby picnic table. He didn't like the look of this fucking jungle, but Frederick had sounded uncharacteristically alarmed when he heard the Englishman had visited the Oderteich and insisted they hit them at the first opportunity.

'All right, you know my feelings about this.' He ran his finger over the line of the Oder gorge. 'It's a shit-hole in there, but we have our orders. Ideally we take them before they descend into the gorge, but if that's not possible we split into two teams as discussed. Like a game shoot; beaters to the north with Jurgen, the gun line to the south under Werner. I will direct from above using the tactical radio and flush them out if necessary. Ideally we want them alive, but the important thing is to recover what they have with them. Anybody fucks up and they'll have me to deal with. Are we clear?'

'What if they start shooting? They killed Arnim and shot Hans.' It was Jurgen, the Hamburg bully boy who liked to think he was tough, but one of these days would find out different.

'It won't happen,' Gustav said dismissively. 'They're amateurs. Arnim was a fluke.'

'But if it does?'

Gustav thought about that. It was true that he owed them for Arnim and when it came right down to it, Frederick said the priority was to recover the journal.

'If they fire on you, kill them. But I want that book.'

XXXI

8 May 1945 We were so close, I could see the snow-caps of Switzerland shimmering in the distance. They hit us just after dawn between Saulgau and some one-horse hamlet that wasn't worth a name. A unit of half-starved SS stragglers and Hitler Youth holdouts who nobody had bothered to tell the war was over. I was in the second jeep, with the three Nazis in the back and Stan at the wheel. Commanding the first, Lieutenant Al Stewart had survived parachute drops in Sicily, Normandy and Holland, but like me he was worn out by war, the instincts that had brought him through half a dozen firefights and won him the Silver Star shaved wafer thin by a cocktail of exhaustion, constant fear and overwound tension. A month ago, even a week, he would have seen the little beech wood and sensed danger, but not today. The war was over, the sun was shining and I could hear his laughter blown back by the breeze from a hundred yards ahead. At least he died happy. The smoke trail of the panzerfaust came streaking from his left front and I screamed a warning I knew was wasted breath. The rocket hit the jeep square on the engine block and flipped it on to its back, throwing three of the occupants clear and crushing Al's body beneath its two thousand pounds of steel. Even as Stan swerved into the roadside and I threw myself into the ditch I consoled myself that my friend had almost certainly died in the explosion. But one of the occupants had survived because I could hear him screaming. I'd heard that scream before, from a man who had been crushed by a Tiger tank in a street in Arnhem, and I knew that, whoever it was, I'd be burying him before dusk. If I lived. At the moment, that was an open question. My mind was in combat mode now, that instinctive, three-dimensional calculating machine that takes you above the action and allows you to work out angles, fields of fire and dead ground without conscious thought. Our ambushers continued to pour fire into the stricken jeep and the bodies of the men who'd occupied it; at least one MG-42 and probably a Schmeisser machine pistol and a couple of rifles. Combat mode told me this was an opportunist attack, or I would already be dead, crushed beneath my own jeep or burned, eviscerated and riddled with bullets, in that overkill that war is so fond of. If they'd had time to set up a proper ambush they would have done it so that the panzerfaust hit the first jeep and the MG-42 took out the second simultaneously. The fact that they hadn't meant they'd probably reached the edge of the woods just as the jeep arrived and someone had decided it was too good a chance to miss. Bad luck for Al, good luck for me. That was the way it went. They'd been so focused on their target that they didn't even know we were here, but that couldn't last for long.

I looked round, and found three pairs of eyes staring. Klosse was calculating the chances of jumping me and taking my M1 carbine. Strasser's were wide with pure terror, but I knew that if Klosse moved the SD man would follow him. Walter Brohm was wearing a little half smile that asked me what I was going to do next.

'Stan!' I kept my voice low and the Pole looked back from where he had been covering the road. He nodded as I signalled him to move into the forest and towards our ambushers' flank. He shot a last look at the three prisoners, grinned at me and was gone into the undergrowth.

'Here.' I tossed my pistol to Brohm. 'If they move kill them.' Then I followed Stan into the wood.

Why did I put my trust in Brohm, who was undoubtedly the least trustworthy of all? Because the one thing I could trust was his instinct for self-preservation. Walter Brohm had a destiny. He was not going to join some ragged band of fanatics whose fate was, at best, to end up in a prison camp, or more probably be hunted down and killed by the Allies. Walter Brohm had placed his faith in America. Now I was placing my faith, and my life, in the hands of Walter Brohm. Stan and I had operated as a team on and off for a year and now we moved sweetly and silently through the trees, taking it in turns to cover each other. We froze as a last burst from the machine gun brought the firing to a halt. I was gambling that the firepower I heard was evidence of their strength. The MG-42 required a crew of two, one to fire and one to load, three more for the small arms and the faust, add two just in case. Say seven. We began moving again and I motioned Stan right, towards the trees edging the road. I heard voices, at first quiet, then high-pitched shouting as they celebrated their victory. In my mind I could see what was happening and what was about to happen and I picked up the pace, taking the chance of being heard and arming a grenade as I moved forward at the crouch. Stan kept pace with me. Thirty yards ahead I could make out movement through the trees and I prayed they were concentrating on their front and not their flank. They would be relaxed now, in that state of post-combat euphoria when a man is at his most vulnerable. They would be hungry and focused on whatever treasures the jeep held. I slowed and dropped to a crawl among the leaf mulch and the dead branches and I sensed Stan mirroring my movements to the right. Then I felt him tense, *stop, half-sensed, half-saw the hand signal. Three, no, four, moving into the road to investigate the jeep. Wait. He nodded, his eyes intense, but not frightened. Stan had been fighting Germans since 1939 when the world had been looking the other way as they raped his country. He was better than I was. Wait. Wait. I imagined one of the men at the burning jeep looking at the mangled bodies, kicking them, just to make sure, turning, seeing the second jeep by the ditch a hundred yards away. A shout. Fire! Stan's controlled bursts raked the road at the same instant I threw my first grenade. The second was in the air as the first exploded and I heard screams as lumps of razor-edged shrapnel scorched the air between the trees, tearing flesh and smashing bone. I ignored the men in the road. They were Stan's. I ran forward, screaming, though I wasn't aware of it, and firing short bursts at the two soldiers by the machine gun and the two who had simply been waiting to share the spoils of the attack. Three of them were down, caught in the grenade blasts, but the fourth blazed away and I felt the hot breath of a passing bullet on my cheek and heard the unmistakable shoop . . . shoop . . . shoop of rounds passing over my head. Inexperienced. Firing too high. I took my time, aimed and he was punched back with two bullets in his chest and another in his throat. A second grey-clad figure struggled to his feet at the edge of my vision and I fired as I turned towards him, the burst folding him in half like a puppet with its strings cut. It was finished, but I was still flying, my mind ranging over the scene around me and the carbine kicking as I automatically fired into the prone figures lying by the wrecked machine gun. I'd learned the lesson the hard way a long time ago. A wounded man can kill you, a dead man can't. As I stood in the disbelieving void of the aftermath, I registered single shots coming from the trees by the road and I willed my protesting body across the pine needles to take up a position a few yards from the Pole.*

'How many?'

'Just the one, hiding behind the jeep.'

I replaced the half-empty clip in the carbine with a full one and he did the same. No point in prolonging this. It had to be done.

'Three-second burst then we rush him. I'll take right. You take left.' On such arbitrary decisions your life hangs. Stan just nodded.

'Go!'

I fired towards my side of the overturned jeep, leaping forward as the last bullet left the barrel. When I was halfway across the road I saw a muzzle flash a heartbeat before someone kicked me in the right shoulder and I went down hard on the gravel. I heard Stan continue firing and a high-pitched voice call out 'Kamerad! Kamerad!', which is what Gerry says when he wants to give up. But Stan hadn't heard from his family since the

Warsaw Uprising in 1944 and he knew what that meant. A single shot was followed by a sharp cry, then there was silence.

I didn't feel any pain yet, only a numbness in my right side, but I knew the pain would come. I lifted my head to see Stan's grinning face looking down at me. He was holding my carbine. The German's bullet had smashed the wooden stock and the impact had knocked me off my feet, but otherwise I was unharmed. He held out a hand to help me up and we walked slowly back up the road . . . where Walter Brohm waited.

XXXII

The soft hiss of the rain filtering through the trees was the only sound apart from the scuff of boots on gravel as Jamie and Sarah made their way along the unpaved loggers' road. Jamie quickly discovered that walking with the hood of his jacket raised reduced his peripheral vision to zero and his auditory perception by about 75 per cent. Any follower could have been wearing steel-shod boots and whistling the *Dam Busters* theme tune and he still wouldn't have known until it was too late. He lowered the hood. Now the misty rain worked its way inside his shirt collar and trickled down his back where it turned the waistband of his boxer shorts into a chilly, sodden trial. Sarah followed his example and the rain quickly plastered her hair tight to her head and face, making her look like an extra from a low-budget zombie movie.

She caught his glance. 'Don't say a single word.'

Spruce trees grew tight to the flanks of the path, but their ordered ranks and the lack of thick undergrowth gave Jamie increasing hope that conditions might not be too difficult once they were forced to leave the road. They'd been walking for twenty minutes when the track took a sharp turn to the south.

He stopped. 'We need to be further west.' He pointed away from the road, into the trees.

'Let me see the map again,' Sarah said. He handed it over and she studied it, grimacing. She sniffed. 'You're right, but it's going to be a lot harder going.'

He shrugged. 'We don't have any choice. We'll stick to the track for another hundred metres; with luck there'll be a spur that goes in the right direction. If not, we take to the trees. It might not be as bad as you think.'

It was much worse. They discovered that the cultivated, evenly spaced plantations by the trackside quickly gave way to wild woodland where fallen branches and rotting vegetation created natural traps designed to break a leg or turn an ankle. Worse, these were covered by a mass of bracken and nettles, and vicious waist-high brambles created impenetrable nests of coiled, inch-thick tentacles that might as well have been made of razor wire. Every step became a lottery, each wrong move a five-minute delay while the hooked thorns were disengaged from clothing and flesh and a new route was found. Within minutes of leaving the path Jamie had forgotten about the rain because he was sweating so much he might have been sitting in a bath.

With each hundred yards they covered his respect for Sarah Grant increased. She accepted every setback without complaint, her eyes narrowed and her face a

257

mask of determination. A bramble had cut across her forehead and a thin line of blood tinted the rain running down her nose pink, but, if she noticed, she ignored it. Eventually, they stopped for a breather and she pushed a damp strand of hair from her eyes.

'Boy, you sure know how to show a girl a good time, Saintclair.'

He laughed and offered her a bottle of water. 'Some champagne, madam? You'll find that life's always an adventure when you're with me.' She accepted it, took a deep drink and handed it back.

'What now?'

He picked up his rucksack. 'More of the same.'

She nodded. 'One thing has been bothering me since I've read the journal—'

His head came up sharply. 'Did you hear something?'

She listened for a few seconds. 'No. What do you think it was?'

He stared the way they'd come. 'I don't know. Just a noise. Back towards the road.'

They waited a few moments. Nothing. As they moved off Sarah continued her thesis. 'From what I've read so far, Walter Brohm only makes vague hints that he has the Raphael, yet you seem pretty certain he did possess it. Certain enough, anyway, for us to be here. But even your grandfather thought Brohm could be making it all up.'

Jamie considered the question as he unhooked himself from another patch of brambles.

'True, but he had his own reasons for thinking that.

Brohm was trying to tempt him, bribe him even, but I like to think that Matthew Sinclair decided – at least then – that he wasn't going to be bought. Matthew knew his art. He'd worked out that the painting was by the contemporary Leonardo feared most. Well, that was Raphael. Two popes, Julius and Leo, were among Raphael's patrons. Leonardo was thirty years older and his powers were waning, Raphael's were at their peak. He feared the younger man was about to eclipse his genius and, if he had lived, who knows he might have done just that.'

'He died young?'

Jamie gave a sheepish smile. 'He was thirty-seven. One theory is that, the er, cause was overdoing it in the bedroom with a lady friend.'

'He died of an overdose of sex!'

'It's possible.'

Her laughter rang through the trees.

'OK,' she returned to her subject, as the ground began to fall away beneath their feet. 'So let's accept that you're right and Brohm was referring to the Raphael? Who's to say he didn't just see it hanging on a wall somewhere. You have an unproven link between Hans Frank and Reinhard Heydrich, but as far as I can see, none at all between Heydrich and Brohm.'

'That's true, but I would refer you to the circumstantial evidence, m'lud.'

'Carry on,' Sarah said graciously.

'We know Hans Frank had the painting, that's a given?' She nodded and he continued. 'In nineteen thirty-nine

Frank became governor of that part of Poland which wasn't incorporated into Germany or Russia. It gave him power of life and death over millions of people, and he wasn't afraid to use that power. In one single *Aktion*, he had thirty thousand Polish intellectuals arrested. Seven thousand were shot.'

'A bastard, then.'

'A bastard, but it seems not a big enough bastard. Some people, most of them in the SS, thought he was being too soft on the Poles. Within months of his appointment they were undermining his authority and challenging every decision he made. By December 'forty-one he was on the brink of being sacked. To survive, he needed an ally, a powerful one.'

'Heydrich?'

'It's possible. At the time Heydrich was chief of the RSHA, the Reich Main Security office, and was probably the most feared man in Germany after Hitler and Himmler. Let's say, for instance, Frank wanted to send Heydrich a sweetener. Well, you don't just wrap a million quid's worth of masterpiece in brown paper and stick it in the post. Ideally, he would have handed it over himself, but Heydrich was busy in early nineteen forty-two and so was Frank. The next best thing would be to send it by a trusted messenger.'

'So?'

'On the twentieth of January nineteen forty-two Reinhard Heydrich and Josef Buhler, Frank's deputy, were in the same building in Berlin, in fact, in the same room.'

He saw he had her. 'How do you know that?'

'Because the twentieth of January nineteen forty-two was the day fifteen men, including Heydrich, Buhler, Heinrich Himmler and Adolf Eichmann, gathered in a Berlin suburb for the Wannsee Conference to resolve the Final Solution of the Jewish Question. The meeting that decided the fate of six million people.'

Sarah choked. 'I'm beginning to think this painting is cursed.'

'You don't have to touch it. I'll take care of that.'

'So Heydrich has the painting. Now tell me how it gets to Brohm.'

'Ah well, this is where the evidence gets even more circumstantial, that is to say . . . flimsy.'

'Convince me.'

Jamie forced a path through a thick clump of bushes that barred their way. 'OK. Everything I've read about Heydrich makes me certain he would have been amused that Frank believed he could be bought with some daub, even if it was a Raphael. As soon as he saw it he would have wanted to find a way of rubbing Frank's nose in it. He would also have wondered if the gift was part of some kind of plot against him. So he'd get rid of it as quickly as he could. But to who? Hitler and Goering would be the obvious candidates – they both wanted the painting when it was originally looted. To give it to Hitler would be to acknowledge its worth, so that was out. Heydrich despised Goering almost as much as he despised his boss Himmler. So why not give it to an old friend?'

'What makes you think Heydrich and Brohm were friends?'

'This is the flimsy part. They were contemporaries in the Nazi party, which was a relatively small organization when they joined in nineteen thirty-one. Heydrich was in the SS from the start, but Brohm wasn't far behind him. Brohm must have needed funding and support for his research in the early days, who better to call on than Heydrich?'

'You're right. Wafer thin.'

'That's what I thought until I remembered that on January the twenty-fifth, five days after Heydrich would have received the Raphael, Walter Brohm celebrated his twenty-ninth birthday and—'

This time they both heard the snap of a branch. For a moment they stared at each other, an identical question in each of their eyes. Run or hide? But the noise had been very close, somewhere in the bushes they'd just come through. Hide. Jamie dropped to the ground and waved Sarah silently back to a clump of fern where the knee-high green fronds formed a sanctuary big enough for one person. While she wriggled away, he crawled through the undergrowth into the closest patch of brambles, ignoring the thorns that twisted around his legs as if they had a life of their own. He almost panicked when something caught his rucksack, but in the same instant the ominous rustle of bushes a few feet away made him freeze. One man? It seemed unlikely. He strained his ears and heard more stealthy movement behind him. More than one, then. But only one to worry about, for now. Footsteps in the undergrowth, slow and deliberate, each footfall measured and testing the grass beneath his boots so as not to repeat the mistake that had given away his position. Jamie heard the instructor's voice from the escape and evasion course in his head and he willed himself to be part of the landscape; a stone, a tree, a bush. He kept his eyes down, relying on his ears, so that whoever was hunting them wouldn't be alerted by a flash of pale skin among the foliage. He picked up the soft whistle of controlled breathing. A whisper of cloth on cloth. That close. A walking boot appeared in the grass and nettles in front of his eyes and he had to suppress the urge to cry out. Every fibre of his being screamed at him to flee. Ever so gently, the boot lifted and was gone. He waited, measuring the seconds, before risking a glance with a single eye that rewarded him with the sight of a retreating back in a green anorak, mousy hair cut short and a single earphone that he doubted was connected to an iPod. Something else, too, that chilled his blood. A red flower among the bracken where no red flower should be. Not a flower, then. Red hair. Sarah's hair.

'Come out where I can see you.' A harsh voice that enjoyed giving orders. North German, from the back streets or the docks. 'I said get out here, or I'll fucking shoot.'

Sarah pulled herself from the bracken. She was partly concealed by the man between them, but Jamie could see that though her eyes were wary, she wasn't frightened.

'Put your hands on your head and take two steps

forward. Good. Now kneel. I like it when the girls kneel in front of me.' There was a pause while Sarah obeyed. 'Good. Now, where's your boyfriend?' Jamie untangled himself from the thorns, wincing at each slight 'tick' as the hooked barbs came free, and rose silently to his feet. He heard the sharp slap of flesh meeting flesh. 'I said where's your fucking boyfriend. Open your mouth.'

'Please don't hurt me.' Sarah's plea was just loud enough to mask the sound of Jamie's three strides through the soft grass.

The reaction to her words was as natural as breathing. No calculation was required. Just a realization that it had to be quick and there must be no sound. His left hand came round to clamp over the man's mouth and nostrils, his right took the back of the head, and the two twisted in opposite directions in an unconscious imitation of Stan's demonstration at the hospital. It took more force than he would have expected, but adrenalin added to his strength and he felt the moment the German's neck snapped. The body jerked and twitched in his hands and there was the sound of tearing cartilage you get when you tear the leg off a Christmas turkey. He held the head until the twitching stopped before he allowed the German to drop. As he stood over the dead man all the strength drained from him. He stretched out a hand to help Sarah to her feet, but she seemed to be part of a mirage because he wasn't able to find her.

'For Christ's sake, Jamie, let's go,' she hissed. She was beside him, tugging at his arm. 'If you want to send him flowers do it later. We need to get out of here. Now.' She picked up the German's pistol from where it had fallen and handed it to him.

'Sorry, it's . . .' His brain seemed to reassemble one small piece at a time. 'Where?'

There was a soft crackle from beside the body, where the earpiece had dropped. Sarah darted a glance to the right, but he shook his head. 'Not there.'

No time for argument. They dashed through the undergrowth knowing the only way to escape now was to outpace their hunters. Jamie could still feel the dead weight of the man he had killed; the warm head resting between his hands as the torso convulsed. The morality of what he'd done could be debated later, for the moment his mind barely acknowledged his surroundings. Sarah dropped back a little, her eyes scanning for danger. A shout from behind announced that someone had found the body and it was echoed from left and right. But not in front.

'Christ.'

If her reactions hadn't been lightning fast he would certainly have fallen. As it was he found himself teetering on the brink of a two-hundred-foot near-vertical drop to the river with Sarah hanging on to one arm and digging her heels into the turf. For a split second he thought his weight was going to carry them both over, but with a grunt of effort she hauled him away from the edge.

'Bloody hell.' He peered over the edge.

'Stop!' A faint rattle accompanied the shout, like a woodpecker at work somewhere in the faraway woods, and the tree above them began to disintegrate, chunks of white bark dropping down like snowflakes amid a curtain of pine needles. It seemed odd that there was so little sound to accompany the violence. Jamie's mind made an unconscious calculation. Machine pistol, silenced, only accurate at short range, but now we're really fucked.

'Stop,' the cry was repeated. They looked at each other.

'Bugger that.' Jamie made the decision for them both. He took her hand and they launched themselves over the edge.

XXXIII

*While I had been fighting my war, Walter Brohm
had been fighting his. The contest could only have
one winner. Klosse's face was pink with rage and
he wore a new bruise on his right cheek. Brohm's
eyes shone with the eerie light of victory and he
twirled my pistol on his finger as if he was Tom
Mix. I retrieved it before he shot himself. 'We make
a good team, you and I, Leutnant Matt. Perhaps
you should come with us to America?' Somehow
I restrained myself from wiping the smile from his
face with the Browning. I signalled him to get to his
feet and told him we had a job to do first. Strange
how you can share your food and your blanket with
a man, but still never really know him. Ted Jack,
my wireless operator, had nursed me through two
bouts of chronic dysentery, but because I was an
officer I'd never called him anything but Sarn't. Ted
was one of those stolid, competent, uncomplaining
types who are the backbone of the British Army.*

He had a wife and two children under five. Now I cradled his head in my hands, wondering at the weight of it, as the others watched me with the kind of look you reserve for a man standing outside a lunatic asylum who suddenly announces that he's Napoleon. Sarn't Jack's eyes were half closed, the way most dead people's are, but at least he still had eyes. Al Stewart didn't even have a head. We hadn't been able to find it. Klosse muttered something about being a gentleman and threw his entrenching tool down. Stan didn't appreciate that and kicked him in beside the tattered, blackened remains of what was left of our four friends. The German looked at me for support. For answer I tossed Sarn't Jack's head at his feet and he got the message and continued digging. Even Walter Brohm didn't complain. We put the bodies of our ambushers into the ditch. I didn't want them sharing a grave with the men they'd killed. Apart from an older SS veteran who had operated the machine gun, they were probably aged between twelve and fifteen and their bled-out, marble-grey faces and surprised eyes made them look younger still. Just children. But they were Hitler's children, indoctrinated since the day they started school to worship the Führer and programmed to give their lives for the Fatherland. Well, they'd got their wish. I looked down at them, the flies already feasting on the drying blood that stained their faces. One particular fly made its way slowly from one side of a staring opaque eyeball to another and I was surprised the dead boy didn't blink. If you asked me then how I felt about killing children I would have told you that they weren't children, they were the enemy, and the moment they had lifted their weapons and fired upon my friends they had forfeited their lives. But I knew that someday these dead boys would come and visit me in the night, the way all the men I'd killed do, and maybe then my answers would be different. At one point my hands started shaking and I kept them busy by replacing the magazine in the carbine I'd recovered from the wreckage of the first jeep. It made a sharp click when I pushed it home. The three men filling in the grave froze and their faces went almost as pale as the corpses in the ditch. Stan laughed.

We marked the grave with a makeshift cross and I scrawled the names of the dead on a page from the journal and placed it under a rock. When we were done, we drove on in silence until we were south of the town of Blumberg about four miles from the Swiss border. Stan parked the jeep along a forest track outside a small hamlet. I told him to make camp there and wait for me. At first I thought he was going to argue, but the discipline of his long service prevailed. Once he was organized I shook hands with him and got back into the jeep with the three Nazis. I'd spent two months before the war walking in this countryside to the west of Lake Constance, what the Germans call the Bodensee, so

I knew the area well. We were on the northern edge of the Hoher Randen, the hill country that straddles the border between Germany and Switzerland, and beyond it, on the far side of Schaffhausen, lay the upper reaches of the Rhine. I drove two miles further up the track before I stopped again. 'We walk from here,' I told them. 'When we reach the border we will be met by a representative from the US State Department who will arrange your onward journey from Switzerland.' The Germans laughed, even Klosse, and talked about what they'd do when they reached America, what they'd buy and what they'd eat. They made me sick. 'You are to say nothing to anyone, not even your guide about who and what you are,' I told them. 'Nothing.' I stared at Brohm. 'Nothing, Walter. You talk too much.' He just grinned at me and clutched his briefcase tighter to his chest.

XXXIV

What started as a slide quickly turned into a roll and eventually a flailing tumble. Somewhere on the way down Jamie lost Sarah's hand. His world gyrated through impossible angles and planes. Rocks that would have bashed his brains out missed his head by fractions so fine he felt them touch his hair. He knew it couldn't last so he closed his eyes to make them go away and prayed that Sarah was as fortunate during the helter-skelter plunge down the steep hillside. A final lurch and a mouthful of dirt announced an unlikely and relatively safe landing and he was just opening his eyes when something landed on top of him and drove all the breath from his body.

For a few ominous seconds Sarah lay unmoving, a dead weight across his ribs, but the rhythm of her breathing told him she hadn't suffered any serious injuries. 'You feel like you're still in one piece?'

'Give me five minutes and I'll let you know,' she

groaned. 'Also, remind me never to go out on a date with you again.'

He dragged her into the shadow of the cliff where they would be out of the line of fire of the shooter with the machine pistol. They'd landed a few feet from the river in a pile of dust and pebbles that had fallen from the cliff above. From here, the Oder looked much deeper and wider than it had from above. Rain-dampened dust caked them from head to foot and Sarah's hair looked as if it had been styled by a 1970s punk. Jamie could see her mentally checking for any damage. She patted herself down and his heart sank when he saw a moment of panic cross her face. She reached into her jacket.

'My mobile.' She withdrew the phone from her inside pocket. It took only one look to know it was smashed beyond repair. A little cry of anguish escaped her lips.

'Better the phone than you,' he pointed out.

'You don't . . . OK,' she said resignedly. 'Let's get to it.'

Jamie studied the dark swirls of the swift-flowing river. 'If we try to cross, we'll only make ourselves targets, and I don't much fancy our chances of getting to the other side in any case. So upstream or down?'

'The going is the same either way. Bad. Down is Braunlage. They'll expect us to head there, won't they?'

'So upstream.'

'Unless they second guess us.'

They froze at a series of shouted orders from above. Clearly it was only a matter of time before their hunters found a route to the valley bottom.

'It looks like we'll need to take our chances.'

Jamie remembered holding the dead German's pistol as he jumped and he felt a momentary panic as he realized he'd lost it on the way down. Surreptitiously, he searched the area where they'd landed, but could find no sign of it. He decided not to mention it to Sarah. He doubted it would be much use against a machine gun in any case.

Staying tight to the valley wall, they made their way north, upstream towards the Oderteich dam. It was almost as tough going in the gorge bottom as it had been through the wild spruce at the top of the cliff. They clambered over boulders, between the roots of upturned trees, or amongst the skeletal branches of others carried into the gorge by generations of floods. Occasionally they were forced to take to the water's edge. The terrain did have one compensation. The further north they went, the narrower the gorge became and the less likely they were to be spotted from above.

In his mind, Jamie saw the valley from the dam wall, fearsome and rugged, hemmed in by the trees and chopped deep into the surrounding landscape. From there it had looked as if you could hide an army in it, but up close it was different. Narrow and constricted, like a winding rabbit's burrow, but with no handy escape passages. He remembered once seeing a ferret sent into a rabbit warren. The squeals of terror and the bloodied, dead-eyed bundle hanging from the hunter's jaws had stayed with him for years.

Yet for all the feeling of being a hunted beast, he was

now calm enough to think on a second level. This valley was where Walter Brohm had pointed him in Matthew Sinclair's journal. His eyes searched for any clue that might tie in with the map or the sun symbol. The same thought had occurred to Sarah and she slowly realized that their original plan had a major flaw. She'd barely said a word since their tumble down the hillside and the sound of her voice startled him.

'Even if the Black Sun wasn't an abstract piece of symbolism, we're talking about something based on the road grid around here sixty years ago. Hell, we don't even know if there were any proper roads. How many of these tracks have been added or have become overgrown in the meantime? And did you see those fancy little trains in the tourist brochure? This would have been a logging and mining area during the war. You can bet your new boots that the rail network in the Harz Mountains was a lot different in nineteen forty-five.'

Jamie didn't pause as he unslung the rucksack and retrieved the journal and the map. 'All right, I'll go with that. But let's look at it from a slightly different angle. There is one constant in this landscape. Water.'

'You mean the river.'

'That's right, so let's assume legs one and five are the river, running directly through the target area. It means we're only looking for two more landmarks to pinpoint the position.'

'Sounds pretty thin to me.'

'It is, but we also have the clue in the diary—'

They were interrupted by shouts from upstream.

Simultaneously they dived into the shelter of a fallen tree. Jamie noticed with alarm that the gun Sarah had taken from the dead Nazi at Wewelsburg had appeared miraculously in her right hand. He tried to think rationally. The men in front of them were making no attempt to conceal themselves and by the sound of their voices they were still something like a hundred paces away. Behind them, the valley curved away to the south at an angle that would always keep them out of sight of their pursuers if they could only stay far enough in front. There was still a chance. He waved Sarah back. She looked at him as if he was crazy and shook her head.

'There are only two or three of them,' she whispered. 'We can take them as they go past. Get your gun out.'

'I haven't got it.'

'What?'

'I lost it when we jumped.'

She closed her eyes and shook her head. 'Jesus, Saint-clair, how did I get stuck with you?'

'We have to go.'

Her expression said no, but she squirmed backwards away from the tree and he followed. When he was certain they couldn't be seen they got to their feet and ran north.

Gustav heard the shouts from the shelter of the trees lining the clifftop. He'd been disappointed when Saintclair and the woman had jumped, but not surprised. Frederick had warned him not to underestimate Saintclair's abilities or resolve. The original position had given him a better

275

view of the bank downstream than up and he'd soon realized that the fugitives must be heading north, which suited his purpose perfectly. From his new viewpoint he scanned the river through the MP5's telescopic sight. His fist tightened on the pistol grip as the two running figures came into view and the stubby barrel of the suppressor ranged on the targets. He moved the rate of fire selector to a three-round burst and caressed the trigger. He was firing from above and at an acute angle, which gave the shot a degree of difficulty that might have made another man hesitate, and he was using a weapon that was far from ideal, but Gustav was supremely confident of his ability. He willed himself to relax, sucked in a breath and slowly released it. And fired.

XXXV

8 May 1945, noon. I pushed them hard and they hated me for it. The way began steeply, at first in the trees where we were all plagued with buzzing black flies and the sweat coursed from their faces in streams, then for a short while in the open. Brohm complained until he ran out of wind. Klosse cursed me under his breath. Strasser looked as if he was on the verge of a heart attack. I took pity on them when we reached a runnel that flowed through a clearing beside a steep ravine, and they gratefully sat down to drink from the water bottles and eat the last of the bread. The intelligence briefing I'd been given indicated that this was one of the quietest sectors of the German–Swiss border. The line wanders erratically and with no apparent reason from the point where it dissects the Untersee, the western part of Lake Constance, as far as Klettgau, where it turns back on itself and takes a huge bite out of Swiss territory, making it entirely arbitrary whether a farm or a hamlet is German or Swiss. From what we'd seen there was no doubt who had the best part of the bargain. Even though they were better off than the people in Germany's bombed-out cities, the inhabitants of southern Bavaria had been on starvation rations for the best part of two years. This was smuggling country and I had no doubt that some food and drink got past the border guards in exchange for gold and valuables, but it must have been galling for a farmer on one side of the valley unable to feed his starving beasts to look across at the untouched land of milk and honey over the way. There would be mines, of course, but only on the Swiss side, and that wasn't my problem. The guards who patrolled the German side of the ten-foot border fences had been low-grade foreign conscripts and in any case were long gone. The Americans would make sure there was no interference from the Swiss.

'Another hour,' Brohm said cheerfully, 'and no more war. Warm sheets and clean American women. And you, Leutnant Matt, you will return to your home and your family?' I didn't answer. How could I tell him I no longer had a home or a family?

XXXVI

The air sang with shards of jagged rock and ricocheting fragments of 9mm ammunition as the first burst struck within yards of Jamie's back. Something hit his rucksack a glancing blow and he staggered over the boulders.

'Keep going.' Sarah turned to look back at him, but she didn't hesitate and he loved her for it. The only chance they had was if one of them drew the sniper's fire. It had been a short burst, just three or four rounds out of a thirty-round magazine. His back tensed for the strike of the next volley. Now. He threw himself left, praying his timing was right, and was rewarded with a second symphony of sharp-edged metal and stone. This time the shots struck further away and he felt a tiny sliver of hope. Maybe the machine-gunner wasn't as good as he thought he was. The first burst on the clifftop had been high. The latest two had been a little behind. The angle was against him and he seemed to be overcompensating for the height of his position.

A loud shout from behind confirmed that the sound of the ricocheting bullets had alerted their pursuers and Jamie charged on, bent low and praying that the curve of the gorge wall would be enough to protect him from the next volley. As his feet raced over the rocks, somewhere in his head a little worm wriggled; a niggling irritation that worked on a level beyond the fear and the adrenalin. He saw that Sarah had slowed and he waved her on. No more bullets now, but he could hear the sound of the followers shouting encouragement to each other, and he knew the man with the silenced automatic was moving through the trees above, reloading and looking for a better shot. Or was he?

He'd fired three bursts, short and controlled. Those bursts said he was a man who knew what he was doing. An amateur would have put the selector to automatic and blazed off a full clip. Yet he hadn't made any attempt to adjust his aim. In his position Jamie would have put the second volley ahead of his target and the third would have shredded it. Throw that into the pot with the pursuers who were doing everything they could to advertise their presence and what did you get?

'They're herding us,' he gasped.

Sarah turned to stare at him, her dark eyes full of questions.

'We need to cross the river.'

He saw the disbelief on her face. The fearful glance towards the right where the Oder swirled and eddied.

'Somewhere downstream there are more of them. Every step south takes us deeper into a trap.'

'He'll slaughter us.'

'No. He's . . . aiming to . . . miss.'

He could tell that every instinct was warning her that to trust him was to die. But he'd made his pitch. He couldn't drag her across. And what if he *was* wrong. It didn't matter. One way or another they were finished. A long moment of decision before she nodded. 'OK, where?'

Jamie led the way back to the spot where they'd made their leap from the clifftop. A fallen tree lay in the water on the opposite bank close to the outlet of a small stream. The tallest branches reached out almost halfway across the river. A slim lifeline, but if they could reach the first of them they could use their support for the rest of the crossing. No time to think about it.

'Give me your backpack.'

She pulled it off and retrieved something from inside before throwing it to him.

'Let's go.'

'Just one more thing. They're too close. We need to slow them down.' She raised the little pistol she'd taken from the dead man at Wewelsburg and aimed it into the undergrowth upstream. The sharp crack of two shots echoed from the valley walls. 'OK,' she said. 'Now we can go.'

From the cliff above, Gustav frowned at the sound of the shots and the deeper bark of the Sig Sauer automatics replying. The firing didn't trouble him as long as his men retrieved the Englishman's rucksack and the journal. All Saintclair had done was shorten his life by an hour. He moved towards the cliff edge where he would get a clear view.

Jamie grabbed Sarah's hand and drew her down to the river's edge. He held the two rucksacks above his head and within two strides the water reached his thighs. Already he could feel the tug of the current against his legs and his boots fought for purchase on the slippery boulders of the river bottom.

'Hold on to my waist and don't let go.'

He felt her arms close around him and a fleeting moment of warmth. Every step took him deeper into the river's power. A buzz of disturbed air, as if a bee had flown close to his right ear, and the dark surface in front of him exploded in a line of white waterspouts. He felt a moment of liquid weakness; the horrible vulnerability of a man waiting for the headsman's axe. But there was no turning back now. He ploughed on through the current, dragging Sarah with him, into the space where the burst had landed. Another line of shots, closer this time, but still ahead. They were trying stop him, but they weren't prepared to kill him. At least not deliberately. Now his only thought was to move forward. The water reached his lower ribs and with every step the current forced him a little further downstream, but the outermost branch of the fallen tree was almost in reach. They were going to make it.

'No.'

Sarah's sharp cry made him look back just as two running figures reached the bank behind them. The first of the two men knelt and using a two-handed grip aimed a big automatic pistol towards them. He was so close Jamie could make out the little dark eye of the muzzle. So close that the man couldn't miss. More bluff. But if that was the case why hadn't he ordered them to turn back? As the seconds lengthened Jamie realized he'd miscalculated. He saw the gun steady. Imagined the finger tightening in the trigger.

'When he shoots me, let go and dive until you're out of range.'

He felt her arms tighten.

From his vantage point high above, Gustav had cursed as he saw Saintclair and the woman enter the river. He'd tried to force them to turn back, but when they had continued to walk into his fire he knew he'd run out of options. He was still watching when his two men burst from the upstream brush and Jurgen knelt and aimed towards the two helpless figures. Without thought, Gustav raised the MP5 to his shoulder, aimed and fired in one movement.

Jamie knew he'd feel the strike of the bullet before he heard the bark of the gun. Instead, there was a repeat of the curious woodpecker sound they'd heard earlier and the man who had been about to shoot him rose and spun before plunging face first into the river. His companion gaped and ran back into the brush.

Jamie turned and forced his way towards the far bank.

'What happened back there?' Sarah's voice shook, but it wasn't clear whether the reaction was caused by fear or the bone-numbing cold as they lay in their soaked clothing among the undergrowth on the western side of the river. Safe, for the moment.

Jamie had been pondering the same question. 'They want the journal. Whoever was on the cliff could have killed us at any time since they tracked us down. For some reason the man with the pistol didn't get the message. Maybe you nicked him or hit one of his friends with those shots you fired. If he'd taken us out in the middle of the river the journal would have been lost. The man on the cliff couldn't let that happen.'

'He must be a cold-blooded bastard, to shoot one of his own like that?'

'Yes, he is, and now he'll be coming for us. They'll put people across the river, maybe even bring in more men. Our only chance is to find a way out of the valley and back to Braunlage. We need to go up.'

They searched the sheer valley walls for a hundred yards above and below their crossing point, but the only place that showed any promise was a narrow gully that cut into the cliff and carried a gushing tributary stream to join the main river.

Sarah wasn't convinced. She stared into the shadowy interior. 'If we go in there and it doesn't lead anywhere we'll be trapped.'

Jamie shrugged. 'Would we be any worse off than we are now?'

'I still don't like it.'

'Look, we don't have time to argue. I'll go in for a recce, you stay here. I won't be any more than ten minutes.'

It took her about two seconds to figure out the implications of his suggestion. 'No way are you gonna leave me behind, Jamie Saintclair.' She hoisted her rucksack and led the way inside.

As they picked their way over the boulder-strewn gully bottom the sides rose sheer and inaccessible alongside them. Here the direct light of the sun seldom penetrated and the deeper they went the more dank, dark and forbidding it became. They'd gone a hundred yards when they were alerted by a sound like muted thunder. Minutes later they found themselves staring at a waterfall that plunged in a dirty white torrent from the lip of the cliff two hundred feet above to form a rocky, foam-flecked pool among the rocks.

Sarah's shoulders sagged in defeat. 'That's it then,' she shouted above the roar of falling water. She turned to go back, but Jamie grabbed her shoulder.

'Wait.' His throat was so dry with excitement that the word crackled. He stared at the cascade for a full minute before clambering over moss-slick boulders to the shallow pool where the fall landed like an emptying bottle of stout.

'Remember that strange phrase Walter Brohm used when he was talking to my grandfather about the painting? He said: *You must look behind the veil.* But what the hell did he mean? A woman's face is hidden behind a veil, but we can't be talking about a scrap of cloth. We've seen moss hanging on the cliff walls, maybe that would count, but it can hardly have been here sixty-odd years ago. So he was talking about something permanent. Something natural. Some kind of curtain. *Look behind the veil.*'

She stared at him. 'There is only one constant in this landscape.'

'That's right.'

'Water!'

'It fits, more or less.' He pulled out the original drawing of the sun symbol. 'Look. The river forms the main horizontal leg of the Black Sun. That means the stream that feeds the waterfall must form one of the others. There could have been another on the eastern bank, or maybe a road that's since become overgrown.'

She frowned. 'So what now?'

'There's only one way to find out.' Jamie peered into the dark void beyond, all thoughts of their pursuers forgotten. Nothing. But what had he expected – a crate with 'loot' stamped on it?

'Keep going.'

He pushed on upwards, ignoring the water thundering from the cliff above. It was pitch black behind the fall. The cacophonous darkness battered his senses, but there came a moment when he knew something had changed. The stone beneath his feet wasn't rounded any more, it was flat.

He experienced a thrill of exhilaration as he ran his fingers over the edged surface. Concrete. He checked a few feet ahead. Concrete stairs. Slowly he felt his way forward until the natural rock of the walls gave way to a different material.

'Well?' Sarah was almost dancing with anticipation as he emerged from the torrent.

Jamie shook his head, spraying water like a wet dog. 'You wouldn't happen to have pinched another set of keys?'

'Why?'

'Because there's a bloody great metal door.'

Her face creased in a determined frown. 'Show me.'

'Watch your feet.' He led the way behind the cascade. When they reached the door she pulled a penlight from her bag. 'Maybe we could hire some equipment from a hardware store; bolt cutters or a hydraulic jack?'

'They'd think you were tooling up for a bank job. I have a better idea.' She rummaged in the rucksack again.

'Dynamite?'

'Why don't you move out of the way and you'll find out?'

She pulled out some kind of metal punch and began to struggle with the lock, emitting little grunts as she worked. It took less than five minutes. 'Yes!' she shouted as the mechanism gave a sharp click. But when she turned the look she gave him was almost apologetic. 'See, I told you there's something to be said for growing up in a tough neighbourhood.'

He put his shoulder to it, but it didn't budge. 'Are you sure you unlocked it?'

She glared at him before disappearing to return a few moments later with a fallen branch as thick as her arm. 'Try wedging the narrow end between the door and the frame.'

It took both their strength to break the rust seal of sixty years, but eventually the heavy metal barrier creaked open like something from a Hammer horror movie. They found themselves in a narrow stairway that led up into the darkness.

XXXVII

The passage smelled of mould and old rust and the iron banister beneath his hand felt as if it was about to crumble away. Whatever he had expected – a damp cellar, some sort of vault? – it wasn't this. 'Careful,' Sarah warned. 'If this really dates back to nineteen forty-five there's got to be a possibility of booby traps.' He wondered why he hadn't thought of that.

They took it one step at a time, sweeping each stair with the torch as they went. After a dozen steps Jamie spotted a darker patch on the grey concrete and stooped to pick it up. It was filthy and covered in dust, but when he rubbed it between his fingers it proved to be made of metal. He spat on it and used his handkerchief to clean away the dirt.

'What is it?' Sarah whispered.

He shone the torch on the object, illuminating a small oval stamped with the distinctive coal-scuttle helmet of a German soldier, overlaid with a swastika. The design jogged something in his memory.

'I think it's what they call a Wound Badge. Anyone who was injured in battle was entitled to one. The Germans probably produced them by the ton at the end. Someone must have mislaid theirs on the way out. That's a relief.'

'Why?'

'I was worried this might be the back entrance to the local knocking shop.'

By the time they reached the top, Jamie counted 144 stairs. Another metal door barred their way, but this one proved to be unlocked. He held his breath as he pushed it open.

'Bloody hell!'

The twin beams of their torches shone on the walls of an enormous arch-roofed corridor perhaps twelve feet wide and the same high. The walls and floor were bare concrete and when they stepped out into it they realized that it stretched further than the torches' reach in each direction.

'We must be in the very centre of the mountain,' said Jamie incredulously. 'They would have removed tens, maybe hundreds, of thousands of tons of rock to build this place. I feel like Lord Carnarvon at the opening of Tutankhamun's tomb.'

'Let's hope we have more luck than he did. Left or right?'

'Left.'

'Why?'

'Because, if in doubt, I always go left.'

'We'll go right, then.'

He bit his tongue and followed her. As she walked, she left a single set of footprints in the dust of decades which had settled on the floor and that she now kicked up to sparkle like a million tiny fireflies in the torch beams. Above their heads a cable ran in shallow loops along the roof, linking a string of covered lights that vanished into the distance. Sarah strode on with the confidence of someone who belonged, though she carried her rucksack in front of her like a shield, but for Jamie the tunnel held an all-pervading atmosphere of doom. He tried to think of the Raphael, but all he imagined was a pair of vengeful eyes on his back. He had never felt more of an intruder. The air tasted foul and damp, like chewing mud, and he tried not to think about some kind of spore he'd read about that proliferated in ancient tombs and multiplied to fill the lungs like concrete. No, he didn't want to think about that at all.

'Look!'

Her torch had identified something glittering on the floor ahead. As they approached, Jamie could see it was window glass from the doors and windows of the wood-partitioned cubicles that now appeared on either side of the passageway. Sarah hesitated.

'Shouldn't we search them as we go?'

Jamie noticed a shape in the dust at his feet. He kicked it clean.

'Probably not.'

Her face paled as she recognized the red skull and crossbones of a chemical warning sign.

'But what about the painting?'

He studied the nearest cubicle, which contained a couple of cheap desks and rusting, open-mouthed metal filing cabinets. 'These must have been laboratories or offices. If the Raphael is here it will be locked in a safe somewhere. That's what we should look for.'

Now they walked with the constant crackle of broken glass beneath their feet.

'Why would they go to so much trouble to cause this amount of damage?' Sarah puzzled. 'It must have taken a huge amount of effort.'

'I don't think they did. The spread is too even for these windows to have been smashed by individuals. The last time I saw something like this was in a documentary about the Troubles in Northern Ireland. You know about that?'

'Of course.'

'Someone had just set off a bomb in a shopping centre.'

For once she didn't have anything to say.

They reached the end of the corridor. To the left a metal stairway led down to the next level, to the right was a compartment whose windows had miraculously survived whatever catastrophe had befallen the others. Halfway down the stairs Jamie stopped, not quite sure why, but suddenly drawn back to the intact office.

'Sarah,' he called.

She halted and glared back at him, keen to continue the search.

'You said—'

'I know, but I have a feeling.'

A minute later they stood in front of the last cubicle.

A thick layer of dust coated the windows and made it impossible to see beyond their opaque stare. Jamie's fingers twitched towards the door handle, but again some instinct drew him back. Why was this room still whole when all the others were not? A dark shadow of fear descended on him and he told himself it was only his imagination.

Sarah caught his mood. 'You think it could be wired?'

'I don't know.' He gently tapped the window. 'This is some kind of toughened glass; that's why the blast didn't smash it like the rest. That makes this place special.'

He noticed that his knuckle had made a tiny circular peephole in the dust. He raised the torch and looked through it.

'Oh, Christ almighty.' He stepped sharply away from the window.

Sarah ran to his side. 'What is it?'

He tried to speak, but no words would describe it. Instead, he took her hand and, slowly, almost reverentially, led her back to the window. He began in the middle of the small space he'd created and in circular sweeps cleared the dust from the glass. Not quite believing what they were seeing, they stared at the image before them. Jamie had never seen anything quite so beautiful and Sarah shared his wonder.

Slightly taller than it was wide, it hung in pride of place in the centre of the wall on the far side of the office behind a large desk. The face was almost feminine, but Jamie knew the subject was a young man, possibly even Raphael himself. He wore a soft cloth cap and white, loose-fitting shirt, and the dark eyes radiated intelligence from confident, aristocratic features. Beneath a thin coating of dust the minutely textured fur of his cape still retained a vibrancy that time had not diminished. Through the open window beyond the youth's left shoulder was an Italian landscape. The arrangement was typical of the artist's later portraits and Jamie knew that the scene in the window might have been painted three or even four different times before Raphael was satisfied. It was a masterpiece in the truest sense of the word.

He closed his eyes and backed off to slide down the far wall before his legs turned to rubber.

'Jamie, are you all right?'

He shook his head. 'Not once did I ever believe we'd find it. Not even when we walked up that stairway and along this corridor.'

'But you have.' Her eyes glittered in the torchlight. 'This is yours. All yours. I have my story, but the lost Raphael will make Jamie Saintclair famous.'

'It's too much. Now that I have it I wish . . . Can you understand? It was the hunt and the following the clues in my grandfather's journal. It was being with you and having this great adventure after my routine, boring, London life. And now – it's over, and I wish it could start all over again, but I know that it can't.' As he came to terms with the enormity of their discovery the excitement began to bubble inside him. He could already imagine the press conference where they would announce the recovery of one of the world's greatest lost masterpieces. He would never have to beg for another commission. There would be a reward that would set them both free to do whatever they wanted with their lives. Television appearances, lectures. And she was right, he would have fame of a kind he could only previously have imagined. They . . .

'Jamie?'

Christ, what was he thinking? They didn't have time for daydreams.

Sarah reached for the door of the cubicle.

'Don't!' The word came out as a sergeant major's bark and he instantly regretted it. She stared at him, her eyes a mix of anger and hurt. He sighed. 'The office has been sealed,' he explained. 'If we open the door and change the conditions we could destroy the painting.'

She shook her head, her expression a combination of disbelief and exasperation. 'We can't just leave it after all we've gone through to get it back.'

He knew she was right. Not after what had happened to them. Think.

A noise. A sort of dull, echoing clank. They'd jammed the metal door shut with the fallen branch. It wasn't much, but it was all they had. Someone had just forced it.

'Jamie.' Her eyes were wide, pleading.

Fuck it.

He gripped the handle and turned. Unlocked. Thank Christ for that. In one movement he opened the door and slipped through the gap into the office, making as little disturbance as possible. A dark heap in the centre of the floor might have been a dead body, but was actually some kind of exotic rug. Clearly Walter Brohm liked his little luxuries. No time for finesse. He unzipped the rucksack and removed a plastic bubblewrap bag from one of the compartments. It had been folded flat, so there'd be very little air inside. He waved it to fill it with the fetid atmosphere of the room. It was crude and probably pointless, but under the circumstances it was all he could think of. He could feel Sarah staring at him through the glass, urging him on, but when he looked into the enigmatic eyes of the young man in the picture a sort of paralysis overcame him. It was as if he was back in the river, but this time his feet were trapped in quicksand. Fortunately, the window rattled like an alarm bell to break the spell. Hurriedly he lifted the painting from its mount and gently slipped it into the bag, which had been selected in a fit of unlikely optimism specifically because it would hold something of the Raphael's dimensions. It had a ziplock fastener which he closed and secured as he retraced his steps to the door.

Sarah was already running for the stairs and when he glanced to his left he understood why. A pale orange glow painted the far end of the corridor where the stairs emerged.

They were coming.

XXXVIII

If anything, Gustav's astonishment when he reached the tunnel was greater than Jamie's. But where it had inspired fear in his quarry, the German only felt a sense of wonder and pride at the incredible feat of engineering his forefathers had created and kept secret for so many years. There had never been any doubt he would capture the fugitives, but this made it simpler and more convenient. No one would hear them screaming from beneath thirty feet of concrete.

In the yellow beam of his torch two distinct sets of footprints disappeared into the darkness. It was almost laughable. He felt like a fisherman reeling in his line. Gustav had watched through binoculars as they scurried like trapped ants along the base of the cliff seeking a non-existent escape route. He'd experienced a few moments of concern when they disappeared into the gully, but when he had reported the problem to Frederick it was almost as if the other man had been expecting the news. Frederick had issued very specific instructions and a warning. In the dying weeks of the war and for unexplained reasons, the Oder facility had been red-flagged by Himmler himself. There could be any number of reasons for that, but one thing was clear. Some secrets must stay secrets. For ever.

Sarah Grant and Jamie Saintclair would not leave the bunker alive.

The threatening silence was always with them. They moved quickly, as if, by their swiftness, they could somehow leave it behind along with whoever had followed them into the complex. But in the vast labyrinth of the tunnels the silence always prevailed. Jamie led the way, with the Raphael tucked under his left arm and the torch in his right hand. As they ran through the echoing man-made underworld he was conscious of the trail they left behind them, but what option did they have? Any attempt to disguise their footprints would leave just as big a signpost and would waste time. Their only hope was speed and the chance that somewhere in the maze was another exit.

They approached a massive steel door which looked as if it was sitting slightly ajar. It was only when they got closer that Jamie saw it was hanging from its hinges. He raced through, into the heart of Walter Brohm's secret world.

Behind the door lay a room the size of a football pitch that contained the biggest junkyard Jamie had ever seen. If it reminded him of anything, it was the wreckage of the Twin Towers on the morning of 12 September 2001. At every point of their vision, twisting, rusted metal created huge modernist sculptures: pyramids of engines, pumps and centrifuges, corkscrewed tubes and broken-toothed cogwheels, mounds of nameless machinery in every shape and size; ovens, gas tanks and even an entire tractor hanging like festive decorations. When they shone the torches over the roof and walls they could see the great white scars where the mass of steel and iron had been hurled by the force of an explosion powerful enough to crack the feet-thick reinforced concrete and expose the steel cables within. For a moment, they stood in silent awe taking in the immensity of it. The power required to create such a cataclysm. The incredible squandering of energy, effort and talent.

Sarah made to set off again, but Jamie pulled her back.

'This place is like a minefield.' His voice was a whisper. 'We've no idea what traps may have been set. There are wires everywhere. Just walking through this lot would be dangerous enough. One foot in the wrong place and you'll start an avalanche. If we run . . .'

'But . . .'

'I know,' he insisted. 'If we slow down, they'll catch us. We have to find a way to delay them.'

He studied their footprints again, Sarah's so much smaller than his own. 'Get behind me.' He took three steps forward. 'Now, as light-footed as you can, walk in my footsteps.' She did as she was told and they scrutinized the result as if their lives depended on it. Two lines of tracks had merged into one.

'Not bad, but they aren't going to buy that I upped and disappeared into thin air, are they?'

'No,' he agreed. 'But see how your tracks stop by the base of that big heap of debris with what looks like a boiler at the top? Well, the first thing they're going to suspect is that I've sent you up there to cover me while I escape.'

'You wouldn't do that,' she pointed out.

'No, but the cold-blooded bastard who is leading these people would. It won't delay them for long, but it might give us a chance. What we really need is to find some way to hurt them. Maybe take out one or two of them altogether.'

She darted a glance towards the doorway. 'Well, you'd better be quick.'

He handed her the Raphael. 'This is one of the darker arts I learned while I was in the OTC at Cambridge.' He pulled something circular from the inside pocket of his jacket and held it up for her to see. 'Fishing nylon. Fifty yards of thirty-pound breaking strain, but so thin you can't see it. You can use it to fish, but it also comes in handy for stitching wounds, putting up a makeshift shelter and for certain rather devious manoeuvres involving a hand grenade.' She declined to point out that they didn't have a hand grenade, but he probably wouldn't have heard her. As he talked he searched the closest heap of metal until he found what he was looking for. First, he tied the spider-web-thin strand of nylon from the leg of what had once been a workbench to a twisted piece of machinery about the size of a football.

'Give me your rope.'

Working quickly, he knotted one end of the rope through a gap in the metal part and when he was done he placed it gently so that a single twitch of the nylon would make it fall.

'Now comes the difficult bit.'

Sarah gasped as she saw what he planned.

'You can't. It will bring the whole lot down. Leave it, we don't have time.'

He ignored her and gingerly began climbing. After the first few feet he turned to look down at her. 'Make your way to the centre room on the far side, but stick to the edges of the aisles and try to keep your feet of the floor. I'll join you if I can.'

The piece he'd identified was about halfway up, maybe fifteen feet from the floor. Hardly daring to breathe, he slowly made his way towards it, knowing that every second was bringing their pursuers closer, but that to rush was to invite disaster. As he went, he pushed the slack of the rope into any gaps in the metal spoil, so it was close to invisible. The motor part was about twice the size of the smaller piece of machinery attached to the fishing nylon and it formed the key to a finely balanced heap, which in turn carried the weight of a massive engine of some kind. With trembling hands he laced the rope around it. Was it unstable enough? He reached out to make sure, but he knew that if he moved it even an inch it could bring the whole mountain of metal down and him with it. Reluctantly, he retreated, taking even more care where he put his feet.

He'd just reached the floor when she screamed, a scream so drenched in terror that it turned his heart to ice.

'Sarah!'

He started to run through the twisted heaps of metal.

XXXIX

The pony-tailed man stared from the enormous picture window of his suite in the corporation's Manhattan headquarters and considered his next move. Normally he barely noticed the dramatic New York skyline, but today it inspired and moved him. The fact that he was the head of the Vril Society did not make him any less of an American. This country had lost its way, thanks to failed politicians who did not understand the new reality. In the decades since the Second World War, the United States had sought to extend its global influence by military and economic means, but in almost every instance it had failed. Korea had been the last just war, and the West had been fought to a stalemate, ground down by the sheer mass of its enemies. Vietnam, Iraq and Afghanistan were largely pointless conflicts, as he saw it, with little profit to be had either politically or diplomatically. The 9/11 attacks had shown how a great power could be rendered militarily impotent. In the wake of the Twin Towers, America had lashed out like a chained bear at her tormentors; the bear had the power to crush its attackers, but the chains of misguided liberalism denied her the chance to use that power to its full extent.

And now the world was moving towards a new phase, but they were still too blind to see it. Energy was the key. It had been the key since the first turn of a turbine during the Industrial Revolution way back in the eighteenth century. The Russians knew that, and Europe would soon be on its knees begging for a whiff of the natural gas reserves the Kremlin controlled. But the Russians would only hold the cards in the short term. He had a far broader vision. A true world leader who combined the best of German and American blood would create peace and prosperity. No government on earth would be able to ignore him when he could send them back to the Dark Ages with the flick of a switch.

But he couldn't delude himself. He didn't just need the Sun Stone to make his vision a reality. He needed it to survive. His analysts predicted that the global banking crisis was much worse than anyone, even the banks themselves, realized. The group of companies he had formed was hopelessly exposed. If one of them went under the effect would be like the bottom brick being removed from a wooden tower. The entire entity would collapse, bringing all the other nearby towers down with it. The result would be catastrophic.

Frederick said his men would soon have Saintclair and the girl, and with them the journal. But Frederick could not be allowed to lay his hands on the Sun Stone.

Frederick was a very dangerous man: the true soul of the Vril, even if he did not yet know it. A fanatic who would take the stone and use it in some pointless mumbo-jumbo ritual at Wewelsburg.

The true power of the Sun Stone lay in its capacity to change the future, not alter the past.

In time, Frederick would have to be taken care of, but Frederick was not the only obstacle in his path. Somewhere out there other forces were at work. Sinister unseen forces who exhibited the same ruthlessness he was capable of himself. The Chinese certainly, though how much they knew of the Sun Stone's true power he wasn't sure. And who had killed their two agents? It was even possible some shadowy organization within his own government had become involved. If that were the case he might be forced to reconsider his long-term strategy. He had always intended to make a gift to his country of the military by-products generated by Brohm's breakthrough. Now he could be forced to play that particular card a little earlier than he'd intended. Soldiers were such simple souls, give them a sniff of a new wonder weapon that would make a bigger bang than anything yet created and they would sit up and beg. But for the moment all that was of secondary importance.

He turned back to the desk, where the grinning silver skull from the casket returned his stare. Secret papers of any kind are a currency, even if they deal with events long past. Surprisingly often they produce the small seedlings from which large profits grow.

305

One of the businesses that formed his many-tentacled corporation was that of producing newspapers. True, as an industry it was in danger of being steamrollered by the emerging technologies and was not the high-profit vehicle it had once been. Still, he enjoyed the prestige that ownership brought with it and the leverage his reporters gave him over small-minded individuals in government and the professions. From the start he had been amused by how artfully dishonest journalism could be; utterly unscrupulous, like espionage, but more cynical and with a little less pointless sacrifice. Through his publications he had created a network of informants among low-paid government archivists across Europe and the United States, retained to cherry-pick their files for papers that might be of interest. These men and women believed they were working for his newspapers and were grateful to accept a relative pittance for the fruits of their researches. Certain categories of papers, including those of curiosity value or which provided the possibility of exploitation, automatically made their way to his desk.

The documents from the records clerk in Cologne were only forwarded to him because of his well-known interest in technology, but he could still remember the dry feeling in his throat as he had read them for the first time. They dated from 1943 and included requisition orders for certain materials, tools and equipment that seemed to point to only one thing – and a name.

That was when he had launched the resources of the Vril Society on this hunt to discover Walter Brohm's whereabouts and the location of his research materials. The first hint of progress had come with an investigation into Brohm's background and the revelation that he had been a member of the 1937 Ahnenerbe expedition to Tibet. Most of the official papers had been destroyed, but enough evidence remained to reconstruct the route of the expedition and satellite images of the Changthang crater confirmed enough of what the Brohm papers hinted at to set his heart racing. It had taken six years to track down the casket and another three before he had the confidence to give the Menshikov operation the green light. In the meantime, his Vril contacts in the State department and the Bundestag were making efforts to discover Walter Brohm's fate. The German authorities had traced a Red Cross document confirming Brohm's incarceration in a prisoner-of-war camp near Leipzig, where he had been placed in protective custody. His rank was given as private and, even more curiously, the paper had later been stamped 'Unconfirmed'. There was no further evidence of Brohm's existence in the camp system. Much later, the State department official found Brohm's name in a list of potential prisoners who might be suitable for what would become Operation Paperclip, a secret OSS programme to recruit Nazi scientists and exfiltrate them to work for the American government. The next big breakthrough had come when some nuisance of a computer hacker had leaked dozens of archived Pentagon files on the internet, including a document marked 'Highly Restricted' which named Jedburgh teams Dietrich and Edgar. The military record showed that Team Edgar had been wiped out in an ambush in the Bavarian Alps on 8 May 1945, the day the war ended. On further investigation, it was found that two survivors from Team Dietrich, Captain Matthew Sinclair and Lieutenant Stanislaus Kozlowski, had been subsequently awarded the Military Cross for their actions on that date. Walter Brohm had never been heard of again.

The pony-tailed man's investigators confirmed that Matthew Sinclair had left the Army and been ordained into the Anglican Church. Between 1949 and 1963 he had carried out missionary work in the African Congo, until, in an altercation that had made the front page of many newspapers, he had physically assaulted the mercenary commander of Katanga province, Colonel Michael Hoare, and been sentenced to death. When he returned to Britain all trace of him was lost.

Stanislaus Kozlowski, the only other member of Team Dietrich, had been traced to a home for the elderly in Rugby, Warwickshire. At first, he had been reluctant to talk about his military service, but eventually he was surprisingly forthcoming about his wartime experiences. Kozlowski's insistence on telling his story to a wider audience had required his removal, but it was from transcripts of the Kozlowski interview that he had learned of the fate of Jedburgh teams Dietrich and Edgar. And of the journal that Team Dietrich's commander had kept so assiduously in the final weeks of the war.

From that moment on, he had devoted every resource

at his disposal to the discovery of Matthew Sinclair and his surviving relatives. How ridiculous that after all this time and effort and investment it came down to one man.

He picked up the telephone on his desk. 'Get me Sumner.'

XL

Jamie reached the doorway where Sarah had disappeared. To his right, her torch lay on the floor, still gently rocking, the beam playing on the base of the far wall. He froze as he heard a gentle shuffling and raised his own torch to illuminate whatever had made the noise.

'Oh, Christ!'

The silent scream in the tormented, eyeless face reflected the terror of her end, the jagged hole in her skull clear proof of the method they had used to snuff out her life. He reached forward to touch her shoulder.

'Why did they do this?' Sarah's hushed voice came from the corner behind him. He almost cried out with relief as he caught her in the spotlight. Safe. Hunched into the angle of the wall, her body seemed smaller and more fragile, her eyes shone huge and liquid in the torchlight.

He turned back to the desiccated body dressed in the remains of a striped grey shift which lay slumped across the steel bench. In the torchlight her still perfect teeth shone like pearls in the ivory skull. Small and delicate. Like Sarah's teeth. Leathery hands with long slim fingers that might have once played the piano stretched out towards him as if in welcome. He heard the shuffling again and a mouse peered cautiously from the eye socket of the skull where it had made its nest. The torch lifted and the beam took in dozens, no, hundreds, of other skeletal bodies. A sea of bones that stretched the length of the room.

They sat in ordered rows, chained to the benches where they had worked and where they had died, some slumped forward, others reaching up, their backs permanently arched in agony from the moment the bullets had struck. The disarticulated remains of still more lay in scattered heaps on the concrete floor below the point where they had hung lifeless for years until time and gravity combined to snap their sinews. He imagined the screams of terror, the shouts of defiance as the SS men had walked along the ranks with their pistols and machine guns barking, the blood staining the work bench thick. Was the woman closest to him the first or the last? Did she know her fate before she was chained to the cold steel bench? He looked at the face again. Oh, yes. She knew.

'To defend the Great Secret. The Wonder of the World.'

'This was Walter Brohm's doing?'

'Shhhh!' He clicked off his torch and forced her back into the corner as the first flickering beams reached

311

the main hall. A brusque voice issued whispered instructions. Jamie crouched low and risked a glance from the doorway. Through a gap in the mountains of metal he counted them. Six, at least, and the leader hadn't been fooled by the tracks in the dust. Jamie had hoped to lead them all down the main aisle, but whoever was giving the orders had held them back and split them into three groups. Two to take the outer passages and one to go through the centre. Once the dispositions had been made they started forward, moving with deadly intent. A torch beam swept across his hiding place, forcing him to duck back.

He pushed his head against Sarah's so that his mouth touched her ear. 'Listen.'

Gustav had been irritated by the enforced delay while his men investigated the office which was of so much interest to Saintclair, but he couldn't take the chance that the Englishman had found or left something there. The empty space in the dust on the wall was intriguing, but the only thing that mattered was the journal and it was only a question of time before he had it. The scream that had just echoed through the corridors proved it. There was no escape from the bunker, apart from the way they had come.

When they reached the main production hall, a hunter's instinct told him this was where his prey had gone to ground. They always went to ground. Fear and hopelessness robbed them of their energy and their courage. But they could still be dangerous.

'Muller and Krauss sweep the left, Schmidt and Ritter the right. Kempner and I will take the centre. This time we take no chances. If you see them, shoot to kill.'

Very slowly they worked their way forward. Gustav allowed Kempner to take the lead, while he provided cover with the MP5. In the torch beam he noted where the two sets of footsteps had turned into one. Did they really think him such a fool to be taken in by a cheap trick like that? Well, they would learn. Away to his left one of the torch beams deviated and he noted approvingly that Muller was searching some sort of side room. Yet the further they moved into the great mounds of twisted scrap, the more the scale of the place worked against his confidence. Should he have secured the bunker and waited until they could rig up some kind of generator? No, Frederick wanted results. It had to be now. It might cost him another man, but the price was worth paying.

One more step and it was as if World War Three had broken out. Gustav whipped the machine pistol round as two shots reverberated like cannon fire around the vast echo chamber of the concrete room. The shocked silence that followed was broken by a burst of almost hysterical laughter.

'What the fuck is going on?' he demanded.

Krauss appeared from another side room backlit by the wavering beam of a torch. 'Just a bunch of soaps who were resettled during the war. Muller almost shit his pants.'

313

Gustav cursed beneath his breath. 'The only corpses we are interested in are Saintclair and the girl.'

He gestured to Kempner to move on. That was when he saw the silken strand of the spider's web tauten and bend against the knee of his partner's combat trousers.

The two figures slumped at the end of the row of corpses slowly raised their heads. Jamie's ears rang from the incredible noise of the shots in the confined space and Sarah's hand shook as she reached for the comfort of his in the darkness. They had taken their places on the bench where two of the dismantled skeletons had fallen to the floor, frozen in position as the torch flicked from skull to skull and the panicked German began firing. Sarah had almost cried out as a bullet shattered the jaw of the dead man next to her and spattered her with teeth and shards of bone, but some deep-set instinct for survival kept her silent.

With the men gone, Jamie pulled her to her feet and retrieved the rucksacks and the bubble-wrapped painting from below the table. Together they crept back towards the door. The closest torches had moved on, but the pair in the centre were taking more care and Jamie could see the glow of another set on the far side of the biggest hill of metal. His heart told him they should make a break for it, but his brain said wait. Ten seconds passed that felt like an hour. *They must have reached it by now.* What if they'd seen the nylon? He squeezed Sarah's hand as a signal to get ready.

*   *   *

For a fraction of a second after Kempner's knee felt the first pressure of the fishing line, the nylon stretched, its natural elasticity brought into play by the force placed upon it. But before the German could react it pulled the smaller piece of machinery from its position and there was a clatter as it fell to the floor. Gustav stiffened at the sound, but when nothing happened he breathed a sigh of relief. Then he noticed the rope.

Twenty feet above them, the weight of the smaller piece of machinery pulled the larger engine part out of its position in the jumble of metal holding together the top of the pile. At first it was just the rattle of a single piece of metal bouncing down the side of the slope, but very quickly it turned into an avalanche. Within a second the fragile shelf holding the big engine disintegrated and the enormous piece of steel alloy toppled to join the wave of tons of twisted metal plunging towards the Germans. Kempner let out a shriek and began to run, but Gustav knew there was no escape. He threw himself sideways in a forlorn attempt to find safety.

Jamie waited until the clamour of the avalanche subsided and wobbling torches had converged on the centre of the room. Moving fast and low he and Sarah crawled silently to the doorway and into the corridor. Right or left? He had no way of knowing whether the direction they'd come would be guarded, but at least he could be certain it was a way out. He chose right.

Ten minutes later they reached the waterfall and for the first time in an hour he felt it was safe to breathe.

They headed downstream towards Braunlage, keeping away from the marked trails, and crossed the river at a hiker's bridge.

Sarah was uncharacteristically silent as they walked, but just before they reached the main road she stopped him.

'I asked you a question back there, but we were interrupted before you gave me an answer. Why?'

He hesitated. 'Walter Brohm couldn't afford to leave anyone alive. These weren't ordinary slave workers. They were the scientists and technicians who had helped create the *Uranverein*. When the Nazi nuclear project was wound down between nineteen forty-one and 'forty-two Hitler decided they weren't needed any more.' He remembered David's words. *That was the year they sent many of their best scientists to Auschwitz.* 'But Walter Brohm needed them, and he had them brought here. The SS ran the bureaucracy of death, it would have been simple enough to arrange. The knowledge their heads contained was as precious as any research file, perhaps more so. They may have been his slaves, but we know from the journal that Brohm wanted above all to be admired. He would have confided in them his plans and his hopes for the future. He would have wanted them to believe that they were part of that future.'

'But they were Jews.'

'Yes, they were Jews. So they had no future. Not in Walter Brohm's Germany.'

She nodded and stared at the distant bulk of the

Brocken, the signpost that had brought them to this dread place.

'Promise me something.'

'Of course.'

'No, wait until you know what I am asking. It's important.'

He stared at her for a moment. Her face was unnaturally white. Pale as death. 'Ask then.'

'Promise me that if we find out that Walter Brohm is still alive you will use whatever money you get for the recovery of the Raphael to hunt him down.'

He didn't even have to consider it. 'I promise. If Walter Brohm is alive, I will follow him to the ends of the earth and bring him to justice.'

'No, you don't understand. I don't want justice. Promise me that if Walter Brohm is still alive, you will kill him.'

At first, her words sent a shock of revulsion through him. The man who died at Wewelsburg had been more or less an accident and the hunter in the woods pure self-preservation. Did she really believe him capable of cold-blooded murder? Then he remembered the long rows of corpses in the chamber and the girl with the musician's hands. Walter Brohm had been responsible for their deaths and if Walter Brohm was alive, it had been Matthew Sinclair who had kept him that way.

He took a deep breath.

'If we find Walter Brohm, I will kill him.'

XLI

'You are free to go.'

Jamie opened his eyes to find the door of the cell open. and a tall, dark-haired woman studying him with the expression of someone who had just found a dead rat in her kitchen. She was in her mid-forties and dressed in a smart business suit that was as much a uniform as anything with badges of rank. '*Polizeihauptkommissar* Lotte Muller.' Jamie got to his feet rubbing his spine as she introduced herself. 'And you are Mr Jamie Saint-clair. You have spent a comfortable night?'

'As comfortable as can be expected.' It had been fully dark by the time they got back to Braunlage and another hour before Jamie located the local police office. The patrolman who had listened to their story had been first annoyed, then perplexed and finally bewildered, before they produced the Raphael. That was when he decided to hedge his bets and arrested Jamie on suspicion of something and told Sarah to go back to the hotel and stay there.

Lotte Muller produced a thin smile. 'Perhaps you are surprised that you are to be freed?'

He shook his head. 'No, as I explained to the officer last night, we did nothing wrong. This is just a misunderstanding.'

'Of course, a misunderstanding.' She had a policeman's way with words. Disbelief was her default position. 'Naturally, there will be certain conditions to your release.'

'Naturally.'

'My colleague from the *Landespolizei* had dismissed you and your . . . travelling companion as publicity-seeking fantasists, but then there was the question of the painting.' What might have been a twinkle appeared in Lotte Muller's hard little eyes and a slight uplift at the corners of her mouth accompanied the word painting. Clearly, the Raphael had made a suitable impression. 'He did not dare open the package, of course, but the more he studied it the more concerned he became. So concerned that he rather belatedly found the courage to disturb my sleep. Since dawn, I have spent a rather trying morning in the Oder gorge attempting to verify, or otherwise, your unlikely story. Fortunately, I found no terrorists with machine guns. No dead men among the trees, or bodies in the river. No blood trails or spent cartridges.' The dark eyes held Jamie's. 'But then my officers discovered the entrance to the bunker precisely where you and Miss Grant said it would be.'

'May I ask how Miss Grant is?'

Lotte Muller's expression softened. 'As far as I know she is well. She should be here in a few minutes. Perhaps you would like to freshen up a little and we can continue this conversation in the interview room when she arrives?'

Sarah Grant might have spent the previous day at a spa rather than being chased around a forest by machine-gun-toting killers. She had relinquished her usual jeans and leather jacket for a candy-striped summer dress that made her look about eighteen. When Jamie rose to give her a restrained hug her perfume smelled of crushed lilac.

'I didn't even know you owned a dress,' he whispered.

'A girl has to have some secrets, Saintclair.'

'May we begin?' Lotte Muller interrupted.

They took their seats on the other side of the desk. The room was like police interview rooms everywhere: small, sparse and functional.

'I understand you are comfortable in German, Miss Grant?'

Sarah nodded.

'You slept well?'

'Very.' The accompanying smile hid the fact that she'd spent the night with a chair jammed behind the door of the hotel room wishing Jamie hadn't persuaded her to dump the pistol she had carried since Wewelsburg. She had passed the time working on a synopsis of the Raphael story that she'd e-mailed to a selection of newspapers and magazines and eventually fallen asleep to wake up to an inbox full of offers that took her breath away.

The policewoman adjusted her reading glasses as she studied a piece of paper on the desk. 'I have read your statements and I must admit to being somewhat perplexed. You say you were hunted through our forest by men with guns, but, as I have already informed Mr Saintclair, there is no evidence of this. No reports of gunshots. No shell cases. No bodies. No signs of any violence whatsoever.'

'That doesn't mean it didn't happen,' Sarah interrupted.

'No, it does not,' Muller agreed. 'But I would have preferred some further evidence. However, we also have the painting . . . and the bunker. You say that you were led to the bunker by indicators provided in this journal left by your grandfather, but only stumbled upon the entrance when you were being pursued.' She turned a page and Jamie recognized a photocopy of the tightly written text of Matthew Sinclair's diary. 'A remarkable document, and even more remarkable that you were able to decipher the clues, if clues they are.' The long pause that followed was an invitation to provide an explanation, but neither Jamie nor Sarah responded and she was forced to continue. 'Still, what matters is that the bunker does exist, and that it provides us with a crime scene for which there *is* substantial evidence.'

'You mean the dead prisoners?'

'That is correct, Mr Saintclair. Just because a murder was committed many decades ago does not mean we can ignore the fact that it happened. I visited the site this morning. Quite astonishing. One does not expect to be confronted with such barbarity. Perhaps one should not be surprised that these things emerge from time to time, but still . . . Even for someone like myself, who has seen many difficult things, it was an emotional moment. To think that this could happen so close to this beautiful place is disturbing. There must be a full investigation, even though the perpetrators are most probably dead themselves. It may be many months before we can even identify the victims.'

Jamie allowed his surprise to show. 'You think you'll be able to find out who they were?'

'Oh, yes, I don't doubt it. In your very concise report to my colleague last night you mentioned the *Uranverein* project. If you are correct in that assumption, it narrows the field considerably. Those involved in the *Uranverein* who survived the war made very detailed statements about their work to the Allied authorities. We have lists of people who were removed – as was thought then – to the concentration camps. By matching physical details and using the latest DNA techniques we should certainly be able to identify most of those in the bunker.'

'They were Jews.' Sarah's voice cut the cosy atmosphere like a chain saw. 'You seem reluctant to mention that.'

Lotte Muller's lips tightened. 'Yes,' she said. 'There is a probability that most, if not all, are Jewish; that would certainly correspond with the times in which they died and the situation in which they are found. But for me, Miss Grant, they are all victims, whether they are black or white, male or female, Christian, Muslim or Jewish, and I will do everything in my power to apprehend whoever perpetrated this atrocity. Does that satisfy you?'

Jamie glanced at Sarah and she nodded, he thought reluctantly.

'Good. Now we may turn to the more pleasant part of your discovery. You will be aware that there are other bunkers in the Harz, at Nordhausen, in particular, where the V2 rocket was manufactured. But Nordhausen cannot boast a famous masterpiece. You have placed Braunlage firmly on the international map, Mr Saintclair, you and Miss Grant. Of course, we must carry out a detailed check to confirm its authenticity, but if, as I have no doubts will be the case, this is the lost Raphael painting, there will be huge international interest. The Polish ambassador is already on his way here. You know, of course, that *Portrait of a Young Man* was removed from the Czartoryski Museum, in Cracow? The trust which now runs the museum is very eager to see its return and is sending a representative to witness the unveiling of the painting, which will be carried out by conservators from the *Staatliche Museen* in Berlin. I am sure the Princess Czartoryski Foundation will be most grateful for the Raphael's return, but that is something you must discuss with the trustees personally. Already,' her face hardened again, 'we have had calls from the press, many calls, regarding the discovery. You are a journalist, I understand, Miss Grant?'

'What about these men who tried to kill us? You seem to have forgotten them.' Jamie interrupted.

Lotte Muller pursed her lips. 'Naturally we will

continue to investigate, but unless there is further evidence . . .'

He opened his mouth to argue, but Sarah kicked him below the desk.

'What will happen to the bunker now, I mean in the long run?' she asked.

'I think that will depend on the structural condition,' the *kommissar* sounded unconvinced. 'As you no doubt saw, the lower floors were quite badly damaged by an explosion. But if it is structurally sound there is already talk of the Federal government turning the bunker into a museum and, naturally, a memorial to those who died there. In the circumstances we are very fortunate that it is there at all.'

'I don't understand?' Sarah said.

'Of course, you would not know.' Kommissar Muller studied their faces. 'The whole complex was wired to explode thirty minutes after you opened the door behind the falls. The only thing that saved you was the rodent that ate its way through the main cable.'

XLII

'Here's to the mouse that chewed.' Jamie raised his glass and took a deep draught of dark Gose beer as they sat outside a bar across the main square from their hotel.

'I'll drink to that,' Sarah acknowledged. 'And to not being blown all over the Harz Mountains.' The grin they exchanged was of the sickly variety and they sat for a while enjoying the novelty of still being alive. 'I was surprised when she started quoting the journal at us. I didn't think you'd let it out of your sight.'

He shrugged. 'They gave it back quickly enough and I didn't think I had a lot of choice. They confiscated the rucksack as possible evidence. It didn't seem to matter much, because the journal has taken us as far as it's going to.'

'So what happens now?'

It was an odd question. In theory, at least, the Raphael would change their lives. Yet he had an odd empty feeling of anticlimax that he sensed Sarah Grant shared. It was as if the hunt had been their true purpose and the discovery only mattered in the abstract. Even then any joy they could take from it had been overwhelmed by the enormity of the other things they'd found in Walter Brohm's bunker.

'I made you a promise last night on the way back here, but it's a promise that may be difficult to keep,' Jamie admitted. Privately he was having second thoughts about his rash pledge, but that could wait for another day. 'I'd like to be able to finish what we started and take the story right to the end. We found the Raphael, but we still don't know what happened to Walter Brohm. My grandfather's last mission has a beginning and a middle, but no end. The answers are out there somewhere, but if there's no more to the diary I'm not sure where else we can go.'

A porter from the hotel approached the table holding a package. 'This arrived for you this morning, sir. Express delivery.'

Jamie frowned, then remembered his phone call to David and the text he'd sent confirming their new location. With the excitement of the last two days he'd forgotten the young Jew's promise to dig for more information. He accepted the padded brown envelope and tipped the young man.

'I hope you've not been holding out on me again, Saintclair.'

He saw himself smile in the mirror of her sunglasses. 'Just a little additional research I commissioned.' He tore open the envelope and spread the contents out on the table top. Four or five photocopies of faded cuttings from German newspapers with the dates they were filed and the name of the publication apparently written in ink on the original. They were all from the mid to late 1930s. On each of the photocopies, someone had highlighted two words with a yellow marker pen. *Walter Brohm*.

Sarah dragged her seat round the table so they could read the cuttings together. 'Tibet?'

'Yes. Brohm told my grandfather that he had *walked in a land of giants* and that was where he found *it*. I asked a friend to check the story out and this is what he came up with.'

'A well-connected friend?'

'It looks like he got lucky.'

The reports all documented the same 1937 expedition by a group of German scientists. He scanned the photocopies one at a time in no particular order, but Sarah organized them chronologically and leaned forward in her chair to study them with a scholar's intensity.

'Do you notice anything?' she asked after a few minutes.

'Only that the papers all hail the triumph of German stamina, ingenuity and scientific achievement over great odds and some of the most difficult terrain in the world. I keep looking for Joseph Goebbels' byline. The main aim of the trip seems to have been to study the natives. No mention of the occult or seeking the origin of the Aryan race. Why?'

'In the earliest cutting, which is the announcement

that the expedition is going ahead, the report is quite specific about the aims, but, more importantly, the destination, the Guzong crater. But the later editions, after the scientists return, only mention the Changthang Plateau in a wider sense, an area of thousands of square miles. It's as if they wanted people to forget the original destination.'

'Or to hide it.'

'What made you ask for this?'

He took a deep breath. 'Because Walter Brohm also said he was certain there was more to find.'

She saw what he was thinking before the idea had fully formed in his own head.

'You can't be serious.'

But he was.

'Don't you see?' his voice quickened. 'This is where it all started. It's where Walter Brohm made his discovery that could change the world. We can't just stop now. We owe it to my grandfather to find the answer. We owe it to all those people who died in the bunker. We have to find a way to get to this Guzong crater.'

'It's crazy.'

'On the contrary, it's the logical next step. We can't go forward, so we retrace Walter Brohm's steps until we find what he did.'

'But you don't have the resources, or the money to finance that kind of trip. Walter Brohm was sponsored by one of Adolf Hitler's cronies. Somehow I don't see any rich folks queuing up to hand you cash.'

He'd thought about that. 'My grandfather's house

will sell eventually. There'll be some sort of finder's fee for the Raphael, probably a substantial one. I'll fund the trip from that.'

'You are the most obstinate, pig-headed—'

'I thought you liked the new adventurous me?'

'Tibet isn't a place you can just walk in to. The Chinese run it now, and they don't encourage visitors.'

'I'll find a way.'

She shook her head and for a moment he thought he'd lost her. 'No, *we'll* find a way. The Raphael story may not make me rich, but it will help stake an adventure holiday with an eccentric idiot.'

He stared at her. 'I thought you had what you came for?'

Sarah Grant pushed the sunglasses into her hair and the challenge in the hazel eyes raised the stakes. 'I thought so, too. Have I?'

For a moment he felt as if his soul had been stripped bare. He'd become closer to this woman in a few short weeks than to anyone he'd ever had a relationship with. The thought of losing her chilled him to the depths of his being. Yes, he had doubts, but about *what* she was, not *who*. Finally, he nodded. 'If you want it.'

'I thought I'd made that pretty clear, Jamie.'

'You—'

'Hi, Miss Sarah Grant, right, and Mr James Saint-clair?'

Jamie glared at the intruder, but the tall man who stood a few feet from their table was unruffled by the coolness of his reception. He had dark, almost Polynesian good looks and a helmet of sun-bleached hair that would stay in place even in the highest winds. The smile that showed off his perfect white teeth didn't budge or the amused – a less trusting person might say mocking – blue eyes lose their sparkle. The tan suit he wore over a cream shirt would have cost Saintclair Fine Arts the best part of a year's profit and fitted tightly across a swimmer's muscled shoulders. He spoke English with an American accent. Jamie took one look at him and couldn't keep the words snake-oil salesman out of his head.

The visitor waited for an acknowledgement and when it wasn't forthcoming, he nodded approval.

'Yep, you're right to be wary, a couple of folks with a valuable commodity on their hands. Guess I'd be much the same if I'd just found that painting.'

'What makes you think we found a painting?' Sarah asked innocently.

The smile was replaced by a self-effacing grin. 'Well, that might be on account of the local police commander pointing you out. Now don't tell me she would be mistaken? Not after I've gone to the trouble of confirming it at the hotel over yonder. That's the hotel where you sent your pitch on the internet from, right?' He pulled a card from his pocket. 'Bob Sumner, I represent the Vanderbilt Corporation.' Sumner saw she was impressed and the grin broadened. Now Jamie understood the level of cooperation from the police. Vanderbilt was one of the world's most powerful business corporations: a ruthless global giant that dominated a dozen industries. The kind his heart told him shouldn't be allowed to exist, but that his head said always would. He read the card. It confirmed that Bob Sumner was the Vanderbilt Media Division's deputy director of European operations.

'Might I sit with you?' the big man requested. 'I have what I hope you'll find an interesting proposition.'

Jamie moved to make room at the small table and Sumner slid comfortably into one of the vacant metal seats. Sarah found herself the focus of disconcerting blue eyes.

'I'll get right down to business, if you folks don't mind. Because in an hour the entire European press pack is going to come driving down that road like ol' Guderian's panzers and they'll be just as hard to stop. You'll notice I'm not hiding the fact that I face opposition for your signature. I'll also talk to you as a partnership, because as you'll see, although Miss Grant has offered us a feature story, we envisage substantially more potential. Like I say, you have a commodity which we at Vanderbilt recognize is of substantial value. We respect your right to get the best possible price for it. I flatter myself that the fact the company has sent me is some kind of indication of that and I hope to convince you that Vanderbilt Corporation can deliver the best commercial environment to exploit your story and bring it to a worldwide audience.'

'I take it that means you'll put it in your newspaper and pay me for it?'

Sumner motioned to the waiter hovering by the doorway. 'Can I get you folks anything?' They shook their heads. '*Kaffee, bitte.*'

The American studied Sarah and shook his head. 'No, ma'am, not exactly. Vanderbilt Media has one hundred and fifty media outlets worldwide. We would franchise your story, in series form, across all those titles. In addition, we would commission you to write, or cooperate with a ghost writer, on a book bringing together all aspects of the story and the history of the painting.' He smiled indulgently. 'Like *The Da Vinci Code*, but true, profits to be split fifty-fifty.' Sarah's eyes widened imperceptibly and Jamie could tell that Bob Sumner's hard sell was cutting through her armour like a welding torch. 'Vanderbilt Media also owns or part owns twenty-five satellite and terrestrial television stations. It would be our intention to commission a film documentary tracing your search for the painting from day one. The film would have a substantial budget and be backed by all the resources of Vanderbilt Corporation. We would leave no stone unturned in the search to track the painting's journey across Europe. We're also intrigued by this mysterious Nazi bunker you found. I personally would be interested to know how you knew where to look?' The grin didn't falter, but just for a millisecond Jamie saw ice chips where there had been none earlier.

'Maybe when the first cheque arrives, Bob, old boy.' He emphasized the lazy Cambridge drawl for all he was worth, earning a puzzled glance from Sarah. 'In the meantime, I don't think we've seen the colour of your money?'

'Vanderbilt Media has authorized me to offer you two

hundred and fifty thousand English pounds for your cooperation in putting this package together, the split to be decided amicably between yourselves.'

Sarah let out a little 'wow' at the figure, which was ten times what she'd been offered by anyone else. Jamie only just managed to maintain his poker face. 'I suppose that's an acceptable starting point for negotiations,' he said carefully.

'There's also the question of the world tour.'

'The world tour?'

The big man nodded solemnly. 'Dependent on the Czartoryski Museum accepting our offer to sponsor the display of *Portrait of a Young Man* in fourteen major cities across the globe, beginning in Cracow. You would commit to providing insight and publicity on the tour over a four-month period for a stipend to be negotiated.' He reached into his leather bag. 'I have contract details he—'

'No.' Sarah's interruption froze the smile on Bob Sumner's face. 'The rest of the package sounds attractive, but we won't be able to commit to any tour. We have further investigations to carry out into the man responsible for bringing the Raphael here.'

Jamie wondered if she was being hasty. The thought of spending four months jetting around the world at the Vanderbilt Corporation's expense, captivating the unenlightened with his wit and wisdom on the subject of the Raphael, had its attractions. He felt an idea forming, just the faintest hint of a possibility. 'Maybe there is a way . . .' The fathomless blue eyes fixed him. 'We'll sign up for the full package, on one condition . . .'

'Mr Saintclair, the Vanderbilt Corporation will be paying you a substantial amount of money—'

'The Raphael story doesn't begin in Europe, it begins in Asia. The condition is that we will provide you with a location and will form part of the documentary team sent to film there.'

It was an outrageous demand and they both knew it, but Bob Sumner didn't even blink. 'I'd have to clear it with my bosses, but I'm not against it in principle. Of course, I'd need to know the exact location we're talking about.'

Jamie held his stare.

'Tibet.'

XLIII

Bob Sumner saw Sarah watching him from across the square as he dialled his boss to discuss the new terms. He smiled and waved as he spoke.

'Our German friend has a photocopy of the journal through his sources in the local police department. Apparently Saintclair became careless after discovering the bunker. I'm signing them up as you advised, but we have a problem.' He described Jamie's ultimatum and was surprised by the rich laughter at the other end of the line.

'Make sure your man hands over the photocopies and get them to me right away. It's perfect. We need to get Saintclair off the scene and out of Frederick's reach until we evaluate what we have. I couldn't have planned it better. If there's anything in the diary Saintclair can help us with, we'll bring him back. If not . . . well, that's too bad.'

Sumner discussed the details for a few minutes before returning to the table. He spread his hands. 'Sounds crazy to me, but my boss, he loves it and the riskier the better. Following in the footsteps of Nazi treasure hunters. Battling against the elements, the terrain and the might of the Communist Chinese in a search to uncover the secret behind the Raphael bunker. We'll have cameras on you all the way and record every drop of sweat and squeal of terror. I hope you know what you're getting yourself into, Mr Saintclair.'

A week later as he sat in the co-pilot's seat of the Bell Long Ranger which normally inspected Vanderbilt Corporation pipelines, Jamie had cause to remember the executive's words.

'We'll get you as close to the border as we can, maybe twenty miles.' The pilot's distorted metallic voice rang in his earphones above the clatter of the helicopter's engine and the rhythmic thump of the rotor blades.

'Why can't you take us all the way?'

'Because any closer and we'd be flying in a restricted zone and if one of the good old People's Republic fighter jets didn't shoot us down, one of friendly India's attack helicopters would. It's that kind of place.'

'Thanks.'

The chopper pilot, a prematurely grey-haired young Texan, grinned behind his sunglasses. Sarah leaned forward from the rear seats and tapped him on the shoulder.

'What happens when we get there?' she asked.

'I flew the camera team in to Joshimath two days ago. They're in touch with a group of Tibetan dissidents.

You'll be going in over an old smugglers' route across the Mana Pass, then up towards Ngari, way up there.' He pointed ahead, where a wall of white dominated the horizon.

Sarah looked out of the helicopter window at the hostile terrain a couple of thousand feet below and felt a shiver run through her. They were still fifty miles short of the Tibetan border and the mountains soared to either side, craggy green-flanked slabs which fell away sheer to rock-strewn river valleys that twinkled deceptively. The snow-capped peaks to their front must be three times as high.

'This isn't going to be a picnic, then?'

'Ma'am,' the pilot said seriously, 'I hope somebody explained to you that you are going into the most inhospitable place on the planet. You can die of thirst in the Sahara or freeze to death in the Arctic, up here you'll get the chance to do both while little slanty-eyed men with automatic weapons shoot at you. The Chinese have been here since nineteen fifty and they have the place sewn up real tight. The only way to enter Tibet legally is through Lhasa. You need a permit to do that and your movements are carefully controlled while you're there. So to get wherever you're going to make this here film, you need to go in *illegally*, which means on your hind legs. There are no physical barriers, because both sides rely on the terrain, but you'll have to sneak past army garrisons who like nothing better than hunting human meat and harmless-looking shepherd boys who'll turn you in for less than a dollar a head. The air is so thin even the birds have to walk and the only thing to drink is yak butter tea that tastes like sediment from the Hudson River. Now, you look in pretty good shape, I see you've got the best of equipment and they'd fire me for saying this, but you and your young fella would be advised to tell that documentary director to go to hell and Vanderbilt to stick their money up their ass and head right on back to Meerut. We could be having a beer on the deck by sunset?'

Jamie turned to Sarah. 'Maybe he's right. You stay with the helicopter and I'll go?'

She gave him the kind of stare she usually reserved for overly persistent door-to-door salesmen. 'No thank you.'

The pilot laughed. 'Thought not. You don't look like a quitter. Here we go.' He twisted the helicopter down towards an insignificant settlement in the valley away to their right. 'Thank you for flying Pelican Airways and have a nice day, y'all.'

XLIV

'Why are you wearing that crazy scarf?'

'Because I thought it might be cold, and I was bloody right!'

Sarah studied the lurid purple and white striped monstrosity with distaste. 'You might as well paint an archery target on your chest and wave a placard that says: *I'm here*.'

'It's my college scarf, and I'm rather proud of it.'

'Well, be proud of it somewhere else, Don Quixote. I'd prefer not to get hit when they're shooting at you. Ganesh thinks you must have altitude sickness.'

Jamie looked at their interpreter, who grinned uncertainly. He tucked the long scarf into his Gore-tex jacket and down into his trousers and the other man nodded vigorously before walking back to check on the few porters the film crew had persuaded to make the trek into occupied Tibet. Jamie had quickly formed an enormous respect for the wiry mountain men. Without them, he knew the expedition wouldn't have lasted twenty-four hours. They were small men, but their slight frames were packed with incredible strength and endurance, and each of them carried a load that weighed as much as the porter himself.

For the first two days they had trekked through an almost alpine landscape of conical hills cloaked with oak, birch and rhododendron, twisting valleys that carried foaming, swift-flowing streams and across broad, flower-carpeted meadows. Rare red pandas, brown bears and even snow leopard roamed these Himalayan foothills, but the only thing they glimpsed was a small troop of squalid-looking monkeys which sat in a tree beside the road and threw rotting fruit at them as they passed. Jamie hoped it wasn't an omen. Narrow, precipitous paths zigzagged up mountainsides making the steep inclines bearable and allowing them to acclimatize for the tougher terrain ahead.

It was only on the third day, as they climbed higher and their guide told them they had crossed the border into Tibet, that Sarah began to feel her lungs fighting to extract oxygen from the air. How could she have taken breathing for granted? What she normally breathed in London had the consistency of chicken soup compared to this. Altitude sickness was a real danger and Jamie insisted they take their Diamox tablets every day, but that still didn't do anything for the splitting headache that had started on the second morning and never left her. Now, they were in the Himalayas proper, two miles and more above sea level, between the tree line and the snow line. The sharp-set, scenic grandeur with its ethereal light and fantastic colours overwhelmed and awed them, but Jamie found the terrain, a rock-strewn moonscape enlivened only by occasional strips of faded, wind-worn prayer flags, eroded his resilience with every step and the long climbs stretched him to the brink of endurance. Flimsy, double-skinned tents provided the only shelter and they slept on wolfish rocks that clawed their way through bedroll, sleeping bag and spine. Tibetan nights were long and chill; plenty of time for talking and thinking and wondering before exhaustion overcame the body's hyperactivity. Each day was a never-ending Calvary of steep, scree-scattered scarps that set their calf muscles on fire and turned their feet into blistered, pain-filled sacs. Jamie marched in a dream, cocooned in his own breathless bubble of discomfort, knowing Sarah was less than twenty feet behind suffering just as much, but without the energy to communicate with her. It was only when the little caravan halted beside a small lake of the most astonishing, opaque, almost toxic blue that they had the chance to speak.

She lay with her back against a rock allowing the sun to warm her face, and he slumped beside her, accepting a bottle of water she retrieved from her ruck-sack.

He drank deeply before returning it. 'I've been thinking,' he wheezed.

'Me too.'

'I'm beginning to regret being quite so clever.'

'Uhuh,' she grunted. 'But it's a little too late to change

your mind, seeing as we've signed the contract and all, and unless you happen to have a handy little helicopter in your pocket to get us out of here.'

Gervaise Pearson, the documentary producer and leader of the three-man film team, ambled over to sit down beside them. He was short and plump and looked out of place amongst the hard edges of the mountains, but the appearance was deceptive. Gerry had made his name filming persecuted Kurds in the no-go zone of northern Iran and documenting the massacre of indigenous tribespeople by Muslim extremists in the jungles of Indonesia. He was tougher than he looked.

'Enjoying our little stroll, are we?'

Jamie smiled through gritted teeth. 'Every moment, Gerry.'

'Only I'm wondering what the hell you're doing here? Not that I'm displeased to have your company.' He gave Sarah an oily grin that reminded her he'd tried to seduce her on the first night and was still owed.

She waved a slim hand to push the dark hair from her eyes. 'We're making a documentary, Gerry,' she said sweetly, 'unless that little guy who keeps pointing the camera at me is some kind of pervert.'

'I'm aware of that, dear heart. But old Gerry likes to be in the know and old Gerry thinks we are going to a hell of a lot of trouble to film what is only going to be a tiny part of it. This documentary is principally about your friend Walter Brohm and the Raphael, the mysterious Tibetan crater will only get two minutes at the start, with a voiceover that could just as easily have gone with a stock picture of the SS and a panning shot across Everest.'

The film-maker produced a schedule, a map and a satellite image from his pack. He opened the map.

'Instead, we are here.' He pointed to a spot just inside the Tibetan border. 'Or so the guide tells me. Personally I haven't a bloody clue. Our destination is here. Another two days' march away.' He placed the satellite image on the map. 'The crater that Brohm and his SS Ahnenerbe chums explored in nineteen thirty-seven and which our lords and masters are so interested in. When we get there we give the crater the once-over, film you and your piece of tottie with anything of particular interest and then you do your "Once more into the breach" piece to camera. As I say, a great deal of effort for little return in a place that gives me the willies. My bosses were most insistent that we filmed in the crater, and I gather the reason they were most insistent is that Vanderbilt Media whistled, and when Vanderbilt whistles my lords and masters roll over and beg. Not that I'm complaining, I'm getting a rather large fee and enough danger money to make a couple of nights cuddling the bedbugs in a Chinese jail just about bearable. I only thought that, perhaps, you had a little more information on the whys and wherefores that would put my troubled mind to rest?'

Jamie gave him his most reassuring grin. ''Fraid, we can't help you there, Gerry. The only thing they told us was that this would be like taking a stroll down

Piccadilly with you in charge, and I must say they've been spot on so far.'

Back in London, Simon studied Jamie's tropical fish with the care of a surgeon about to make his first cut, a cardboard cylinder held steady in his hand above the tank. For the second or third time in a week he wished to God he'd never agreed to feed the bloody things. How much? That was the question. Too much and he'd kill them. Too little and they might starve to death before Jamie came back. A knock on the door saved him from having to make a decision..

The man who filled the frame looked as broad as he was tall and the bruises on his face seemed to suggest he'd been in some kind of accident. Simon wasn't the kind of person to start at shadows, but he found his presence intimidating.

'Can I help you?' he asked.

'Can you hear anything?'

'No,' Jamie yawned, blinking against the brightness barely filtered by the thin material of the tent.

'That might not be good.'

'Why?'

'Because every other morning we've woken on this trip the porters have been making breakfast and being darned noisy about it.'

'Stay here,' he ordered, struggling out of his sleeping bag and putting on his trousers. He wrapped his scarf around his neck, pulled on his hiking boots and his jacket. He was reaching for the tent flap when something occurred to him. 'Aren't you going to argue with me?'

She had her arms behind her head outside the sleeping bag, like a butterfly waiting for the right moment to leave the chrysalis.

'I reckon you can handle things until I'm ready.'

He shook his head, then crept back and kissed her on the lips. 'Thanks.'

'For what?'

'For nothing.'

He pulled back the flaps and emerged into air the texture of raw silk and stark morning sunshine that created razor-edged shadows among the rocks and hollows. They'd made camp in a stony, sheltered bowl close to a stream of cloudy green meltwater. In that first second he knew Sarah had been right. Everyone else was sitting in a circle in the centre of the tents with their hands on the back of their heads. The lip of the bowl seemed to have sprouted trees, or maybe, since they hadn't seen a tree for two days, that should be statues. Their stillness reminded him of the saints on St Peter's Basilica as they stood overlooking the circle of tents. Only saints didn't carry AK-47 assault rifles.

'I think you'd better join us,' he called back over his shoulder.

A rifle barrel twitched a silent command, but, despite an empty feeling in his guts that had nothing to do with missing breakfast, Jamie stood his ground and waited until Sarah came out of the tent.

'Trouble, huh?' She surveyed the armed men on the rocks around them. 'Who are—'

They didn't need an interpreter to tell them that the barked command meant shut up and join the rest, and they took their places at the edge of the little group of porters and film-makers and assumed the same hands-on-head position of surrender.

Jamie kept his face down, but his eyes checked out their captors' equipment and weaponry. They didn't appear to be regular soldiers of the People's Liberation Army, but that wasn't necessarily reassuring. The Chinese authorities had created a paramilitary police force of immigrants, the *wujing*, to patrol the frontier, and no doubt there were plenty of men among the impoverished tribes of the plateau ready to accept Peking's bounty for fugitives or interlopers attempting to breach the porous border between the Tibet Autonomous Region and India's northern provinces. They were armed with what looked like Soviet SKS carbines and AK-47s, but he guessed they would be the Chinese variant, the Type 56, which was virtually indistinguishable from the Moscow version. The only difference was the folding bayonet attached to the barrel, but he hoped he wouldn't get close enough to make the comparison. He had handled the AK during his time preparing for Sandhurst and he remembered it for the vicious kick and the awfully large hole the 7.62mm bullets made in anything unfortunate enough to get in their way. The weapons appeared clean and well cared for, unlike their owners, who were uniformly hatchet-faced, filthy and wrapped in a variety of layered outer clothing that would be well-suited to the ever-changing climate of the mountains. Low over heavy brows, they wore the type of long-eared, knitted caps that young men in Britain sometimes put on for a joke during wintry weather and their footwear was an incongruous mix of battered climbing boots and branded track shoes. He felt Sarah move beside him and he willed her not to draw attention to herself. One thing was certain, they had to wait this out and deal with the cards as they fell. No chance of fighting. No chance of running. These men would hunt them down within minutes. It was much more sensible to cooperate. If they were lucky it would mean a couple of days trekking and a couple more in a Lhasa jail before they were booted out. He didn't like to think about what would happen if they weren't lucky.

Two men scrambled down from the rim of the bowl and snapped an order before hustling Ganesh away from the rest of the group. One gunman sat cross-legged in front of the terrified Tibetan, while the other kept his Kalashnikov conspicuously sighted on the captive's middle.

From Ganesh's near hysterical replies, Jamie guessed that he was being questioned about the identity of the westerners. Eventually, the interrogator nodded and his companion shouted a command. Four more men descended into the bowl, ordered the porters to pick up their loads and herded them off down the trail along with the terrified interpreter.

Despite the intense cold, Jamie could feel rivulets of

sweat running down his spine. The scenario reminded him of stories he'd read about Vietnam and Cambodia. No witnesses to testify to the fate of the filthy western capitalists or CIA stooges. From the desperate glances Gerry was darting at him, he guessed the film-maker had read them too. He shook his head. Making a run for it would only make things worse. At least this way he'd get a chance to plead for Sarah's life before someone put a bullet in him.

By now the remaining militia men were going through the tents and removing anything of value. Gerry winced as they fumbled with the expensive camera equipment, but Jamie only had eyes for the interrogator who walked towards the remaining captives with a high-stepping mountain man's stride. The gunman had tawny, leopard's eyes and unsmiling, mongoloid features. The eyes surveyed them, deliberately going over each man in turn, then, with a slight frown, turning to Sarah. What did the frown mean? Maybe she reminded him of someone. Maybe killing women was against his rules. Then again, this man didn't look as if he had any rules.

The Tibetan rapped out a string of orders. Immediately, half of the remaining men pushed the film team towards the entrance of the hollow, gesturing at them to pick up the camera equipment on the way. Gerry shot Jamie a helpless glance as they were led off with a pair of gunmen on either flank, but he had worries of his own. One of the remaining captors attempted to usher Sarah away, and as she was led off protesting loudly, he moved to go with her. The result was a rifle butt in the belly that doubled him over and left him dry-retching into the earth.

'My wife,' he choked. 'I have to stay with my wife.' Christ, he felt as if he'd been kicked by a donkey. His spleen was somewhere in there and a ruptured spleen was going to be bloody inconvenient in the middle of the Himalayas. He let out a long gasp and fell forward on his knees with his face to the ground. A pair of scuffed leather boots appeared in front of his nose. He noticed that one was laced up with packaging string.

He raised his head and looked up into a pair of merciless amber eyes. The barrel of the Kalashnikov hooked on to his scarf and drew him upwards.

'King's, isn't it?' the interrogator said in perfect public-school English. 'I went to Trinity myself and we thought you chaps were nothing but a bunch of smelly, beer-swilling Reds.'

XLV

The blank-eyed buildings of the ruined monastery perched precariously on a cliff at the head of the long valley, clinging like moss to the fractured grey stone. They'd marched for hours without a break and Jamie and Sarah were dead on their feet by the time they arrived just as darkness fell. Throughout the trek the Englishman's head had been filled with questions for the commander of what he now realized was a group of Tibetan insurgents loyal to the deposed Dalai Lama, but the leader only smiled grimly and told him to save his breath.

When they reached the monastery they were allocated a tiny monk's cell on the second level. While Jamie checked the contents of his rucksack, Sarah spread her sleeping bag on the stone bed and closed her eyes. Before she lapsed into sleep she whispered, 'What was that stuff about the wife, Saintclair? You haven't even asked me yet.' He tried to come up with a suitably clever reply, but her breathing told him she was already unconscious. Exhausted beyond words, he leaned against the bare mud wall and allowed his head to fall between his knees.

After what felt like only seconds, a hand touched his shoulder and he opened his eyes to find one of the young Tibetans smiling shyly at him. He followed the boy down to the ground floor where the commander sat by a yak dung fire reading what appeared to be the documentary producer's diary.

He looked up as Jamie entered.

'Tell me why you wish to visit our sacred place?'

'This is madness, of course,' he said when Jamie had finished. 'The *wujing* and the PLA patrol the roads and the passes. It was only a matter of time before you were discovered. If the *wujing* had taken you they would have raped the woman and shot you all, then left your bodies in a gully for the vultures. You were fortunate that we found you first. I have sent the film-makers back; we cannot afford to have our faces emblazoned on Sky or the BBC. The porters will also return once they have helped replenish our stores.'

'Why have you kept us here?'

He found himself fixed by the unblinking predator's eyes. 'Because you intrigue me. Your story is so unlikely it could well be true, but there are other possibilities. Perhaps you are CIA, who abandoned us many years ago, but who have lately been attempting to woo our representatives in Washington. Or maybe this is one of those subtle puzzles the Chinese are so fond of and you have been sent to spy on us, or draw us into a trap. If that is the case, we will all die together.'

'I told the truth.' Jamie waited for a reaction, but none came. 'You know all about us, but I know nothing about you?'

The guerrilla stared from the window into the darkness. 'We do not go by our given names, for it could endanger our families here and in India, but you may call me Tenzin. As to *what* we are,' he paused for a moment, seeking the precise definition, 'why, we are ghosts.'

The word, in the faint, flickering light from the tiny fire, with the shadows dancing on the grey mud walls, sent a shiver through Jamie. Tenzin removed his heavy woollen jacket to expose the maroon robe of a Tibetan monk.

'Yes, I am of the Gelug, Mr Saintclair. But I am also a patriot. Why should it surprise you? The tradition of the warrior priest has been part of your own culture since the dawn of Christianity. Did not an entire sect, the Knights of St John, fight in the Crusades?'

Jamie had placed Tenzin in his mid-forties, but now he could see the monk's face properly he realized he was at least a decade younger, his features prematurely aged by the privations of the life he chose to live. 'I had the impression that the only opposition to the Chinese in Tibet was of the non-violent variety.'

'Aye, and it has been a spectacular success, has it not? More than a million Tibetans dead since the invasion in nineteen fifty, hundreds of thousands still being tortured in Chinese prisons, our people brutalized, our land plundered and polluted, our children taught lies, our religion drowned in the blood of our nuns and monks. Six thousand monasteries destroyed. What you see around you was once a great centre of learning, now it is home only to spiders, bats and vultures – and ghosts.'

The tone was flat and emotionless, but the words evoked images of whole lifetimes of pain and suffering. Jamie struggled for the right response and failed to find it. 'I'm sorry, I didn't know.'

Tenzin laughed. 'Why should you? A dispute between neighbours in a faraway place. The strong overcome the weak, but Quomolonga is still open to your mountaineering tourists. Tibet was not the Falklands. The oppressed did not speak English, so why should you care about us?'

'You speak English, and speak it very well,' Jamie pointed out.

'Of course. I was sent to school in England from Delhi, where my father was one of the fortunate few who grew rich in exile. At Winchester I proved to be intelligent, but exotic, and was treated the way exotic boys are in your public schools. That was where I learned the futility of passive resistance. When I went to Cambridge I did not stand out quite so much. I made many friends, some of whom now support my little Crusade here in the mountains. Kundun, the Dalai Lama, does not approve of what we do, but we do it all the same. A patrol or a convoy ambushed up in the passes. A *wujing* garrison attacked while they sleep in their fort. We try to protect those who wish to flee to India. Futile pinpricks, you might argue, but enough to remind the invaders that Tibet still has teeth and they are not welcome here. Then we drift away, like smoke, across the border. Tibet is a place where myth and legend and truth quickly become indistinguishable, Mr Saintclair. Word of our deeds is whispered among the oppressed and gives them hope. So we are the Ghosts of the Four Rivers, the Kamba guerrillas reborn, and proof that some Tibetans are still willing to fight and die for freedom.'

A young fighter entered the room with a rifle on his shoulder and while Tenzin gave him his orders Jamie pondered the reality behind the softly spoken statement. *We drift away like smoke.* He knew the truth must be brutally different. The Chinese would send whole divisions of specially trained mountain troops to hunt down men like these. The dead eyes of Tenzin's followers told their own tale. Of men living on the edge, or perhaps beyond it. Men who knew their time was short and their end inevitable. For the Ghosts of the Four Rivers every new breath and every heartbeat was another battle won.

When the young man left, Jamie said, 'I would have thought Beijing would put pressure on India to stop you from making these incursions?'

Tenzin leaned forward over the fire and allowed the flames to light the leaves of a twig, which immediately gave off fragrant, perfume-scented smoke. He handed Jamie another twig and invited him to do the same.

'Now you have committed an act of defiance against the regime and are as liable to imprisonment and torture as I. The burning of juniper branches pleases Buddha, but displeases the oppressors. The Indians ignore us, because the Chinese do not acknowledge our existence. To do so would be an admission of failure, a loss of face. They wish the world to believe that after fifty years of their benign rule Tibet is a peaceful, ordered society. In their misplaced pride lies our strength.' He raised his head to look directly into Jamie's eyes. 'When we talked earlier of the sacred place, it seemed to me that your story was not complete.'

Jamie studied him warily. He'd limited his tale of the expedition to what the documentary team had known and meant to keep it that way. 'Why would you think that?'

'Perhaps it is a coincidence that a special unit of Chinese engineers have also been taking an interest in it for the past month?'

'Tell him, Jamie. Tell him it all.'

He looked up to see Sarah standing at the top of the stairs. 'All right.' He nodded. And told Tenzin about Walter Brohm and the discovery that would change the world.

The crater was enormous and as Jamie watched through binoculars from a sheltered hide on the rim a mile away, he realized Tenzin had been right and there had never been any chance they would get close to the shaft, never mind inside it. Chinese soldiers swarmed round the entrance while bulldozers and earth-moving equipment stripped the earth for hundreds of yards around and loaded it on to lorries that shuttled back and forth up a roadway of crushed rock that had been dug into the crater side.

'Let me see.' Reluctantly, he gave the binoculars up to Sarah who had been twitching impatiently at his side.

'Make sure the sun doesn't catch the lens,' he warned.

'I'm not an idiot, Saintclair.' She focused on the digging operation. 'This has to be costing them millions. Most of the equipment would have been flown in by helicopter. Whatever they're mining here must be incredibly valuable.'

'It is not a mine, it is a shrine,' Tenzin said patiently. 'A sacred place for a thousand years. And they are digging up nothing but worthless earth and rock. They seek the Sun Stone, or traces of its passing, but you cannot steal what has already been stolen.'

Sun Stone. The hair stood up on the back of Jamie's neck as he heard the phrase for the first time.

'Long before Buddha's time, a meteorite landed here.' Tenzin saw Jamie's look. 'Yes, Mr Saintclair, I'm something of an amateur geologist – I picked it up at Cambridge when I was studying applied physics, and a monk has plenty of time for reading. As you can see, it must have been very large to cause a crater of this size. Ninety per cent of the object would have burned up in the atmosphere and when it struck it would have disintegrated on impact, creating a huge dust cloud. This is an area rich in such craters, though most are much smaller. Once, a man could become rich collecting the residue of fallen meteorites, glassified minerals known as tektites. But this was a meteorite like no other. It contained a substance so indestructible that it drove a tunnel eight feet in diameter a mile and a half into the living rock. If you move a little to the left, Miss Grant, you will see the entrance to the shaft.'

'How do you know so much about all this?' Sarah asked.

'It has been passed down through the generations,' Tenzin said simply, as if no further explanation was required. 'The Holy Men of that time believed the devastation the meteorite caused was the wrath of the Sun god. They came here to carry out a ritual that would appease the god.'

'A sacrifice?'

Tenzin nodded sadly. 'They were less enlightened times. Seven prisoners were led down the shaft the meteor had driven into the earth, but as they prepared the victims for the sacrifice they discovered something astonishing.'

Jamie found he was holding his breath and when he looked at Sarah, he saw her eyes were wide, like a little girl listening to a frightening bedtime story.

'The Sun Stone. It was like nothing they had ever seen before – dark, perfectly spherical – and it had a quality that amazed them. It was not subject to the laws of gravity. Or more correctly it was gravity neutral. It floated. The ancients believed that the Sun god had sent them the seed of the earth's destruction and they feared it. They decided that it must never again be touched by the light of its creator. For two hundred generations the Sun Stone was kept in its lead-lined casket, never again to pollute the earth or the water or the air. Then the Germans came.'

XLVI

Back in the relative sanctuary of the monastery, Sarah stared into the flickering, oxygen-starved flames of a tiny fire. Thick cloth squares covered the windows of this lower room to ensure no light could escape, and the smoke filtered up through a hole in the roof to dissipate through openings in the upper storeys. She could hear the soft snicker and rustle as the building's population of bats prepared for their nightly hunt. The contrast between now and the immense focusing of technology they had witnessed earlier made her head swim. It was as if she had been sucked into some kind of time warp that had swept her back to the fourteenth century. Yet the reality of the crater had accompanied them like some vengeful spectre and was here all around them in the room.

'So the Sun Stone is the key? Walter Brohm discovered a substance from another world and was determined to exploit it?'

'Whatever we happen to think of Brohm, he was a

brilliant physicist,' Jamie agreed. 'Right up there with Oppenheimer, maybe even Einstein. It wouldn't have taken him long to work out that this was something completely outside his experience.'

'And he spent the next eight years working to divine its secrets.'

'Yes, and if he'd had the chance to work on it exclusively he might have done it, except the war got in the way. When he was recruited to the project to build Hitler's nuclear bomb nobody would have given a damn about his obsession. From what my grandfather said in the journal he was forced to work in secret. That would have been at best disloyalty, maybe even treason. Walter Brohm was the original misunderstood genius.'

'But he never gave up.'

'Not Brohm. He was ruthless and ambitious and he saw in the Sun Stone an opportunity to carve his place in history. Ethical or moral dilemmas would never have entered his mind. Somehow he discovered what the material was and what it could be used for. It was his misfortune that by the time he had proof of its true potential Adolf Hitler had lost faith in his nuclear scientists.'

'He also feared it. What does that tell us?'

Tenzin's voice cut across the conversation. 'It tells us the ancient priests were correct, Miss Grant. The Sun Stone has the potential to destroy the world.'

They stared at him.

'Don't you understand?' the Tibetan went on. 'In the Sun Stone lies the power of the sun. It is the material that fuels the stars. A source of infinite energy but also a source of infinite destruction. What has more potential than nuclear fission? What is the Holy Grail of science?'

Still they didn't grasp what he was telling them.

'Nuclear fusion. Controlled, limitless power from the joining of two atomic nuclei to form a heavier single nucleus. Fusion was first achieved in the nineteen thirties, but it has never been harnessed as a reliable source of nuclear energy. Whoever discovers a way to control it will have the economic power to hold the world to ransom. And the military power. Because with controlled nuclear fusion, comes the fusion bomb. Potentially a hundred times more powerful than a conventional nuclear bomb.'

'If they know so much about nuclear fusion and have been working on it for so long why can't they control it?' Jamie asked.

'Because they have never been able to discover the necessary catalyst that would give them both the high energy output they need and the control to contain it in a fusion reactor. I think this Walter Brohm believed he had discovered that catalyst.'

'The Sun Stone?'

Tenzin nodded and his unsmiling face darkened, but Sarah interrupted before he could continue.

'You said a fusion bomb could be a hundred times more powerful than anything we have now? That would be hugely destructive but it still wouldn't destroy the world.'

'That is correct, but it assumes that whoever builds

the bomb understands what they are dealing with. A fusion bomb is basically uncontrolled nuclear fusion, a chain reaction that results in a thermonuclear explosion. What if there is no limit to that chain reaction? If the stone is truly the material that fuels the stars, it could be the catalyst not for an unlimited source of energy, but one that turns the earth into an inferno that burns for a hundred million years.'

For a few moments, they were each lost in their own vision of the end of the world. Eventually, Jamie said quietly, 'Why did you bring us here?'

Tenzin's eyes narrowed and his voice became solemn. 'It seems to me that some force has linked you irrevocably to the Sun Stone. You were given the journal, which in turn provided you with Walter Brohm's name. Now it has brought you here. You were sent to me for a reason. I think every step of your journey has been guided towards one outcome.'

'And what is that outcome?'

'You must return to Europe and continue your quest. I believe that only you can ensure the Sun Stone never falls into the hands of those whose greed or ambition or foolishness will destroy us all.'

Sarah stared at him, confusion plain in her eyes – along with something else that Jamie couldn't read.

'But how are we supposed to do that? You can't place this responsibility on us. We're just . . . just two ordinary people. We don't have the strength, or the resources.' She shook her head. 'It's too big. This is something for governments to deal with.'

'On the contrary, Miss Grant.' Tenzin's face was grave. 'It is governments you must beware. Governments like the one that has invaded and oppressed my country would give anything and do anything to lay their hands on the Sun Stone and release its power. Communism has no soul, just as fascism had none, but what about capitalism? Do you think the Americans would be different? In nineteen seventy-one Richard Nixon betrayed my people for a handshake and a smile from Mao Zedong; are we to expect any better from the current president?'

'But what can we do?'

'When the time comes you will have a decision to make, only then will you know what to do.'

Sarah shot an anguished glance towards Jamie, but he had already made up his mind. He felt as if he was bathed in the aura created by the monk's strength and resolve. This had been his fate from the start. This was the final chapter of Matthew Sinclair's story. He would finish what his grandfather had started.

'We should leave in the morning.'

Tenzin set a punishing pace as the fourteen-strong column headed back towards the border, but on the second and third days he became progressively warier. Twice they took cover beneath the rocks at the sound of an aircraft flying at altitude somewhere above them.

'We are fortunate that they do not have the spare parts to keep their Black Hawk helicopters in the air,' the Tibetan confided to Jamie. 'The J-7 and J-11 jets based up at Lhasa are too fast to do us any harm among the mountains, but there are reconnaissance planes flying from smaller airfields all along the frontier and if they spotted us, they would call in a patrol to intercept us.'

'I thought the Black Hawk was an American helicopter,' Sarah said.

'That is correct, Miss Grant. Your American defenders of democracy sanctioned the sale of twenty UH-60s to China during the nineteen eighties, which they swiftly used to suppress any resurgence of democracy in Tibet. Ironic, is it not?'

Late in the afternoon, one of the insurgents who had been covering the rear of the little column jogged up and conferred with Tenzin. The monk nodded and his face was grim when he turned to Jamie and Sarah.

'They are coming.'

If Jamie believed the pace had been hard over the past three days he quickly discovered how wrong he'd been. The Tibetans relieved them of their rucksacks and Tenzin set off at a trot that quickly had Jamie's lungs screaming for oxygen. Only the knowledge of what would happen if the Chinese caught them kept him going, but, even so, after ten minutes he was willing the monk to ease off or turn an ankle, anything to stop the pain in his chest. It wasn't until Sarah began reeling on her feet and two of the insurgents were forced to support her that Tenzin slowed to a brisk walk.

'We must stay ahead of them until dark,' the Tibetan

leader explained. 'If they are *wujing,* they have learned to fear the night and the Ghosts of the Four Rivers and they will halt, while we carry on.' Jamie's heart almost stopped at the thought of crossing this unforgiving landscape in the inky blackness of a Himalayan night, but Tenzin's next words sobered him still further. 'It is possible the soldiers who follow us are mountain-trained special forces troops. These men fear nothing and are equipped with night-vision equipment.'

'How will we know?' Jamie gasped.

'If they are still with us at dawn,' Tenzin said, and picked up the pace again.

What followed was the longest night of their lives. Tenzin kept up the relentless rhythm of the march for hour after hour, stopping only once to allow them to rest and take a drink. Ten minutes at the trot, followed by ten minutes at the walk to conserve their dwindling strength. Jamie and Sarah ran with a Tibetan on either side whispering incomprehensible words of encouragement as they kept their faltering charges upright through the rocks. In the gossamer-aired darkness every breath felt like a dying gasp, every heartbeat the hammer blow that preceded a seizure. Eventually, they travelled as if in a dream, their bodies pushed beyond the human norms of pain and exhaustion, their movements automatic and their minds seeking refuge in some weightless nirvana. Time or distance had no meaning, they could have marched three miles or thirty. It was only with the gathering Himalayan dawn, that soft, roseate light which garlanded the faraway peaks like a pink halo, that they realized they were alive, would live, and with it came the dread knowledge that soon they would know whether the martyrdom in the darkness had been worthwhile.

Thirty minutes into the new day Tenzin ordered a halt, but insisted everyone stay on their feet. Jamie hated him for it, but he knew that if he had slumped to the ground he would never have risen again. Sarah swayed between her two minders with her eyes closed, mumbling to herself. The Tibetan stared at the far horizon. Jamie followed his gaze, but could see nothing but barren grey rocks.

'They are here. Two miles.'

'How do you know?'

'The wind carries their message. I do not know how, I only know.'

'Then we're finished.' Jamie fought the urge to let himself collapse to the ground. He and Sarah might be kept alive, but there was no hope for this man he had come to respect and admire.

'Perhaps not,' Tenzin said. 'Like most special forces, they operate in small units, perhaps only four or five strong. If they originally accompanied a *wujing* patrol they will have left them behind during the night. It's possible they may look at us and decide we are too strong for them. Then again, they are the best trained troops in the People's Liberation Army – the equivalent of your Special Air Service – and they have pride. That pride may keep them coming. One thing is in our favour: we are less than two miles from the border.

If we can stay ahead of them we will reach Indian territory.'

'Will they stop at the border?'

Tenzin shrugged. 'We will see. It depends on what orders they have and how important to them we are. If they came across our trail by chance and decided to track us, they will not cross. If they know we were at the crater . . .'

He shouted a command and the column moved off, with two scouts in the lead and two guarding the rear. The man on Jamie's left grinned at him, but the grin didn't reach his eyes. Above the usual aroma of yak butter and unwashed body Jamie could smell something else, rank and strong. Fear. He knew the other man would have the same scent in his nostrils.

He turned to encourage Sarah, but she was beyond encouragement, hanging between the two Tibetans like a rag doll. He gritted his teeth and ran.

The first shot came when they had covered less than a mile, a whipcrack in the thin air that echoed like a volley from the mountains around them. Jamie staggered to a halt and looked backwards along the track. He could see them now, six tiny figures dogging their trail the way a stoat follows a rabbit.

'Come.' Tenzin shook his shoulder. 'That was just a warning shot. They will be in range soon. Keep going.'

Jamie willed his legs to move and took up the mental refrain of the military route march. *One foot in front of the other. One foot in front of the other.* Another shot cracked out and he heard the distinctive zzzip-zzzzing of a bullet ricocheting from a boulder to their left.

Tenzin barked a new order and two of the Tibetans peeled off and moved into the rocks by the side of the trail. Jamie felt sick. The two men were the price of his life, and Sarah's. No matter how determined the pursuit, the Chinese soldiers would have to deal with the threat to their flank. It would delay them. Not for long. Two barely trained guerrillas against the élite of the Chinese army. But long enough for Tenzin to get them to the border.

With the knowledge that they were going to survive, his legs found new strength and he shrugged off the man beside him, staggering along under his own power. More shots followed but none came close. They had reached a broad escarpment fringed by jagged, boulder-strewn hills that first rose then plummeted away almost vertically to the south. The only way out was ahead where two peaks were split by a pass that Jamie assumed must mark the border.

He risked a glance back just as a rattle of automatic fire confirmed the first contact between the pursuers and the two men left behind. Jamie knew it would only be a matter of minutes, but the pass was closer now and—

A muted thunder turned into a paralysing, gut-shaking roar. For a split second a monstrous shadow blotted out the sky, then it was gone. He looked up to see a turbo-prop plane similar to an RAF Hercules sailing towards the pass. As he watched the pilot banked across their route and a string of white dots left the big plane. Within seconds they had blossomed into fifteen or twenty massive parachutes. At first he thought it must be some sort of supply drop, then he realized that the size of the parachutes was to compensate for the thin air in the mountains and what hung below them was not canisters, but more of the special forces troops who pursued them. They were trapped.

XLVII

Tenzin reacted instantly. He broke right towards the hills a quarter of a mile away where the boulders offered more cover than the open trail. Chiru, the youngest of the guerrillas, attached himself to Jamie's shoulder and shepherded him away from danger, all the time darting wary glances back to where the paratroops were now deploying in loose formation. The Tibetans formed a protective circle round the two outsiders, but Jamie knew it was only a matter of time before they were overwhelmed. Against six, even six of the Chinese élite special forces, they would have had a chance, but not against four times that number. They were hopelessly outgunned.

A rock formation in front of Jamie shattered and a heartbeat later he heard the distinctive ripsaw clatter of a burst of automatic weapons fire. As a storm of lead savaged the air around them the man to his left gave a sharp cry and fell to the ground. Without thinking, Jamie picked up the fighter's rifle and stripped him of his ammunition while Chiru checked the fallen man for signs of life. The boy shook his head and they ran together to the base of the hills where Tenzin had set up a defensive perimeter among the rocks, with Sarah, who looked dazed and sick, at its centre.

'What now?' Jamie demanded.

'We can hold them here for a while, I think,' Tenzin said, his dust-coated hawk's face creased in a frown of concentration.

Jamie saw he was right. The Chinese paratroop commander now faced the choice of attacking over the open ground the Tibetans had just crossed or a long flanking movement to the east. The first would cost him casualties, the second might give the beleaguered insurgents a chance to escape. It all depended on just how determined he was to kill them.

A sustained burst from a dozen assault rifles on fully automatic signalled his decision. Jamie curled into a foetal ball as the rocks around him exploded. For the first time in many days he thought of his grandfather. This combination of exhaustion and sheer terror was the life Matthew Sinclair had lived for six long years. The knowledge lit some spark in him and he raised his head and sighted the Type 56 carbine on the open ground just as a dozen green-clad soldiers broke cover and rushed forward, shooting as they ran. All hell broke loose around him as the Tibetans opened fire and Jamie joined in with short controlled bursts that set the rifle shuddering in his hands. The man who had found Matthew Sinclair's journal would have fired warning shots over the attacker's heads. The man who had read it and fought for it took deliberate aim at the chest of the leading attacker. His first shots flew high and he automatically sighted lower, watching as the shots kicked up dust among the charging men. First one went down, spun by a burst that caught him in the upper chest, then a second who dropped like a stone. In an instant, the landscape was empty, the survivors melting into the dusty ground.

Tenzin called out an order and the firing died away, apart from a few desultory single shots from the Chinese four hundred yards off on the far side of the track.

Jamie turned and saw Sarah struggling to get to her feet. He ran to her at a crouch and pulled her down. 'Do you want to get your bloody head shot off?'

'Hey, Saintclair,' she mumbled, 'I can look after myself.'

Jamie lifted her chin and wiped flecks of vomit from her lips. Her eyes were dilated. His heart sank as he recognized the signs. Altitude sickness. The longer they stayed at this height the worse it would get. Unless he could get her out of here and down to the foothills she could die.

'Sure you can, tough guy.' He matched the words with a reassuring smile, but she wasn't fooled.

'Screwed, huh?'

''Fraid it looks like it, love.'

'We gonna surrender?'

'I'm not sure they'll give us the option.'

A soft plop like a bubble of mud bursting in a hot

spring punctuated the sentence and he threw himself on top of her.

'Christ, Jamie—'

'Mortar!'

The explosion twenty yards to the right sent razor shards of shattered stone whizzing through their refuge and Jamie cried out as he felt the sting of something slicing across his brow.

Sarah reached out and touched his head and her fingers came away red. 'You're hurt?'

'It's just a scratch,' he insisted, because it was, but for a moment he felt like a bit-part actor in a cowboy movie and the thought almost made him smile. Tenzin and Chiru were huddled in conversation behind a nearby rock and as Sarah dabbed ineffectually at his forehead with her sleeve, the Tibetan leader crawled to where they lay.

'There may be a way to get you out of here, it will be dang—' The next mortar blast was much closer and to their left. Tenzin frowned. 'Ranging shots. You know what comes next. Chiru will lead your way; with him you have a chance, stay and . . .'

Jamie knew what staying meant. The next round from the two-inch mortar, or the one after that, was going to land in the little circle of rocks and kill or disable them all. It was the simple arithmetic of war. Two or three ranging shots and one in the bull's-eye. But there was something else. 'What do you mean he will lead us? What about you and the others?'

Tenzin's amber eyes were lit with the same inner glow

373

as the night he had burned the juniper leaves over the fire. 'We stay. The Ghosts of the Four Rivers will cover your retreat.'

Jamie shook his head. 'But—'

The Tibetan was already moving. 'There is no time for buts, Mr Saintclair. If you go, it must be now.'

'No,' Sarah gasped. 'We can't leave you.'

Tenzin gave a sad, almost embarrassed smile. 'But you must, Miss Grant. Only you can ensure that the Sun Stone is never used for what Walter Brohm intended. Please.' His voice was urgent now. 'Go now. You have your job to do; I have mine.'

Chiru plucked at Jamie's jacket, and the Briton took Sarah by the arm, but there was still one thing he had to do. He unwrapped the King's College scarf from his neck and placed it formally round Tenzin's.

The monk's eyes softened and he bowed. 'Now go,' he hissed.

Chiru led them away to the left, hugging the base of the hills and staying low among the boulders. The slight figure of the young Tibetan seemed to merge with the rocks around him and he moved silently over stone and scree. Jamie, with his arm supporting Sarah's weight, struggled to keep up. When they had gone thirty paces the gunfire resumed and he knew that Tenzin was drawing the attention and fire of the Chinese. His mind counted down the seconds to the inevitable explosion and it came half a minute later, but the bomb must have fallen short because the shooting continued without pause. Chiru hissed at them and he guessed the boy was telling them to hurry. He risked one last look backwards but all he could see was rocks.

He knew that back in the clearing, Tenzin would be issuing his orders to his guerrillas. In his mind he saw the young men check their weapons. This day was always going to come. In some ways it was a comfort to them to be dying in the company of their friends. Better this than to die in the cold on some bleak mountainside with only prayers for companionship. He waited for the inevitable, saw the bomb arcing towards them, a black blob against the blue sky, first slow, then incredibly fast as it passed the top of its flight and plummeted down. His body cringed as he heard the blast and imagined the carnage in that confined space among the rocks.

This time the explosion was followed by silence and Jamie had to force himself to keep moving and not think about what was happening behind them. Sarah seemed to be drifting in and out of consciousness. Her body was almost a dead weight and combined with the weapon he carried made it almost impossible to maintain pace with their guide. Chiru moved out of sight around a buttress projecting from the hill and he resolved to call the young Tibetan back to help out. By the time he dragged Sarah to the corner Chiru was forty paces ahead. As Jamie opened his mouth to shout, a figure in grey-green camouflage rose silently from the left of the path and took aim at the Tibetan's back. Jamie brought up the assault rifle and dropped Sarah in the same movement. The Chinese commando heard the sound of her outraged protest and half turned as the gun kicked in Jamie's hands, a four-round volley that stitched the soldier from belly to chest and threw him back among the boulders. Chiru turned, his face pale, and ran to where the man lay groaning by the path.

The boy looked at Jamie and called something in Tibetan. When the Briton didn't move he retrieved the commando's spare magazines and threw them towards him. Jamie picked them up and stuffed them in his belt, then pulled Sarah to her feet. Her eyes rolled like the numbers in a slot machine and it was clear she barely knew where she was. Chiru took her other arm and they set off without another word.

The mortar blast threw Tenzin against the base of the hill in an eruption of heat and flame and his ribs cracked as he hit the rocks. For a few seconds he lay stunned, but when he looked up at least one of his men was still firing. He struggled to his knees as the staccato clatter of the machine guns rent the air. His padded jacket was torn in several places and blood and body parts painted the area where the bomb had fallen. The Tibetan was only alive because two of the guerrillas had taken the brunt of the explosion. One more was dead, and two others too badly wounded to fight, but a second man dragged himself to his feet and began firing at the commandos. Tenzin crawled to one of the men and filled his pockets with the Chinese-manufactured grenades he carried. Then he picked up his rifle and set off after Jamie.

*   *   *

Jamie had no idea where Chiru was leading them, all he could do was put his faith in the Tibetan. The firing resumed, which meant at least one of the guerrillas had survived the latest mortar blast, but he doubted they would last long against a sustained Chinese attack. The commando he had shot must have been one of the original group who had been tracking them, possibly sent ahead while the rest dealt with the two-man ambush Tenzin had set. That meant the others would be coming this way. Tenzin had said Chiru knew a way out, but if they didn't find it soon it would be too late. The young Tibetan pushed ahead without speaking, dragging Sarah's arm, but gradually he slowed and Jamie understood he was looking for something. Chiru searched the rock at the base of the hill with a puzzled frown.

'Christ, don't tell me he's looking for a cave.'

Sarah's eyes focused on him for a moment. 'What?'

'I think he's looking for a bloody cave.' Jamie heard the hysteria in his own voice. 'It'll take them about five minutes to find us.'

She muttered something before her head slumped forward again. He smoothed back the hair on her brow. 'What did you say, Sarah?'

The eyes were dimming quickly and though her next words were only the slightest whisper, he understood them.

'Trust him.'

Chiru glared at him. '*Tshur log pa.*'

'What?'

The Tibetan gestured back the way they'd come.

'*Tshur log pa!*'

'You mean back?'

'*Tshur log pa.*'

Jamie closed his eyes. 'There must be easier ways of getting killed.'

It took them another few minutes to find the opening. It wasn't a cave, or a tunnel. It was a fissure. A simple crack in the rock caused by God only knew what geological combination. Even Chiru's sharp eyes had missed it, because the entrance, if the narrow cleft could be graced with the word entrance, was dappled with shadows that were as good as a coat of camouflage paint against the bare stone of the hill. The opening was barely wide enough to accommodate one person at a time and to Jamie it appeared like the entrance to Hell. After the tunnels of the Hartz bunker complex he could hardly be accused of claustrophobia, but this was pushing luck to the limit. The crack split the hill in two, but no light reached its jagged depths and he had a horrible feeling that just the slightest tremor in the mountains would be enough to close it again. That feeling was reinforced as he pushed Sarah after Chiru. A few feet into the rock the young man turned to him and made a calming motion with his right hand. Or maybe he wanted them to get to their knees? No it was definitely a calming motion, which he reinforced by raising his eyes upwards. Jamie followed Chiru's gaze – and froze. Above them, like a pile of money in one of those fairground games that looks as if it needs just one more penny to make it fall, were tons, maybe hundreds of tons, of loose rock and scree. Jamie's eyes met Chiru's and they exchanged a sickly smile. He nodded, slowly, so as not to disturb the air, to show he understood.

'Where the hell are we?'

Sarah's shout sounded like a bomb blast in the enclosed space and Jamie automatically wrapped a hand across her mouth.

'MMM mm MMMMmmm mm.'

He turned her head towards him and looked into her eyes. With his free hand he put a finger to his mouth. 'Shhh.'

'Mmmm?'

He nodded and pointed upwards, allowing her to ease her mouth free.

'Jesus, Saintclair,' she breathed, 'you sure do know how to show a girl a good time.'

Chiru led them on, one painstaking step at a time. They moved silently, because they understood they were a knife-edge from destruction. Sometimes the crack narrowed so that they were forced to turn side-on to continue and Jamie had to drag the assault rifle behind him, but, gradually, they made their way through the hill until it widened and they could see daylight ahead.

Chiru halted at the exit, and slipped out of sight to one side. Jamie managed to squeeze past Sarah into the gap.

'Fuuuuck!'

He tried to merge with the rock as he teetered above one of those towering, limitless voids only the

Himalayas can produce. The vertiginous nothingness below drew him like a magnet, altering his centre of gravity and dragging him towards oblivion. All of India seemed to be laid out in front of him, the vibrant green of the foothills finally giving way to the hazy ochre of the faraway plains. The only thing between Jamie and the rocks a thousand feet below was air, and air had never seemed so insubstantial. He turned to go back, but Chiru, who perched comfortably on a foot-wide ledge to one side of the entrance, grabbed his arm. They stared into each other's eyes and Jamie was ready to rage at the younger man for leading them into this trap, but the look on the young Tibetan's face froze the words in his mouth. The desperate appeal required no translation. There was no other way. Jamie looked again into the depths below. Behind him, Sarah stirred restlessly.

Chiru pointed to a second, wider ledge that must have been a hundred feet below them, and signed to Jamie to follow his finger across the cliff. He had to look twice, but it was there, not even solid enough to be called insubstantial. A path. A fractured formation of stone perches fit only for mountain goats, but a path just the same. If they could get there, the Tibetan appeared to be saying, he could lead them to safety down that path. But how to get there?

Chiru read the look on his face and nodded. He slipped past Jamie on the sheer face and edged his way another six feet along the ledge to where a thin seam of scree split the cliff face. A dusty stream of frost-shattered rock and small rounded stones that led directly to the second ledge. At first glance, it looked vertical. Look again and there might be five or six degrees in it. But close enough to vertical to make it part of the cliff.

Chiru pointed down, grinned and stepped straight off the ledge.

'No!' Jamie grabbed at his arm, but it was too late.

At first it seemed Chiru must plummet down that awesome drop, but by some miracle his feet found enough purchase in the scree to support him. He slid swiftly down the river of stones in a cloud of thick dust, his body almost perpendicular to the cliff face. The soles of his designer sports shoes surfed the scree and controlled his speed and an inbred sense of balance kept him upright. Jamie watched him, waiting for the inevitable moment when the Tibetan stumbled and the controlled descent turned first into a tumbling rush before hurtling him into the abyss. But the moment never came. Chiru had lived and breathed these mountains for the seventeen years of his existence. The cliff paths and the scree slopes were his highways and he was as much in charge of his destiny as any civil servant walking down Whitehall. He glided to a halt as he reached the ledge and looked back towards Jamie and waved for him to follow.

For a moment, Jamie felt utterly abandoned. He realized Chiru hadn't deliberately left them; the Tibetan was a hill man, brought up in the harshest environment on the planet and taught from birth to be utterly independent. The show was designed to give them the confidence to follow him. But Jamie looked at that thin river of stones and experienced stark, paralysing terror. Would he have the courage to take that final step even if he didn't have Sarah to look after? And with her? No, it was impossible. The only thing they could do was turn back. He had already made the decision when he heard the rattle of machine gun fire echoing through the passageway. The Chinese would be here in moments.

No time to consider the consequences. Sarah was leaning against the side wall of the cleft only barely conscious and with her eyes closed. Jamie pulled her on to the ledge beside him and led her cautiously to the top of the scree slide. When they reached it, he dropped down to sit with his legs over the lip of the void and somehow manoeuvred her on to his lap. He placed the rifle by his right side and wrapped his left arm across her chest. She mumbled quietly and tried to turn her head towards him and in his terror he cursed her to stay still. The sound of gunfire grew more intense.

'Trust me,' he whispered in her ear. He closed his eyes and with a final plea to the God he only consulted in the direst of emergency he allowed himself to slip off the edge.

That first second when gravity took control was probably the most terrifying of his life. It seemed certain their combined mass must throw them out into the emptiness and carry them away to the rocks half a mile below. Instead, he found the scree scoring his back and his feet automatically seeking purchase among the stones. He slid toes first with his head forced back and he could feel the knife-edged rock ripping at his scalp. Sarah's weight forced his body into the scree, compounding the agony and slowing them still further. It was comforting that they weren't repeating Chiru's headlong rush, but Jamie knew that if they slowed too much it would be just as fatal. If they stopped, they would never get going again. He pushed with his arm to maintain their momentum. Strangely, after that first adrenalin surge of fear, he never felt in any danger until Chiru's hands lifted him to his feet and he had to open his eyes again.

Sarah sat groggily among the loose stones at his feet. 'That was fun. Can we do it again?'

He resisted the urge to throw her off the edge and exchanged a nerve-shattered grin with Chiru.

They were still grinning at each other when the solid thud of an explosion shook the earth beneath their feet and Jamie looked up to see dust and smoke vomit out of the passage where they'd emerged.

XLVIII

Tenzin passed the body of the slain Chinese commando and his sharp eyes caught the fissure that Chiru had missed on the first pass. He coughed sharply as another knife thrust of pain speared his chest and drove blood into his mouth. Every minute increased his exhaustion and dulled his senses. He realized that his wounds and the effect of the explosion were combining to sap his energy and blunt the power of his mind. Somewhere inside him the blood was pooling. When the amount of blood that escaped into his body was outweighed by the amount in his veins, he knew he would lapse into unconsciousness. He studied the crack in the grey wall and checked the first few yards of the narrow rock channel. He could hold them from inside, but only for a few minutes at most, probably less. There was a better way.

He began to climb the sheer outer slope, his hands and feet unerringly finding the tiny scuffs and crevices another man might miss. His blood stained the rocks and they would see it, but that could not be helped. Perhaps it even suited his purposes.

When he reached the point where the surface sloped away towards the crack in the rock, he crabbed his way towards the massive pile of stones and scree that loomed above the fissure like a giant cairn. Carefully, he placed the contents of his pockets among the stones at the base of the pyramid before settling down in its lee where he had a view down into the cleft. He tucked the stock of the assault rifle below his right shoulder and waited.

His mind drifted back to his days in England, the gentle countryside and the gentle climate, and the hard-eyed little rich boys who had made his life there such a hell. He had learned to love England at Trinity, where he had been surrounded by men of learning with a passion to pass it on, but he would never be able to call it home. No, this was his home, this towering citadel of stone that treated the unwary with such brutal impartiality. In no other place on earth could a man feel closer to his ancestors, or to himself. The Himalaya begrudged her people their every breath, but her savage beauty drew them to her and bewitched them so that neither harshness nor want would ever part them from her. Even when they were forced from her embrace, they stayed within sight of the high peaks, their hearts and souls forever among the mountains, even if their bodies would never be again.

It was only good fortune that he heard the sound, the clatter of a rifle barrel on rock, and woke from something more permanent than sleep. He raised his head. The noise hadn't come from the two men who were moving stealthily through the cleft below. He had company, but whoever it was couldn't see him because of the mound of rock that separated them.

The rifle sight drifted over the two soldiers. It was an execution really, but he felt no shame, which made him a poor Buddhist and a poorer monk. They had murdered so many of his people that he looked upon it as a mere balancing of the scales. His finger caressed the trigger and the short burst shredded the two Chinese, the bullets ricocheting from the narrow walls to cause multiple wounds. His ears were still ringing from the discharge of the weapon, but he identified a soft grunt as one man or more fell on his stomach on the far side of the rocks. A fusillade of automatic fire sliced through the air on both sides of the cairn, but he was safe enough for now. Eventually they would find a way to reach him, but it would take time and time was all he wanted. He changed the magazine for a fresh one and waited for the next attempt to force the cleft.

The lieutenant of the four commandos who had followed Tenzin's blood trail was forced to admire his enemy's choice of position. He had been exterminating these vermin, and religious fanatics like them in China's autonomous provinces, for more than a decade, but he had never come across an adversary as formidable as the leader of the Ghosts of the Four Rivers. Well, now they truly were ghosts, apart from this one, whom he had no doubt was their commander, a man hailed as a legend among the peasants who populated this wilderness.

But he had made a mistake. He was trying to buy time for the westerners who were the commandos' prime objective, but when his time ran out, as it inevitably would, there was no escape. They were trapped. Unless they could fly.

One of his men pulled a fragmentation grenade from his belt, but the lieutenant signalled him to replace it. That was a measure of the rebel's guile. He had deliberately drawn them here to a place where one grenade would do his work for him. In addition, the rock-strewn slope that swept down to the mound was almost impossible to cross at speed or by stealth, the two elements which, along with their ruthlessness, gave the commandos their feared reputation. Still, the lieutenant knew he would have to take a decision. Every one of these men was an élite specialist who had taken years to train. He had lost too many already. He was prepared to sacrifice more. But only if it gave him final victory. He waved two more forward into the cleft and signalled the soldiers around him to get ready to rush the mound.

Tenzin was weakening fast. The Chinese were back in the cleft, but he'd been too slow to fire a telling shot. Time was running out. Movement beyond the cairn indicated that his enemies were manoeuvring to attack. If there was a time for regret, now was it. According to the teaching he lived by, his actions in this life would deny him an elevated position in the next, but he would have done nothing differently. No man should stand aside and watch his country die and people suffer. Kundun taught that one should prepare for death by doing only good and keeping the heart and mind pure. But what if one could only achieve purity of heart and mind by acts which might be defined as evil? Was it evil to kill men who were evil-doers and were even now coming to kill him?

He took a calming breath and reached for his last grenade. Partially removing the pin, he placed it among the little nest of its egg-shaped companions he had made in the rocks.

A burst of fire from the passage below shattered the rocks to his left. He ignored the threat and moved to the far side of the mound just in time to greet the four commandos clambering across the rocks towards him with a volley of shots. One man was thrown backwards with a shriek of pain, but Tenzin had exposed himself to the guns of the others and he felt the stallion's kick of bullets hitting his shoulder, chest and stomach. He felt no pain, only a gentle fading towards what came next. Still, he had one more task. From somewhere, he found the strength to roll over and his fingers closed on the pin of the last grenade and pulled it the final few millimetres.

The Chinese commander warily approached the prone body on the rocks and turned it with his boot. Strange that a man could approach death with such a look of serenity on his face. His final thought before the world exploded was that it was what made these people so dangerous.

XLIX

Jamie watched the smoke billow from the narrow passage in the hillside and he understood exactly what it meant. Tenzin's fate had never been in doubt from the moment he had sent them away with Chiru. Still, he felt overwhelmed by a terrible sense of loss. But there was no time to mourn. The Tibetan may have managed to delay their pursuers, but they were still stuck like flies on a wall eight hundred feet up a sheer cliff. Somehow he had to find a way to get Sarah down. He signed to Chiru that they would need to work together and was relieved when the Tibetan boy seemed to understand.

Chiru had been squatting nervelessly on the very brink of the ledge with his rifle across his knees. Now the Tibetan stood up and signalled to Jamie to get Sarah to her feet. His face wore an untroubled smile that promised, whatever the perils they faced, he would somehow get them to safety. Jamie smiled back and Chiru's calm seemed to reach out to him. In slow motion, he saw the moment the boy's eyes changed

JAMES DOUGLAS

shape. Heard the butcher's block smack of the bullet hitting flesh. His mind screamed denial as Chiru was catapulted backwards off the ledge and into the void. Unthinkingly he crawled to the edge and watched the boy's body tumble end over end in a fall that seemed to go on for ever. Blind panic froze him in position before some deep buried instinct saved him. He rolled sideways and squirmed backwards just as the sniper fired his second shot and the bullet screamed off the rock where he'd lain only a split second before. His hands scrambled for the rifle and he used his body to cover Sarah's as he frantically scanned the clifftop above. Nothing. It took him a few seconds before he realized that the shape of the cliff concealed the inner part of the ledge from the marksman. They were safe, for the moment, but he knew it couldn't last. Sooner or later the shooter would find a vantage point that would give him the angle for a clear shot. When that happened they were finished. Carefully, he crept to the end of the ledge where Chiru's 'path' led diagonally down the cliff face. He identified a few possible hand- and footholds in the first twenty or thirty feet, but even alone he would quickly run out of options. Then it would be a matter of whether his strength ran out or he died of exposure. In any case, he couldn't leave Sarah. The end result would be the same, but better to stay together. Maybe the Chinese would send someone down to rescue them? He laughed bitterly at his own innocence. The commandos were on a seek-and-destroy mission. They wouldn't rest until everyone who had been with Tenzin was dead. The Tibetan's face swam into his head and he found strength in the solemn features and the gentle, mesmeric voice. *Only you can ensure that the Sun Stone never falls into the hands of those whose greed or ambition or foolishness will destroy us all.* Well, the world would have to look after itself. He still had the rifle and he checked the action to make sure it hadn't been damaged during the slide. If . . . No. Not that. Not yet. He put his arm around Sarah's body and she snuggled into his shoulder for warmth. A cloud of exhaustion blanketed his brain and he closed his eyes and inhaled the scent of her body. There were worse ways to go.

His wandering mind conjured up a scene from *Apocalypse Now.* The opening scene where Captain Willard is lying drunk in his Saigon hotel room and the sound of the ceiling fan morphs into the mesmeric 'whump, whump, whump' of helicopter blades and heralds him back to a reality he doesn't wish to be part of.

It was only when Jamie opened his eyes that he realized the sound was real and growing louder with every passing second. He grabbed the assault rifle and pushed Sarah down low, but even as he reacted a gigantic mechanical monster rose up before him with an almighty clattering and he was engulfed in its hot breath, the draught from the helicopter's blades threatening to buffet him from the ledge. Through a Plexiglas shield men in flying helmets studied him like a trapped insect from behind mirrored visors. He found himself staring into the mouths of four lethal-looking rocket pods and a pair of remotely operated machine guns moved remorselessly to fix him with their little black eyes. He laid down the rifle and did his best to shield Sarah's body, knowing just how pointless it was. His final thought was that somebody had gone to a hell of a lot of trouble to kill them.

'If it was up to me I would throw you in prison and leave you there.' The Indian Army major's manner was polite but chilly, but then Jamie could hardly blame him. When the air force Mil-35 began its training flight out of Joshimath, the last thing the pilots were looking for was a confrontation with élite Chinese special forces which had all the signs of developing into a full-blown international incident. 'Not only did you put yourselves at risk, but our airmen, and, if we are to believe you, the poor deluded Tibetan peasants who were bringing you back to India. Your partner, Miss Grant, was fortunate to survive her altitude sickness, but I am happy to say she has a remarkable constitution and will be released from hospital later today.' He picked up a piece of paper from the metal desk. 'Our prosecutors have formulated a list of charges against you that makes very grave reading indeed, Mr Saintclair, but, for reasons I find somewhat disconcerting, my superiors have ordered me to offer an alternative solution. This is a statement of your activities in Chamoli region which I will require you to sign. You will note that there is no mention of Chinese commandos, parachute drops or gun battles. No explosions and no dead bodies. Mr James Saintclair and Miss Sarah Grant unadvisedly decided to leave their guided walk to the Valley of the Flowers and strayed into Tibetan territory, where they ran into difficulties and had to be rescued by the Indian authorities, to whom they are extremely grateful.' He offered Jamie a ball-point pen from the breast pocket of his olive-green shirt.

'What happens if I sign?'

'You and Miss Grant will be transported to Delhi and placed on the first flight to London.'

'And if I don't?'

'I hope you like ghee, Mr Saintclair.'

L

They arrived at Heathrow airport still in the clothes they'd worn to climb the Himalayas. The two travel-stained pariahs held in isolation at the back of the Air India flight had attracted the curious stares of their fellow passengers – the consensus seemed to be drug smugglers caught in the act – but in their weariness and with the memory of Tenzin's sacrifice still fresh, they barely noticed.

Sarah insisted on stopping off at her flat for fresh clothing before they continued to Kensington and after they'd showered it seemed sensible to fall into bed where they slept for the best part of the afternoon. It was only when they were up and dressed that she noticed the red light flashing on her telephone that indicated a new voice message.

Jamie busied himself in the kitchen while she listened. When she joined him the news was clearly not good.

'Vanderbilt have cut us loose. They say we breached the conditions of our contract. I'm not sure how it works, but I suspect we weren't supposed to get involved in a shooting war. There was also a suggestion that the museum won't let the painting out of Poland again. They'll pay me for the feature, but we can forget about buying a yacht.'

'Does it bother you?'

'Being poor again?'

'Yes.'

'It doesn't seem to matter.'

'No, it doesn't.'

'So what happens now? We can't just stop.'

He smiled and kissed her hair. This was the old Sarah talking.

'I've arranged to speak to an old friend who knows all about that stuff Tenzin told us about. Nuclear fission and fusion. The Holy Grail and all that. I also think we need to find out more about the secret American operation to smuggle Nazi scientists out of Germany at the end of the war. We're not finished yet.'

Mike Oliver had known Jamie long enough not to expect him to be on time. He was sipping his beer patiently in the corner of the pub when the familiar rangy figure walked in. What did surprise him was his friend's choice of companion. Here was something much more exotic than the fragile and often rather dull English roses who normally lasted a couple of months with Jamie before mutual apathy prised them apart. Sarah was wearing tight leather trousers and a short, tailored jacket that emphasized her slim figure. With her golden complexion and high cheekbones she could have had star billing in one of those commercials for Italian designer gear, but something told him this girl was much more than a clothes-horse. He ran a hand through his thinning hair, and not for the first time, wished he had more of it.

'What'll you have? Mike Oliver, this is Sarah. Mike is a mad scientist.'

They shook hands while Jamie went to the bar. 'Have you known Jamie long?' he asked.

She stared at him and he wondered if she was reading more into the innocent enquiry than he'd intended.

'About a month, but it seems like years. Every day with Jamie is one big adventure.'

Caterpillar brows elevated in surprise. 'Then you must be good for him. It's only about eight months since I last met him and he looks about five years younger. How did you get him out of his tweed jacket? Actually, forget I said that. What I mean is you've improved his clothes sense, er, made him more fashionable.'

'Why, thank you, Mike,' she said, giving her drawl the full works and studying his own cherished, but well-worn leather bomber in a way that made him blush. 'Like all you men, all he needed was a little push in the right direction. Come to think of it, you don't look like my idea of a mad scientist. I imagined a little more hair and a white coat. What is your speciality?'

He grinned, accepting the gentle mockery in the spirit it was intended. 'I keep my madness well hidden, madam. It only comes out when there's a full moon.

Then again, I'm a humble jobbing astrophysicist and it is a well-known fact that all astrophysicists are certifiable.'

'Don't let him kid you.' Jamie appeared, grinning, with two pints and a glass of white wine. 'There's nothing humble about Professor Michael Oliver MSc and bar. The man's a genius. Certifiable, yes, but never humble.'

Mike accepted his pint.

'So what can I do for you? You said you wanted to bend my ear. Sarah tells me you've been having a few adventures and I have some questions of my own about that giant burrow you stumbled across in Germany, but you have the honour.'

Jamie looked at Sarah and chewed his lip. He hadn't been joking about Mike being a genius. The scientist was one of the cleverest men on the planet, with more degrees than Jamie had GCSEs. What to reveal and what not?

'We were musing on the subject of celestial objects, as you do of an evening.' He ignored the other man's scowl of disbelief. 'I know it's in the realm of science fiction, but what are the chances of finding something previously unknown from a meteorite?'

Mike shot him a tight smile. 'You're taking the piss, right?'

Jamie shook his head.

The scientist sighed. 'Something tells me we're not a million miles away from the hole in the Harz. What do you mean by *something*? Are we talking bacteria or *something* more substantial?'

'More substantial.'

'A *material*, right?'

'Right,' Jamie and Sarah said simultaneously.

Mike sat back in his seat and his voice took on the formal tone that Sarah guessed he usually kept for the lecture theatre. 'Science fiction has a curious tendency to become science fact. Look at Jules Verne and H.G. Wells. You can follow a direct link between what Wells wrote through to the development of the V2 rocket and the Americans putting Neil Armstrong on the moon. What we know now is most definitely not what we will know in ten years. Has anything been found? No. Is there a possibility? That's different. Maybe we're looking in the wrong place or in the wrong way. Maybe we don't yet have the tools to understand what might be there. But we *are* looking and the possibilities are interesting enough to have the Yanks and the Russians sending out teams to study impact sites all over the world. The Chinese, too, more recently; that's one of the reasons why they're investing so heavily in Africa.'

'What about the practical implications?' Jamie asked.

Mike gave him a shrewd look. 'So that's what this is all about. The rumours have been flying about that place you found in Saxony. Obviously, the practical applications depend on exactly what it is you discover. But whatever it is, it will open up whole new areas of scientific study. Maybe even whole new branches of science. Science spawns research, which spawns development, which spawns technology, which spawns

398

industry, which spawns profit.' The possibilities were reflected in his voice, which grew in power as he spoke. 'The current big thing is nuclear fusion. It's a pipe dream at the moment, but think of it as harnessing the power of the sun. A perpetual source of energy. Enough output from a swimming pool full of sea water to fuel the entire planet for a year. Of course, like nuclear power it would have weapons applications as well. There were stories during the war of some kind of German breakthrough, but they turned out to be as real as Mr Hitler's wonder weapons. Unless . . . ?'

Jamie shrugged and kept his voice low. People were staring at them. 'It looked like a scrap metal yard to me, Mike. We were more interested in the painting.' He could see that Mike didn't believe him.

'So why have you suddenly become so interested in my, albeit fascinating, branch of science, Jamie? And don't give me that musing bullshit. You know something. Well, if you tell me what it is, maybe I can help you.'

Jamie opened his mouth; why not tell Mike about the sphere? But the warning look in Sarah's eyes forced a change of direction.

'Believe me, Mike,' he said regretfully, 'if we knew anything solid we would tell you, but this is all entirely theoretical.'

'Then why do I have this feeling that somebody's tugging on my chain? If we didn't go way back I'd be out of here and you and your new girlfriend could go to hell. But since we do I'll have another pint.'

Sarah picked up the glasses and Jamie carried on as if nothing had been said.

'Let's just say this pipe dream is a possibility: who would be the big winners?'

Mike shook his head. 'Jesus, Jamie, what happened to old, boring, non-confrontational, wouldn't-say-boo-to-a-goose Mr Jamie Saintclair? I think I liked him better.'

Sarah reappeared with the drinks. 'Why, he fell under a train, Mike. This is the new improved version.' Her laughter was so infectious that Mike couldn't help joining in.

'Ach, to hell with it. Who'd win? Whoever got there first. The Yanks, the Russians, who've already got us by the balls with their big gas reserves, or, God help us, the Chinese. They're way ahead on research, but they haven't made the big breakthrough yet. So, governments. And corporations. One of the big global industrial companies would, literally, pay the earth for something like this.' He sobered. 'In fact, they'd kill for it. Any of them. So maybe you're right and your Uncle Mike doesn't need to know. Then, of course, there is the potential down side. You've heard of the Hadron Collider?'

Jamie shrugged. 'Vaguely.'

'Christ, where have you been? Cern. A four-*billion*-dollar investment. A seventeen-mile tunnel dug through France and Switzerland to bury the biggest particle accelerator ever created so that they can mimic the conditions of the day the universe was born. The Big

Bang. And if that bang isn't big enough they're also hoping to find the God particle and shed light on what we know as Dark Matter. Taken all together, it could open the door to what we're talking about. Sustainable nuclear fusion.'

Jamie frowned. 'So if they're already doing this, what's the big deal about it all?'

'Because no one knows whether it will work and there's that teeensy-weensy down side.'

'Teensy-weensy?'

'The very small matter of it going out of control and creating a Black Hole that could swallow the planet.'

'And you really think that's a possibility?' Sarah demanded.

Mike smiled at her naivety. 'The whole point of scientific experiment is to push back the boundaries of our knowledge. To do that, scientists have to stick their noses in some dark and sometimes dangerous corners. Just ask Marie Curie. How likely does a global catastrophe have to be for a scientist to back off from a big experiment? A couple of guys, including the president of the Royal Society, looked at the Collider and worked out that, based on astronomical evidence and assumptions about the physics of a few hypothetical particles called strangelets that we don't really understand, the odds of turning the earth into a dead planet were about fifty million to one. Good odds, eh? About the same as my chances of winning the lottery. Only someone out there wins the lottery most weeks. Scientists are as fallible as the next man, Sarah. The Hadron Collider is playing with the building blocks of the universe, and the truth is that nobody has the slightest idea what the true risk is. Hell, they must cross their fingers every time they press Start.'

LI

They reached the landing outside Jamie's flat just as an elderly woman was disappearing through the door opposite and the atmosphere lay heavy with the scent of freshly sprayed air freshener.

'Hello, Mrs Laurence,' Jamie greeted his neighbour.

She turned to glare at him. 'I don't know how you dare show your face after all that noise the other night.'

'What was that all about?' Sarah said after the door had slammed shut.

Jamie shrugged. 'Search me. I thought we'd always got on pretty well.' As he put his key in the lock an unsavoury odour caught in his throat. He groaned. 'The fish. That dozy bugger Simon has forgotten to feed them.'

The moment he pushed open the door the smell hit him like something solid, instantly reacting with his gut to fill his mouth with bile. Someone had closed the thick velvet curtains and it took time for his eyes to adjust to the gloom. When they did, they were drawn to a bulky object in the centre of the room that shouldn't be there. His brain seemed to fragment into a thousand pieces, but somehow he managed to grope for the light switch and Sarah stifled a scream as the full horror of what they'd walked into dawned.

'Oh, fuck.' Jamie's legs threatened to give way and he crouched down with his hand over his mouth. The sound of his thundering heart almost overwhelmed the buzz of the hundreds of flies that had risen from the alien object and now filled the room.

Blood everywhere. Old blood that stained the walls and the carpet a deep brown. But that must have come at the end.

He forced himself to study the scene as if the central figure was not his friend. They had tied Simon – yes, Simon was present somewhere in that bloated, heavily marbled caricature of a human being – to a kitchen chair. He was naked to the waist and his feet were bare. That must be one of his own socks stuffed into the thing's mouth. Internal gases had inflated the body until the darkened skin threatened to split and vile black fluids flowed from his nose, ears and where the eyes should be. Despite the decomposition it was possible to work out what they had done to him. The faint cooked-meat smell just detectable beneath the overpowering stench of death must have been caused by the blow torch or soldering iron they had used on his nipples and chest. At least four toes, and as many fingers, were missing, which presumably meant they were lying around somewhere among the mess of papers and household items strewn across the carpet. Once they had what they'd come for they had slashed his throat with an obscene, terrible violence that had splattered his life blood across the room, but which must have come as a blessed relief to its victim.

'They were looking for us.' Sarah's voice shook.

Jamie nodded, not trusting himself to speak. He tore his eyes away from the horror that had been his friend and surveyed the rest of the room. Every drawer had been ripped open and turned out on to the floor. The cushions of the sofa were sliced apart and the stuffing scattered. Even the furniture itself had been gutted, leaving the springs sticking out of the cloth. He glanced through to the study and saw a similar picture. In addition his computer had been taken apart and he knew that the hard disk would be missing.

'I'm to blame for this. I underestimated how much the Sun Stone meant to Frederick and his thugs. When we vanished from Braunlage this is the first place they would have looked for us.'

'No. You could never have predicted this. No one could. These people are psychopaths; they'll kill anyone who gets in their way. Maybe we should just give up now?'

Jamie forced himself to look at Simon. Frederick and the Vril would never give up while he and Sarah were still alive. The only way they would ever be free of them was to find the Sun Stone.

'No.'

*　　*　　*

Three days passed before the police were satisfied with their statements. It seemed clear to the inspector in charge of the investigation that Simon's murder was linked in some way to the find of the Raphael in Germany. Jamie had spent two of those days convincing him that he wasn't trading in stolen artworks from a secret warehouse that the dead man had been tortured to identify.

When they were allowed to leave, Jamie decided to set up home at his grandfather's house on the grounds that it would be much easier to spot any watchers in the leafy lanes of north Welwyn than in central London. It turned out to be a good decision because a hand-delivered letter was waiting for him inviting him to visit the family lawyer, which presumably meant there was some movement on the sale of the house. While he walked into the town centre, Sarah continued her research.

'This stuff on Operation Paperclip is incredible,' she called as she heard the front door opening an hour later. The lack of reply puzzled her and when she went to investigate she realized instantly that something was very wrong. Jamie's face wore the haunted look of a man walking away from the fatal accident he'd just caused.

'What's happened, Jamie? Is it about the house?' She saw he was clutching two envelopes, one larger and white, but the paper so aged as to be a faded, marbled yellow, and the other a narrow dun-coloured oblong that might have been from the tax man. He brushed past her into the lounge and collapsed in a chair at the table. He put the larger of the two envelopes on the table in front of him and laid the second aside.

Sarah sat opposite him. She noticed that the yellowing envelope had words written on it in a tight, almost archaic script and she understood instinctively that it wasn't the solicitor's writing. With a little effort she made out the inverted words. *For the attention of Master James Sinclair.* The use of Sinclair proved it had been written and deposited before Jamie's mother had changed their name to the more upmarket version. It was padded, but not bulky, and clearly contained more than a single sheet. She knew better than to reach for it. Instead, she waited while the silence lengthened to the point where it became unbearable.

'My grandfather instructed the solicitor to only pass it on after he was dead.' Jamie's voice came out cracked, as if all the moisture had been sucked from his throat by the dry, aged object in front of him.

'What is it?'

The green eyes filled with a combustible mixture of grief and pain, anger and loss that almost made her turn away. 'The final pages of his diary.'

Her fingers made an involuntary lunge for the envelope, but he put his hand, palm down on top of it. He saw that he'd hurt her feelings, but the hand didn't move.

'I need to think about this, Sarah. I've read the first few pages, but I couldn't . . . I want to see it through his eyes as it happened. We need to go back to Germany.'

She reached out and placed her hand over his. The

flesh was cold. 'Then that's what we'll do,' she reassured him. 'Just tell me where you want to go and I'll book the flights. Do you want to hear about Paperclip?'

He shook his head. 'Paperclip can wait. First you have to know what I know.' He reached into the envelope and counted out four lined sheets of paper, identical to those from the blue journal.

He began speaking in a flat monotone and the first thing she noted was that Matthew Sinclair was no longer in the foothills of the Bavarian Alps, but was recording his memories of the period four years earlier, in the summer of 1941. It began as a love story.

'We met in that old church hall by the cathedral, the one that smelled of stale sweat, flat beer and Capstan Full Strength. It was a time of hate, but you drove it away with your laughter. My soul was blackened and rotten, but you healed it with your goodness. My heart had turned to ice, but you melted it with the warmth of your love. When I picture your eyes they are the shifting colours of a tropical sea on a sunlit summer's day; sometimes blue, sometimes green, their surface sparkles but in their depths lies the smoke and the fire that makes you you.

'Your mother disapproved of me and the army disapproved of you, but you were clever enough to defeat them both. I can never smell the musty earthiness of old straw or feel the kiss of the sun on my bare flesh without thinking of you. You came

to me bathed in the scent of elderflower and new-mown grass, your skin soft as velvet and hot as naked flame, and together we found a new place, far from war, far from pain, and far from fear.

'I had forgotten how to live. You gave me life.

'When the war found us again, your courage humbled me. Who would have believed we would ever become a target in our harmless old town? But then Hitler is a serial devourer of all that is good, with his Junkers and Heinkels, his incendiary bombs and his aerial torpedoes.

'On the best day of my life, but one, you made me prouder than any man, standing tall before the priest even as the ground shook beneath our feet in the big shelter under the railway station. Remember how we laughed when he said, "Do you Margaret . . ." because you will never be anything but Peggy to me? When we emerged into that living hell, shattered buildings were our guard of honour and our confetti the falling ash. You smiled through your tears and spent our wedding night mending torn bodies and splinting broken bones, while I dug the living and the dead from the rubble that had been their homes. Coventry, 14 November 1941. And still we were happy. Because the seed had already been sown.

'They appeared, like snowdrops at the end of March, earlier than expected but never more welcome. Elizabeth and Anne. Anne and Elizabeth. I held them in my arms and felt the life I had created *squirm and bubble within them. I looked into their eyes and saw your eyes. Perfect. Have two new human beings ever been more perfect? How many hours did I have with them, and with you? I count them every day, but somehow I can never reach a proper tally. Did I ever see them smile? I dream that I did, but I do not truly know.*

'I try not to remember that day, Peggy, but the devil perches on my shoulder and whispers the details in my ear. I know I was at the camp when I heard the sirens. I ran, God knows how I ran, until the breath was like a knife in my throat and my legs collapsed under me. What is there in bricks and mortar to make them burn so? Flames, leaping from the roof like a giant funeral pyre. Flames, spewing from every window so it was as if I peered into the very mouth of hell. Flames all around. A sea of flames. No, an ocean of flames. I knew you would have been taken to the shelter, so why did I run to the hospital? But Elizabeth was sick, and Elizabeth couldn't go to the shelter. So you stayed. You all stayed. I wept for you as I watched the hospital burn, all the time praying that you had escaped. All the time knowing – knowing – you had not. Then you were there. In the doorway. A shimmer in the heat. A smudge of darkness against the gold and the red. Of course, you would get them out, brave Peggy. You would smell the smoke and carry them through the wards and down the burning stairs and into the burning hall and out

into the burning world. I called out your name, but the fire devoured it. Just as it devoured you. And Anne. And Elizabeth. You were on fire as you walked towards me, a pillar of flame with a halo of gold around your pretty head. Was it your feet that melted first? Or was it the tarmac? Did you hold them out to me as I ran into that wall of burning air? Did you cry my name as they held me back from you? I can't remember, Peggy. All I remember is lying on the hot ground with my hair on fire and watching you melt, sinking slowly down until you and my babies became one with the burning earth.

'And then I went mad.'

Jamie's emotionless voice faded and the only sound in the room was Sarah's sobbing.

'You realize what this means?' he said harshly. 'My grandfather had another wife. Another family. If the Germans hadn't killed that woman and her children Jamie Saintclair wouldn't have existed. They died, so that I could live. How do you think that makes me feel?'

Her reaction astonished him. She lifted her head and her eyes flashed. 'They had names,' she snapped. 'Peggy and Elizabeth and Anne. Don't try to kid yourself that if you don't give them names they don't exist as real people, the way the Germans do by not mentioning the Jews. Spare me your fucking self-pity, Jamie. Matthew left you those pages so that you would understand. Don't tarnish his memory and theirs by using it as an excuse to feel sorry for yourself. If you want to sit here and mope, that's fine by me, but I'm going to pack.'

He let her get to the door.

'We fly in to Munich, but we do this my way.'

She turned and gave him her hard stare.

'All right,' she agreed. 'We'll do it your way. But just remember, Jamie Saintclair, that I like you how you are now. The guy who was prepared to take on the Chinese army and the Indian air force just for little ol' Sarah Grant. Not the way you were before somebody threw you under that train. Don't go all boring on me.'

He nodded and when he lifted his head the old Jamie was back. 'At least we know what we're fighting for. Maybe you should tell me what you found out about Operation Paperclip?'

She shook her head. 'I need to book our flights for tomorrow and I suspect it will mean an early start. I'll explain on the plane.' They headed for the stairs and she glanced back at the table. 'You forgot your other envelope. What is it anyway?'

He picked up the letter and put it in his inside pocket.

'Just a detail my mother left me to sort out.'

LII

'We lost him.'

Bob Sumner couldn't believe what he was hearing. 'What do you mean you lost him?'

'You told us to keep him on a light rein, so that's what we did. His secretary said he was due back in the office this morning, but he called her last night and said she should take a couple of weeks off once she'd cleared his diary.'

'The girl?'

'We think she's with him.'

Sumner allowed himself a few moments of menacing silence, while the other man fidgeted at the end of the phone.

'Get everybody on it. Two weeks means they're going travelling. That means airports. I want to know where they're going, what their seat numbers are and what they've taken along to read. Everything. You have until noon.' He didn't say *or else*, he didn't have to. He put down the phone and immediately picked it up again for the call he wasn't going to enjoy making.

'Operation Paperclip.' Sarah read from her notes and wriggled herself into a comfortable position in the cramped economy-class seat of the Gatwick–Munich flight. 'As the war was ending the good old US of A belatedly realized that with the Red Army overrunning most of Germany they also had their hands on most of the Nazis' military secrets, including their nuclear programme. This was about the time when what became the Cold War looked like it might be pretty hot, so it was suddenly very important to get any scientists and technicians in Allied hands back to America where they could be squeezed of what they knew. President Roosevelt had specifically ruled out offering these guys any guarantees, but Harry Truman overturned that decision – on condition they weren't involved in war crimes.'

'Truman was one of your more naive presidents?'

'Yes, he was, or maybe he knew that the people he was letting loose on Operation Paperclip didn't have the time or the morals to make such fine distinctions. In the end, the OSS smuggled out more than seven hundred scientists and their families. According to their documents they were whiter than white, but now we know better. Werner von Braun was the best known. He had designed the V2 rocket and went on to play a key role in the NASA space programme, but he was originally tagged a security risk to the United States.

He was an angel compared to some of the others. Kurt Blome infected hundreds of concentration camp prisoners with plague vaccines. He got a job with the US Army Chemical Corps. Arthur Rudolph ran the Mittelwerk factory at Dora-Nordhausen in the Harz, where they made V2s and twenty thousand prisoners died from hanging, beating and starvation. He became a US citizen and designed the Saturn 5 rocket for the moon landings. A couple of guys called Hermann Becker-Reysing and Siegfried Ruff carried out medical experiments on inmates at Dachau, including placing them in an altitude chamber and decreasing the pressure until they died. They were paid to write their findings by the USAAF. And so it goes on. Klaus Barbie, for Christ's sake. You'd think being labelled the Butcher of Lyon might have given them a clue?'

'So Walter Brohm was part of Paperclip?'

Sara shook her head. 'Not officially. Paperclip was spawned by a couple of earlier freelance operations involving the Special Operations Executive. It looks as if Brohm and the others were part of that experiment. What bothers me is that they just vanish from the record. Sure, a lot of these guys disappeared to Argentina and Brazil after they arrived in the States, but we know that they reached there. Maybe Brohm handed over his big secret and they gave him a one-way ticket to Buenos Aires, but if he did, what happened then?'

She turned, expecting an answer, or, if not an answer, at least a theory, but Jamie had his head back with his eyes closed and was snoring gently.

'Bastard,' she mouthed, and turned to stare at the clouds, failing to notice the Chinese man in the business suit who had been studying them from the aisle seat three rows behind.

Munich's Franz Josef airport is a vast modernistic barn of a place fifteen miles north of the Bavarian capital. Only the language rapped out by the hard-faced security men differentiated it from a hundred other charmless landing places in a hundred other cities. When they'd cleared passport control, Jamie hired a Volkswagen at the airport's Europcar desk. Before they set off they decided to have a coffee and a pastry at one of the cloned chain restaurants clustered in the glass-roofed shopping centre that connected the two main terminals.

Sarah finished her drink quickly. 'I gotta go powder my nose and make a phone call.'

He smiled. 'I won't go anywhere without you.'

'Just see what happens if you do.'

Jamie was sipping his coffee when the Oriental who had been on the plane sat down uninvited at the table. He rose to his feet, but a second man put a hand on his shoulder, and he felt a third, running professional hands under his arms and over his chest, before he was pushed back into his seat. He looked around, but no one appeared to have noticed what was happening.

'Please excuse my companions, Mr Saintclair.' The man spoke precise language school English and his tone oozed reason, but Jamie allowed himself to ease into what Matthew described as combat mode. Instinct told him that this striped bespoke suit represented a greater danger than any gun. 'I see your Himalayan adventures have not put you off foreign travel? But, please, that is in the past. My name is Lim, and I am a rather lowly representative of the People's Republic of China.' Mr Lim had dark, soulful eyes and a cheerful smile that might have been painted on his broad face. Without moving his lips he passed a message to one of the two men accompanying him, and the bodyguard went off in the direction Sarah had disappeared. He continued: 'I would have prevented it if I was able. There has been far too much miscommunication. Would it surprise you if I said that two of my colleagues exceeded their authority in London, leading to your unfortunate . . . accident? No? Of course, it does not make us friends, but perhaps the fact that I am prepared to give you this information will help us trust each other.'

'After my experiences in Tibet, I wouldn't trust you as far as I could throw your minders, Mr Lim. Perhaps you could get to the point, if there is one.'

Mr Lim's smile grew appreciably wider. 'Certainly. You have proven yourself very resourceful and very persistent. My superiors felt that you were an obstacle to us, but I have persuaded them otherwise. I believe you will find what you are looking for. This object rightly belongs to my government.'

'I think the Dalai Lama might have something to say about that.'

'But the Dalai Lama is no longer of consequence, Mr Saintclair, and what you call Tibet is, and always has been, part of China. What is of consequence is that my country is currently home to 1.3 billion people and that despite our best efforts this will rise to 1.5 billion in the next thirty years. In a few years we will overtake the United States as the world's largest energy user. My people are hungry for power, Mr Saintclair, and will only grow hungrier. We are spending unthinkable amounts on alternative sources of energy, but in the long term there is only one solution: nuclear fusion. We are already many years ahead of our rivals – it is even possible that we have outstripped the progress made by your Walter Brohm.'

Jamie froze. 'He's not my Walter Brohm.'

'Oh, but he is, Mr Saintclair. Why else would you have pursued him halfway around the world? But to return to my point, we are close to having the technology, but we need the return of the Sun Stone to ensure the project's success. As I said, I believe you will find this object. When you do, my country is prepared to pay a large bounty to get it back.'

'We don't need your bounty, Mr Lim.'

'No? Then the matter would go before the German courts.' He shrugged. 'I can assure you that we have an extremely strong case and those courts will rule in our favour. But even in that event, I believe we would be honour bound to recompense you for your efforts. As you see, Mr Saintclair, we wish to proceed in a civilized manner.' He placed a card on the table. 'I implore you to call this number when you find the Sun Stone. If you do not, I fear you will place both your lives at risk. Do you want to be responsible for putting Miss Grant in danger?'

Jamie fought the urge to take Mr Lim by the throat and shake the smile off his face. 'Is that a threat?'

'You misunderstand me, Mr Saintclair.' Lim shook his head sadly at the wickedness of the world. 'You must be aware by now that we are not the only party with an interest in the Sun Stone. Others may be less inclined to negotiate. If there is a threat, it is from those who do not have the same concern for your welfare as my humble self.'

He rose from the table. 'When your companion returns, perhaps it would be wiser not to mention our conversation. She appears to have a great deal on her mind already.' Jamie stared at the large envelope the Chinese had left on the table. 'Call that a down payment. Please, open it.'

Jamie peeled back the flap. The envelope contained two 8x10 black-and-white photographs.

'I could have had them done in colour, but I felt monochrome suited our particular situation so much better,' Lim explained cheerfully. 'I'm sure Mr Le Carré would be impressed.'

'I don't understand.' Jamie stared at the top picture. It showed three men talking on a country path. One of them was a slight figure in an overcoat that was too large for him.

'Oh, I think you understand most clearly, Mr Saintclair. You will note the dates.' Lim lifted the photograph, so Jamie could see the second picture. A shot of the same two men sitting in a car outside a house that was instantly familiar. Jamie's heart lurched as he recognized the closer of the two as the man he'd found in his grandfather's lounge.

'As I say, a down payment. To receive the second instalment all you have to do is call the number I have given you at the appropriate time.'

Sarah reappeared a few moments after the Chinese had left. 'You look thoughtful?'

He tried a smile that didn't quite make it. 'I've got a lot on my mind.'

Their route took them from the airport past the north of the city. Jamie tried to keep his mind on the road, but as he drove it was difficult to keep Mr Lim's reasonable voice out of his head. The claim that there was no threat was less significant than Lim's presence, which, of course, was a threat in itself. It struck him that it might have been the Chinese, rather than Frederick and the Vril Society, who had been responsible for Simon's murder, but he immediately dismissed the thought. He suspected that while Mr Lim was perfectly capable of the killing, he would have been much more subtle in its execution. What mattered was that every word the man spoke had been like a gentle touch on the rudder to steer him in a certain direction. He had felt like a horse on a light rein just waiting for the sting of the whip. And then it came, in the form of the photographs. The photographs that appeared to show old Stan with the men who had almost certainly murdered him and the same two men outside the house where his grandfather had died. The implications of that turned his vision red and his hands tightened on the wheel. He willed himself to stay calm. Hadn't he always suspected? His grandfather's missing walking stick. Two deaths linked by the past in such quick succession? An unfamiliar gloom settled over him. He could take the pictures to the police in Britain, but on their own they proved nothing. They were circumstantial evidence at best. He opened his mouth intending to tell Sarah what had happened, but something stopped him. *She has a lot on her mind.* Like everything else that had been said, the cryptic sentence held a warning and a message. He just hadn't yet worked out its significance.

Sarah must have caught his mood, because she was uncharacteristically silent. The sun broke through the clouds and they had a view across the city to the mountains beyond. Neither of them mentioned the signpost they passed for the little town of Dachau. It seemed nowhere in Germany was free from the shadow of the war. Sarah kept her eyes on the stunning panorama to the south. 'Nice place. But it gives me the creeps.'

He drove on until he came to the outer ring road and after a few miles he picked up the exit for Augsburg and turned north-west.

'I still don't understand why we aren't heading directly for the Swiss border,' Sarah said. 'You know more or less where they crossed? It would save time.'

'Because I want to see this unfold through Matthew's

eyes,' he insisted. 'Or as much as it's possible after sixty years. Maybe these final pages of the journal hold the key to the Sun Stone and maybe they don't, but the best way to understand them is to take the journey with my grandfather and Brohm. I want to get as close to him as I can.'

They by-passed Augsburg and the multi-laned highway carried them swiftly through a thickly wooded area that the map told them was the local nature reserve. 'Hey, we just crossed the Danube,' Sarah announced. 'I thought the Danube was in Hungary or Romania?'

'I suppose it has to start somewhere. We turn south around here.'

She consulted the map. 'Looks like we should wait until we get past Ulm. What makes you so certain Matthew came this way?'

'I'm not certain. But Bad Saulgau is our next reference point and we have to get there somehow. I suspect most of these roads didn't even exist during the war.'

She looked again. 'To get to Bad Saulgau we take the B30 after Ulm and turn left after about an hour, at Schweinhausen.' She paused. 'Look, Jamie, I'm sorry I've been such a bitch since we got back from Tibet. I think maybe it's a delayed reaction to all those poor guys being killed. Tenzin would still be alive if he hadn't run into us. Simon too.'

'Simon didn't deserve what happened to him,' Jamie said bitterly. 'At least Tenzin died for what he believed in. He thought the war he was fighting mattered and that his cause was worth dying for. When he found out what we were mixed up in he decided that was worth dying for too.'

'Do you think it's worth dying for?'

The question took him by surprise. 'I don't know,' he admitted. 'For me, this is more about my grandfather than the Sun Stone. Can you understand that? All that stuff about the end of the world is just an abstract. Matthew Sinclair is real. If, by discovering who *he* is, we find a way to track down the Sun Stone then I'll do everything in my power to fulfil my promise to Tenzin, but if I can't I just hope we can walk away alive and unscarred. We're just two people caught up in events that are too big for us, Sarah. We can't be held responsible for everybody on the planet. Maybe once a year I'll burn a juniper branch and raise a glass to Tenzin's memory, but then I'll get on with my life.'

'What if Tenzin is wrong and Walter Brohm was right?'

At first he wasn't sure if he'd heard her correctly. 'Sorry?' He shot her a glance, but her eyes never left the road ahead.

'Tenzin believed the Sun Stone had the potential to destroy the world, but that belief was based on an ancient myth passed down through a hundred generations from a culture that thought the best way to defend themselves against it was to cut the throats of seven innocent people and sprinkle their blood over it. By that logic we should still be burning witches every time the milk goes sour.'

'Mike said much the same thing and I don't think he's into human sacrifice.' He tried to keep his voice even, but he was confused at the turn the conversation had taken.

'I know that, but he also said the chances were about fifty million to one. We're talking about something that could solve the world's energy problems for ever. No more burning up the planet's irreplaceable resources. No more global warming. No more famine. Isn't that worth taking a chance on? And we could find it, Jamie. Us. Not some faceless corporation, corrupt government or bunch of crazies like Frederick and his storm troopers.'

He shook his head, remembering Mr Lim's benign certainty. 'You're talking about Walter Brohm's legacy, Sarah. A discovery that is tainted by blood and greed. You've read the journal. Do you really believe the world would benefit from something a man like that had a hand in? Yes, we could find it, but for how long could we control it? That was Tenzin's warning. We can't trust anyone. The moment we lay our hands on it we become a target for every big-time crook and international terrorist, every lunatic dictator and religious fanatic. It would only be a matter of time before we were begging someone to take it off our hands. Your government or mine? Which would you trust? No, if we do find it, we have to destroy it or put it somewhere it will never be found.'

She smiled sadly. 'That might be more difficult than you make it sound.'

'We owe it to Tenzin to give it our best shot.'

LIII

'They flew into Munich this morning and hired a car. Current location unknown, but it looks as if they are following the route taken in the journal, so we know where Saintclair will end up and we'll be waiting for them.'

The man with the ponytail listened to Sumner's explanation with increasing irritation. 'Not good enough. Your report states that Saintclair paid a visit to his mother's solicitor?'

'That's right, but despite repeated attempts by our sources the lawyer refused to reveal why our man went there.'

'Yet within hours of attending that meeting Saintclair discovers a sudden renewed interest in the journal. That means he has new information, or he's been given something that has made him re-evaluate the information he already has. Somehow, the journal is still the key to the Sun Stone. Saintclair is the key to the journal. I want him found.'

He put down the phone and pressed a key on the intercom on his desk. 'Have the plane prepared. We'll be flying to Europe first thing in the morning.'

Jamie turned off the autobahn and on to a much narrower road that took them through a patchwork of heavily cultivated fields. Small agricultural communities flashed by the windows and within ten minutes they were on the outskirts of Bad Saulgau, which was a much larger town than Matthew's journal had hinted. Clearly it had prospered and expanded in the years since the war. They negotiated their way to the centre and parked.

'Where do we go from here?' Sarah asked.

'I'd like to see the site where they were ambushed and Matthew won his Military Cross.'

She looked sceptical. 'I don't see how we're going to find it. We have no idea which road they took out of this place. How will you know?'

'I'll know.' He took the map from her and studied the country to the south-west. 'This is the most direct route to Blumberg, the next place mentioned in the journal.' He traced his finger along the line of a road leading south-west towards the town of Ostrach. 'There are a couple of places that might have been nothing but a few scattered houses back then. What we really need is a nineteen forties map.'

'We have one.' Sara grinned and retrieved the silk escape map from the rucksack, along with the journal. She opened the journal at the page recording the ambush. '*I could see the snowcaps of Switzerland shimmering in the distance. They hit us just after dawn between Saulgau and some one-horse hamlet that wasn't worth a name,*' she read aloud, comparing the silk map with the modern road map. 'Look, you're right, there are a few places that fitted the description back then.'

Jamie drove slowly from the outskirts of town, studying the terrain around them. It was raining again and where the Alps should be there was nothing but filthy grey murk.

'If we're looking for a forest we've come to the right place,' Sarah said helpfully, as they passed yet another broad stretch of woodland.

He ignored her sarcasm. 'These are conifers, evergreens, Matthew said the wood where they were ambushed was beech. At this time of year the leaves will be bright, emerald green.'

'You mean like that,' she said a few moments later.

He drew to a halt and studied the copse she had indicated. It didn't look much. The trees were mature enough to have been growing for more than sixty years, great broad trunks and wide canopies, but there didn't seem to be enough of them to be called a wood. Behind the stand of beeches another conifer plantation spread into the distance. A couple of miles up the road stood a few isolated buildings that might have fitted the description *some one-horse hamlet that wasn't worth a name*.

Jamie studied the buildings across the wind-ruffled

wheat fields. 'I suppose the only way to find out is to ask.'

The first door they knocked on was opened by a young woman who answered their questions politely, but was unable to help them. She directed them to the house furthest away from the road. 'Talk to old Werner. He was here then.'

'*Guten tag.*' The thick-set figure worked steadily with a hoe in the centre of an immaculately tended vegetable garden. He looked up and nodded at Jamie's greeting. Werner had pale unreadable eyes, a bulbous nose and ruddy, time-worn features framed by heavy grey whiskers. As Jamie and Sarah waited by the house he came towards them using the hoe as a crutch to offset a pronounced limp.

'May I help you?' he asked.

Jamie explained why they were in the area and Werner's face clouded.

'Englanders, yes?'

Jamie nodded. He didn't see any point in explaining Sarah's ancestry.

The old man gave a bitter laugh. 'What is it you English say – "Don't mention the war"? Good advice. It is a long time ago, better to forget, especially around here. Don't be deceived by the pretty scenery. Bad things happened, just as they happened everywhere. Bad things.' He leaned on the hoe, and sighed heavily, staring at the ground.

Sarah opened her mouth to protest, but Jamie shook

his head. There was no point in stirring up unwanted memories. He thanked the German for his time and turned to go.

They were halfway to the car when Werner surprised them. '*Ach*, wait,' he called. 'It was a long time ago, but maybe an old man keeps things locked away for too long. Perhaps it is time to face it. Come, I will make coffee.'

While they sat in the tiny kitchen, Werner served his coffee without asking how they liked it; strong, dark and with a liberal lacing of schnapps. He hunched over his mug and stared at the table, his face wearing the pained expression of a man entering a confession box. Eventually he said: 'Yes, it happened as you said. Right across there. Of course, most of the old trees are gone now, replaced by that olive desert you see. Not many people left to remember it, but I was here.' He looked up from under the thick grey brows. 'You say your grandfather was one of the men in the second jeep?'

Jamie nodded.

'Then your grandfather probably killed my brother.'

The room seemed to go cold and Jamie felt Sarah's hand close on his beneath the table.

'I'm sorry.'

Werner shrugged. 'It was a long time ago. Erich was seven years older than me, loyal and brave; he died fighting for what he believed, but he killed a lot of my friends and he gave me this.' He thumped his leg and they heard the sound of hollow plastic muffled by his thick Tweed trousers. 'You have heard of Werewolf?'

'My grandfather mentions it in his journal. Some kind of Nazi guerrilla organization.'

The old man shook his head. 'A joke. Broken-down SS like Erich leading boys who should still have been at school against men with machine guns and tanks. He was convalescing here, after being wounded in the head on the *Ostfront*, when the local gauleiter ordered him to organize a Werewolf cell and harass the enemy. I was fourteen years old and frightened. Just a boy. Hitler was dead. People said the war was finished, but Erich would not believe it. I just wanted it to be over and be at home with my mother. You are surprised? You thought we were all fanatics in the Hitler Jugend?'

Jamie smiled politely.

'There were nine of us. Myself, Erich, my friend Pauli and a few others from the school. We made camp in the woods on the other side of the road – like being a boy scout except we had a machine gun and a few old Mauser rifles and a couple of fausts. Truth is, I think the war had driven Erich mad. He said we should take the fight to the Amis. Some of the boys started crying. I told him: "No we are going home." He was my brother, I thought he would listen, but he screamed that I was a traitor and hit me in the mouth with his pistol. When I said I would not fight, he shot me in the leg.' He turned to Sarah. 'Do not be sorry for me. I was fortunate. In Erich's eyes I was guilty of mutiny and he had every right to shoot me dead or string me up from the nearest tree. It happened to many. Of course, the other boys were too frightened then to do anything.

430

They carried me to this house, my mother's house, and left me here.'

Werner slurped at his coffee and licked his lips.

'Mama did her best with the leg, but when the gangrene came . . .' He shook his head at the memory. 'But that was later. Three days after Erich wounded me I heard the shooting and the explosion, over there. I wanted to go, but I couldn't move and I think Mama would have stopped me in any case. But I could see from the window the jeep burning and the flashes of the tracer rounds from the woods. When the firing stopped I was torn. Should I be elated at my friends' victory? Was I a coward, who had walked away from them? And what would the Amis do when they discovered this thing? Erich had boasted about a place in France that the SS had taught a lesson, and I had heard him talking in his sleep about things that happened in Russia that freeze my blood even now. Surely the Amis would burn our farm and hang us all? Then the shooting started again and I knew that the weapons doing most of the firing were not German. It only lasted for a moment. Then silence. All I could hear was Mama sobbing. I think she knew even then that Erich was dead. A few minutes later there were four or five individual shots. Very slow, very deliberate. Each one like a punctuation mark. I knew they were shooting the wounded. Before they went, the Amis buried their dead and left our boys for the crows.'

'They shot wounded children?' Sarah demanded incredulously. 'But the war was over. They knew that.'

'Oh, yes, young lady, they shot little Pauli and the

rest. I saw the bodies when they were brought here to be buried. You say the war was over, but war doesn't end just because someone says it is ended. It finishes when people stop shooting at each other. Erich's war was only ever going to finish when he was dead. The pity is that he took so many good boys with him.'

Jamie struggled to make sense of what he was hearing. He had read Matthew's account of the ambush as a heroic charge against a determined enemy and superior odds. The references to boys and children were clear enough, but somehow, in reading the journal, his mind had only absorbed one side of the story. Matthew's enemy had been hard-eyed fanatics, however young. They had struck, like cowards, from the forest and he had paid them back in their own coin. Only now, as old Werner rummaged through a drawer and produced a sepia-tinged picture of a grinning schoolboy football team, did he fully understand how young they had been. Had Matthew looked into an injured child's eyes and pulled the trigger? If he had, it turned everything he had learned on its head.

'I'm on the right, the big lad with the blond hair. Star centre forward. Pauli is the dark-haired kid in the front row. He was a good pal, Pauli. A good pal.'

'What happened afterwards. Was there some sort of inquiry?'

The German laughed – *haw, haw, haw* – as if Jamie had made a hilarious joke. 'You think anybody cared about a few Bavarian farm boys who were too stupid to surrender when they had the chance? Back then, the only

432

war crimes were German war crimes. The only victims were the Jews. A few months later a graves registration unit turned up and they eventually buried the dead Amis in the military cemetery at Dürnbach, with the shot-down Allied airmen, escaped prisoners who didn't make it home and the poor bastards the SS marched to death when they closed the PoW camps. Erich and my friends are over there at Saulgau.'

They finished their coffee and sat in silence for a while. Jamie stood up to go. There was nothing else to learn here.

Werner looked up, but the rheumy eyes were still somewhere in the past. 'Before they moved the bodies to Saulgau, they were stored in the barn. I sneaked in to see Pauli one last time. It was a mistake. He had been under the earth for three months, you understand, and he was no longer the Pauli I remembered. My advice to you, my young friend, is to turn back now. There is no profit in digging up the past. If you continue, all that lies in wait for you is sorrow.'

LIV

They reached Blumberg in the early evening but any chance of continuing on Matthew's route towards the Swiss border just five miles away was fast fading along with the daylight. Sarah bought a local map from the tourist centre as the staff were closing the doors and Jamie booked them into a *gasthaus* in the centre of town. When they met outside the hotel, he pointed to hills that formed the southern boundary of the valley.

'Those must have been where Matthew took the Germans.'

Sarah studied the map she'd bought and shook her head. 'I don't think so. I think maybe it's those high ones in the distance. See . . .' She showed him the map. 'There are two hamlets to the south between Blumberg and the Swiss border. Epfenhofen and Futzen. Beyond them is the start of that miniature mountain range he mentioned.'

'The Hoher Randen?'

'That's right. By the look of this, both of them are

possibles.' She studied him seriously. 'Jamie, why don't you just read the final pages of Matthew's journal and get this over with.'

'Do you think I haven't been tempted? I'm like an addict with a drugs stash. My fingers keep twitching towards the journal. But I won't give in because I'm certain this is how Matthew wanted it to be. In a way, this is his true last will and testament. When we go up there tomorrow he'll be with us. I have a feeling that if we break his rules we'll never find the answers.'

'What if you're wrong?'

'If I'm wrong, we go home. Maybe we forget the Sun Stone ever existed?'

'I don't think so.'

'No, I don't either. Since Tibet, I feel as if it's part of me. I suppose we'll just have to go back and start all over again. Walter Brohm's Black Sun led us to the Harz and the research facility. On the day he walked away from there he took his research papers, or at least a summary of them, with him. Remember what Matthew said about the day he first met him?'

'He said two of them were the most evil men he'd ever met. Did that mean he'd already formed some kind of instinctive bond with Brohm?'

'I think maybe he had, but that's not the point. One of them had a briefcase on his knee. It has to be Brohm. He must have cut a deal with the Americans. Brohm was a player. He would always keep an ace up his sleeve. When he left the Harz bunker and got rid of all the evidence he had already made sure the crown jewels were hidden in a safe place. The papers in the briefcase were just bait. Enough to tempt whoever saw them, but with the key elements missing. The Sun Stone was Brohm's passport to a new life in the United States and he would only hand over the location, and that of his main research, when he was in neutral Switzerland.'

'But once he reached Switzerland, he disappeared, along with the others?'

In the gathering gloom she saw his eyes fix on the fading blue line of the distant mountains. 'That's right. And tomorrow I think we'll be a step closer to finding out why.'

Next morning they set out for Epfenhofen, a tiny community of farms and houses distinguished by an astonishing hangman's loop of railway line that encircled the place like a noose. From beneath the railway viaduct they studied the tree-covered slope which rose almost vertically from where they stood. To their right, a narrow path led into the trees.

'This could be it,' Jamie suggested.

'Let me see the journal.' He handed it over and she turned the pages until she reached the passage she was looking for. 'Matthew says here that after Stan got out of the jeep at the beginning of the track he drove a further two miles before ordering the Germans out. I don't see how anyone could drive up that track.'

They searched the base of the escarpment, but it quickly became clear that she was right. The only drivable route south from the village was the main road. Epfenhofen was a dead end.

'It must be the next one then,' Jamie said with more confidence than he felt.

The village of Futzen was just over a mile to the west and as he scanned the countryside around him Jamie felt his heart beat faster.

'This looks more promising,' Sarah said, echoing his thoughts. From the road they saw that farmland sloped gently up from the village towards the hills and Switzerland, and even from a distance they could make out tracks linking the fields.

The landscape reminded Jamie of something from his past and he tried to remember the artwork it came from. An image popped into his head from nowhere. '*The Great Escape*!'

'What?' Sarah looked at him as if he was mad.

He laughed and pointed to the view. 'I thought this reminded me of a painting, but it's a film. They used to show it on TV every Christmas before we had a hundred satellite channels.' Still, she looked mystified. 'Surely you remember? Steve McQueen on a motorbike trying to jump the barbed wire between Germany and Switzerland. The scenery was just like this. Meadows and dirt roads and the Alps in the distance.'

She shrugged. 'Maybe it wasn't my kind of movie. Did he make it?'

He looked at her curiously. 'No, but it was a good film.'

'Did it have a happy ending?'

He shook his head. 'Not really. The Gestapo shot fifty unarmed prisoners of war.'

When they reached the village they worked their way along a network of streets to the south, where they were able to look across the fields towards the wooded hills beyond. The same railway that strangled Epfenhofen formed the southern boundary of the village and as they sat in the car an ancient steam train huffed its way past trailing a stream of green carriages and emitting a cheerful whistle. They looked at each other.

'You sure we woke up in the right century?'

'I'm beginning to wonder.' Jamie studied the track directly ahead of them. Bounded by trees on one side and a marshy ditch on the other, it cut, arrow straight, across the fields and rose into the trees. 'This is it.'

Sarah shot a glance at him. 'You can't be sure.'

He reached behind him and picked up the mottled envelope from its place on the back seat.

'This is it.' He put the car into gear and bumped across the railroad on to the gravel track and they drove south, towards Matthew Sinclair's destiny.

'You are sad, Leutnant Matt?' As usual, Walter Brohm sat apart from Klosse and Strasser and his words cut across my thoughts. Sadness was too inadequate a word for the mixture of emotions I felt at that moment. Up here among the trees with the breeze softly fluttering the oak leaves and with the warmth of the sun on my face it was easy to believe it really was all over. I should have been happy or at least relieved. I had fought a good war, a war that one day other men would tell me I

should be proud of; the best of wars because it was a war that I had lived through. Not survived, you understand. Lived through. The Matthew Sinclair who had disembarked in 1939 at Cherbourg, pink-cheeked and bright eyed, with the walking ghosts of the Royal Berkshire Regiment, was long gone. Part of him died with Sergeant Anderson on the retreat from Dyle and in the madness of broken bodies, blood and iron that followed. What was left had walked willingly into the inferno of the Coventry hospital and added his flesh to the flames that consumed his family. True, an empty shell remained, an empty shell with no soul and a single purpose. The SAS had taken the shell and created a new Matthew Sinclair, a Matthew Sinclair who could endure and survive and who could kill in many different ways without conscience or remorse, hard as the steel of the double-edged, fighting knife he carried. But now the armour of the new Matthew Sinclair has been worn down by the proximity of peace in a way never achieved by the proximity of death. He can feel himself fading, the barrier he has created to protect him from the madness and horror being worn away with each passing second that brings him closer to the end.

I shook my head and picked up the journal from the grass at my side, hoping Brohm would leave me alone with my ghosts. But he noticed that the brass clasp which held the book closed had broken.

He grinned and ambled across to me, reaching into the breast pocket of his khaki tunic which he could not help patting every time he talked of the great painting he owned. 'Here, Leutnant Matt, you must protect your work.' He handed me a piece of silver cord just long enough to tie the book together. 'Better you have it. A memento. Part of Brigadeführer Walter Brohm's uniform. One day you will look back with pride and say: "I knew Walter Brohm." When I reach America I will not forget what you have done for me. Soon the world will be a different place, a better place, where we two can be true friends. My work will change life for everyone. You understand that I cannot give you the details,' he smiled, 'but you must believe me when I tell you this. For now, only Astra can find the answer. Of course, we must first deal with the Ivans. Where Hitler failed, America will succeed, because America knows that if it does not succeed it will be destroyed, just as Germany has been destroyed.' His eyes narrowed and he glanced back to make certain Klosse and Strasser could not hear. I knew he was going to tell me then. 'A bomb,' he whispered. 'I will give them a bomb greater than any bomb ever invented. A bomb with the power of the sun.'

LV

They parked in a semicircular clearing just off the main trail and Jamie felt the electricity in the air the moment he stepped from the car beneath the overhanging canopies of ancient lime and oak trees. The tyre tracks of a mountain bike and the distinctive indent of horseshoes showed that not only walkers travelled the route and he guessed that it was used much more than it had been when his grandfather had passed this way. For if he was certain of one thing, it was that Matthew Sinclair had been here.

'But how do you know?' Sarah demanded.

'I don't *know*. But I can feel him all around me. He was exhausted in body and mind by the time he reached here. He just wanted it to be over. When he stepped out of the jeep with those three men they were less than two miles from the Swiss frontier and safety.'

'So what happened?' Her voice was almost desperate.

'Let's find out.'

The air was cool when they started climbing the path,

but they were quickly forced to remove their sweaters as the sun's heat began to force its way beneath the canopy and the vegetation closed in where the trail narrowed. Jamie studied the ground around them for the few clues his grandfather had left in the diary.

Behind them, ten minutes after they left the car, a Mercedes four by four with darkened windows drew slowly, almost silently, into the car park clearing.

'Make it quick, but make it certain,' the driver snapped to his passenger.

The second man took a rucksack from the back seat and walked quickly to the little Volkswagen. It took him less than twenty seconds to break into the car using an electronic key. After a quick search revealed nothing of interest he took a tiny magnetized metal circle shaped like a rivet head from the rucksack and placed it beneath the driver's seat in a position he knew no one but a mechanic or auto cleaner would ever find it.

Once the combined microphone and tracker was placed, he popped the bonnet of the car and opened the engine compartment. This time the package he took from the rucksack was larger, a heavily wrapped rectangular block, one side of which he sprayed with quick-drying cement and attached to the chassis at the driver's side wheel arch. It was a little more haphazard than he would have liked, because he had only been told the make of car that morning and didn't have time to make the kind of precise calculations of thickness of metal and blast potential he would normally do, but he consoled himself that he was using so much explosive that very little would survive of the car. Once he was certain it was firmly attached and the receiver was working properly, he nodded, closed the bonnet and locked the car.

'Set?' asked the driver.

The man nodded. 'Just say the word.'

The driver smiled. 'Patience. We can't afford any mistakes this time.'

As Jamie and Sarah climbed, the path became steeper and less well defined, just a scuff of brown dirt winding between the trees, crossed by twisted tree roots and with occasional natural stairways of worn grey rock. Sarah stopped with her hands on her hips and breathed in deeply. 'You can see why three unfit, middle-aged Nazi war criminals might find this difficult. I almost feel sorry for them.'

'Don't. They were bastards, and they probably ended up sunning themselves in Santa Barbara with skins like leather and mojitos in their fists while they watched their pneumatically enhanced mistresses frolic in the pool. I hope I'm that misfortunate.'

'What?' She stuck her chest out provocatively. 'You mean I'm not pneumatic enough for you, Saintclair. You ever even think about a busty blonde mistress, mister, and I'll replace the olives in my martini with your cojones.'

'In that case,' he bowed, 'let me assure you that it never crossed my mind. Let's go.'

'What's your hurry? We've got plenty of time.'

'I'm not so sure. The clock is ticking and we know we're not the only people who are looking for the Sun Stone. Just because we can't see them doesn't mean they aren't out there somewhere.' He studied the trees crowding the edge of the path. 'At least when Matthew Sinclair came this way he had a gun and he knew how to use it.'

They climbed on, through the sultry heat of mid-day, only once having a clear sight of the sun when they reached a broad clearing in the woods which had been planted with some kind of grain crop that was just beginning to ripen. They stopped to eat and through a gap in the trees they had a view of the hills to the north and west and the patchwork of cultivated fields in between.

'Listen,' Sarah hissed.

Jamie tensed, and wished, not for the first time, that he had some sort of weapon. Even a kitchen knife would be better than nothing. 'What is it?'

She sat motionless for a few seconds until a faraway machine-gun rattle broke the silence.

'A woodpecker.'

He felt like strangling her. Instead, he kissed her.

They lay side by side in the grass, staring up at a perfect cupola of pale eggshell blue. Sarah's hand searched for his and her fingers held him tight. 'Seriously, Jamie, do you ever wonder what happens after?' There was a wistful regret in her voice that sent an icicle through his heart.

'After?'

'When it's over. When you know Matthew's story. When we've found the Sun Stone or we haven't. When we don't have the pot of gold at the end of the rainbow to chase.'

He shrugged, which was awkward lying on his back. 'If I do think about it, I think about you and I together, having fun,' he said, aware that his words lacked conviction. 'There are still plenty of things we have to do and see. Together.'

She squeezed his hand.

'Sure there are, Jamie, but don't you sometimes worry that we'll be different people then?'

'Do you?'

She rolled over so she could look into his face. 'Look, the first day we met, you'd just been pushed under a train, that's hardly normal circumstances. Since then it's been a roller-coaster of World War Two puzzles and crazy quests, rabid Nazis, lost masterpieces and long-dead Jews, and this mysterious discovery that might not even exist except in our heads. Hell, we've been living on adrenalin and coffee and sex for the last month. Don't get me wrong, I wouldn't have missed it for anything, but while we've been chasing rainbows we've been completely different people from the ones that scrounge a living back in London. Do I know the real Jamie Saintclair? I'm still not sure. And you sure as hell don't know the real Sarah Grant.'

He got to his feet and dusted himself down, trying not to let her see his disappointment. There were certainly things he didn't know about Sarah Grant and things he suspected, but didn't want to know quite yet, but he'd been prepared to discover them in his own time. 'Maybe that's true, and maybe it isn't. But the one thing I'm certain of is that I'd like the chance to find out.'

He set off up the slope, expecting her to follow, but when he looked round a few minutes later, she wasn't with him. He turned back along the path just as she appeared through the trees, head down and deep in thought. She looked up and he saw she'd been weeping.

'Hey. Things aren't that bad. We'll work it out. I'll take you for a swanky dinner in the West End when we get back home and we can talk it over. Unless you'd prefer to have a quiet night in.'

She grinned through the tears and nodded. 'Look, it's . . . it's just that I'm confused, Jamie. Everything has happened so fast and there's been so much going on. I don't know what's up and what's down. Just give me time, huh.'

He bent and kissed her on the forehead. 'Sure. Come on, it can't be far now.'

They reached the clearing with the stream after another ten minutes of climbing. Sarah recognized it first. She stopped in her tracks. 'A runnel through a clearing beside a steep ravine, that's what Matthew described. I had to look up runnel in the dictionary.'

'This is it.' Jamie tried to keep the tension from his voice. He walked to the edge of the gully that slashed the woods. This was the moment he'd been waiting for since he first opened the journal. His imagination had painted a dark, gothic landscape of jagged rocks and brooding, dangerous forest, but it wasn't like that at all. Around him, the sun's rays turned the summer leaves into a hundred thousand sparkling emeralds and bird-song echoed among the trees. Still, he had no doubts. 'This is it.'

He fumbled in his rucksack and his hands shook as he withdrew the yellow-white envelope containing the final diary entries.

LVI

'*8 May 1945, 1 p.m., 3 miles south of Blumberg.
We have travelled two hundred and fifty miles over
the past seven days and throughout that time I
have felt as if a volcano has been building up inside
me. Klosse and Strasser might look like a pair of
mismatched British Army cooks in their ill-fitting
battledress, but the miasma of evil surrounding
them is as corrosive as mustard gas. They literally
stink of death, or perhaps it is truer to say that the
stink of death has never left my nostrils. I have done
many things that sickened me during six years of
war, but I have never felt dirtier than while helping
these men to escape the justice that awaits them
back in Germany. I knew now that Klosse was the
Nosferatu of the camps. I had seen the camps. The
awfulness of Belsen will never leave me; the living
turned into walking skeletons, the dead discarded
like so much refuse, the smell of decaying flesh and
the taste of burning bodies on my lips, the staring*

eyes of doomed children pleading from the faces of old men. The beaten, the starved, men torn apart by dogs, shot or hanged. Physically destroyed by the inhumanity of their treatment and mentally by the misery of their existence and the removal of all hope. Casual violence is symptomatic of war. The systematic annihilation of a race is beyond comprehension. Yet, if I am to believe Brohm, Klosse's crimes went beyond even that. He had hovered unseen in the smoke from the ovens and chosen his victims from among the living dead below: men, women and children, every individual specifically selected to suit his purpose; measured, weighed, injected or dosed, analysed and inspected in their agonies, each convulsion recorded, until the last, and finally eviscerated, dissected or disassembled for the knowledge their abused bodies would provide, their organs and parts bottled and stored for comparison with those who had gone before and those still to come. Not human beings. Not even animals. Things. Experiments. And all of it justified in the name of progress. There is no remorse in Klosse; it is plain on his smug Prussian face as he contemplates his new life. I think I have never hated anyone more. By comparison, Strasser is a babe in arms in the pantheon of genocide, a mere torturer; extractor of teeth and toenails, and twister of genitals. A dull bureaucrat driven by ambition and flattery to exchange his pen for a cattle prod and a soldering iron. Strasser is already doomed. Escaping to America will not save him, because he cannot escape from himself. For the same reason, he will never know forgiveness or absolution. The things he has seen and done are devouring him from the inside and the only escape will be oblivion. I can feel no pity for him. His crimes, paltry as they are in this terrible war, surely cannot just be forgotten.

'Yet it was only when Walter Brohm told me about his bomb "greater than any bomb ever invented" that I finally came to my decision.

'He sits directly opposite me, beneath a tree on the bank of the stream, watching me write, smiling that knowing smile of his, well fed and satisfied, certain of his own greatness, his genius merely dormant and soon to flower again beneath the benevolent rays of a Californian sun. I know of no crime Walter Brohm has committed, apart from the crime of complacency. He is a garrulous, almost likeable man, who, but for a tendency towards arrogance, would make a perfectly acceptable dinner companion. In a world full of enemies, Brohm wishes to be everyone's friend.

'Why is Walter Brohm more dangerous than a hundred Klosses? Because his curiosity knows no boundaries. Because no price is too high if it proves him right. Because no risk is too great if it enhances his genius.

'I carefully placed the journal in my pack and roused them from their rest. Klosse and the Ox

were reluctant to move, but I explained that our contact was waiting for us across the border less than an hour away.

'Klosse laughed. "Gut," he said to me. "At least the Amis will treat us with the respect we are due. I intend to report you for your treatment of your prisoners. You will be reprimanded."

'Strasser eventually pushed himself to his feet, grumbling quietly and scratching his fat backside.

'Walter grinned at me. "You will visit me in America, Leutnant Matt? They say we will have fine houses and big cars. Perhaps even a swimming pool. Who would believe such a thing? That is how precious my work is to them." He took my hand and shook it. "I thank you for bringing us here. Do not mind Klosse. His opinion counts for nothing against Walter Brohm."

'I detached myself and told them we wouldn't be stopping again. If they wanted to take a pee now was the time to do it.

'They stayed together, as men do in such circumstances, and lined up along the ravine as I had predicted they would.

'I had the Browning ready, with the safety catch off and I walked quickly up behind them. I shot the Ox first, in the back of the skull, and his body was thrown forward on to the rocks below. Klosse turned, prepared to attack me, but a man with his penis in his hand is peculiarly vulnerable and I had time to aim the gun directly at his heart. He *died cursing me, as I suppose was his due. Walter Brohm calmly finished what he was doing and turned to face me . . . '*

Jamie's voice faded. He had read the final paragraph automatically, not taking in the meaning of the words and the shocking reality dawned on him only slowly. This was a confession of cold-blooded murder. The scene replayed itself in his mind, but his brain wouldn't connect the man who pulled the trigger with the picture he had of the real Matthew, a smile on the kindly face and eyes that glittered with gentle humour.

LVII

'Read the rest, Jamie. Matthew wanted you to see this. You won't understand why unless you stay with him to the end.'

'I . . .'

'Read it. What happened to Walter Brohm? What happened to the Sun Stone?'

'At first Brohm didn't believe he was to die with the others. He was Walter Brohm. He was guilty only of genius. Klosse and Strasser were war criminals. He was a scientist. It was only when I kept the muzzle of the .45 pointed at his chest and he saw the implacable resolve on my face that the smile faded. He began to plead for his life.

'He offered me the contents of his briefcase, which, he said, were worth a king's ransom. When I kicked it aside he reached for the top pocket of his tunic. I almost shot him then, and he knew it, because his hand began to shake. He took out a

silk escape map with some sort of Nazi symbol on the reverse. This, he said, would lead me to the Raphael and everything else. He explained how to decipher it, but I wanted nothing from Walter Brohm. I knew that whatever he offered would be poisoned by contact with him. I despised him. He thought he was better than the two men I had just killed, but he was the worst of them. In his arrogance and his conceit he was prepared to unleash Armageddon upon this world in the name of science. A thousand Coventrys in a single explosion of white light. How many Peggys and Elizabeths and Annes must die to prove Walter Brohm right? Worse, he was prepared to risk the End of Days, and for what?

'He attempted to justify his work. It was the wonder of the world and only he, Walter Brohm, had the skills and the genius to make it happen. Unlimited energy, Leutnant Matt, think about it. Heating for every house. Power for industry. And that was only the start. Ordinary people would ride in cars and automobiles and trains designed to use his technology. Air travel would be so affordable and swift any man could go anywhere in the world, yes, and take his family too.

'He tried to tell me about the Sun Stone, but I wouldn't listen. I almost spat in his face. "What about the bomb, the bomb with all the power of the sun?" I demanded. "What about Peggy and Elizabeth and Anne" He looked bewildered, he

knew nothing of any Peggy or Elizabeth, I was trying to trick him. By now he was weeping and I almost wavered, but I knew I had to harden my heart for the sake of the world.

'*He went down on his knees and asked me to hear his confession, as if that single gesture would gain him absolution for all the sins he forced me to listen to. The deaths of Tibetan monks and Russian slave labourers. Jews shot down for having clumsy fingers or slaughtered for having the temerity to know too much. Yet his greatest sin of all he would not confess. The sin of certainty.*

'*When he was finished I shot him through the head and carried his body to the ravine and threw it over. Then I climbed down and did what I could to cover them in a decent fashion.*'

In a daze, Jamie walked across to the edge of the gully and looked down. After sixty years there was nothing to see except a jumble of moss-covered rocks twenty feet below and a thin stream barely worth the name running amongst them. 'He killed them all. They were unarmed. He executed them. It was murder, Sarah, cold-blooded murder. They would have hanged him if they'd found out.'

'But they didn't,' she said firmly. 'And I'm not sure they would have . . . hanged your grandfather, I mean. The three men he killed were monsters. Each one of them was responsible for hundreds of deaths. Even thousands. You heard what Matthew said about Walter Brohm's confession? *Jews slaughtered for having the temerity to know too much.* Well, we found the evidence of that massacre, didn't we? That alone would have been enough to have Walter Brohm hanged at Nuremberg. And Klosse, with his vile medical experiments on children. Strasser, the executioner. Do you know how many Jews were killed at Kiev in September nineteen forty-one? Thirty-three thousand innocent men, women and children. Come on, Jamie, these people were scum. If anyone deserved killing, they did. Matthew Sinclair did the world a favour when he fired those three bullets and you know it.'

'Who they were doesn't change the fact that my grandfather murdered three men in cold blood. He brought them here, he let them eat a last meal and he killed them. He and my mother brought me up to believe in justice, Sarah, but my grandfather set himself up as judge, jury and executioner.'

She gave a long drawn out sigh. 'Christ, Jamie, you're doing it again. This isn't about Jamie Saintclair. It's about Matthew and the war and the Sun Stone. You read what the journal said about his family. He watched his wife and children being burned alive by German incendiary bombs. That's enough to drive any man crazy. Yet he fought back. He endured the rest of the war and took part in some of the toughest battles of them all. He was tired and he was sick and what happened in Coventry had overwhelmed his mind. When he met a man who promised to build a bomb that would create a thousand Coventrys in a single night what the hell was he going to do? What the hell would you have done? Don't tell me you would have watched Walter Brohm and Klosse and Strasser walk away into the sunset en route to their cosy retirement in the States and then waited for the news that America had dropped the world's most powerful bomb on Moscow, because I won't believe you. In the same circumstances both of us would have done exactly the same thing, and you know what? We would have been right. Maybe it wasn't legal, but any way you look at it, it was justice. Remember the bunker? You seem to have forgotten what you promised, but that doesn't matter any more because Matthew Sinclair, your grandfather, did the job for you. It's simpler this way.'

Jamie turned away from the ravine. He remembered the hatred he had felt for Walter Brohm in the depths of the bunker, and the silent vow he had made to the girl with the pianist's fingers. Sarah was right. Justice was done. It was over. 'What about the Sun Stone?'

He saw the moment of indecision before her eyes hardened. 'Forget about the Sun Stone. Burn the diary. If we can't find the Sun Stone with the information we have, what chance is there of anyone else finding it without the book. Give me it. Right now.' She unhitched her rucksack from her back and opened one of the zipped compartments to pull out a box of matches. 'Give me it.'

He looked at her outstretched hand, the palm raised, and it reminded him of the hand in the bunker. He was tempted. Sorely tempted. It would be so easy to give it to her and watch the flames eating it, then go home and forget everything. No one else would ever know about the Sun Stone. No one would ever know about Matthew Sinclair and the murder of three Nazis he'd been ordered to protect. 'It's not that simple.'

She shook her head and now her eyes were filled with a mixture of anger and pity. 'You're wrong, Jamie, it is that simple. Give me the book.'

'We owe it to Tenzin not to give up. Have you forgotten that he sacrificed himself to save us? Just because it happened six thousand miles away doesn't make it any less real.'

'Tenzin was a dead man walking and you know it. He's not here now, but maybe if he was he'd be giving you the same advice. Let's walk away from this now, Jamie. For us. Let's go back to London and get on with our life and forget we ever heard of the Sun Stone.'

He noticed the way she said life singular, not lives, and a little bolt of hope shot through his heart. She was saying she would be his and that made it all the more sensible to hand over the journal. There was only one problem.

'If I give up now, I wouldn't be the man you met at the Tube station, or the man who was going to fight a helicopter gunship for you. I'd just be the same old loser I was before I found you. Matthew would have wanted us to see this through.'

He walked back to the gully edge and studied the long drop. 'I need to go down there.'

She came to his side. 'Are you crazy? You'll break your neck.'

He laughed. 'You're talking to someone who's climbed the Himalayas. This is a piece of cake.'

She shook her head. 'All you'll find down there are a few mouldy old bones picked bare by rats.'

He ignored her and dropped to his belly, slithering backwards until the bottom half of his body was over the edge and his feet scrambled for a toehold. Before he started climbing down, he looked up at her. 'What if Walter Brohm didn't have one map, but two? What if he waved the Harz map at my grandfather as a decoy while the map that points the way to the final location of the Sun Stone was hidden somewhere else? It could be down there, still in his pocket. I can't take the chance.'

With a rush of falling soil he was gone, half sliding, half scrambling down the sheer dirt face. He grabbed a tree root to slow his progress, but it only unbalanced him and he ended up rolling the last few feet and landing in an undignified dusty heap among the rocks beside the trickling water of the stream.

'I'll give you a two for style, but you get top marks for comic interpretation.' Sarah's voice came to him from above. 'What can you see?'

He looked around. Matthew said he had covered the bodies in a decent fashion. That meant there should be some kind of cairn.

'Nothing.'

'What do you mean?'

'There's nothing down here. No burial. Nothing that would mark a grave. The rocks are scattered about. Wait.' Something a little further downstream caught his eye and he worked his way towards it. He picked up a fallen branch and dug at a ragged piece of material sticking out of a patch of sand between two large boulders.

'What is it?'

His heart quickened and he excavated deeper. Cloth? No, something more substantial than cloth. Leather.

'For Christ's sake, Jamie!'

'I think I may have found Walter Brohm's briefcase.'

Getting back up took longer than coming down, but eventually he made it caked in dirt, sweat running down his face and some shapeless, weather-stained remains under his left arm. Sarah accepted it with distaste, brushing off sand and wriggling aquatic insects.

'You sure this is Walter Brohm's case? It looks like crap to me.'

'You'd look like crap if you'd been buried in mud for sixty years. If you look closely you can see the SS insignia stamped in the leather. I'm surprised it's survived at all. It must have been made for Brohm from some kind of specially reinforced hide, crocodile or buffalo, maybe. Look, the brass catches are still intact.'

He took the case from her and studied the furred green locks.

'Let me,' she demanded. 'What makes you think there'll be anything in there? Surely Matthew would have searched it before he threw it away.' She rummaged in her rucksack, came up with a substantial Swiss army knife and opened the largest blade.

'I'm not so sure. You heard what he said about Brohm.

460

He wanted nothing to do with his research or the Sun Stone.'

Sarah worked at the brass with the knife point. 'He took the map of the Black Sun,' she pointed out.

'Yes, but only because Brohm said it would lead him to the Raphael, which would have had some value to him.' As he said the words, it was as if someone whispered in his ear, but he couldn't catch the message. He looked at the trees, thinking it must have been the breeze, but there was no wind.

'Are you all right?'

He blinked. 'I think so. I thought . . . Anyway, I don't think Matthew would have wanted to dirty his hands with what was in the briefcase. Whatever was in it – Brohm's research papers, maybe even some clue to the location of the stone – will still be in there and it might have survived. Stranger things have happened. You only have to look at the Dead Sea Scrolls or the Vindolanda Tablets.'

'Got you.' She'd given up on the locks and used all her effort to slice through the thick leather at the back of the case. 'You were right, it was made to last. I suppose you should do this.' She handed it back to him and he pulled apart the leather, allowing them both to peer inside.

'Bugger.'

All that was left of the contents was a sodden mass of brown sludge.

'So what do you think happened to the bodies, if there were any bodies here at all?' Sarah asked as they were

461

packing up, the galling disappointment of failure still creating a barrier between them.

'Oh, the bodies were here.' Jamie looked around the clearing distractedly. 'I think the briefcase proves that. You saw the SS flashes on the leather and it was exactly where it would have been if my grandfather had thrown it away. In a way it makes sense. This must be a popular hiking trail, and probably has been for decades. Matthew wouldn't have been able to bury them properly, only cover them with rocks and a few branches. The corpses could have been exposed by animals or the first decent spate. With dozens of people a week passing on the trail it was only a matter of time before they were discovered. Three skeletons in the remains of British uniforms, but without any form of identification. Remember old Werner telling us about the cemetery where they buried the escaping Allied prisoners of war who didn't make it to the Swiss border. I'm betting that's where Walter Brohm, Gunther Klosse and Paul Strasser ended up. Three British soldiers "known unto God". I don't know whether Matthew will be laughing or crying.'

'And now?'

He hesitated because he wasn't quite sure how to explain. The sensation had been so strong that it had been like someone physically standing beside him. 'You asked me earlier what was wrong. It was because I suddenly had a feeling that we were very close to something important, but I was missing it. It was as if someone was screaming at me in a vacuum; I could see their lips moving but I didn't know what they were saying. Can you understand that?'

'Yes, but I still think we should take this chance to walk away, go right back down that hill and leave all the dead bodies behind us. Old Werner was right when he said digging up the past would only bring us grief.'

Jamie shook his head. 'I can't, Sarah. I'll take you back to the airport and you can go home, but I have to keep looking. Maybe I'll never find it, but I have to try. If I gave up now I'd be letting too many people down. You as much as anybody.'

She smiled, but when she replied there was a catch in her voice. 'Don't be an idiot. If we do this, we do it together. Christ, what have I done to us, Jamie?'

It seemed an odd question and he decided not to answer, because there was no answer. Instead, he asked: 'What was I saying when I suddenly came over all queer?'

Sarah laughed and it rid her of the melancholy that seemed to permeate this place. 'The one thing you'll never be is queer, Mr Saintclair. You were talking about the Raphael, how Brohm had told your grandfather that the map would lead him to the Raphael.'

'Yes.' She could almost feel his excitement as he scrambled for the journal. 'But that wasn't exactly what he said. In the journal Matthew is always very careful to be precise, even when he's under pressure. Here, you read it, exactly as he records it.'

She accepted the book and opened it where he'd placed the final page. '*He took out a silk escape map with some sort of Nazi symbol on the reverse. This, he said, would lead me to the Raphael and everything else.* Is that enough, or do you want more?'

He frowned, his face lined with concentration as he spelled out the words that had seemed to whisper to him earlier. What was it? What had he missed? The first sentence couldn't have any hidden message, it was just a general description of the map. So it must be in the second. *This, he said, would lead me to the Raphael and everything else.* Ten words, without the attribution. Ten little words. Christ, could it really be that simple?

'*Everything else.*'

'What?'

'Brohm told Matthew that the silk escape map would lead him to the Raphael *and everything else.* We were so blinded by the Raphael that we missed it. It was right there under our noses.'

LVIII

She stared at him. 'If the Sun Stone has been in the bunker all along surely the authorities would have found it by now? They will treat what's left in the complex like an archaeological dig, cataloguing everything and removing anything of even the slightest value.'

'Not necessarily. Remember what I said about the maps?'

'About Brohm offering the Harz map to Matthew as a decoy?'

'That's right. Well, I was wrong. There was no other silk map. But Brohm was pleading for his life. He knew he was going to die, so he would have offered every-thing, even the Sun Stone to save himself.'

'But you said the Sun Stone wasn't there?'

'No, but what if there *is* another map. Only it's not a silk map. It's the real thing. The original . . .'

'. . . like the Black Sun at Wewelsburg.'

They arrived back at the car. Jamie used the electronic

switch to open the boot and they put their rucksacks inside. He reached for the door handle.

'Wait!'

His fingers froze a centimetre from the black plastic.

'You can't get in the car.'

'Why not?'

'Because your jeans are covered in mud.' She pointed to his backside where he'd slid down the gully. 'You'll get the seat filthy. Here.' She handed him his jacket. 'Sit on that until we get back to the hotel.'

He glared at her. 'You scared the bloody life out of me.'

'Good. I think you have every reason to be scared. We both have. The closer we get to the Sun Stone the more dangerous this is going to get.'

The next day, he pushed the Volkswagen to its limit on the autobahn. A hundred miles into the journey the temperature gauge began to rise ominously and Jamie thought he felt a vibration in the engine that hadn't been there earlier.

Sarah noticed the car slowing.

'What's wrong?'

'I think we have a problem. There's a rattle somewhere there shouldn't be.' He pointed to the temperature gauge, which still hadn't fallen back towards normal since he'd eased off the accelerator.

'Maybe it's something to do with your driving?'

He bit his tongue and kept his eyes on the road.

'Do you think you can fix it?'

'I can take a look under the bonnet and give a few bits and pieces a good shake, but that won't mean I have any idea what I'm doing. What about you?'

She waved her manicured fingers in front of his eyes. 'Does this look like the hand of an auto mechanic?'

'Do you think it would be able to press a few buttons and call Europcar?'

He felt her staring at him. 'I wish . . .'

'What?'

'Nothing.'

Two hours later – after a short stop in town – they drew up next to the police station on the western outskirts of Braunlage. Jamie knew there was no point in going directly to the bunker. It would be sealed off to keep out the kind of treasure hunters and ghouls who were always drawn to such sites. He went into the building while Sarah called the car hire company and asked them to send a mechanic.

'May I talk to Kommissar Muller?' The officer at the desk gave him the look cops reserve for ordinary mortals who disturb them while they're doing something much too important to be interrupted, like drinking coffee and reading the sports pages.

'The guy who found the bunker, right?'

'Right.'

'You are fortunate, she's just going off duty.' He picked up the phone and spoke quietly into it. 'She'll see you now.'

'Herr Saintclair, this is a surprise.' Lotte Muller greeted him with a handshake. 'Is Miss Grant with you?'

He explained about the car and she shook her head gravely. 'Yes, hire cars. But what can you do? You are here for a pleasure visit to see our lovely town again?'

Jamie had considered his approach on the drive north. There was no way he was going to tell anyone about what he believed was hidden in the bunker. He also realized it was unlikely that even the people who had discovered it would be allowed back inside just because they asked. That left one option. To lie. 'I'm afraid not. We've been touring. Now we're on our way to the airport at Paderborn and decided that we would like to pay our respects to the people who died in the bunker.'

'Respects?'

'A tribute. It is a British tradition. Just some flowers and the opportunity to say a few words. I'm sure you'll understand that we were unable to give them the respect they deserved at the time.'

'You are aware that the bodies have been removed? There is nothing to see.'

Jamie allowed his face to harden. 'I can assure you that we saw more than enough on our last visit, Kommissar.'

She nodded distractedly. 'Of course, forgive me. So you would like to go inside the bunker?'

'If that would be possible. It would take only a few moments.'

Lotte Muller hesitated. She had orders to keep the bunker secure, and she was a great believer in obeying orders. But Jamie Saintclair and Sarah Grant had found the bunker and the Raphael, and despite the extra workload it had brought, she was grateful to them for the opportunities it created. She made her decision.

'Very well.' She smiled tiredly. 'I finish my shift in a few minutes. I will drive you there. No,' she raised a hand as Jamie opened his mouth to protest. 'I insist. Your car will stay here. There is a rental garage in town and I'm sure the mechanic will be here very quickly. They are extremely efficient.'

Ten minutes later she joined Jamie and Sarah in the car park. Sarah carried a large bunch of colourful flowers and Lotte nodded approvingly. 'They are lovely,' she said. 'We have very similar blooms in the town square. They are just reaching their peak in time for the summer.'

As they got into the black BMW Sarah attempted to disguise the fact that the bouquet had no florist's wrapping and some of the stems still had the roots attached.

Lotte Muller took the southern route from the town. She noticed Jamie's puzzlement.

'This is not the most direct route, but it will save another hike through the forest,' she explained. 'We discovered the main entrance to the bunker in the hills to the west of the river. It was a working quarry and a sub-camp of the Dora-Nordhausen *konzentrationslager*, but it closed towards the end of the war and never re-opened. The current owners of the site, a company registered in the Cayman Islands, have gone to great lengths to keep people away. Given the circumstances, the company is naturally part of our inquiry, but so far we have had little success discovering who is behind it.'

After crossing the river they turned north, and a little later left the main road on to a forest track.

'Of course, the bunker is still a murder scene, but we have completed our initial investigations in the area where the bodies were discovered. The strangest thing is that they were all already dead.'

'I don't understand.' Sarah leaned forward from the back seats.

'You noticed that many of the bodies were in a remarkable state of preservation? It seems that conditions within the bunker were conducive to partial mummification. Our initial forensic investigations showed that several victims had similar tattoos on the inside of their left forearm. You understand the implications of this?'

Jamie shook his head, but Sarah said she did.

The police chief explained. 'Whatever you think of the Nazis, Mr Saintclair, they were extremely thorough. Every concentration camp prisoner received a personal identification number. At first, the numbers were sewn on their prison clothes, but because of the nature of the camps the clothing must be reused: again and again and again. So instead of on the clothing, the number would be written on the prisoner. Much more economic and efficient, yes? When the prisoner was disposed of, his number was disposed of with him.

'Fortunately, some records from the camps still survive and we have been able to identify those victims whose tattoos are still readable.'

'Who were they?'

'To the best of our knowledge, they are all either scientists or technicians.' She pointed to a file in the compartment beneath the passenger window. 'Please. The most well known was a man called Abraham Steinberg, a Berlin physicist who, before the war, worked closely with some of the scientists who were eventually involved in the *Uranverein* project. Many of his Jewish colleagues found ways to escape Germany, but poor Herr Steinberg elected to stay with his family.' Jamie opened the file and found himself staring into the face of a stern, bearded man standing behind a workbench filled with scientific equipment. He turned to the next sheet and his heart lurched. 'Another of the victims – the youngest we have identified – is his niece, Hannah Schulmann, a laboratory technician who worked closely with him.' Lotte gave a sad smile. 'She was nineteen years old.' In the black-and-white photograph Hannah Schulmann had the ethereal, cinematic beauty that in other times would have won her a place on the screen. A softness and a sensitivity that surrounded her like a halo. Her dark eyes sparkled with humour and her smile showed tiny pearls of perfect white teeth. The eyes drew him in, and he choked, making the women stare. So much life. So much potential. Wasted. A terrible darkness descended on him and he felt a hatred for Walter Brohm and his like that made him wish it had been his finger on the trigger and not Matthew's.

'All of the dead have one thing in common,' Lotte Muller continued gently. 'They were part of a transport of three hundred prisoners from Mauthausen which arrived in Auschwitz-Birkenau on the twenty-fourth of February nineteen forty-three. On arrival they were taken directly from the train to the gas chambers. Odd, don't you think, that for two years this facility appears to have been staffed by ghosts?'

LIX

The van with the Europcar logo drew into the police station car park and pulled up beside the Volkswagen. While the mechanic retrieved his toolbox, an officer emerged from the station to sign him in.

'Is this the one I'm supposed to take a look at?'

'That's it. They didn't leave the keys, though.'

The mechanic laughed. 'Tourists. Not a problem. I have a spare set.'

'Well, if you need to get in touch with them, just let me know. They're with the boss.'

'Thanks.' Not a bad guy for a cop, he thought. He waited until the man was back in the building before he opened the bonnet.

They reached a rutted track where the roadside vegetation appeared to have been recently cut, and a few minutes later the car approached an iron gate. The gate was badly rusting, but the razor wire that topped it and which stretched into the trees on either side of the road couldn't have been more than a few years old. Two bored-looking policemen hurriedly stubbed out their cigarettes at the sight of the approaching car. The men saluted Lotte Muller, but she still had to produce her identity card before the gate was opened. They drove into a wide, dusty bowl below a great scar in the hillside. At the base of the scar, a dark shadow showed where a tunnel had been cut into the rock.

'I doubt this place would ever have been found,' the police chief said as she led the way towards the passage. 'Of course, some people believe it would have been better if it had not been. They wish to forget that things like this ever happened.'

Sarah gripped the flowers in both hands. She looked towards the impenetrable forest beyond the barbed wire and tried to imagine what it had been like for the three hundred men and women who had seen their last glimpse of sunlight here. She shivered and hesitated before the entrance, but a generator kicked into life somewhere behind them and a line of bulbs strung along the roof illuminated the tunnel with dim, unnatural light. They followed Lotte inside.

Fifty metres into the passage they reached a massive reinforced steel door with a smaller entrance set into it. Lotte reached inside her shoulder bag and brought out a set of keys.

'The locksmith took two days to break in. My minister did not have his patience, he wanted to blow the doors with explosive. Fortunately, he was persuaded to wait.'

The key turned easily in the lock and the door swung open to reveal what looked like a small aircraft hangar. At the far end were sited a pair of a concrete bunkers with narrow horizontal slits that would each allow a belt-fed machine gun to cover the entire area. Between them a set of metal stairs led to the next level.

'They didn't encourage visitors.'

'No, they did not, Mr Saintclair. This way please.' She ushered them below the stairs to where a corridor led to a tunnel similar to those they had run through when they were being hunted.

'Would it be possible for us to spend some time alone where we found the bodies?' Jamie asked.

Their host frowned. 'I do not know if that would be permitted. This is a place of many dangers, Mr Saint-clair. We have not yet begun work on clearing the main production hall.'

'I realize that, Kommissar, but it is very important to us. We – Miss Grant and I – discovered this bunker and what we saw inside that room will remain with us for ever. At the very least, we deserve the oppor-tunity to come to terms with it.' Sarah moved to his side and together they looked into Lotte Muller's eyes. Her expression softened and she sighed.

'Of course, you must. I understand. I saw what you saw and it haunts me also. I . . . This tunnel eventually leads to what we call the production hall, it is lit the entire way. You will recognize it by the door, which is badly damaged – I am sure you remember it – the room where you discovered the bodies is the third on the left. Please be careful. It would be very regrettable if anything were to happen to you.' She nodded and turned away. 'I will wait for you here. Shall we say ten minutes?'

Jamie thanked her and led the way inside.

'That was smooth, lover boy,' Sarah whispered. 'You had the dragon eating out of your hand. I can see I'm going to have to watch you.'

'It's your corrupting influence,' Jamie said airily. 'Can you remember the way to the office where we found the Raphael?'

'Nope. Not exactly.'

'I think I have a vague idea. But we have to hurry.' He broke into a jog and she kept pace by his side. They reached the twisted door to the production hall. 'You take the flowers to where we found the bodies. I'll go on to the office. We'll meet back here.' He saw she was about to protest. 'It makes sense. Lotte Muller will expect to see some evidence we've been there.'

'That's not what I was going to say, idiot. Just because this section is lit up like a Christmas tree doesn't mean to say everywhere else is. Do you have a torch?'

'Aaah, no.'

She reached into her jacket and came out with her penlight. 'This might help.'

He grinned. 'I suppose it might.'

She reached up to kiss him on the lips.

'Now git!'

Jamie set off down the passageway. He ran swiftly, never hesitating at an intersection or a corner, because he'd lied. He knew exactly where he was going. But he was glad of the torch.

The bunker should have been filled with ghosts, but even though he had seen the horrors that had been perpetrated down here, the corridors held no threat. The dead no longer called out for retribution, because Matthew Sinclair had avenged them sixty-three years earlier when he had put a bullet in Walter Brohm's skull.

When he reached the stairs he took them two at a time and the rusting metal creaked beneath his feet. At the top was the office where they'd found the Raphael. The door hung open and he stepped inside. He swung the torch across the walls, spotlighting the dust-free oblong where the painting had hung behind Walter Brohm's mahogany desk. Strange that it didn't really matter any more.

Now he turned his attention to the rest of the office. It was just as he remembered from that single glance before the Raphael had bewitched him. Spacious, but functional. One wall filled with the empty filing cabinets that would have contained Brohm's research and all the minutiae of running the bunker with its hundreds of irritating, petty human hindrances. Jamie suspected Walter Brohm had hated it here. Brohm the genius would have preferred to be in his laboratory dealing with problems he could understand. But Brohm was a cultured man who did himself well, with his Old Masters, his fine French wines . . . and all the other luxuries the new Nazi empire could provide.

Only Astra can find the answer.

He had puzzled over Brohm's odd reference from the moment he read it. Astra was the Latin word for stars and he'd assumed it was a reference to the potential of the Sun Stone. Yet in the context of their conversation it had seemed out of place. Then it had struck him that Walter Brohm and Matthew Sinclair had been speaking in whispers to keep what they were saying from Klosse and Strasser. What if Matthew had misheard?

Not *'Only Astra can find it'*, but *'Only Astra can hides it'*. Astra can. Astrakhan.

The Oriental rug made of the distinctive black fibres lay in the centre of the floor, trampled and disfigured by dusty footprints, more or less where Brohm had left it. Like Jamie, anyone who entered this office would only have had eyes for the space where the painting had been, or the desk.

Taking a deep breath he kicked the musty heap of cloth to one side, exposing the marble floor beneath. And suddenly everything was clear.

'You bastard. You cunning bastard.'

He was looking at a mosaic of a third Black Sun, the style identical to the first two, with a distinctive pattern in the centre that would represent some combination of rivers and roads. What was different was the inscription below the circle. The inscription that finally revealed what he had been looking for.

Die kreuzung wo die frau betet.

The crossroads where the women pray.

He pulled out his mobile phone and dialled the number on the card he held in his hand. For a moment he thought the signal in the bunker would be too weak, then the ring tone purred twice before it was answered.

'May I speak to Mr Lim, please?'

LX

Lotte Muller parked outside the police offices and Jamie retrieved what looked like the decaying carcass of a long-dead animal from the boot of the BMW. 'I think you should hold on to this,' he suggested.

'This is a police station, Mr Saintclair, not a recycling depot.' Her long nose wrinkled with distaste at the scent of decay, 'Although I believe whatever it is may already be beyond recycling.'

Jamie grinned. 'I hope not. Because I think it could be a very valuable Oriental rug. The man who hung a Raphael on his wall wouldn't have any old carpet on the floor. At least have an expert look at it.'

Reluctantly, the police chief stretched out her hands for the mouldering heap of cloth. But Jamie was already on his way into the police office. 'No need for both of us to get our hands dirty.'

Lotte Muller followed him inside while Sarah stayed by the car. 'Put it there.' She pointed to a corner, close to a rubbish bin, which is where she would have preferred him to deposit it.

He dropped the carpet where he was told, raising a cloud of dust.

'I have a favour to beg.'

She stared at him, her patience beginning to wear thin. 'The *Herren* is through there on the left.'

'Not that kind of favour.'

They drove south until they picked up the autobahn close to Nordhausen and Jamie turned east, following the signs for Halle and Leipzig. The atmosphere in the car was like a physical barrier between them. He deliberately kept his eyes on the road, but he could feel her anger building as if it was the heat from an open fire. It couldn't go on. There were things that had to be said and there might not be another chance to say them. He pulled off the motorway at the next turn-off and drew in to a car park overlooking a series of man-made lakes. He got out of the car and waited until she followed. They stared out over the nearest lake, avoiding each other's eyes. When Sarah eventually spoke her words were an explosive mix of pain and suppressed fury. 'What the fuck is going on, Jamie? When are you going to tell me what the hell you found in that bunker?'

'I'm not certain yet.'

'Then where the fuck are we going?'

'South.'

'I have eyes. I can see that.'

'I need you to trust me.'

'You what?'

'I need you to trust me . . . and I need to know exactly what's going on.'

She turned to stare at him and now the anger had been replaced by something else, but he couldn't read what it was. 'Who do you think you are, Jamie Saintclair? Haven't I trusted you every day since we goddam met? I thought we were partners? I thought we were more than partners.'

'We are.'

'Partners don't hide things from each other. People who love each other don't hide things from each other.'

There it was. The first time either had dared to mention love, even though its presence had grown so powerful it had sometimes threatened to suffocate them. It took all his resolve not to surrender. 'No, they don't, Sarah, and that's why I need you to tell me the truth. The time for games is past. If I'm going to save our lives I have to know everything.' He knew he'd won when the first tear rolled down the velvet of her cheek.

When she spoke it was as if each word was being torn from her. 'First I was to follow you. Then they wanted me to get close to you. When you fell under that train I thought it was over before it had begun, but it gave me my chance.'

'Who is they?'

She hesitated, reluctant to take the next irrevocable step. 'Israeli intelligence. My controller. I don't know how, but they somehow learned about the Sun Stone and the link to Walter Brohm. My family is Jewish and I spent a year in Tel Aviv doing my Masters degree. They were on the lookout for people with backgrounds like mine. That's where I was recruited.'

He'd known, or at least he'd suspected. All those handy little criminal skills. The way she handled a gun so expertly. He remembered the meeting in the Kensington pub. Simon's ever so cooperative friend. 'Is David your controller?'

She sniffed. 'That's one of the names he uses.'

'So it was all just part of the job, getting close to me and the rest of it? You played me for a sucker and I fell for those big brown eyes of yours. Dumb old Jamie Saintclair rolled over to have his tummy tickled whenever Sarah Grant smiled. Jesus, you must have had some laughs.'

'No.' She shook head so hard he felt her tears on his face. 'Not the rest of it. That was my choice. You have to believe me, Jamie. What happened between us mattered. Don't taint it by thinking it had anything to do with *them*. I tried to stop this. I tried to get you to turn back, but you were too damn stubborn.' He wanted to reach out to her, but it wasn't yet time.

'And then?'

'We had a team close by all the time. They were to provide protection and as soon as we'd located the Sun Stone I was to call them in.'

His laugh was short and sour. 'Protection? Your Mossad geniuses didn't make much of a job of it. Where the hell were they while we were dodging bullets in the Harz?'

'My phone, I was supposed to contact them . . .' She swallowed and took a deep breath. 'So now you know . . . everything.'

The unspoken question hung between them. He answered it by taking her in his arms and kissing her eyes, tasting the tart salt of her tears.

'Listen,' he said gently, 'there are a lot of things we need to talk about, but this isn't the time. I should kick your spying backside out here and now, but I won't because I've fallen a little bit in love with whoever the real Sarah Grant is.'

'We could still turn back, walk away from all this. I'll tell them I won't work for them any more and we can fly back to London and see if we can make it as two ordinary people.'

'No. We've come too far now. We owe it to Matthew and Tenzin and Simon and Magda, all the people who have died, to see it through.' He looked out over the rippling waters of the lake. 'Can I assume David, or whatever he's calling himself today, is nearby?'

She nodded. 'There's a satellite tracking device in my new phone.'

'Good. When we get closer to where we're going, we'll let him know exactly where to find us.'

She held back as he got into the car. 'So you still won't tell me what you found back there?'

'Trust me.'

*   *   *

Two miles behind them the driver and passenger in the grey Mercedes listened to the final exchange.

'Lovers' tiff?'

'I'll give you odds of three to one he tells her in the next hour.'

'And then?'

The other man said nothing. They both knew the answer.

After another thirty minutes the driver studied the locator device on the screen in front of him. 'Looks like they're pulling in for fuel. Not a bad idea. I could do with a piss.'

The passenger frowned. He didn't like it, but they didn't have much choice, he didn't want to get in front of his quarry. 'We'll stop there too, but we'll stay in the car until they move again. Then you can have your piss.'

They passed Leipzig and began to see the first signs for Prague. 'What will you do if you find it?' Sarah's voice was devoid of emotion, as if the question had drawn all the strength from her.

Jamie shook his head. 'I don't know. I thought we could destroy it, but the closer we get the less likely that seems. Maybe hire a boat somewhere and drop it into the ocean. Chuck it into a volcano.'

'Christ, Jamie, you're not in Lord of the fucking Rings,' she said. 'This is real life. This is dangerous. Please, for my sake, turn back now.'

He didn't look at her. He didn't want to see the tears.

Instead, he glanced out of the window to check if the helicopter that had been flying parallel with the road for the last ten miles was still with them. The next sign said eight kilometres to Dresden.

'I told you. It's too late.'

After five minutes he turned on to a slip road towards the city. Sarah stared at him and he nodded.

'Walter Brohm hid the Sun Stone in the safest place in Germany, which also happened to be the place where he was born. When he closed down the bunker early in nineteen forty-five, Dresden was the only major city in Nazi Germany that had never been properly bombed by the Allies. They called it Florence on the Elbe. It was a centre of huge cultural significance with some of the most beautiful architecture in Europe, a place of grand palaces and theatres, opera houses and museums. More importantly, there was no heavy industry, no tank production lines or ball bearing factories. And it wasn't on any of the *Wehrmacht*'s main supply routes. The kind of stuff that attracts target allocation officers. Dresden was a military backwater.'

She looked out over the city unfolding below them. 'Where, Jamie? Where did he hide it?'

'I found the last Black Sun on the floor of Brohm's office in the bunker. No one had noticed it in all the madness surrounding the Raphael. The road and river network matches what I know about the city. But even if I hadn't known how to decode the Black Sun, the inscription beneath it would have told me. *Die kreuzung wo die frau betet.*'

She looked puzzled. 'The intersection where the women worship?'

'The crossroads where the women pray. When I found out Walter Brohm was born in Dresden, I did a little reading on the city. Remember the journal entry where Brohm was talking about the centre of the earth? The one I missed that pointed us towards Wewelsburg? In the next line, my grandfather said that everyone has a different centre of the earth and Brohm's would always be his mother's spiritual home. That was Dresden, but not just Dresden. The most famous building in the city isn't a palace or a museum. It's a church. The Frauenkirche. The church at the crossroads where his father was pastor and his mother would have worshipped. He knew every stone and every potential hiding place. It must have seemed perfect. Walter Brohm hid the Sun Stone and all his research papers in the crypt of the Frauenkirche.'

Sarah leaned forward against the dashboard and put her head in her hands.

'Why didn't you tell me this before?'

The driver of the Mercedes turned to his partner. 'Did you get that?'

'I got it. Paydirt.'

'You know what to do. I'll call the old man.'

The passenger didn't hesitate. Twenty years in special forces and a month that had seemed like a lifetime in a dusty shithole called Fallujah had long since eroded his belief in the sanctity of human life. He reached for the mobile phone on the dashboard, chose speed dial and pressed one. His face wore a look of intense concentration as he listened to the phone dialling up the number.

The bomb was a simple enough device, smaller and less crude than the one he'd set in the Menshikov Palace, but more than big enough to do the job. He'd copied the signature – the specific design features used by a known bomb maker – from a bomb discovered during a raid on an al-Qaida safe house in Hamburg three years earlier. A kilogram of shaped C-4 high-energy explosive detonated by a mobile phone that was one of a batch of Nokia 2300s bought by the now-deceased terrorist in 2004. Normally, he prided himself on being capable of manufacturing a bomb precise enough to take out an individual target within the car. But using the Hamburg bomber's signature also meant using his methods. A kilogram of HE would tear the car apart and destroy everything within about a thirty-metre radius. As a professional, the overkill offended him, but he also recognized the need for certainty.

Several factors dictated how the next millisecond would affect the occupants of the target car. The shaped charge and the quality of build of the engine bay combined to direct 80 per cent of the explosive force towards the passenger compartment. They started dying when they were hit by a blast wave which expanded within the enclosed space at a speed of 9,000 feet per second, causing a catastrophic pressure change that ruptured lungs, ear drums and bowels and resulted in what trauma experts call 'full body disruption' – multiple amputations. The nervous system is not built to withstand the kind of stress created by proximity to such an event and immediately shuts down. This was fortunate for the victims who by now had been enveloped by the 3,000 C flash which instantly followed the initial wave and inflicted first-degree burns over any exposed flesh, burned away hair and clothing and caused further internal damage as the super-heated air was drawn into already damaged lungs. In the third wave of the explosion, precisely one third of a millisecond after detonation, the combined materials which had divided the occupants from the engine compartment, now consisting of chemical dust from various vapourized plastics, white-hot molten metal and many thousands of shards of jagged steel shrapnel, caused devastating penetrative injuries from abdomen to skull. By this point the two victims were already clinically dead, their brain function fading and the memory of the previous half a millisecond merely a single white flash. In a quirk of physics which the bomb maker could hardly have calculated, the combined forces of the blast catapulted what remained of the car's driver through the gaping hole where the roof had been, at the same time as the fireball from the exploding petrol tank. The body of the passenger – or at least the charred trunk from the knees upwards – remained in its seat to be consumed by the flames as the mangled wreckage of the German automobile spun to a stop next to the centre barrier of the autobahn.

The resulting investigation and the clean-up operation would close the highway for the next twenty-four hours.

'What was that?' Sarah reacted to the muffled 'crump' of the explosion and looked round in time to see an expanding fireball a few miles back on the autobahn. 'Must have been some kind of crash. Looks like a bad one, maybe a petrol tanker or something.'

Jamie considered stopping, then shook his head. 'There's nothing we can do about it.'

She sank back in her seat with her chin on her chest. 'No, there isn't.' They would never know that David had spent most of the previous night debating with his superiors whether tampering with the bomb Mossad's tame mechanic had found would compromise the operation. Or that he had eventually lost the argument and in the end had ordered the switch at the final fuel stop on his own authority.

Jamie drove into the city centre and turned off just before the broad ribbon of the River Elbe on to a road that led them past railway tracks and run-down factories. Halfway along it he stopped. For a few moments there was silence as they stared ahead at the broken skyline of Dresden's Old Town.

'I made a mistake. I should have trusted you.'

'Damn right you should.'

'If this doesn't work out will you forgive me?'

She turned quickly and kissed him on his lips and in the soft glow of the setting sun he realized she

490

had never looked more beautiful. 'There's nothing to forgive.'

'Are you sure?'

'Sure. Let's get this thing done.'

He nodded.

'Let's.'

He put the car in gear and they drove on. To find Walter Brohm's Sun Stone and the discovery that would change the world.

LXI

Dresden's Old Town was a curious mix of the old the new and the unlikely. Sprawling Renaissance palaces and layer-cake opera houses evoked the glory days of Saxon culture while rubbing shoulders with the thronging modern shopping malls, hotels and cinema complexes that are the ever-present advertisements for consumer capitalism in any twenty-first-century city worth the name. Yet the building that caught Jamie's eye, as he drove through the centre hunting down a place to park, was an enormous Stalinist sports hall covered with multi-coloured mosaics of Dresden's Soviet-era heroes; a reminder that this city had spent forty-five years in the very heart of Communist East Germany. All around them on the banks of the River Elbe, giant cranes dwarfed the buildings they helped construct and the constant machine-gun rattle of jackhammers shattered the early-evening silence. Despite all the building work, Jamie noted an unlikely number of empty, weed-infested sites and the kind of structural ruins that would have looked more at home in the forum in Rome. If Sarah noticed, she didn't comment. In fact, since they'd entered the city proper she hadn't said a word.

They reached the *Altmarkt*, the Old Market, which, in true Dresden style, seemed to be surrounded mainly by modern buildings. On the far side of the street Jamie spotted the sign for an underground car park. He pulled in at the roadside outside a shop that sold fine china. For a moment he felt like an Olympic ski jumper waiting at the top of the slope and when he laid a hand on Sarah's shoulder he could feel the tension in her body. 'I'll drop you here, so you can make your call to your boss. Just be natural and tell him exactly what I told you. I shouldn't be more than five minutes.' She turned and gave him a long, searching look. He wondered what she was seeing. He hoped it wasn't the truth. A moment of decision and, finally, the hazel eyes softened. She leaned across and brushed her lips against his.

'I'll be right here, waiting.'

The first floor of the car park was full, so he took the narrow, curving ramp down to the lower level. Here, the cars were all parked in the spaces closest to the lifts and he drove to a vacant spot at the far end of the low-roofed cavern. As he sat in the car with the engine running he felt the weight of everything he'd set in motion threatening to crush him into his seat. What gave him the right to gamble with other people's lives? What if it all went wrong? Then his mind filled with old Matthew's face and he heard Tenzin's words and he realized he'd never had any other choice. The next thirty minutes were mapped out before him like the acts of a play. All he needed was the courage to play his part. He opened the car door just as the squeal of synthetic rubber on dust-coated concrete announced a second vehicle entering the building. The car park smelled of motor oil and petrol fumes, but it wasn't the smell that made Jamie's stomach lurch. As he walked towards the lift he was conscious of another presence keeping pace with him on the upper floor, which was just visible through a narrow gap close to the ceiling. He stopped for a second. From above, three soft footfalls and then silence. The lift was ten paces away and he felt the panic rising inside him as he made for the metal doors. What now? Breathe and think. There's no rush. Think! With fumbling fingers he attacked the knots of his shoes and removed them, then, standing in his socks, he pressed the 'up' button. An arrow showed that the car was ascending from the floor below. He sent up a silent prayer that it would be occupied by someone who'd just parked their car. A family, including a couple of schoolchildren who'd giggle at the idiot in his socks holding his shoes in his hand. The 'ting' as the lift arrived startled him even though he'd been expecting it. The doors parted and he felt a physical pain as he stared into the empty compartment. He hesitated. Was he being paranoid? Sarah would be waiting. It didn't matter. A little paranoia was good for the blood pressure. He stepped inside and pressed the button for street level, immediately leaving the lift and jogging silently towards the far end where a ramp led up towards the exit. He hit the slope at a run, and when he reached the top he could see the barriers and ticket machines. The upper floor was empty and away to his right the lift doors were just closing. A draught of fresh air made him smile at his own foolishness.

He was still smiling when the arm locked around his neck like a steel clamp.

Shock and fear slowed his reactions, but he knew the first few seconds of a situation like this were crucial. He managed to stab his elbow into the ribs of the man behind him with enough force to make him grunt and his right leg twisted round the other's in an attempt to unbalance him. At the same time, he reached both hands over his left shoulder to get a grip of his unseen opponent's collar and threw his weight forward, bending his left knee and trying for a hip throw that would use the attacker's bulk against him. He might as well have tried to shift a block of concrete. In desperation he smashed his head backward, anything to loosen the grip that was choking him, but he only managed a glancing blow that made the other man laugh. His stockinged heels scraped on the concrete as he was dragged helplessly towards a darkened alcove off the main car park.

'Twice you have missed our appointment. There will not be a third time.'

The voice sounded familiar, but before he could place it Jamie's legs were kicked from under him and massive hands slammed him to the ground so the back of his skull bounced off the floor. While his head still spun, some kind of filthy rag was stuffed into his mouth. He was positioned head first towards the garage with his feet into the alcove. An enormous weight settled on his chest, pinning his arms at his side and he found himself looking up into a grinning face that was too small for the head it inhabited. He searched for a name and his heart stopped as he found it. Gustav.

'I took this from a Taliban who was trying to cut my balls off outside Farkar, up in Kunduz,' the squat German said conversationally, producing a long curved knife from inside his zipped jacket. 'Guess who still has their balls?'

He brought the knife down close to Jamie's face, so he could see every shade of blue on the shimmering blade, and drew the razor edge across the Englishman's cheek. Very slowly. First the left side, then the right; the blade rasping effortlessly through two days of stubble.

'You didn't have time to shave? No need now, eh? Frederick, he thinks you're planning to auction the Sun Stone, but that will not happen, OK?' He slapped Jamie's cheek for emphasis. Now the wicked twinkle of the knife point hovered directly over Jamie's right eyeball. 'It won't happen because you are going to tell Gustav exactly where it is or you end up like your friend. The stone belongs to us, the keepers of the truth; the successors of the ancients. Only we have the knowledge to use it for the purpose it was intended.' The words came out stilted and mechanical, as if they'd been learned by constant repetition in a school room. Jamie shook his head to try to dislodge the gag, but the German interpreted the movement as rebellion or defiance. 'No? That's good, because now we're going to have some fun, you and me.' Gustav studied him impassively, like a butcher contemplating a cut of meat. 'The eyes, the ears or the nose? Not the tongue. You will need the tongue later.' His free hand reached down to caress the side of Jamie's head. 'The ears then.'

Desperately, Jamie used all his strength in an attempt to shift the German.

'Shhh,' Gustav said gently. 'The more you struggle, the worse it is for you.'

Rough fingers closed on the lobe of Jamie's right ear and pulled it taut. He tried to scream behind the gag that filled his mouth, but he knew no one would ever hear him. He thought he was losing his mind when a red spot appeared like a cancerous mole beside Gustav's left lip. The spot wavered and Jamie's eyes followed it. The German must have read something in his captive's face, because he hesitated before making the cut. Another bright spot appeared over his left breast, and a third almost exactly in the centre of his forehead. Gustav frowned and his eye drifted down to the spot on his chest. It took him a split second to recognize it for what it was.

'No!'

The knife rose high before the blade descended in a deadly two-handed arc towards Jamie's exposed throat. Three sharp cracks split the silence.

Sarah saw Jamie emerge from the car park lift and went to meet him. The Englishman's face was pale, almost grey, and at first he seemed to look right through her. When she took his arm, he blinked and forced a smile.

'Hey, you're shaking,' she said.

'I had a bit of a run-in with the car park attendant. I'll be fine in a minute.'

They walked in the general direction of the river. It was busy now, the offices and banks were emptying and the streets filled with shoppers. At the intersection of two streets they found a tourist sign that pointed them towards the Frauenkirche and, when they crossed, there it was, on the far side of a small park in the centre of the square.

Sarah gave an involuntary gasp when she saw the soaring, octagonal confection in honeyed stone that dominated everything around it, the enormous dome topped by a twenty-foot bell tower. As they walked across the square, Jamie hesitated, torn between what he knew was right and what he knew was best. He could turn away now and they could get on with their lives as if this had never happened. But could they? Frederick and his thugs would never stop looking for them as long as he thought they would lead him to the Sun Stone. Every time they opened the door it could be to some human meat grinder like Gustav. No. It had to be this way. In any case, there were things he had to know and things Sarah had to understand.

She felt his steps falter and thought he was delaying to get a better view of the church. 'I wonder what your grandfather would have thought of it?'

Jamie squeezed her hand, the last doubt gone, and

led her into the hallowed silence of the interior, where the gilt Baroque ceiling soared above just as it had done three hundred years earlier, supported by lavishly painted marble columns and layers of galleries, the windows allowing in an almost ethereal light that made the whole church glow. In the cupola of the dome, they could see the faces staring out from the glass front of the ramp that led in a long spiral up to the viewing platform. Several dozen tourists wandered the aisles taking in the wonder around them. Sarah followed him to a place in the front pew in front of the astonishing golden masterpiece of the High Altar and waited as he bowed his head as if in prayer.

They'd been sitting for a few minutes when they were joined by a pony-tailed man in a denim jacket who looked as if he'd just escaped from a 1970s pop group. Gradually, recognition dawned. Howard Vanderbilt never voluntarily appeared on TV business shows, but despite his best efforts a few images of him survived. The pictures they used were either photos from a time when the ponytail had actually been in fashion or blurred shots of a distant figure on the hundred-million-dollar yacht that transported him around the Bahamas every summer. Jamie tried to tell himself he'd been expecting this, but it was still a shock to be sitting within feet of one of the richest men in the world – especially when that man was holding a gleaming 9 mm pistol that appeared to be aimed in the direction of his heart.

'Mr Saintclair, I'm glad to meet you at last.'

'I wish I could say the same, sir.'

The fact that Howard Vanderbilt was carrying a gun told Jamie everything he needed about the billionaire industrialist's state of mind. Just like Walter Brohm, Vanderbilt had been driven beyond logic and reason by the Sun Stone. Why else would a man who could buy and sell whole countries be running around with a pistol when he had half a dozen perfectly good executioners sitting within fifteen feet? Their relative positions meant they were forced to talk across Sarah, who seemed not to have noticed the pistol and was showing similar signs to a volcano about to erupt. Her hands clutched at the shoulder bag in her lap and Jamie hoped she would keep them there.

A commotion at the back of the church signalled a new influx of visitors and Jamie turned his head to see a dark-suited figure he recognized as Frederick push his way past Vanderbilt's bodyguards. Four shaven-headed minders in leather jackets and jeans accompanied him, sweeping the interior of the Frauenkirche with their eyes and evidently not liking what they saw. They'd still be trying to figure out Gustav's mysterious disappearance and it would make them jumpy, but Jamie hoped not too jumpy. He was reassured when a word from Frederick brought them to heel. He noted a flaring of the nostrils when the previously impassive German recognized the man sitting beside him. Interesting, but they'd have to wait to see how interesting.

The German took his seat in the second pew, off to Jamie's right but within touching distance of Howard Vanderbilt's left shoulder. An aide approached the tycoon and he visibly stiffened when he heard whatever information he'd been given. Vanderbilt snatched a glance towards the man seated behind him and Frederick's pale eyes hardened, confirming the surveillance information Mr Lim had provided in exchange for the location of the Sun Stone. Of course, the trade had been a little one-sided and Mr Lim hadn't expected to be part of a delegation, but Jamie hoped he was a man who appreciated irony.

For a few seconds the two sets of bodyguards jockeyed for position in the open spaces around the pews as if they were part of a carefully choreographed ballet. Vanderbilt frowned, his patience evidently wearing thin. 'As you can see, Frederick, I have this situation under control,' he said over his shoulder. 'Your presence is not required. We can talk about this later, but for now I think you and your friends should leave.' The only answer was a short laugh and at some unseen signal one of Vanderbilt's bodyguards moved to Frederick's right where he could cover the German's gun hand.

Howard Vanderbilt sighed and when he spoke, Jamie detected a lack of certainty in his voice. The weariness of a man who had run out of time, or ideas, or both. Obviously this wasn't going according to the industrialist's plan.

'You have caused me some trouble, Mr Saintclair. I have spent a great deal of time and money seeking out what has brought us to this place. It ends here. Am I clear on that?'

'Very clear, Mr Vanderbilt.' He thought he heard the

word 'chicken' but Sarah might only have been sighing. 'But I would have thought that in your world everything was a matter of negotiation?'

Vanderbilt leaned closer to Sarah. 'I can buy it, or I can take it, son, it's up to you. Name your price. We're finished playing games.'

Jamie shook his head and looked around. 'Do you think you and your stormtroopers are the only people who've been following me? Bugging my phone? There's probably an NSA satellite up there right at this moment, listening to every word we say. The cheerful Oriental gentleman at the back with his two friends is to my certain knowledge a representative of the Chinese government. Everybody wants the Sun Stone, Howard, and frankly you're the last person I'd give it up to. All you want to do is exploit it, whatever the cost. Just like Brohm.'

Vanderbilt's face hardened. 'Have it your own way, son.' He moved the barrel of the pistol from Jamie to Sarah. 'Tell me where the stone and Brohm's documents are or I'll kill the girl.'

Jamie stared at him. Not even Howard Vanderbilt could get away with murder in a church full of witnesses, but suddenly the church wasn't so full. Young men in dark suits began ushering the tourists out. Most went, but Jamie could hear Mr Lim politely refusing the offer of assistance to leave, and the distinct sound of a pistol being cocked seemed to indicate that the pro-Frederick members of the Vril Society were prepared to stand their ground. Jamie hoped that he hadn't misread the cast who'd assembled here, the last thing they needed was a shooting war in the Frauenkirche.

Vanderbilt took a big breath. 'I . . .'

It wasn't often a man like Howard Vanderbilt could be rendered speechless, but the muzzle of the little pistol Sarah Grant was screwing into the flesh beneath his right ear achieved what presidents and prime ministers had routinely failed to do.

'The Sun Stone belongs to the State of Israel,' she said loudly enough for everyone in the church to hear.

'Perhaps I should have mentioned that, Howard,' Jamie said patiently. 'Miss Grant and the handsome gentleman who has the drop on us from the walkway up there are here to represent the people who were sacrificed to help Walter Brohm unlock the potential of the Sun Stone.'

It was time. He got to his feet and addressed everyone in the church. 'Gentlemen.' He raised his voice and it rang around the enormous space that had been designed precisely for that purpose. He allowed himself a smile at Sarah. 'And lady. This is a place of worship, let us not turn it into a war zone. As you can see, we have a number of competing interests for the legacy of the late Brigadeführer Walter Brohm. Mr Vanderbilt here believes he has a divine right to exploit it and the gun in his hand suggests he is probably prepared to go further than any of you to get it. The shadowy gentleman behind him, representing the paramilitary wing of the Vril Society, may have a legal point were he to suggest that what Walter Brohm called the Sun Stone was in the gift of the then Tibetan government and that the investment which brought the major breakthrough in exploiting it was made by his countrymen. I suppose the German government could make a similar claim, though I doubt that they would want to press it. Mr Lim,' the Chinaman bowed his head, 'of the Chinese People's Republic, would argue that his country has a more legitimate claim to it than any of you, because the Sun Stone was first discovered in the soil his people lay claim to, although I know the supporters of a Free Tibet would dispute that claim. And finally, Miss Sarah Grant, representative of the State of Israel, who can give evidence, which I'd be happy to support, of the human sacrifice her people were forced to make by Walter Brohm in the pursuit of his obsession.

'But,' he continued, 'as I said, this is a place of worship. It is not a law court. You are all here because you want to know the story of the Sun Stone, particularly how it is going to end. My grandfather, like Walter Brohm's father, was a churchman, so please indulge me if I preach you a short sermon about greed.

'When Walter Brohm returned to Germany and opened the casket he found in Tibet, he suspected he had in his hands something enormously significant: a substance hitherto unknown to man. As a scientist it was his duty to discover the properties of that material and, at a time of great upheaval for his country, their significance and potential value. Yet the very upheaval which spurred him proved to be his greatest obstacle, because with war on the horizon no one was interested in possibilities – a dream that promised some distant panacea – only in certainties.

'But Walter Brohm, for all his faults, was a man with several admirable qualities, not the least of which were persistence and self-belief. Somehow, he found the time and the resources to carry out his experiments. We don't know the mechanics of it, but it appears that some time before early nineteen forty-one he came to the conclusion that the Sun Stone consisted of what we now call Dark Matter. That led in turn to the possibility, even the probability, of creating controlled nuclear fusion.'

A stir ran through the men in the church at the mention of the goal which had brought each of them here.

'Now, he was able to turn directly to Hitler for support, but his beloved Führer failed him. Why? Because Hitler feared the power the Sun Stone was capable of unleashing. But one man had no such reservations. Walter Brohm sold his soul to the devil and the devil's name was Heinrich Himmler.'

He waited for some reaction to his words, but none came.

'Brohm needed to operate in total secrecy. That meant the labour to build the bunker in the Harz Mountains had to be expendable. Hundreds, perhaps thousands, of Russian prisoners, Polish slave workers and, of course, Jews were rushed off to the gas chambers the moment the bunker was complete. But the killing didn't stop there. Scientists and technicians. Even the SS guards. When the time came to close the bunker down . . . when he was on the very brink of another breakthrough . . . Walter Brohm sacrificed them all to save himself and his precious secret.

'And, just as Brohm never questioned the ethics or the danger or the morality of what he was doing, he knew his value to the last dollar. Germany could burn, her soldiers could be slaughtered in their hundreds of thousands, German boys could throw themselves at tanks, but Walter Brohm and his work must survive. As the war ended, he dangled the Sun Stone under the noses of people with even fewer morals than himself, and they took it: hook, line and sinker.

'Within a month, he would have been welcomed to America and given more resources than he could ever have dreamed of to complete his project. But for one man.

'One man recognized the true danger of the Sun Stone and Walter Brohm. That man was my grandfather. He shot Brohm through the head and hoped that when he died, the Sun Stone would die with him. But, of course, it didn't, which is why we are here.'

'Enough of the history lesson, Saintclair. We came for the stone. Where is it?'

Jamie shook his head. 'You had my grandfather killed, Mr Vanderbilt, and a Polish war hero called Stanislaus Kozlowski who was his friend. Who knows how many more have been sacrificed on the altar of your greed? You were even prepared to betray your own kind.' Vanderbilt flinched as if someone had slapped his face. 'Oh, yes, Mr Vanderbilt. You're not the only one who can bug a telephone. I suspect you and your friend Frederick will have lots to talk about when this is over. But the more I discovered about Matthew Sinclair, the more certain I was that he would have died to keep the Sun Stone away from men like you.'

'The old man was an accident and the Pole was in the way.' Vanderbilt's voice was almost a plea. 'Don't you understand that this is more important than life or death? The Sun Stone can assure the future of the planet and the survival of our civilization.'

Jamie ignored him and looked around the cathedral, meeting the eyes of Mr Lim and Frederick in turn, before focusing his attention on Sarah Grant. 'I came to the Frauenkirche prepared to sacrifice everything to make sure Walter Brohm's legacy remained unfulfilled. To do so I would have blown up this place and everyone in it.' They looked at the building around them, wondering if they'd been lured into a trap, all except Sarah who had forgotten Howard Vanderbilt and whose eyes never left Jamie. 'But fortunately, I don't have to do that.'

'What do you mean?'

Jamie stared at the industrialist, wondering what was going through his head. 'When he left the bunker in February nineteen forty-five Walter Brohm believed he had chosen the safest place in Germany to hide the Sun Stone. Little old Dresden, famous for nothing more than its crockery and its culture. Untouched by six years of war and likely to stay that way. He knew every stone of this great church, because his father had been pastor here. In particular, he knew the stone vaults below it as no one else did. Where better to keep the Sun Stone and his research papers until they were needed? Brohm probably calculated it would be lunacy to waste resources on bombing Dresden at that late stage of the war.' The church had gone very still. He could probably have whispered and they would still have heard him. 'But Brohm forgot that lunacy and war go hand in hand. There's some suggestion the decision was taken because the *Wehrmacht* was likely to retreat this way from Czechoslovakia, as it was then. The more likely reason is that somebody at Bomber Command was looking for another box to tick on his long list of targets.'

He heard a grunt of bitter laughter. It wasn't surprising that Frederick had worked out what was coming. Frederick was German, and Germans knew all about the history of Dresden.

'Walter Brohm believed Dresden was the ideal place to keep the Sun Stone safe. He was right . . . up to a point. That point came on the night of February the thirteenth nineteen forty-five, probably about a week after the stone was brought here, when a formation of 723 Lancaster bombers proved him wrong. The bull's-eye for the raid was to be a sports stadium about three hundred metres from here in the Aldstadt, but the Pathfinder mosquitoes dropped their target markers over the cigarette factory about a mile to the east. If every plane had dropped its bombs on target, everything would have been fine, but there was a phenomenon during the war called bomb creep, where every subsequent crew tended to drop its bombs a little further back than those that had gone before. Bomb creep resulted in an arrowhead pattern one and a quarter miles long and one and three-quarter miles broad at its widest point. In the next twenty-four hours that arrowhead would become the most dangerous place on earth. The first RAF attack would be followed by a second, a few hours later, and a daylight raid by B17 bombers of the USAAF. Twenty-seven hundred tonnes of high explosive and incendiaries rained down from planes flying at eight thousand feet and the flames of Dresden could be seen by air crew from as far as five hundred miles away. In the middle of the arrowhead was the Old Town; in the middle of the Old Town was the Frauenkirche. At least twenty-five thousand people were killed, crushed beneath falling buildings or incinerated in the firestorms that followed.' He paused. 'Nothing was left but rubble.'

Mr Lim appeared to be praying. Frederick's vengeful eyes never left the back of Vanderbilt's head. Sarah and the industrialist stared at the church around them.

'Oh, yes, this too,' Jamie assured them. 'The Frauenkirche may look like an eighteenth-century Renaissance masterpiece, but it was built – or rebuilt – as an exact replica of the original only after the Communists were kicked out and it was finally completed in two thousand and five. All that's left of the old Frauenkirche are those little black stones you see decorating the exterior. The church that was here in nineteen forty-five was blown to bits by at least one four-thousand-pound blockbuster bomb. The RAF in their schoolboy fashion called them Cookies and they were designed to bury themselves deep in the earth before exploding. They were among the most destructive weapons of that uniquely destructive war. The bomb reduced everything, including the vaults of the Frauenkirche, to dust and bricks. Whatever was down there ended up with the millions of tonnes of rubble from the rest of Dresden.'

Vanderbilt's face had turned ash grey. 'What happened to it?' he whispered. 'What happened to the Sun Stone?'

Jamie took Sarah Grant's hand and she didn't resist as he walked her steadily towards the doorway. No one tried to stop them. Through the door he could see the flashing lights of half a dozen parked police cars. He didn't envy Lotte Muller the job of cleaning up the diplomatic mess, but the pictures and phone transcripts from Mr Lim should help.

'It's out there, Howard,' he continued. 'The rubble from the old city was used to build the foundations for the new Dresden, and to pave the roads for a couple of hundred miles around. About half a million people are living on top of the Sun Stone.'

They emerged into the early evening sunshine.

'It's all yours.'

THE END

Acknowledgements

Special thanks go to my friends Shirley and Kenny Allan for lifting the lid on the beautiful city of Dresden and keeping me straight on my German, and to fellow writer Gabriele Campbell for helping me negotiate my way through the Harz mountains. Heinz Hohne's masterful book *The Order of The Death's Head* gave me the fine detail I needed on the world of the SS and Matthew Sinclair's diary probably owes more to *With the Jocks* by Peter White, one of the best memoirs of the Second World War by a fighting soldier, than any other history I read. Finally to Simon my editor and his fantastic team at Transworld, and to Stan, my agent at Jenny Brown in Edinburgh.

James Douglas is the pseudonym of a writer of popular historical adventure novels. This is the first thriller to feature art recovery expert, Jamie Saintclair.